HALF-WITS

Gerard Goggins

Ambassador Books, Inc.
Worcester • Massachusetts

ISBN 1-929039-01-8
Library of Congress Control Number: 2001116346

Published in 2001 in the United States by Ambassador Books, Inc.
71 Elm Street, Worcester, Massachusetts 01609
(800) 577-0909

Printed in Canada.

Half-Wits was originally published in hard cover (ISBN 1-55612-174-1) by Sheed & Ward in 1988.

For current information about all titles from Ambassador Books, Inc. visit our website at: www.ambassadorbooks.com.

DEDICATION

For Deanna,
who walks in beauty,
and for those far off.

Author's Note

We live in a shallow time.

We embrace the trivial and despise the profound.

We mistake glibness for intelligence and sarcasm for insight.

We are being buried by the trivial and the mediocre.

We think of evil as something committed by poor people and deranged children.

Goodness, we believe, is subjective and relative.

We simply do not acknowledge a spiritual dimension to life.

Christ is seen as irrelevant.

God is an interesting concept.

And life only has meaning as long as it is fun.

But even in a mediocre age, human beings still find themselves at the edge of the abyss.

Even in a shallow age, people still must choose between self-annihilation and facing the darkness—and, yes, facing the infinite, the other, the one, that which, as Augustine says, we call God.

Life's most compelling question remains—what happens when we are alone and we face the infinite?

Half-Wits is not for the faint of heart.

It is an unflinching look at the reality of evil in the universe. And it is a struggle to use art at its most forceful in expressing what cannot be articulated and comprehending at a deep level what is beyond the grasp of the intellect.

Evil does not only use language that is acceptable at the dining room table, and its deeds are often unspeakable. To soften evil is to make it something less than evil.

And it is only when we recognize evil as it is, in ourselves, in others, and in the universe, that we begin to understand the power, the beauty, the reality, and the necessity of the good.

— G.G. May 2001

PROLOGUE

THE CAR ROLLED ANOTHER TWENTY FEET AFTER THE HEAD-lights had been shut off and then came to a stop in the middle of a wide, dark puddle. The door on the driver's side opened and a man wearing a dark raincoat got out. He paid no attention to the steady rain and the quick gusts of wind which blew with such force that they occasionally shook the car, and he did not seem to notice that the water on the pavement came to the top of his shoes. He opened the trunk of his car and took out a shovel and a small black plastic box, then he walked quickly off.

In the distance the lights of the city could be seen reflecting off the low clouds, but here there was no light, and the man stumbled as he strode across the uneven terrain. He stopped after taking forty steps and took a pencil flashlight out of his raincoat pocket and, for only a split second, flashed it on the ground. There was nothing to be seen except loose, sandy soil.

The man put the flashlight back in his pocket and began to dig, but he stopped after a moment and stood up straight. He cocked his head slightly and listened. The only sounds were the wind and the rain. He walked quickly back to the car and opened the trunk. Again, he used the flashlight for a split second, just long enough to see a large bulging piece of green canvas. He reached into the trunk and in one clean motion, he lifted the canvas and what was in it out of the car and swung it onto his shoulder. Then he shut the trunk and retraced his steps. Again he used the light, this time to find the shovel, and then he resumed digging. It did not take him long.

Within a few minutes he had dug a hole about five feet long, two feet wide and two and a half to three feet deep. He slid the canvas to the side of the hole, took an edge of it in his two hands and pulled the canvas straight up. The object inside rolled out of the canvas and into the hole.

The man straightened up again and listened. Again, only the wind and the rain could be heard. He picked up the plastic box and flipped up its top. He pointed it at the hole and pressed a button. There was a sudden flash of light, and the eyes of a young boy stared up at him from the shallow grave. He had died with his mouth wide open and a look of terror on his face.

In an instant, the body disappeared into darkness, and the man waited as the camera whined and pushed out the photograph. When the whining stopped, he thrust the picture into his raincoat pocket and put the camera back on the ground. He quickly shoveled sand into the hole. When he finished filling it, he got on his knees and smoothed the area over with his hands. He stood up and flashed the pencil flashlight on the ground.

The area where he had dug looked almost the same as the area around it. By morning, with the wind and the rain, he himself would not be able to find the grave. He folded the canvas and put it under his arm. Then, as he bent over to pick up the shovel and the camera, he spit on the newly smoothed sand.

"Pussy," he said in a rasping whisper edged with contempt.

He stood up and walked unhurriedly to his car.

PART ONE

CHAPTER ONE

FITZSIMMONS STOOD IN THE DIMLY LIT HALLWAY FINGERING through the change in his pocket for the key to his mailbox. A theme from Mozart found its way to his lips and escaped in a thin, breathy whistle.

A small, yellowed globe with a weak light bulb hung from the ceiling, and shafts of sunlight cut through the three tiny, dirty windows in the front door. The hallway was immutable. The painted walls were streaked with dirt and the floor needed to be swept, just as it had the day Fitzsimmons rented the apartment.

He stopped playing with the change and listened to the tune that was on his lips. It was from one of Mozart's later piano concertos. It had been a long time since he had whistled Mozart.

The windows in the door were too streaked to see through, but even their dirt could not conceal the brightness of the morning outside.

"May is so lavish," he said aloud.

"Hi," a voice behind him said.

Fitzsimmons turned slowly to face the woman who had moved into the apartment across the hall from him a few weeks earlier. He had seen her before, but he had never been this close to her. Her long black hair fell to her shoulders, and her dark eyes were set in a distinctively attractive face. She was young, in her middle or late twenties, but there was an aura of maturity about her. It was not the way she dressed. She was wearing a gray sweater, jeans and canvas tennis shoes, an outfit common on Beacon Hill in the spring. It was something in her face, a hint of pain in those dark eyes that gazed directly at Fitzsimmons and made him feel that he was being given a kind of summary judgment.

"Bad habit," Fitzsimmons said.

"I talk to myself sometimes, too. But not usually in the hall." She smiled, a friendly, but guarded smile. "I think we're neighbors. I'm Karen Easton," she said.

Fitzsimmons took her hand. It was cool and lean and her handshake was firm. "I'm John Fitzsimmons. And you're right. We are neighbors."

They looked at each other in silence for a long moment, and then she slipped past him, gave a little wave, and disappeared through the door. The light fragrance of her perfume lingered briefly and then that, too, was gone.

Fitzsimmons found the key, put it in the mailbox lock and turned it. "Four years," he said aloud. The sound of his voice startled him, and he looked over his shoulder, but this time he was alone in the hallway. "Four years," he said again.

He opened the small stainless steel door. There was a folded newspaper clipping inside. He opened it carefully. "Ax Murderer Slays Family of Three in Seattle," the headline said.

Fitzsimmons crumpled the clipping into a ball and dropped it on the floor where it lay at his feet. After a moment, he kicked the clipping into the corner near the front door where there were two others like it. He closed the mailbox and followed the woman into the street. May was, indeed, lavish. The air was warm and full of sweet smells, hints of lilacs and budding trees, but Karen Easton was nowhere to be seen. Too bad. He would have liked to have had another moment with her.

The walk up the hill and down past the State House swept away the dark feelings that the clipping had caused. Spring was stirring in him. The Common was green again, the air smelled of new life. His step quickened as he headed for Park Square.

"You wanna paper?" The questioner had a runny nose and wore a misshapen black topcoat and sneakers. He clutched a stack of tabloids against his body with his left arm. In his right hand he held one folded in half which he offered to Fitzsimmons, who did not even look at the man as he went though the doorway that led to the subway. He despised tabloids.

"Good to see you, John," Peter said as he swung the door open. "Unfortunately, not as good as I expected it to be."

Fitzsimmons stepped inside without responding.

"I'm afraid I can't go with you today. The bishop's office called. They have a chore for me. I would have telephoned you, of course, but how can you telephone a man who won't install a phone?"

He held his hand up as if to fend off a protest by Fitzsimmons. "You didn't make the trip for nothing. I have some fantastic Italian pastries and the coffee will be ready in a few minutes. So we can relax and chat a little before I have to run off."

They went to the study, and Peter settled himself behind a large, ornate mahogany desk. Fitzsimmons sat across from him in a red velvet easy chair. The room was still, peaceful. Some sunlight filtered through the curtains, but heavy floor-length drapes blocked most of it. The two men sat quietly. Peter leaned back in his swivel chair, and Fitzsimmons studied the room as he had several times before.

Peter looked comfortable at his desk, as if he had been made for the room, and perhaps he had. He fit in well with it. He was quiet-spoken and calm, perhaps just a bit overweight, and he seemed unhurried as if he always had more time than he needed and as if things were always under control. The room was calm, too. Hanging on the wall behind Peter were pictures of the Sacred Heart, the pope, and the cardinal. Over the filing cabinet there was a print of a Renaissance painting depicting the Annunciation.

"I think the archdiocese uses an interior decorator who was trained during the Victorian era," Peter said. "Any time a rectory is going to be redone, they take him out of mothballs and put him to work."

"I like it. It's got that proper mix of temporal peace and other worldliness."

"True," Peter said with a smile. "You wouldn't find a room like this out in the world."

"You don't care for it?"

"It's all right. I don't dislike it. It's just that—well, you would have to be a priest to understand. Rectories are so impersonal. They're like lobbies in motel chains. Over there you have the Sacred Heart, the pope, and the cardinal. Over the filing cabinet is the Annunciation. There is not one personal touch in the room. No pictures of family. No favorite books or paintings. There is nothing in here that suggests a single, identifiable personality. It's a room for strangers and transients."

Fitzsimmons smiled. "Maybe that's why I like it."

"Maybe it is," the priest said.

Fitzsimmons looked away. They were quiet again. After a minute, Peter coughed. Fitzsimmons shifted in his chair.

"Come on," Peter said, breaking the silence. "Let's go out to the kitchen and have a cannoli.

"How long have we known each other? Six months? Eight months?" Peter asked as he poured coffee into a mug. "Since before Christmas—we're becoming buddies."

He handed the mug to Fitzsimmons. "I pride myself on the fact that I don't pry."

"An uncommon virtue," Fitzsimmons said.

The priest offered Fitzsimmons a tray piled high with cannoli, and Fitzsimmons took the one on top.

"I guess I'm not as virtuous as I'd like to be," the priest said.

Fitzsimmons took a bite of the pastry and nodded but said nothing.

Peter's eyes focused on Fitzsimmons and then drifted away. Even with his Roman collar on, Peter did not look like a priest. He was in his early fifties, short, perhaps five-foot six, and hefty. With his bald head and glasses, he looked like he would be at home working behind the meat counter in an Italian market. But, from the first, when they happened to have seats next to each other at a concert in Symphony Hall, Fitzsimmons recognized that Peter Genaro had special qualities.

Peter had been dressed in street clothes and Fitzsimmons did not guess that he was a priest. Instead, he assumed that Peter was an academic, perhaps a professor of philosophy. Peter had that quality of detachment which only comes with experience, and his face, while it was clearly that of a man in his fifties, was also quite youthful. For Fitzsimmons, that should have been the clue to Peter's vocation because he had found that the quality of a youthful countenance was peculiar to spiritual people. Even now, when Peter seemed to be upset with him, Fitzsimmons was struck by the serenity of the priest's countenance.

"I want you to know that I value our friendship, John. My life is sometimes a bit cloistered. You give me the opportunity to get out in the world."

"I thought you had at least a couple hundred relatives around here."

"I do. I have three sisters and cousins and nieces and nephews, and I love them all. But, even so, I sometimes suffer from a kind of spiritual loneliness. Please don't misunderstand me. I'm a pretty happy man doing what I have been called to do, but as I've gotten older, I've found that I don't have as much in common with people whom I used to be very close to, not only relatives, but other priests. It's nice to have a friend who enjoys the theater and listens to Prokofiev."

Their eyes met briefly. "It's good for me to have a friend, too," Fitzsimmons said.

"Then let me ask you a question."

A hint of a smile crept over Fitzsimmons' face.

"That is, if you don't mind," the priest said.

Fitzsimmons shrugged.

"You were not cut out to be a night watchman," Peter said.

"I do more than that," Fitzsimmons said. "I sweep floors, too."

The priest returned his smile. "Yes, well, somehow I thought that you were trained for another calling."

"I was," Fitzsimmons conceded. "I used to teach."

"College?"

"Yes."

"Mathematics?"

Fitzsimmons looked puzzled. "No. English."

"Got your doctorate?"

"Yes."

"I never would have guessed English," the priest said.

"Oh?"

"Your taste in music. Very analytical, very modern, very anti-romantic."

"Well, it's been years since I've taught. I've gotten away from romance."

"Last question. Did you have a special area of study?"

Fitzsimmons nodded. "Medieval, Elizabethan. My dissertation was on Marlowe."

"What was it called?"

"*Marlowe and the Nature of Evil.*"

"That was a subject of special interest to you?"

"I guess it was, at the time," Fitzsimmons said.

The priest started to ask another question, but stopped and looked at his watch.

"Are you free Friday night?" the priest asked.

"Yes. Concert?"

"I thought maybe we could try that little theater on Beacon Street. They're doing *Waiting for Godot,*" the priest said.

"Sure, and if you've got time we'll go out for dinner, too."

"Sounds good."

"I'll call you," Fitzsimmons answered as he rose from his chair.

CHAPTER TWO

THERAPY PRODUCTS, INC. WAS A SMALL PLANT IN THE NORTH END. It employed about 200 people, most of them physically or mentally handicapped, who did light assembly and packaging work—work which could not be done by machine and would be too costly if done by more skilled and therefore higher paid workers.

The company was located in an ancient three-story, red-brick building which had high ceilings and oil-soaked floors. Only two of the floors were used. The first floor contained a large, open room where most of the assembling and packaging was done, and behind that, a shipping and receiving room with a loading dock. On the second floor, there were offices and a large, clean cafeteria. The third floor was closed.

Fitzsimmons had worked at the company for more than a year. His duties were varied. He started at three in the afternoon and worked until five completing packaging and moving the finished work to the shipping room. He spent the next two hours cleaning the assembly room, sweeping the floor, straightening out the chairs, and tidying up the tables. The final four hours he was left mostly to himself. Once every hour he would patrol the building, stopping at stations scattered on the first and second floors and insert the keys which hung from the wall on linked chains into the night watchman's clock. The rest of the time he would read or listen to the radio. Occasionally his solitude would be broken by a rather moody, unpleasant man named Sarz who cleaned the bathrooms, the cafeteria, and the offices.

Sarz kept to himself most of the time, but once every week or two he would seek out Fitzsimmons, and in a conspiratorial way, almost as if they shared a common but unspoken secret, Sarz would complain about something, usually the state of the women's bathroom. Fitzsimmons would listen, responding as infrequently as he could until Sarz's harangue ended, and then he would go back to sweeping, leaving Sarz to stare at him.

Sarz invariably made Fitzsimmons feel uncomfortable, but that was the only thing about the job that Fitzsimmons disliked. Four months earlier, Barbara Wright had tried to interest Fitzsimmons in taking a more responsible job and working days, but he told her that he was happy doing what he was doing and that he had no interest in bettering himself.

She had been visibly disappointed. "You seem to have a natural talent for dealing with our people, and they like you. I think they sense a gentleness about you," she had said.

He had remained unmoved, and since then, Ms. Wright, as he and most other employees called her, had seemed more distant toward him.

"Hey, Jay."

Fitzsimmons looked over at the smiling face of Tommy Quercio, who sat on a stool at one of the assembly tables, dangling his feet. Everything about Tommy was retarded except his eyes. He had stopped growing before puberty, and he was less than five feet tall. Most of the skin on his face was soft and clean with only a few patches where tufts of light gray beard grew. And when he smiled, Fitzsimmons could see the face of a ten-year-old—except for those eyes. They were mature, penetrating, and self-conscious. They usually had an ironic glint, as though at some deep level, Tommy understood better than Fitzsimmons what life was all about.

"How you doing, Tommy?"

"Good, Jay. Good. Even working with all these half-wits. I'm good," he said and laughed. His laugh was a peculiar one, high-pitched, almost a shriek, but muffled.

"They're good for you," Fitzsimmons said.

Tommy stopped smiling and went back to fitting small pieces of metal together.

"What are you making?" Fitzsimmons asked.

"I don't know. Those half-wits don't tell us. They don't think we'd understand. Sometimes I wonder who the real half-wits are."

"You're into philosophy again," Fitzsimmons said.

Tommy's mouth twisted into a half grimace, half smile. "No, Jay. Half-wits can't get into philosophy. You know that." There was no laugh this time, but his eyes glinted with mischievous irony.

Fitzsimmons started to move away.

"But there's a philosopher looking for you, Jay."

"Who's that?"

"Sarz."

"I didn't know he was a philosopher," Fitzsimmons said.

"Sure you did, Jay," Tommy said with a wicked smile. "You go up to his room, don't you?"

"I don't even know where he lives," Fitzsimmons said.

Tommy looked up into Fitzsimmons eyes for a long moment, and his face became somber.

"You're a funny guy, Jay," he said. He went back to doing his work, ignoring Fitzsimmons as if he had already left.

Fitzsimmons turned and began to walk toward the staircase to the second floor.

"See you later, half-wit," Tommy called after him.

Fitzsimmons looked back. Tommy was staring fiercely at the piece of metal in his hands. Except for his crooked smile, Tommy's face hardly looked different from any one of the more than one hundred faces in the room. When Fitzsimmons started to work at TPI, he had unconsciously stereotyped all the handicapped employees. As he had gotten to know some of them, he was surprised to discover that each one had a distinct personality. They all felt pleasure, and they all felt pain. They had egos and emotions and bad days and good days. Tommy had the most flamboyant personality, but Fitzsimmons now understood that each person in the room was an individual, and he was careful to respect their individuality.

Before Fitzsimmons had gone halfway up the stairs, he met Sarz coming down.

"She's looking for you," Sarz said. There was something threatening in his tone and the half-smile which showed two straight, gleaming white teeth.

"Okay," Fitzsimmons said.

Sarz stopped two steps above Fitzsimmons. His fingers played with a gold chain which hung from his neck. "She's got a hair across her ass. She found a porn magazine on her desk. She thinks one of us left it there." The smile was gone from his face, and his tone was less menacing.

Fitzsimmons was used to Sarz's abrasiveness and he ignored it. He started up the stairs again.

"She may be after your ass," Sarz called after him.

Fitzsimmons looked back at Sarz and saw, as he expected, the malice in Sarz's eyes. Fitzsimmons had heard the rumor that Ms. Wright was a lesbian. He didn't know if it was true, but he knew that Sarz believed it. He did not give Sarz the satisfaction of a response.

As soon as Fitzsimmons got to the second floor, Ms. Wright called him into her office. Ms. Wright was a heavyset woman, indeed so heavy that when she walked, the insides of her thighs rubbed together and her stockings made a scratching sound. She was, however, a stylish dresser and a generally meticulous woman who paid great attention to details.

Her office, except for the new wall-to-wall carpeting, reflected the rest of the building: the walls were drab and the furnishings unattractive.

"Do you know anything about this?" she asked, handing Fitzsimmons a magazine.

It was a sex magazine with almost no pretensions. The magazine fell open to a picture of a nude woman with stringy blond hair and large, sagging breasts, thrusting her genitalia at the photographer's lens.

Fitzsimmons shook his head and handed the magazine back to Ms. Wright.

"I didn't think so, but I had to ask," Ms. Wright said. She put the magazine face down on the desk and straightened her eyeglasses. "It's not the kind of thing you want staring up at you from under your morning coffee. Please sit down for a moment."

Fitzsimmons paid little attention to the people at TPI, and so he knew very little about Ms. Wright. He could not escape knowing the basics—that she was divorced and that her son, who had Down syndrome, had died as a teenager. And, of course, he was familiar with the office gossip that held she was a lesbian. He guessed that she was now in her mid-forties, and that her life was not a very happy one.

"Do you have any idea how this could have gotten here?"

Fitzsimmons suspected that Sarz had been reading it the night before and had left it there by accident.

He shook his head.

"I can't imagine what would have happened if a parent of one of our clients had come into my office this morning and had seen that on my desk," she said. Ms. Wright usually referred to the handicapped workers as "clients." The rest of the people who worked at TPI were called employees. "But I can tell you it would have been extremely embarrassing, and it would have been damaging to TPI."

Fitzsimmons remained silent.

"When you made your rounds last night, was there anybody in here?" she asked.

Apparently Ms. Wright and Fitzsimmons had reached the same conclusion. He shook his head.

"I can't imagine one of the clients or even one of the office staff coming in here and leaving this. Do you think it could have been a practical joke?" she asked.

He wondered if Ms. Wright disliked Sarz as much as Sarz disliked her. "I don't know," he said.

"This isn't the first time something like this has turned up. A few weeks ago one of the male clients had a magazine like this at his table, and when we asked him where he got it, he said he found it in the men's room. We had no reason to doubt him, and that worries me. He could have easily put the magazine in his pocket and brought it home. And if he had, I'm sure his family would have been outraged, and they would have had a perfect right to be.

"This is a unique work environment. Every one of us who works at TPI are called upon to be role models. The clients imitate us in ways that fully endowed workers would not. If this did come from one of our employees, I really think that person is a danger. We simply cannot tolerate what is tolerated at other plants. Our people have the minds of adolescents. They're impressionable and vulnerable. I, for one, don't want them to think that this kind of thing is acceptable or that the majority of healthy adults go around reading this trash."

Fitzsimmons nodded.

"If I find out who left this on my desk or left the other one in the men's room, I'll fire him," she said. She picked up a letter opener and began to jab the desk blotter with it in a slow, gentle motion.

"From now on," she continued, "I want the offices locked at night after they are cleaned, and I want you to make sure there are none of these magazines lying around before you lock them up."

"Okay. Anything else?"

"Well," she hesitated, and her manner became more relaxed, "just one thing. I wish you would give some more thought to what we talked about earlier. The people you work with all think highly of you, and the clients all like you and trust you."

Fitzsimmons started to speak, but she raised her hand to stop him.

"I couldn't help but find some things out about you when I checked your references. Everyone I spoke to thought the world of you. Of course I didn't tell them the kind of job you were applying for. I'm sure they all would have been surprised if I had."

Fitzsimmons gazed at her; his face was expressionless.

"But that's not really the point," Ms. Wright continued. "I just wonder if you aren't ready to do a little more with your life than you're doing now. You might think it's selfish on my part, and maybe it is a little. But I never expected you to stay here too long. I almost didn't hire you because of that. In fact, you've stayed a lot longer than I thought you would. And I hope that someday you'll come in here and tell me you've decided to go back to your profession. But in the meantime, I think it might be good for you, and I know it would be good for TPI, if you take on a supervisor's job."

The first time she had made the offer, Fitzsimmons dismissed it out of hand. This time he did not. "Let me think about it, Ms. Wright," he said.

"Well," Ms. Wright said as she got up from her chair, "that's a step forward." She smiled for the first time. "One other thing, feel free to call me Barbara," she said.

"Okay, Barbara," Fitzsimmons said as he, too, stood up.

As Fitzsimmons walked past the rows of assembly tables on his way to the shipping room, he glanced at scores of clients' faces. They had stopped working and were waiting quietly for the 3:30 buzzer so that they could leave. How many of them, he wondered, were like Tommy Quercio—innocent and yet tainted by the world? Each of them was missing something, some component of the human personality. They reminded Fitzsimmons of toys which had been misused. They did not work quite right. Fitzsimmons liked them, and they knew it, and they liked him in return. Maybe, too, they knew that Fitzsimmons was like them, that something inside of him was also broken. As he passed them, many of the clients looked up and said, "Hi, Jay." It was the nickname Tommy had given to him, and the rest had picked it up. He responded with their names and was careful not to overlook anyone. He knew from past experience that it was easy to hurt their feelings.

"Hi, Jay. We've got most of it done, but those two pallets have to be brought over to the loading dock," Shanny called as he got to the shipping room. Shanny was the foreman. He had started calling Fitzsimmons Jay as a joke, but now called him Jay more often than not. "You're a little late today."

"I was up with Ms. Wright," Fitzsimmons answered.

"Yeah. I heard about that magazine. It don't take Sherlock Holmes to figure out who left it there," Shanny said.

Fitzsimmons laughed. "No, but Sherlock Holmes would have a hell of a time trying to prove it."

"He's a slippery bastard," Shanny said. The comment surprised Fitzsimmons since he often saw Shannon and Sarz in private, indeed, guarded conversation. "Listen, I've got to run. My wife's outside waiting for me. I'll give you a call later just in case I forgot anything."

As Shanny walked away, the buzzer went off and the clients suddenly became animated. Some stood up slowly, but a number jumped up and scrambled for the door.

Fitzsimmons slipped the hand forklift under one of the skids and began to move the skid toward the loading platform.

"She's making an awful big stink over nothing," Sarz said. He had come up behind Fitzsimmons without making a sound. Fitzsimmons kept moving the skid without looking up.

"It's too bad she's a dyke. All she really needs is a good screwing to straighten her out. If she could just go out and get laid she'd forget about all this nickel and dime shit."

Fitzsimmons stopped and turned to face Sarz. "Don't leave your magazines lying around anymore. If she catches you, she'll fire you," he said.

For a split second Sarz looked away from Fitzsimmons, just long enough to let the defiance bubble up inside of him. Then he looked directly at Fitzsimmons. "Fuck you," Sarz said.

Fitzsimmons shrugged and started to turn away.

"Did that bitch tell you to watch me?"

"No," Fitzsimmons said. "But she doesn't want those kinds of magazines lying around. She's afraid the clients might get their hands on them."

"The clients? Those dirty little bastards. They're the ones who bring those magazines in. Not me. I wouldn't spend good money on that crap. I might look at them if they're lying around, but I wouldn't buy them. She ought to get her head examined. She thinks the clients are innocent virgins. They're perverts. Every one of the little bastards. They may be half-wits, but all they think about is sex."

"Look, it doesn't make any difference to me. I'm just letting you know how she feels."

"She already told me how she feels. She ought to find out how I feel. That bitch. If she knew how it felt, she wouldn't be such a pain in the ass." He looked at Fitzsimmons as if expecting him to agree.

"I don't see anything wrong with Ms. Wright," Fitzsimmons said.

Sarz glared at Fitzsimmons. "That doesn't surprise me," he said. "Nothing seems to bother you."

Sarz used the words as if they were a knife and he was jabbing Fitzsimmons. For just a moment, Fitzsimmons felt a foreboding, an uneasiness which he didn't understand. He turned back to the hand forklift and began pushing the skid. Sarz's mood changed instantly.

"Hey, I didn't mean to get heavy. I suppose she's all right. Just doing her job and all that shit." He began to walk along with Fitzsimmons.

"Listen, do you ever do anything after work?"

"What do you mean?"

"Well, we've been working together for over a year. I thought maybe we could go out for a drink after work some night."

"I don't drink," Fitzsimmons said.

"You don't? Well, so what? Come along anyway. There's a place I go to—The Good Sports Cafe. Ever heard of it?"

"No," Fitzsimmons said. "I didn't know you were interested in athletics."

"Not that kind of sports. It's just a place that a lot of interesting people go to. People like us. They talk about more than the Red Sox and the Celtics. How about it? We could go after work."

"No, thanks."

"You're not married are you?"

Fitzsimmons shook his head.

"I'm not either. So neither one of us has to hurry home."

"Sorry," Fitzsimmons said.

Sarz's mood changed again. "What's the matter? Something wrong with me?"

"No. I'm tired. I don't feel like going out."

"Well then maybe we can do it another night."

Fitzsimmons felt as if he had been manipulated into a corner. "Yes. Maybe some other night."

"Good," Sarz answered. "You'll enjoy yourself. I'll look forward to it." He walked away before Fitzsimmons could respond.

Bob Shannon called at nine o'clock.

"Jay, this is Shanny. Did you notice the boxes on the last table in the corner?"

"I finished them up."

"Good. Well, that was the only thing I forgot to tell you. Everything else okay?"

Fitzsimmons sometimes wondered about Shannon's constant concern with the shipping room. He frequently called Fitzsimmons after leaving for the day to make sure everything was okay, almost as if he expected to find that something was wrong.

"Everything's fine," Fitzsimmons said. "But before you hang up, have you ever heard of a place called The Good Sports Cafe?"

"Yeah, I've heard of it. Why?" His tone had changed. It had become cold and defensive.

"I'm just wondering what kind of place it is."

"It's a strange kind of place," Shannon said.

"In what way? It's not a gay bar, is it?"

"I don't think you have to be of a particular persuasion to go there. It gets all types. It's different. I'll say that. Sarz goes there. Is that why you wanted to know about it?" Shanny asked.

"Yes."

"Well," Shannon said, "It's his kind of place, and his kind of people. It's not the kind of place I would get comfortable in if I were you. It's the kind of place where you have to watch your ass."

CHAPTER THREE

WHEN FITZSIMMONS GOT BACK TO THE APARTMENT HOUSE THAT night, he found Karen Easton standing in the hall with her raincoat over her arm. She was wearing a sparkling white nurse's uniform, and she was, Fitzsimmons thought, startlingly attractive. He felt a mixture of excitement and satisfaction in seeing her again.

"Hi. Lock yourself out?" he asked.

"No. I thought I heard something inside. I didn't know whether to open the door or not."

"Here. Let me." He took her key and inserted it in the lock and turned it. When he heard the bolt snap back, he twisted the handle and pushed the door until it swung wide open. The room was brightly lit.

"Did you leave the lights on?" he asked.

"No. Maybe we better call the police."

Fitzsimmons took one step through the doorway. Even though he was not paying attention to the furnishings, he was struck by how different this living room was from his own.

"Where's your telephone?"

It's over there next to that bedroom door," Karen said, pointing toward a closed door.

Fitzsimmons realized it was a two-bedroom apartment.

"You're sure nobody else is home?"

"I live alone," she said.

At that moment a crashing sound came from the bedroom Karen had pointed toward. It was followed by the loud clanging of footsteps on the metal fire escape.

Fitzsimmons went to the bedroom door and opened it. The lights were on but the room was empty. A portable television and a stereo had been placed next to the open window. A night table lamp lay smashed on the floor. He opened the bedroom closet. It was empty. Then he checked the bathroom, the other bedroom and the kitchen. They, too, were empty.

"They've gone," Fitzsimmons said. Karen had entered the apartment and stood in the middle of the living room. She looked upset, as if someone had injured her.

"I don't know how much they got away with. Your television and stereo are still in the bedroom."

She looked at Fitzsimmons but said nothing. He could see the pain in her eyes.

"The joys of urban living," he said.

"How can they just come in here like that?" She dropped her pocketbook to the floor. "I feel violated."

She looked away from Fitzsimmons and then back at him.

"And suppose I had been here? My God. I really could have been violated."

She was so deep in her own thoughts that she did not, at first, notice that Fitzsimmons had suddenly become visibly nervous and ill at ease, and his face had lost some of its color.

She cocked her head and scrutinized him. "Are you all right?"

"I'm fine," he said. He bent his head and rubbed his thumb and forefinger across his eyelids.

"Are you sure? You look as white as a sheet."

"I'm all right," he repeated. "Probably just low blood sugar."

"Here, sit down," she said.

Fitzsimmons sat down. The color began to return to his face. "I'm really all right. Why don't you look around and see what they've taken?"

"Shouldn't I call the police?"

"I suppose, but if they didn't get anything, it might be more trouble than it's worth."

She stared into his face. "Are you sure you feel all right?"

"I'm much better. As soon as I get something in my stomach, I'll be perfect."

She threw her raincoat on the sofa and took hold of his wrist.

"Karen, I'm. …"

"Quiet," she said. She placed two fingers on his pulse and stared at her wristwatch.

He caught the light fragrance of her perfume, and he could feel his pulse rate increase. He stared at the window and cleared his mind.

"You're okay," she said, dropping his wrist. "This is really strange. Something like this has never happened to me before. How can people just come into somebody else's apartment and take whatever they like? Has this ever happened to you?"

He shook his head. He looked haggard again—ashen.

"You're not diabetic are you?"

"No."

"We'd better get something in your stomach. I have bacon and eggs in the refrigerator. I don't have anything heavy because I don't usually eat dinner here."

"Don't go to all that trouble. You've just been robbed. You really ought to look around and see what they made off with."

"That can wait. I'm hungry myself. I'll go make us something. Scrambled or fried?"

"Either," he said, as she disappeared into the kitchen.

A moment later she was back. "Here, drink this," she said, handing him a glass of orange juice.

As he sat smelling the bacon cooking, he looked around the room. It was ablaze with color—blue and red and beige—and it seemed crammed with furniture. There was a sofa, three chairs, a coffee table, end tables, lamps, wall-to-wall carpeting, a mirror, and three paintings hanging from the walls. The apartment seemed warm and comfortable.

By contrast, his own apartment was sparsely furnished and austere. The walls and drapes were white, as was the divan. There was a low table, a brass stand-up lamp, and a stereo with speakers. On the floor was a rectangular, pale blue rug, but it was not wall-to-wall carpeting, and between the edges of the rug and the walls the shiny hardwood flooring was exposed. It added a stark quality to the room. There was a bookcase on one wall and an abstract painting on the wall opposite it. He had not realized it was so ascetic.

When the food was ready she called him into the kitchen. There were bacon, eggs, toast and coffee.

"This is really very kind of you," Fitzsimmons said.

"It's not all that kind. There's a selfish motive involved. I really wanted some company until I calm down. This neighborhood. Sometimes it just makes me a little nervous."

"Oh really? I always thought it was pretty pleasant."

"It is. It really is. I like it, but I guess I'm not used to living alone in a large city. Murders and robberies are so commonplace. Do you remember the Boston Strangler?"

"Vaguely. That was quite a while ago, wasn't it?"

"He killed a woman about a block from here."

Fitzsimmons cleared his throat.

"There are still some nurses at the hospital who talk about it. Sometimes it makes you wonder what goes on in a city. That and some of the cases we get. Right now we have a six-year-old girl who was raped and burned in about twenty places with a cigarette. It's terrible."

Fitzsimmons stood up and his leg jostled the table.

"I'm sorry," he said.

"Are you sure you're all right?" Karen asked.

Fitzsimmons smiled and shook his head. "Probably not. Probably not."

Karen looked puzzled.

"That was an excellent breakfast," he said. "Before I leave, why don't I go around and lock all the windows?"

"Okay."

He stopped at the door as he was leaving. "Your apartment is very nice, very warm. It makes mine look like a cell. That painting over the sofa ... ." Fitzsimmons pointed to the soft expressionistic portrait of a woman in a white dress.

"Oh, yes. I love that painting. It's a copy. I found it in one of those shops on Newbury Street."

"It's very striking. Who painted it?"

"I can't remember. But it was painted in the late 1800s. It's American. But I really don't know anything about art." She seemed apologetic, almost remorseful.

"Well, you've got nice taste," Fitzsimmons said.

Karen smiled. It was a relaxed, quite charming smile, and Fitzsimmons felt something stir deep within him.

"Perhaps I can pay you back for all of this by taking you out to dinner," Fitzsimmons said.

There was a pause, and then Karen said, "I'd like that."

"Saturday?"

"Fine."

Fitzsimmons did not fall asleep right away that night; though he was not restless. He felt change taking place within him; involuntary change which had nothing to do with his intellect or his will. He felt as if he were being shepherded toward an unknown object by an interior force over which he was powerless. It was a little like being a bystander witnessing his own life take shape.

The sign of that change was Karen Easton. He had met other attractive women in the past four years, but they had evoked no inner response. Karen Easton had. His eyes were drawn to her beauty and his nostrils to her perfume. As he was leaving her apartment, he had had a sudden urge to reach out and touch her hand, but he resisted because he was afraid that he would have offended or frightened her.

Now, as he lay on his back staring up at the darkness, he tried to visualize her and to imagine the scent of her perfume, but he could see only her dark eyes. He saw a vulnerability in them and an anguish which perhaps only another wounded human being would detect. It wasn't there most of the time, certainly not when she was taking charge of a situation as she had when Fitzsimmons felt faint. Then she had fallen back on her professional training, and he guessed that she was a very good nurse. But the anguish was there nevertheless—below the surface, to be seen only for an unguarded moment.

They had spent an hour together, but they had said nothing about themselves. He did not know her marital status or her age—but he guessed that she was seven or eight years younger than he—and she did not know his. Neither had boasted of accomplishments or spoken of family. They had revealed nothing of their histories, and yet they had revealed something of themselves. He had found her unpretentious and likable, and he suspected she found him to be likable, too, if just a little puzzling.

There was something else they knew about each other. For whatever reasons, they were both alone.

CHAPTER FOUR

"THE OLDER I GET, THE MORE AWARE I AM OF MY FAILINGS," PETER Genaro said as he stirred his coffee. They were sitting in Angelina's restaurant in the North End. It was a friendly, family-run Italian restaurant not far from TPI and a place where Father Genaro was well-known and well-liked. "And then sometimes, I think I get my failings confused with my virtues and vice versa. I think discretion, for example, can be a vice. We can use it to avoid taking risks and to keep from becoming involved."

He dipped the spoon in the sugar bowl and dropped another spoonful of sugar in his cup. "You can see that I'm not a real coffee drinker. Real coffee drinkers are like you—no milk, no sugar—just straight, black coffee. My spiritual adviser in the seminary told me I would never be a man until I could take my coffee black. And here I am fifty-eight years old, and I still drink it very sweet and very light."

He paused, but Fitzsimmons did not reply.

"How long have we known each other? Six months? It was last fall, wasn't it?"

Fitzsimmons nodded, still silent.

"If I practiced the virtue of discretion to a fault, I suppose I'd just keep my mouth shut. But I'm not going to."

The two men eyed each other for a moment and still Fitzsimmons did not break his silence.

"You've come a long way since last November," the priest said. "There are moments when you actually get outside of yourself."

Fitzsimmons rubbed the point of his nose with the knuckle of his right forefinger and studied the priest.

"When we met—I don't know whether you know this—you were frozen. I don't mean outside. You functioned well enough. At least you seemed to. You made small talk and appeared to get along. But inside, John, it was another story. I don't think I have ever met anyone who has walled himself off the way you have."

Fitzsimmons continued to study the priest without flinching.

"I was faced with a mystery: an educated man, perhaps even a brilliant man, has shut the door on all that has gone before—not only to other people, but to himself. We've known each other for six months, and I know almost nothing about you. And what I do know I've arrived at by the process of deduction.

"Take art, for example. Ives, Becket, abstract impressionism. It's all very cerebral. There is an absence of feeling and an absence of personal involvement. However intellectually drawn we may be to Charles Ives, we do not become emotionally involved with him, no more than we become emotionally involved with a geometric abstraction. Now Beethoven or Wagner or Verdi or Puccini—there we cannot help but become emotionally involved, except of course in some of Beethoven's late quartets, which you admire so. And their beauty is like the beauty of the desert."

The priest tapped the palm of his right hand on the table. His usual gentle countenance was gone. He looked strong, forceful, and determined.

"I've done a lot of thinking about this, and I'd like to continue if you don't mind," the priest said.

Fitzsimmons' gaze had dropped to the red checked tablecloth. He looked up at the priest and shrugged, and then he bent his head again. With his index finger he pushed several granules of sugar into a small pile.

The priest spoke to the top of Fitzsimmons' head. "You are a man who has come to terms with himself by sealing off emotion. Most people, when they don't like the way they are feeling, try to feel differently. Some people despair of feeling differently and try not to feel at all."

"More coffee, gentlemen?" The waitress stood next to them holding a glass coffeepot.

Fitzsimmons nodded. The two men were silent while she filled their cups. When she left, the priest continued.

"It's not an easy task to avoid feeling. It's a little like walking a tightrope. There is feeling in so many aspects of life—in art, in human relationships, in our vocations. To protect ourselves from feeling, if that is what we want to do, we have to shut a lot of doors on art, on human relationships, at least the ones that are not superficial, and on our true vocations. There is even an emotional relationship between a man and his work."

Fitzsimmons lifted his head and looked directly at the priest. "That's right," he said.

"Shall I go on?"

"If you wish. It doesn't matter."

"Do I sense that this friendship is in trouble?" Peter asked.

Fitzsimmons waited a moment before shaking his head. "No. I suppose I'm surprised it has taken you this long."

"So am I," Peter said, and smiled. It was a gentle, friendly smile. "Sartre would say that when you chose to become friendly with a priest, you chose to have this conversation."

"Perhaps," Fitzsimmons answered.

"I know you have suffered something. At first I wondered if you had committed a crime, but you're just not the type. Then I thought that perhaps you were a recovering alcoholic or a compulsive gambler. I've met a number of them who have lost wives and children and jobs. But people who have lost because of something they themselves have done try to recover what they lost. If you had been the cause of your own trouble and had now straightened out your life, you would be anxious to get back to where you had been. But you don't want to go back. You've cut yourself adrift, and you want to stay that way."

"That's right," Fitzsimmons agreed.

"Forgive me for being a priest," Peter said. "But it's not right. I don't mean morally. It's not humanly right. Eight cylinder cars were not meant to run on three cylinders. It's not mechanically right. Human beings are not meant to forcibly restrict their spirits. When they do, they are not operating the way they were made to operate."

The priest examined Fitzsimmons' face to see if what he was saying was making any impression. Fitzsimmons was a tall, fair, slender man with an introspective air about him. He was obviously a man who knew how to keep his own counsel, and yet for all his aloofness and detachment, he had a certain vulnerability which he could not conceal.

"Am I troubling you?" Peter asked.

Fitzsimmons picked some wax from the short red candle sitting in a stubby holder in the center of the table. He rolled the wax into a little ball and dropped it into the flame. It hissed and, for a moment, the flame shot up. Fitzsimmons waited until it died down before he answered.

"Not really," he said. He slumped back in his chair and looked directly at the priest. "I've been over all this ground before, with myself, Peter. I have done what I have had to do. You're right. I'm not a felon or a reformed gambler or drug addict. I am not recovering from something I have done." He extended his hands, palms up, toward Peter. "I am not guilty. I have done nothing. And you are right. I have shut it off. I've taken a sabbatical from life."

Peter leaned toward him, and seemed on the verge of speaking, but Fitzsimmons held up his right hand as if to say, "Stop."

The priest slouched back in his chair and neither man spoke. Fitzsimmons watched the bus boys clean up tables and scurry off to the kitchen. He saw a waitress with white, rubber-soled shoes and a pencil behind her ear hurry through the room carrying on her shoulder a heavy tray loaded with plates of spaghetti and veal, and he saw a plump, late middle-aged woman in a flowered purple dress standing a few tables away, watching the priest very closely. When she caught Fitzsimmons looking at her, she abruptly came to the table.

"Father Pete, so nice to see you."

"Angelina, the meal was delicious," Peter said. He started to get up, but she put her hand on his shoulder. "This is a friend of mine, John Fitzsimmons. John, Angelina owns this marvelous place."

Fitzsimmons was already on his feet.

"No. No," she said. "Sit. Sit. You sit. Ah, Father, these well-mannered Irishers. They have to learn to sit and relax." Her smile was huge. "Mr. Fitzsimmons, did you have a nice meal?"

"It was wonderful. I loved it."

"That's good. That's good. I'm pleased. And you, Father Pete? How was your veal?"

"Exquisite."

Angelina's smile grew. "Yeah?" she said.

"Angelina, it is positively miraculous what you do with veal."

"A miracle," she laughed. "Ha, ha. This whole place is a miracle. Father, if you only knew what a miracle it is." She turned to Fitzsimmons. "Sometimes I ask Father Pete to say a special prayer for me." She waved her hand at the room. "And it's working. See, Mr. Fitzsimmons?"

Fitzsimmons nodded without conviction.

Angelina looked pained. "Father, is that all you've had? Just coffee? No dessert?"

"I'm trying to watch my weight," the priest replied.

"You watch your weight at somebody else's restaurant. When you come here, you relax and eat and worry about your weight tomorrow. We have some beautiful Italian cheesecake. It was just made. I'm going to have the girl bring you each a piece. A little piece for you, Father, and a big piece for Mr. Fitzsimmons. He can't be watching his weight. And maybe a little Galiano and some more coffee. Or would you like espresso? Mr. Fitzsimmons, how about you? You have to set a good example for Father Pete."

"The cheesecake and espresso sound good to me."

"I'll send two of everything," Angelina said. "Two of everything. She winked at Fitzsimmons and spun away from the table before Peter could reply.

"A sabbatical from life, huh?" Peter said.

Fitzsimmons looked away, and the two men lapsed into silence again until the waitress came with the desserts. When Fitzsimmons had eaten about half the cheesecake, Angelina returned to the table.

"How's the cheesecake?" she asked.

"It's delicious," Peter said.

Angelina smiled and nodded as if agreeing with him.

"And yours, Mr. Fitzsimmons?"

"I don't ever remember having cheesecake this good."

"Good, good," she said and turned back to Peter. "Father Pete, don't look for the check. It's already been taken care of."

"Angelina, come on now. We talked about this last time. I can't keep coming here if you don't let me pay."

"You can pay. But not this time. This time is special. Mr. Fitzsimmons, you understand, don't you?"

Fitzsimmons nodded.

"You see, Father Pete, Mr. Fitzsimmons understands."

"And what does Mr. Fitzsimmons understand?" the priest asked.

"I understand a good heart."

"But this is an expensive check!"

"No. No," Angelina insisted.

"I'll make it up tomorrow night," Fitzsimmons said. "I was looking for a place to take a woman I know. This is so good, we'll just come here."

"You see, Father? Bread cast upon the water," Angelina said.

"All right, Angelina. Thank you. But this really is the last time."

"Of course, Father," she said and gave Fitzsimmons a wink.

When she had left, the priest leaned toward Fitzsimmons.

"A date?" he asked.

"Yes."

The priest smiled. "Is this something new?"

"As a matter of fact, yes. Very new. I just met her."

"That's good," Peter said.

"You seem surprised," Fitzsimmons said.

"I guess I am, a little. Pleasantly surprised."

"So am I," Fitzsimmons said.

CHAPTER FIVE

KAREN EASTON OPENED THE DOOR AND VERY NEARLY TOOK Fitzsimmons' breath away. It was the combination of her perfume and the way she looked.

"Is this dressy enough?" she asked. She wore a beige sweater and a plaid skirt. A gold locket hung from her neck. The light from the apartment gave her hair a radiance.

"It's perfect," Fitzsimmons said.

"I could change into a dress."

"No. No. It's perfect. I thought we'd go to Angelina's, if that's all right."

"Italian?"

"Yes."

"Great. I love Italian food."

The cab ride was short and pleasant enough. Karen talked easily. She chatted about the weather and the city, and Fitzsimmons found himself listening and enjoying the conversation. But he also felt something within him that he had written off as dead a long time ago. He felt a strong attraction to Karen. It was not merely sexual, although he felt that, too; it was a human attraction. If he could, he would have inhaled her. She seemed happy, and she was amusing, beautiful, young and stimulating, and Fitzsimmons, who had been living like an anchorite for four years, was drawn to her.

"Did you call the police?" he asked.

"Yes. They came over and looked around. They said I was lucky that nothing was stolen. There was really nothing they could do."

"No. I guess not."

"Are you fully recovered?"

"Recovered?" Fitzsimmons asked. He felt an unexpected embarrassment.

"Yes. From whatever made you so pale the other night."

"Oh, yes. Yes. I'm fine."

Angelina spotted them as soon as they entered the restaurant.

"Mr. Fitzsimmons, you're a man of your word. I'm holding a table for you."

"Angelina, this is Karen Easton."

"How do you do, Miss Easton," Angelina said shaking her hand. "Mr. Fitzsimmons was here last night with Father Pete. Do you know Father Pete?"

"No. I'm afraid not."

"That's too bad, but maybe you'll meet him," Angelina said, and her face burst into a smile. "Mr. Fitzsimmons told Father Pete and me last night that my place was so good that he was going to bring a beautiful lady back tonight. And here you are."

They all laughed. Karen looked at Fitzsimmons and he shrugged, still smiling.

"She really likes you," Karen said, after Angelina left the table.

"She's very nice."

"Do you come here often?"

"Last night was the first time. A friend of mine brought me. He swears it's the best Italian place in Boston."

"Father Pete?" Karen asked, raising one eyebrow slightly.

"Yes," Fitzsimmons answered. "You seem surprised."

"I guess I am. I don't think I've ever known anybody who had a priest for a friend. You know, somebody they went out with."

"Peter's a good guy. He has a parish out in Brighton."

"Have you been friends long?"

"Six months or so. Why do you ask?"

"I don't know," Karen answered. "Just wondering. But... ."

"But?"

"Well, you look ... oh ... you look a little like a priest. You've got that kind of face."

Fitzsimmons laughed. "Me?"

"A little bit," Karen said. She was starting to become embarrassed.

"And you were wondering if I'm a priest?"

Karen blushed slightly and smiled.

"I feel like I'm digging a hole for myself," she said.

"No. No. I'm just curious. It's not every day I get taken for a priest."

"It's silly, I suppose. But not that silly. I guess it's your face and my imagination. Everybody in our apartment house is either married or living with somebody. And across the hall from me there's an attractive man who lives alone. You read about all the people who are leaving the Catholic Church these days, and this man has a priest for a friend." She let the thought hang in the air.

"You're right. I am alone, and now you're going to tell me that you used to be a nun."

"No. I've always been a nurse. But I'm alone, too."

The waitress came to take their drink orders. Karen asked for a whisky sour on the rocks, Fitzsimmons for a quinine water with lime.

"Don't you drink?" Karen asked. She seemed suddenly somber.

"No."

"How come?"

"No reason. I just never liked the stuff. Why do you ask?"

Karen smiled again and seemed to relax.

"Just curious," she said.

Fitzsimmons did not pursue the conversation. Instead, he, too, relaxed and began to luxuriate in the pleasantness of his surroundings and company. From time to time, trying not to be obvious, he would study Karen's face. She was, he decided, quite beautiful with dark hair and dark eyes and a warm, full smile. Her face was lively, at one moment full of brightness and the next tinged with irony or gentleness.

But there was something else; something he had noticed before. There was a vulnerability in her face, especially around her eyes, as if they had seen their share of pain. It was just a fleeting thought, something he did not dwell on. He could not dwell on it because her presence was intoxicating to the point that he felt almost flushed and slightly embarrassed, hoping that she would not notice.

The questions began after dinner.

"What do you do for a living?" Karen asked.

"Not much. I work at a company called TPI. I'm a watchman."

"A watchman?"

Fitzsimmons seemed slightly amused. "Well, I also sweep floors," he said.

Karen looked bewildered rather than disappointed.

"Are you kidding?" she asked.

"No. That's what I do. I hope you don't mind."

"Why should I mind?"

"Well, I really didn't think about it, but there are probably a lot of women who might turn down an invitation to dinner from a night watchman," Fitzsimmons said. He was apologetic with no trace of irony.

Karen smiled gently, almost consolingly. "I'm having a nice time. I don't think my social standing has been damaged. I guess there's probably a story behind how you wound up sweeping floors."

"There is, but I'd just as soon skip it for tonight."

"Okay," she said. Then, after a pause, she added, "But I'll bet that you haven't always been a watchman."

Fitzsimmons threw up his hands.

"No. Not always," he said. "I taught English at a college on Long Island."

"No. Please. I don't mean to pry," Karen said. Then she smiled again. "But there is one other thing I'd like to ask."

"What's that?" Fitzsimmons said and he, too, smiled.

"Are you married?"

"No."

"Ever been married?"

"Yes. How about yourself?"

"Same answers. I'm not married, but I was."

As if by mutual consent the cross-examinations stopped. They talked about the meal and Angelina and the decor of the restaurant, and as they spoke about inconsequential things, they warmed to the conversation and to each other. Fitzsimmons found himself laughing at Karen's small jokes, and she, in turn, smiled almost continually.

After they left Angelina's they found a club with a small combo that played slow music. They sat for a while sipping their drinks—he had another quinine and she had an after dinner liqueur, and then they rose to dance. She slipped her body against his very gently, but even the light contact made his blood rush. She felt soft and warm, and they moved slowly and easily. Her temple touched his cheek, her breasts pressed gently into his lower chest, and her leg brushed his. His intoxication was complete.

When he asked Karen to dinner, he had anticipated nothing. His human contacts, with the exception of Peter, had been so impersonal that it had not occurred to him that his encounter with Karen would be anything more than polite.

Now, as he swayed with her on the dance floor, smelling the perfume from her hair and feeling her warm body nestling against his, he was astonished by the pleasure that he was taking in the moment.

Fitzsimmons had an analytical mind, and he was aware, even as he danced, that his senses were being overwhelmed, and he wondered if it had less to do with the woman with whom he was dancing than the mere fact that, after four years of celibacy, he was holding a warm and beautiful woman in his arms. He decided he did not care. He was dancing with a woman who seemed open and alive, a nice person without pretense or prejudice, and he was taking great pleasure in it. That was enough.

"I enjoyed that," he said when the music ended.

She smiled. "It was very nice." She squeezed his hand and they went back to the table.

Karen took a sip of her drink and then traced a semicircle around the base of her glass.

"Divorced?" she asked.

"No. My wife is dead."

"Oh. I'm sorry."

"It was some time ago."

"Do you have any children?"

"We had one. A little girl. She's dead, too," he said.

Fitzsimmons' face did not change expression, and the edge to his tone was almost imperceptible.

After a long silence, Karen spoke. "I'm divorced," she offered. "I have a little girl, but right now she's staying with my mother.

"How old is she?"

"Seven. Almost eight." Karen reached for her handbag, but thought better of it and stopped. "Her name's Amy."

Fitzsimmons nodded. His mood had changed swiftly. They were silent, and the silence made him uncomfortable.

"Do you want to go?" he asked.

Karen looked surprised.

"There's no rush," Fitzsimmons said quickly. "The band should be back in a minute."

"It's up to you," she said.

"I wouldn't mind another dance," he said.

"Neither would I," she answered.

They stayed until almost midnight.

When they left the club they took a cab to Park Square, where Karen suggested they walk the rest of the way.

Karen took his arm as they climbed past the State House.

"I enjoyed myself tonight," she said.

"Me, too."

"Really?"

"Yes, really," Fitzsimmons said.

They took a few more steps.

"You weren't bored?"

"No. Of course not. Why? Did I look bored?"

"No," she said. "But sometimes people who don't drink find it difficult to be in that kind of atmosphere."

"Why is that?"

"Well," Karen said, "they find it's a temptation."

"Temptation?" Fitzsimmons asked, and then he laughed. "You're not kidding, are you? This is strange. This is the second night in a row that I've had dinner with a person who thought I might have been an alcoholic. Do I have an aura?"

"And you're not?" Karen persisted.

"No."

"You're sure?"

Fitzsimmons stopped walking and turned to face Karen. He could see by her face that his answer was very important to her.

"I'm sure," he said.

He did not ask her reason for concern. He was not ready to bring the past into their relationship, neither hers nor his. They walked the rest of the way in silence.

"Good night," Karen said at the door to her apartment. "I hope you didn't mind my questions."

"I didn't mind. I enjoyed the entire evening. Every bit of it."

Karen smiled broadly.

"You're a nice guy," she said.

"You're pretty nice yourself," he said. "I think we ought to do this again."

She rose up on her toes and kissed him gently on the lips.

"I think so, too," she said.

A moment later she had slipped into her apartment and shut the door, and Fitzsimmons stood alone in the hall savoring the taste of her lips on his.

CHAPTER SIX

AT ABOUT FOUR O'CLOCK THAT MORNING, THE RECURRING DREAM returned. Fitzsimmons had not had it for almost six months, and he was hoping that he would never experience it again.

He was immersed in a warm, thick liquid. Great weights were tied around his body, yet his arms and legs were free, and he was struggling to swim to the surface. As he swam upward, even though he was submerged, he could shout, and he did shout, "Sarah, Eileen. Sarah, Eileen."

But his voice lacked power. He could hear it, but he knew that it could not penetrate the thick liquid, and he knew that no one else could hear his shout.

"Eileen, Sarah," he called again. It was in vain, but he continued to call the two names. As he swam, he was filled with anxiety, and he could feel himself being taken over by panic. He tried to swim more rapidly, but the faster he moved his arms and legs, the less progress he made. He knew he would go faster if he stopped thrashing about, but he could not help himself. He kept thrashing.

Finally, despite his efforts, the huge weights began to drag him down. The liquid got thicker and darker and at last Fitzsimmons could swim no more. He was ready to drown, and he accepted his fate. He opened his mouth and the liquid rushed in. He could taste it. It was blood. It was the blood of Sarah and Eileen.

He woke up trembling and covered with perspiration. In his mind he could see the red pentagram on the wall and the huge knife on the floor. He scrambled from the bed and ran to the bathroom. When he turned on the light, the images disappeared, but he could feel his heart beating and his mind racing. He turned on the faucet and scooped cold water up and splashed it on his face and on the back of his neck. He straightened up. Strange eyes stared back at him from his gaunt reflection in the mirror.

"No," Fitzsimmons said to the image. "I will not go insane." His face glared back at him without answering.

Fitzsimmons went back to the bedroom and began to dress. By the time he had pulled on a pair of pants and tucked in his shirt, his breathing and his pulse rate began to return to normal. He thought of going back to bed, but he knew he would not sleep. He took a pair of tennis shoes from the closet and put them on. He decided to walk it off.

A few hours later, Fitzsimmons knocked on the rectory door.

Peter was surprised, but pleased. "You're up early, John."

"I was in the neighborhood. I hope it's all right."

"Of course it is. I'm glad to see you. Come on in. I'm making coffee and there are fresh doughnuts. I don't have Mass for another hour, so we have plenty of time."

In the kitchen, Peter pointed to a brown cardboard box on the counter. "The doughnuts are over there," he said. He waited until Fitzsimmons had lifted a jelly doughnut from the box and had taken a bite. "You look a little harried."

Fitzsimmons nodded. "I am."

"Do you want to sit down?"

"No, thanks."

"Do you want to talk?"

"I don't know."

The priest took two coffee mugs out of a cabinet and set them next to the coffee maker which was still dripping. He started to speak and then stopped.

"Go ahead," Fitzsimmons said.

"I was going to say that priests learn very early to be patient," he said. "Things always take much longer than I expect them to. I have a tendency to look for instant results." He turned to look at the coffee maker. "But if you want instant coffee that's all you get. If you want good coffee, you have to wait."

Fitzsimmons did not answer, and Peter did not speak. The two men sat in silence at the kitchen table sipping their coffee. Occasionally their eyes would meet, and they would look away. When they emptied their mugs, Peter took the glass coffeepot and refilled them. He sat down again, and again they sat without speaking. If the silence made them uncomfortable, neither one of them showed it.

After about fifteen minutes, Fitzsimmons spoke. "Well, I'll move along and let you get ready for Mass," he said.

As Fitzsimmons was walking out the front door, Peter stopped him.

"See those tulips?" the priest asked. The edge of the flower bed which ran along the front of the rectory was dotted with tulips.

"They're very nice," Fitzsimmons said.

Peter nodded. "They are, aren't they? They remind me of something. Do you have a second?"

"Sure," Fitzsimmons said.

"I see them every spring, and every spring they remind me of when I was fifteen years old. I was a sophomore in high school, and my father died. He had a heart attack one night as he was coming home from work. He had just gotten off the bus, and he collapsed on the sidewalk. Nowadays they probably would have saved him, but not then. They pronounced him dead on arrival at the hospital. You can imagine the shock."

The eyes of the two men met. Fitzsimmons nodded and looked away.

"My father was more to me than a father. He was a father and an older brother and a best friend combined. He was a very gentle man, but he was very strong, and he understood. I could bring my troubles to him and my fears and my mistakes and we'd talk about them. I think he would have made a great priest. He was always talking about forgiving, about canceling debts. If I did something wrong to somebody, he would tell me to forgive myself for being wrong and to forgive the other person for being right. If I achieved something he was overjoyed, and if I failed he was still happy that I tried. I think it was impossible for me to disappoint him.

"He was just a little guy. He was pudgy, not fat, but stout, and he used to smoke cigars—not in the house, my mother wouldn't let him.

He wasn't much to look at, but he was wonderful to be with. He was full of love. He loved to take us places—Fenway Park, Boston Garden. And then just before Christmas, he died without a word, without a warning.

"I was devastated. I couldn't believe it. I couldn't accept it. I was so, so angry. I was angry with my father for dying, and I was angry with God for letting him die. And I withdrew. I quit the basketball team and I decided not to go out for baseball. I stopped hanging around with my friends. I stopped going to Mass on Sundays—I didn't tell anybody, I didn't want to upset my mother—but I didn't want anything to do with God. I felt he didn't have any right to take my father, and I certainly had no intention of being a hypocrite and honoring him with my lips when I was angry with him in my heart.

"I stayed mad the rest of the winter and into the spring. Before my father died, I had felt a strong calling to become a priest. We had talked about my entering a seminary, but my father wanted me to wait at least until my junior year of college. That winter I decided that I was no longer interested in the priesthood. Indeed, I decided that I would become a man of the world and that as soon as I possibly could, I would end my teenage celibacy.

"Then one day in May, a beautiful day just like this, as I came home from school, I noticed tulips sprouting by the front steps to our house. The bulbs had been planted the previous fall by my father. I had watched him, but I had forgotten. I stood there and I could see my dad with the trowel, dressed in an old sweater and old pants, down on his knees, digging holes six inches deep and six inches apart. He had a dead cigar stub sticking out of one corner of his mouth and he was singing 'E lucevan le stelle' from *Tosca*. He couldn't really sing, but he loved Puccini.

"I sat down on the steps and I wept. I thought about the tulips and about my father. It came to me that just because my father had died it did not mean he had been taken out of my life. Just as he had planted the tulips months before and they came up after he died, he had planted things in me before he died, things that were growing in me and which would continue to grow in me if I let them—things like love and respect, tolerance and forgiveness.

"The tulips would not last into the summer, but the gifts my father had planted in me would last a lifetime. I still thought it was wrong for my father to die and wrong for God to let him die, but I decided to forgive my father for dying and God for letting him die. Looking back on it, I think it was on that afternoon that I entered my manhood.

"A couple of afternoons later my mother came home and heard the phonograph playing Puccini. For just a moment she thought my father was in the living room and that he had put the record on. And then she realized that it was me and that I was better."

Peter Genaro smiled. It was a wistful, slightly sad smile, and then he brightened. "I got more from my father than just a good example. I got my height, my good looks, and my singing voice."

Fitzsimmons started toward the street, and then he turned back to face the priest.

"Did you plant the tulips?" he asked.

"As a matter of fact, yes, I did. Last November. Just about the time that I met you," the priest said.

CHAPTER SEVEN

FITZSIMMONS HAD PLANNED TO WALK TO COMMONWEALTH AVENUE and take a bus back to Beacon Hill, but as he passed in front of the church he changed his mind.

St. Camillus was in the Gothic tradition, but it was a small church and, to Fitzsimmons, it looked inviting. He had not been inside a church since the funeral, and there was something even now that made the prospect unpleasant, but he was also curious about Peter. He wanted to see him in his role as priest, and his curiosity overcame his reluctance.

He entered through the center doors and, with only a glance at the holy water font, passed through the vestibule and went into the church itself.

It was still early, about a quarter to eight, and the church was not crowded. The lights had not been turned on, and the main altar was shrouded in darkness. On a small altar to the right, a red vigil candle glowed signifying, Fitzsimmons recalled, the presence of Christ in the Eucharist. The atmosphere was reverent and, except for the harsh breathing of an elderly man, the church was hushed. It reminded Fitzsimmons of his youth when, as an altar boy, he would serve the early Mass. Everything had seemed unblemished, the priest, the people, himself, as if the early morning carried with it a special reverence and purity. He could feel traces of that here. The stained glass windows, the stations of the cross, the feeling that in this place there was peace.

Loud clicks snapped out from behind the altar as, one after another, the rows of lights came on, first over the altar and then over the congregation. Fitzsimmons moved about halfway up the aisle and found a pew next to a massive stone pillar. He did not use the kneeler. He wondered if he would be able to sit through an entire Mass. The last time he had been in church, he had been half-mad and had fought a compulsion to suddenly bolt from his pew and run screaming to the outdoors. Now, however, he sensed a tranquility in the atmosphere that made him feel quite calm.

After a few minutes, a thin man in his mid-sixties walked to the center of the altar, turned his back to the congregation and bowed, and then mounted the pulpit. He cleared his throat and adjusted the microphone.

"Today is the feast of Pentecost," he said. "The proper for the Mass is found on page forty-two. Please rise and greet our celebrant, Father Genaro, by reading the entrance antiphon with me."

After a pause so that people in the congregation could find the right page in the missalette, he and the congregation read, "The Spirit of the Lord fills the whole world. It holds all things together and knows every word spoken by man, alleluia."

As they were reading, Peter came out onto the altar preceded by an altar boy. The priest was dressed in red vestments, and he seemed strange to Fitzsimmons, as if the vestments gave him another personality, one that Fitzsimmons had not anticipated. He seemed in one way to be a busy little man, straightening things out, putting the chalice in its place, opening the large, red book and flipping the pages, and then finally walking to the microphone and reading the opening prayer. But in another way, it was as if he had adopted a larger-than-life persona, as if he were somehow a public official carrying out official acts for the body of people in the church.

After he read the prayer, Peter sat down in a chair which was on a raised platform behind the altar, and the elderly man went back to the microphone.

This time Fitzsimmons did not pay attention to what the man said. Instead, he let his gaze wander around the church. Things had changed since he had been a very young altar boy. The Mass was in English, and some of the readings were done by lay people. The priest faced the congregation instead of quietly praying in Latin with his back to the people. The altar rail was gone and so were most of the statues. As he glanced around, he could not see one pair of rosary beads, and everyone in the church seemed to be intent on what was happening on the altar.

"Alleluia," the congregation proclaimed.

Peter was standing in the pulpit. "The Lord be with you," he said.

"And also with you," the congregation answered.

"A reading from the Holy Gospel according to John," Peter said.

"Glory to you, Lord," the congregation said.

After a moment, Peter began to read. "On the evening of the first day of the week, even though the disciples had locked the doors of the place where they were for fear of the Jews, Jesus came and stood before them. 'Peace be with you,' he said. When he had said this, he showed them his hands and his side. At the sight of the Lord, the disciples rejoiced. 'Peace be with you,' he said again. 'As the Father has sent me, so I send you.' Then he breathed on them and said: 'Receive the Holy Spirit. If you forgive men's sins, they are forgiven them; if you hold them bound, they are held bound.' "

When Peter finished reading the gospel, he paused for a moment and looked around the church. "Peace be with you," he said and paused for another long moment.

"When the Lord said those words, he was confronted by a room full of disciples who were anxious, frightened and confused. They had seen evil triumph over good and great hope turned to great despair. They did not know what the future held for them, but they knew enough to view it with great misgiving. And so Jesus Christ, who had just recently been put to death in a humiliating fashion, enters that locked room and tells them, 'Peace be with you,' just as he enters this church this morning and says to us, 'Peace be with you.' "

"You think that's far-fetched? To draw a parallel between the disciples in the upper room and the parishioners at St. Camillus? Where, after all, is the confusion? Where is the anxiety, the fear? Where is the despair?

"It's all here in the church this morning. It's staring up at me and out at you. I am sure that there are people here who know they are dying, or who have a loved one who is dying. There are people here this morning whose homes are in shambles, whose children are in prison, whose wives or husbands are in mental institutions. There are children here whose homes are ravaged by alcoholism, whose brothers and sisters have become addicted to drugs. And there are those who haven't come to Mass this morning, who can't come this morning because they are burdened by grief and guilt, women who have sought love outside of marriage and found self-hatred, girls whose emotions have been frozen by the decision to have an abortion, men who have turned their backs on loving relationships in favor of power and sensuality—people who are crippled by self and by a depraved world. And we wonder, where is God?"

Peter looked at the congregation and nodded his head.

"Oh, yes," he said, "priests wonder, 'Where is God?' There have been times when I have wondered and times when I have seen others wonder."

As he scanned the congregation, his eyes fell on Fitzsimmons.

"Thirty years ago, when I was a seminarian, I had a mentor, an old priest who used to take time to chat with me and give me advice now and then. He was an instructor in moral theology and he seemed to me to be one of the wisest men I had met. One morning, I bumped into him as he was on his way out of the residence hall. He seemed his usual self, cheerful and full of energy. He told me he was on the way to the hospital to visit a woman—I think she was a relative, I'm not sure. Anyway, I wished him luck and watched him go, and I remember envying him—his wisdom, his self-assurance. That afternoon I happened to meet him again, just as he was coming back. He looked very tired and very depressed, and when I asked him how the woman was doing, he just shook his head. 'I wouldn't do that to a dog,' he said. We both knew that he was talking about God's Providence, about God's care for that woman. God was letting that woman be treated in a way that you and I wouldn't even treat a dog."

Peter's voice was steady, and he spoke without any touch of drama. But the congregation was transfixed by his words. Even the altar boy was wide-awake and staring at the priest.

"A few years ago I met a man named Frank," Peter continued. "Frank was a reformed alcoholic. He had had a lot of trouble, but about ten years before I met him, he got his life straightened out. He stopped drinking and he got back to church. He spent a great deal of his time working with other alcoholics. He would go to great lengths trying to help them. He even brought some of them into his home. One time Frank brought a sick and suffering human being home; and then he got a call and went out. While he was gone, the fellow that he had brought home murdered Frank's wife."

Peter looked around the church as if he was speaking directly to each person sitting in a pew.

"Where was God?" he asked.

Fitzsimmons' and Peter's eyes met.

"Where was God?" the priest repeated. "You and I would never have allowed that woman in the hospital to suffer the way she did or Frank's wife to be killed as a direct result of his charity. But God did."

Their gaze stayed locked. "Yes," Fitzsimmons whispered to himself. "Where was God?" His whisper was soft and questioning, without anger.

He looked away from Peter to the crucifix suspended above the altar, and he wondered if Peter was talking to everyone in the church or just to him, and he wondered how Peter knew Fitzsimmons' question.

Peter continued in the same conversational tone of voice.

"Do you think, for a moment, that this is all there is? Do you think that life ends in a cancer ward or with a knife in a kitchen? And that is all? If that is all, then we may very well ask where is God.

"But the reason you and I are here this morning is that there is more to life than burdens and pains, joy and hope, and death. And you know that, and I know that. In our heart of hearts, we know that this is not all there is. Deep within us, much deeper than intellect can see, we know that there is something more, we know there is a promise we have not received, a dimension we have not entered. But we will enter that dimension, and when we do, whatever pain we have experienced, whatever sorrow we have known, whatever tragedy we have borne, will seem a very small price to have paid for admission.

"But that's later. That's not now, and we live in the now. What about now? I spent a lot of years thinking about the woman who died of cancer and thinking about Frank's wife lying in a puddle of her own blood on her kitchen floor. And I've thought about myself and the pain I've experienced and about my eventual death, and I asked myself a question. Suppose God came up to me and said, 'I'm going to give you a choice. I'm going to let you go back to the moment before your conception, and I'm going to let you choose to either be born or not to be born. And, if you are not born, you will escape all consciousness, all worry, all anxiety, all fear, all pain. But if you choose to be born, only

I know what you will go through.'

"My answer to that question is: 'Give me life.' I'll take whatever I can get. If it means I can only live to be ten years old, I'll take that. If I die at thirty, I'll take that. If a heart attack takes me this morning, or I get run over by a bus this afternoon, that's all right. I accept it. That's a risk I took when I came out of the womb.

"Right now, at this moment, my life has meaning. As I stand before you, I know in my heart that I am a happy man, a joyful man. I know that I have been touched by the power of God, just as those others were touched on that first Pentecost, and I have been changed from a man of fear to a man of hope, from a man of despair to a man of love, from a man of anxiety to a man of peace.

"That is what Pentecost is all about—freedom from the burdens of life and the burdens of self. And if you don't have that freedom, then you have not yet had your personal Pentecost. You have not met the risen Christ and received his power.

"So this morning, I have a message for you—for you who are in pain and without hope, for you who look at life and shudder, and for you who lock yourselves up in rooms to keep the rest of the world away. It is time to stop running. It is time to stop fearing. It is time to stop hiding. God has come to set you free. It is Jesus Christ himself who says to you this morning, 'Peace be with you.' "

When Peter stepped down from the pulpit, Fitzsimmons got up and slipped quietly out of the church. He had seen another side of Peter, one that surprised and disturbed him. The priest, despite his understated approach, was a powerful speaker, and he knew and talked about what goes on inside of human beings.

A slight breeze rustled the new leaves as Fitzsimmons walked toward Commonwealth Avenue. The world was renewing itself in another dazzling May morning, and it made Fitzsimmons feel uncomfortable because he knew that as much as he had changed, as much as he had come alive in the last several months, he still had one foot firmly in the grave, and he wondered if he did not want to keep it there.

There was something else that bothered Fitzsimmons. He had always believed in God, but he had always believed that God was an observer of man's actions and not a participant in them. Peter seemed to have another view.

Chapter Eight

Fitzsimmons had just finished shaving when he heard the knock on his door. He buttoned his sports shirt and tucked it in his trousers. He was feeling much better.

"Hi," Karen said. "You don't have a telephone." She was wearing a tan raincoat over her white nurse's uniform.

"No. What's up?"

"I just got off work. I was going to grab something for dinner. A sandwich at a deli or a pizza. I thought maybe you would like to join me."

"I'd love to," he said.

Karen hesitated. "I don't mean to be forward."

"Don't be silly. It's a great idea. I'm glad you thought of it."

Her smile was warm and confident. "In about an hour or so?" she asked.

"Fine. I'll come over at six."

As soon as he closed the door, Fitzsimmons began to have misgivings. Karen was a striking, beautiful woman. When she entered a restaurant, men's eyes followed her. Fitzsimmons had noticed that the previous night. She was a woman who should have no trouble finding a date or a partner. He knew instinctively that she was not looking for a shallow relationship or a casual sexual encounter. He, on the other hand, was not sure what, if anything, he was looking for—a pleasant evening out, some light conversation, the company of an attractive woman.

He had enjoyed himself immensely the night before. Something in him had awakened. He had half expected to be sexually aroused despite his celibate existence, or perhaps because of it, but something more than that had happened. His entire personality had been aroused. He had felt courtly, warm, exuberant. He had wanted to give of himself. He had wanted their personalities to embrace.

But that was last night. His talk with Peter Genaro had put things back in perspective. Peter had said that a healing process was going on, and he was right. Fitzsimmons felt that he was hardly more than a shell. He had forsaken life and human companionship for four years, and he was not sure that he wanted to resume living. She was starting over. It seemed unfair that their paths had crossed. She needed to meet someone who was healthy and whole and not someone who had renounced life. And yet, he enjoyed her company. At the same time, he knew that elements of an old selfishness were still in him. It would not be right to let selfishness dominate his behavior. He decided he would tell her.

He had the opportunity as they sat eating submarine sandwiches in Horace's Delicatessen. He stared down at the French bread with the onions and peppers and provolone gushing out and he tried to get started, but there was a huge weight within him blocking his words, blocking even his effort to begin to talk about his past. It was not that he did not want her to know; it was just that he did not want to talk about it. He could not bring himself to open his mouth and let the words come out.

Karen sensed something. "You seem pensive," she said.

"Do I?"

"A little. Anything wrong?"

He shook his head. "No. I'm just thinking."

"About anything in particular?"

"About the way people get to know each other. How we reveal ourselves—slowly. How we disclose our personalities and our pasts."

"Slowly," Karen said. She looked up from her sandwich into his eyes. "Because we're afraid of scaring people off."

"Or because we don't want to open the box."

"The box?"

"I used to think human beings packed their past into a box, day by day. Sort of like a dirty laundry basket with a spring at the bottom. And if you let the lid up, everything would pop out and you would have to live it all over again," Fitzsimmons said.

"You wouldn't want to live the past over again?" she asked.

Fitzsimmons looked grim. He shook his head.

"Neither would I," Karen said.

They were silent for a few minutes while they finished their sandwiches. Fitzsimmons went to get them coffee and came back to the table.

"My husband was an alcoholic," Karen said. "I mean he still is an alcoholic, but he is no longer my husband. I left Detroit after the divorce became final. I wanted to walk away from the past and start over again. So I came to Boston. Once I'm sure this is where I want to stay I'll send for my daughter. Right now she needs stability and friends. I didn't want her changing schools if the move wasn't going to be permanent."

Fitzsimmons looked around the delicatessen. It was quiet. Only half the tables were filled. It was a stark sort of place; the walls were painted light green, and the floor was covered with dirty yellow tile. Except for a green plant hanging by a large plate glass window at the front of the store, there were no decorations.

"I guess it's about the same for me. I left Long Island after Eileen and Sarah died and I wound up here." He paused and thought for a moment. "I don't think I was looking for a new life so much as just to get away from the old one."

Karen started to say something but stopped. Then after a moment, she did speak.

"So we both came to Boston to start over," she said. She smiled at Fitzsimmons. It was a gentle smile that had just a hint of a hidden robustness.

Traffic was light on Beacon Street. Karen took Fitzsimmons' arm and they walked slowly toward the Public Gardens. It was a cool twilight. Some of the cars still drove without their headlights on, others used only parking lights.

Fitzsimmons usually associated cool spring nights with melancholy, a gentle sadness that he had felt, perhaps as a child, on such nights. But this night was different. He felt light-hearted. He was very conscious of Karen next to him, conscious of her shorter steps, her more relaxed gait. It took him half a block to adjust his stride to hers.

"Smell that?" she asked.

"Yes. Spring," he said.

"Even in the city. I am really getting to like it here. Especially Beacon Hill. I was so surprised to see gaslights and cobblestone sidewalks."

"There's something friendly about it. It's built on a human scale." Fitzsimmons replied.

They spent almost two hours in the Public Gardens, lingering here and there, watching the breeze make ripples in the pond. They talked about little things, mostly about what they observed around them—a teenage boy on a bicycle, an elderly man walking a Doberman, other couples.

By nine o'clock the moon was up and the gardens took on a hushed quality. They spoke softly as if not wanting to disturb the subdued atmosphere. As they were about to leave the gardens, Fitzsimmons began to hum softly.

"What's that," she asked.

"What?"

"The tune you're humming."

He hummed for a moment and listened. "It's an aria from *Tosca*. 'E lucevan le stelle.' Just this morning Peter was telling me how his father used to sing it. That must have been what put it in my head."

"It's very pretty. I think I've heard it before. What do the words mean?"

"Something about the stars shining and the earth being filled with perfume and a beautiful woman in a garden. It's very appropriate."

She smiled and took his hand and they continued to walk slowly.

"Do you like opera?" she asked.

"I was nuts about it."

They took a few more steps. "I don't know anything at all about opera," she said.

"It can be magnificent. I used to think that something happens at an opera that doesn't happen anywhere else."

"What's that?"

"A kind of freeing of the spirit. Would you like to go? Caldwell's doing *Rigoletto* next week. I could get tickets."

"I don't know," Karen said. "I'm afraid I'm rather limited. I'm not the intellectual type."

"You don't have to know anything about opera to enjoy it. If only people who knew something about opera went to see it, the opera houses would be half-empty. I can't even remember the last time I went to an opera. Keep me company. It will be fun. First, we'll eat downstairs at Lockobers, and then we'll go. You'll love it."

"I'll keep you company," she said. Then, after a moment, she asked, "Do you think you'll ever teach again?"

"Why do you ask?"

"Your love of opera. It just seems so out of character for you to be doing what you're doing."

"It's funny that you should ask. I've thought about it lately, but I haven't decided. It may be a while before I do."

They walked on without paying much attention to where they were going. A half-hour later they found themselves in front of Filene's staring at a mannequin dressed up like a young girl.

"Isn't it pretty?" Karen asked.

The mannequin was wearing a summer outfit, light blue shorts and a floral print blouse. Fitzsimmons only glanced at it.

"Yes, it's very nice," he said. As he looked at Karen he saw that her eyes had filled.

She looked away from him. "Sometimes I feel very unmotherly," she said.

"It's very difficult," Fitzsimmons said.

"For you, too."

"It's not as bad as it used to be," he said.

He took her hand and pulled her away from the window and they began to walk back to Beacon Hill. They did not speak, and there was a kind of intimacy in their silence, an acceptance of the other's struggle.

Then as they walked, an unspoken question arose. Fitzsimmons instinctively knew that Karen was facing the same decision. He was ambivalent. He had an almost adolescent uncertainty, and he felt that she did, too. It had been twelve years since he had faced a similar ambivalence, and that woman, all those years ago, had been Eileen who had become his wife. Fitzsimmons had never been able to do anything casually. Relationships had been either deep or non-existent, and now he had a curious detachment as if he were a third person observing Karen and himself and wondering what would develop.

When they got back to the apartment house they stopped in front of Karen's door.

"John, we're adults living across the hall. We're both experienced, and I suppose at our age there are no rules."

Even in his detachment, Fitzsimmons felt his pulse quicken.

"There are always rules. It just depends which ones you want to play by," he said.

Karen's back was against the door, and she seemed smaller and more vulnerable. She looked him squarely in the eye.

"What rules do you play by?" she asked.

"It's been a long time since I've played," he answered with a half smile. "But the rules I used to play by were honesty and unselfishness."

"Those are good rules," she said. "Where do they leave us?"

Fitzsimmons thought for a moment. "I am in the company of a beautiful woman whom I find attractive and stimulating. I have immensely enjoyed being with you. I feel like I am being propelled toward you, that I'm being called back to life from where ever it is that I have been. But there is a part of me that is looking back, a somber part of me that doesn't want to let go. And another part of me wants to bend and kiss you and to hold you close to me."

Karen closed her eyes and they kissed, slowly and gently, and he felt a tremor go through his body as if the kiss had touched a central nerve.

"And what about you?" he asked.

"I'm scared. I wanted to meet you. I wanted to get to know you, but you're very deep, and I'm sort of shallow."

Fitzsimmons was puzzled. "What do you mean, shallow?"

"Just shallow. I've had my ups and downs, but I've never thought about them. I've just sort of bounced along. You look at things in a way I never have. You're different from me—from the people I've known."

They were silent again and in the silence, there was a new consciousness, an awareness that they were alone, that they were isolated from the rest of humankind and that together, without speaking, they were in the process of making a decision. It was an awkward silence, filled with inhibition, anticipation and exhilaration.

The dispassionate side of Fitzsimmons observed his physiological reactions with a clinical detachment. He felt his blood rush and his body ache as if it were someone else's blood and someone else's body. A voice within him wondered, "Is this it?" But the answer was irrelevant. Something was happening to him quite apart from intellect and will. It was already a closed issue.

He took her hands in his. "What shall we do?" he asked.

"I don't know," she said.

"Neither do I."

There was another silence.

"If … " she said.

"If what?"

"If we …"

They kissed again, and their bodies came together. This time the passion overwhelmed the distant detached part of Fitzsimmons, and he could feel the barrier inside of Karen had been similarly overwhelmed. It no longer mattered what each of them thought was best. The reality was that their bodies were pressed against each other and neither could pull away.

"Let's go inside," she said.

CHAPTER NINE

THE EUPHORIA STAYED WITH FITZSIMMONS THROUGHOUT THE DAY. He walked with a carelessness which he could not remember experiencing before, although he was certain he had experienced it. It was as if his cadence was determined by an inner music that he could feel but could not hear. He felt whole even though he knew that he was not, and he was filled with an emotion that was quite foreign to him. It was an inexpressible tenderness that softened everything within him. A friend of his had once told him that he had always felt uncomfortable after he had had sex with a woman whom he did not love. Fitzsimmons had not felt uncomfortable at all, and neither, as far as he could tell, had Karen. They had been gentle and giving and there had been an underlying unity, an agreement, unstated, but real nevertheless.

"Hey, Fitzsimmons."

"Yes," he answered, still listening to his own thoughts.

"Tonight?"

"Tonight?"

"Yeah. We'll have that drink tonight."

Sarz's stare brought Fitzsimmons out of his reverie.

"Tonight?" Karen was working from 11 to 7. He would not be able to see her anyway. "Why not?" Fitzsimmons answered.

"You goin' out with Sarz?" Tommy Quercio asked after Sarz had walked away. Irony shone in his eyes, and he smiled a sly smile.

"I guess so," Fitzsimmons said.

"Jay's goin' out with Sarz. Whoopee," Tommy giggled. He fidgeted with two pieces of metal. "You goin' up to his room, Jay?"

"No, Tommy. I'm just going out for a drink. I'm not going to his room."

Tommy's eyes went blank for a moment and then his face lit up.

"Hey, Jay, you gettin' much?"

Fitzsimmons was startled. He had not heard that expression in years. Was it just a coincidence, or was there something different about Fitzsimmons that told Tommy that he had been to bed with a woman the previous night?

"Why do you ask, Tommy?"

At once Tommy became shy and self-conscious. He stared down at his hands. The shyness did not last long. He looked up and his eyes gleamed with a secret irony.

"How come you're goin' out with Sarz? Huh, Jay?"

Fitzsimmons shook his head.

"God only knows," he said.

"Don't say God," Tommy shot back. His face had turned sad. "Don't say God, Jay. There is no God."

Tommy put his head down and went back to work as if Fitzsimmons was no longer there. Fitzsimmons' eyes lingered on Tommy, and Fitzsimmons realized for the first time that Tommy was aware that he had been cheated out of life. Fitzsimmons scanned the others who sat at the long rows of tables staring down at their hands, and he wondered how many of them felt the same way Tommy did and how many of them were unable to articulate their resentment and anger.

The Good Sports Cafe was dark, crowded and noisy. Hard rock blared through the bar, and the air was dense with smoke and the smell of beer. It was a long, narrow place with a bar running half the length of the wall on one side and booths on the other. In the back, booths lined both walls and there were a few small tables in between.

Fitzsimmons checked the bar where people were standing three and four deep. Most seemed to be in their late twenties or thirties; some were older. The Good Sports Cafe was not a place that catered to the college crowd. Fitzsimmons did not see Sarz at the bar so he started moving toward the rear, looking into each booth as he went. Many of the patrons, both men and women, were drinking shots and beers. "Hey, what are you lookin' at?" a man in a booth asked. He was large. He wore a tan, V-neck sweater with no shirt. A plain gold chain hung from his thick neck.

"I'm looking for someone I'm supposed to meet here," Fitzsimmons said.

"Well, look some place else. They ain't in this booth."

Fitzsimmons moved on. He found Sarz sitting alone in the third from the last booth. He was smoking a cigarette and a half-empty beer glass was on the table in front of him.

Sarz looked up at Fitzsimmons with the hint of a twisted smile. "Hey, Fitzsimmons, glad you could make it," he said.

"It's quite a place," Fitzsimmons answered.

"Yeah, you've noticed. Tough place. Tough people. No bullshit. Sit down. Have a drink."

Fitzsimmons slid into the booth opposite Sarz. "Do you come here often?" he asked.

"Yeah. Pretty often. This is my favorite place."

Sarz seemed to have been just slightly affected by the beer he had consumed. His eyes were slightly glassy, and his face was flushed, but his speech was deliberate, and his words were clearly enunciated.

"What's the attraction?" Fitzsimmons asked.

Sarz hesitated. "You mean, why do I like this place?"

Fitzsimmons nodded.

"It's real. Real life. Not that anemic shit most people waste their time on. People in here can do whatever they want to do. That's the attraction—freedom."

Sarz drained the glass of beer. "What are you having?" he asked.

"I'll just have some ginger ale."

"You're an amazing guy," Sarz said. "You don't drink. You don't smoke. You don't screw. Are you a defrocked Carmelite or something?"

Fitzsimmons did not respond.

"Not the first time you've been asked?"

"No," Fitzsimmons said.

"Well, have something. I was figuring on having a pretty good time. I mean a real blow-out," Sarz said. His smile seemed lewd.

Fitzsimmons' discomfort showed on his face, and Sarz reacted to it immediately. He began to talk about routine things—the spring, TPI, the problems of the handicapped, and television.

Fitzsimmons bided his time, matching Sarz ginger ale for beer, speaking only when necessary, and waiting for an opportune moment to leave. After about an hour, Sarz fell silent and Fitzsimmons started to get up.

"Wait, wait, wait," Sarz said. "This conversation hasn't even warmed up. We're just at the preliminaries. I haven't even begun my famous cross-examination."

"Maybe some other time," Fitzsimmons said.

"Just spend a few more minutes with me. Humor me. I'm a student of human nature. I really am. I study people. That's what I do. You think I'm a floor sweeper. You see me as one-dimensional. But you don't really see me. I study human nature. I explore it. I look at what you would call the dark side of it, and what I call the suppressed side of it. I examine it in others and in myself in all its aberrations—oppression, brutality, sex, violence—what the theologians would call evil."

Fitzsimmons started to say something and stopped.

"What were you going to say?"

Fitzsimmons was going to ask why sex was included in Sarz's list of evil things but he did not. Instead he asked, "Are you writing a book?"

Sarz stared intently at Fitzsimmons, perhaps to see if he was being mocked. "No. I don't believe in books. Nietzsche believed in books and he wound up in the nut house. No, I'm not writing a book. You've got to actually live things. You can't do it vicariously by writing about them."

"Oppression, brutality, violence?" It was a question on which Fitzsimmons did not elaborate.

"Haven't you experienced them?" Sarz responded. "We all do—at least as victims. And some people experience them as perpetrators."

"Prisons are full of them," Fitzsimmons said.

"So is this place," Sarz added. He waved to the waitress and signaled for another round of drinks. "But we're not talking about me. What about you?"

"There's nothing much to me," Fitzsimmons said. "I'm a guy who wandered around for a while and came to rest in Boston."

"Bullshit," Sarz said roughly. "I told you that I study people. You've got a history."

Fitzsimmons' tone changed from casual to sharp. "And if I do?"

"I'm curious. That's all." The rough edge was gone from Sarz's voice. For a moment, he seemed unexpectedly vulnerable and Fitzsimmons immediately sought to turn the tables.

"What about you? I'm sure you've got a history," Fitzsimmons said. Sarz surprised Fitzsimmons. Instead of becoming defensive he seemed pleased by the question. "I've got a history all right," he said. "A long history. A long, dark history."

He paused as if recalling the past. "Dank. Unpleasant." He nodded his head. "It's quite a history. Fascinating. Really fascinating."

He leaned across the table and spoke in a low voice. "You have no idea what an interesting character you're talking to. Unique. Absolutely unique. No question. Fascinating."

Fitzsimmons wondered how much of an effect the beer was having on Sarz.

"I'm not drunk," Sarz said as if reading his mind. "Mellow, but not drunk, and I'm not a braggart. Nobody knows my history. Nobody. I do, of course, but nobody else."

Fitzsimmons refused to give up the advantage. "You seem like an ordinary guy to me," he said.

Sarz's mellowness seemed to evaporate.

"I'm not trying to bait you," Fitzsimmons said. "I'm just wondering what's unique about you."

Sarz was on the defensive and he was obviously uncomfortable. He crumpled an empty cigarette package and dropped it on the table. "I'm out of cigarettes. I'll be right back." He slid out of the booth and disappeared into the crowd.

Sarz was gone for a long time. Fitzsimmons wished that he had told Sarz that he was leaving. Now he was forced to wait for him to return. He drained the glass. It was mostly water. He wondered how well they washed the glasses and what kind of viruses were passed around in the place.

"There was a ten minute wait in the line to the men's room," Sarz said when he finally reappeared.

"Well, I was just hanging around to say good night," Fitzsimmons said.

"You can't go yet, the waitress is bringing another round. Have one last ginger ale, then we'll call it a night."

A new waitress brought the drinks to the table. She was in her thirties and had bleached blond hair. She looked wary and distracted.

"Here's what you ordered," she said, putting a ginger ale down in front of Fitzsimmons and a shot and a beer in front of Sarz.

"Nightcap. This will round it off," Sarz said.

Fitzsimmons was surprised. He thought that Sarz had left the table because he was upset by the question.

"I was just wondering what makes you unique," Fitzsimmons said.

Sarz smiled. "I don't know whether you're ready to hear it," he said.

"Try me," Fitzsimmons said.

"It's a long story."

"Condense it."

Sarz lit another cigarette and then took a sip from the shot glass. "I'm bad," he said. "If you condense it, that's what it comes down to. I'm bad. I was born bad, I've lived bad, and I'm gonna die bad."

Fitzsimmons took a long pull on the ginger ale. Sarz watched him and waited until he put the glass down before he spoke again.

"I came into this world a bastard, and I've never changed. I've done some fascinating things. You'd call them terrible, but to me they're fascinating."

"Like what?" Fitzsimmons asked. Despite the noise and the smoke, he was beginning to feel comfortable, even beginning to feel a bit friendly toward Sarz. He took another drink from his glass and finished the ginger ale.

"Have another," Sarz said.

"Why not?"

"Hey," Sarz called to the waitress, "We're going to have exactly the same thing," he said.

"Exactly?"

"Yeah. Hey, Fitzsimmons, you want to sleep with her? She's pretty good."

The waitress stood impassively waiting for Fitzsimmons to answer.

Fitzsimmons shook his head.

"She's moderately priced, and she's thorough. What she lacks in beauty she makes up for in hard work."

"Screw you," the waitress said and walked away.

"She's a bitch, anyway," Sarz said. "Whatever she had, she lost by the time she was thirteen."

"What about your story?" Fitzsimmons said.

"I'm getting to it. I have to warm to my subject. You ever kill anybody?"

"Kill anybody?"

"Yeah. I don't mean in a traffic accident or Vietnam or something like that. I mean somebody you didn't care for. Somebody that was disturbing you or had something you wanted. That kind of thing."

"No," Fitzsimmons said.

"I didn't think so. You can tell. It's like being a virgin. There's an innocence there, a lack of knowledge. You can talk about it, you can think about it, but until you do it, you really don't understand it. Killing somebody puts you over the line."

"Are you talking from experience or is this philosophical speculation?" Fitzsimmons asked.

"I'm working my way into the story," Sarz answered. "It's not easy. I've never really told it to anybody."

The waitress set the drinks on the table.

"That was fast," Fitzsimmons said.

"Yeah. Thanks for the quick service, honey," Sarz said. He patted her on the thigh. She seemed not to notice.

Sarz took a big sip from the shot glass. "I don't want to shock you," he said. "So I'm trying to establish a common ground. For example, what about your sex life? Are you heterosexual, homosexual, bisexual?"

"I'm just your basic heterosexual," Fitzsimmons said. He took another sip from the ginger ale. It didn't taste like ordinary ginger ale, but he paid no attention.

"You like girls?"

The question seemed ambiguous. "Women?"

"No, girls. Young girls. Before their breasts grow."

Fitzsimmons wondered if Sarz was to be taken seriously. "No," he said.

"You don't know what you're missing."

"No, I guess not." Fitzsimmons heard his voice as from a distance, and he could feel a half-smile on his face.

"It's like killing somebody," Sarz said. "You cross the line and you can never come back."

Fitzsimmons strained to concentrate on Sarz's words. "What's it like killing somebody?"

"Having a ten-year-old girl."

There was no doubt that Sarz was to be taken seriously. Fitzsimmons could see it in his eyes. As he reached for the glass of ginger ale, he could see something else in Sarz's eyes—a look of cruel triumph.

Fitzsimmons began to take a sip from the glass but stopped. He suddenly realized that the ginger ale was drugged. That was why his brain was working so slowly, why he felt so agreeable, and why Sarz was taking such delight in watching him put the glass to his lips. Fitzsimmons fought off a feeling of panic. He was almost at the mercy of the man sitting across from him. Almost, but not quite. He stared at the glass with half-drunken eyes for a moment and then he looked at Sarz.

"What line have you crossed?" he asked.

"Both lines," Sarz said, "And I've crossed them both at once."

"Hmm," Fitzsimmons answered.

Sarz was disappointed. "Is that all you can say?"

"I'm not clear on those lines," Fitzsimmons said, slurring his words.

"It's very simple," Sarz said glaring across the table, "you find an innocent little girl and you fuck her and then you kill her. Is that clear enough for you?"

"I think so," Fitzsimmons said slowly. "You are one sick bastard, Sarz."

Sarz blinked, almost as if he had been slapped. "That's a twentieth-century concept," he said.

Fitzsimmons reacted slowly. He felt that he was in danger, but he did not know why. He wanted time to think, time to plan, and he knew that it was important for Sarz to believe that he had Fitzsimmons in his control. He wanted to get out of The Good Sports Cafe and away from Sarz, but he also knew that he was severely handicapped. He could not physically fight off Sarz or anyone else. But he had two things in his favor—Sarz did not know that he was aware of the drugged ginger ale and that he could still think.

"What is a twentieth-century concept?" Fitzsimmons asked. He took great care with his words, as if making an extraordinary effort not to slur them, while at the same time a deceptive plan of escape was forming in his mind.

The tension disappeared from Sarz's face. "Sickness is a twentieth-century concept. Society—you—have substituted the concept of sickness for the reality of evil. I am not sick. I know exactly what I am doing."

"You are going to have to elaborate for me," Fitzsimmons said, still speaking slowly and deliberately.

His mind flashed back to a time when he was in college and he and a friend had beaten a check in a beer hall in Yorkville. They were both broke and the waiter who served them had sensed it and had kept a close eye on them. Instead of just trying to sneak out, they decided to throw him off the track by ordering another round. When the drinks came they asked two women at an adjoining table to dance. The waiter must have been certain that they would not leave full drinks, and he stopped watching them just long enough for Fitzsimmons and his friend to abandon the women in the middle of the dance floor and run out the door. It had been a stupid thing to do, and Fitzsimmons had later regretted it, but it had worked. Maybe, he thought, some variation of that would work now.

"You are the kind of person who thinks the Nazis were sick. You cannot explain men crushing the heads of babies against their hobnailed boots, so you call them insane; you call them sick. They were not sick, they were evil. They reveled in what they did.

"Maybe some poor fool who makes obscene phone calls is sick, or a schizophrenic personality who hallucinates is sick, but someone who deliberately violates another human being, and who does it in order to exercise power, is not sick. The reason you call him sick is that you are afraid to admit there is evil.

"You can deal with sickness, but you don't know what to do about evil. You don't want to admit it exists. If you did, you would be challenged to join it or to join its antithesis. But those are the two things you do not want to embrace—evil and good. You do not want evil and you do not want God. They each make too many demands. So you ignore them both.

"There is a cosmic war going on, and you cover your eyes and refuse to look because you don't want to take sides. You do not want to surrender to God, and you find the logical alternative to be repugnant."

Sarz paused and sipped from his beer glass while Fitzsimmons looked at him through glazed eyes.

"Do you understand what I'm saying?" he asked.

Fitzsimmons nodded.

"Then understand this," Sarz said. "On one occasion, I found a girl—she was about nine years old—walking home from school. It was a late winter afternoon, cold and gray and almost dark, and I told her that I was a plainclothesman. I walked with her for a block or two, talking about her school and her teachers until I had her confidence, and then I dragged her into an alley, and I held my hands over her mouth and I raped her."

Sarz leaned across the table and his eyes were fixed on Fitzsimmons.

"As I raped her, I stared into her eyes, and I saw the horror and the fear and the pain and the disgust, the disbelief and the terror. She looked for help, but there was no help. She tried to scream, but she could not scream. She was just a little girl walking home from school, and she was overwhelmed by the reality of evil.

"When I was finished with her, she no longer felt the pain. It was over. She had endured it. She thought I would leave, and she thought she could be left alone to sob in the alley or to find her mother and be comforted. But she was faced by the enormity of evil. She had to know that evil—real evil—is merciless. That is part of its strength. So, as she sobbed her silent sobs, I stared into her eyes and I took her scarf and strangled her. Believe me, she knew that evil exists."

Fitzsimmons forced a drunken grin. He felt as though he was drowning and that there was nothing to hang on to.

"Is this fantasy?" he asked Sarz. "Or is this reality?"

"Don't you understand? You. Haven't you wondered what a little girl must feel when she is raped? Haven't you ever thought about being helpless in the presence of evil?" Sarz's stare was angry and yet jubilant.

"He knows," Fitzsimmons thought. "He knows and he wants to destroy me." He did not ask why. At the moment that was unimportant. There was a terror inside of Fitzsimmons and it was not at the thought of death, but it was the terror that the little girl must have felt, the terror that Eileen must have felt, at being powerless in the face of evil. He did not want to die that way. He did not want Sarz to be victorious, and the only weapon he had at his disposal was subterfuge.

"You're putting me on, Sarz," Fitzsimmons said, waving his hand. "Order another round of drinks, will you, while I go to the men's room? That will give you time to make up some more stories."

Fitzsimmons slid out of the booth. He was unsteady on his feet, "Are you all right?" Sarz asked.

"I'm fine," Fitzsimmons said, still smiling the half-smile.

"Maybe I better go with you."

"I told you, I'm a heterosexual. You order the drinks. I'll be back in a minute or however long it takes the line to move," Fitzsimmons said.

He moved slowly toward the end of the bar where the door to the men's room was located, walking on his heels and threading his way through the clusters of people who stood with drinks in their hands. The waitress who had brought him the drugged ginger ale was leaning against the bar watching him.

"Where's the cigarette machine?" he asked her.

She measured him with her eyes for a moment, and he looked at her blankly. "Up near the front door," she said.

He handed her a five-dollar bill. "Give me some change," he said.

She made the change from her apron pocket, and then he moved on toward the front of the bar. When he got to the cigarette machine, he looked back down the bar and saw that the waitress was still observing him, but when she saw that he was looking at her, she turned away. He dropped several coins into the slot, and glanced down the bar again. The waitress was still looking away. Without bothering to push the button for the cigarettes, Fitzsimmons stumbled away from the machine and lurched through the front door and out into the street.

Outside, he was hit by another wave of panic. He had a frantic urge to run, but there was no place to run to, no place to hide—there was no easy way to escape. The street was wide. There were no nearby alleys and the nearest side street was four hundred yards away. By the time Fitzsimmons went a hundred yards, Sarz would have left The Good Sports Cafe and spotted him.

"Oh, God," he thought. "God help me."

He looked behind him expecting to see Sarz, but the door to the bar had not opened. He turned back to face the street, frozen by fear and a drug-induced indecision.

"Excuse me," an effeminate voice said as a heavily cologned man brushed by him.

Fitzsimmons looked to see where he had come from and saw a taxi-cab at the curb with the rear door still open. He stumbled to the cab and managed to squeeze himself into the backseat.

"Park Square," Fitzsimmons said as he struggled to shut the door.

The driver looked wary. "Are you all right?" he asked.

Fitzsimmons took out his wallet and found two twenties. "Park Square. Now," he said.

"Okay," the driver said. He flipped the flag, put the cab in gear and started to drive off. As he did, Sarz came running out of The Good Sports Cafe waving his arms.

"You want me to stop?" the driver asked.

"Not if you want these twenties," Fitzsimmons said.

The driver pressed the accelerator pedal down hard, and the taxi quickly pulled away. Fitzsimmons turned to look out the back window and saw Sarz standing with his hands at his side staring after the taxi. There were no other cabs in sight.

Fitzsimmons gave the driver forty dollars and got out of the cab at Park Square. He felt physically ill, and his sense of panic had been replaced by paranoia. He expected Sarz to show up at any moment, and yet he could not force himself to hurry. He fought off wave after wave of nausea as he waited for the cab to pull away. When it was gone, he stepped slowly and unsteadily into the street and hailed another cab. This time he told the driver to take him to his apartment.

Fitzsimmons could not focus his eyes on his wristwatch. He guessed that it was about midnight, but it could have been later. He could not tell. He gave the driver a ten-dollar bill and did not wait for the change. Every step was an effort. He dragged himself up the three flights, and after some difficulty, managed to get his key into the lock and open the door to his apartment. He shut and bolted the door after him and stumbled into the bedroom. He vomited before he could turn on the light. He leaned against the doorjamb and threw up on the floor, again and again, until there was nothing left in his stomach, and then he kept vomiting despite his empty stomach—his muscles contracted and his stomach heaved and heaved until, finally, it was over. His mouth was dry, and he was sweating. He did not think he had the strength to get to his bed or to get undressed.

"Oh, God," he said. "Oh, God, I'm so sick. I'm so sick."

He dropped to his knees and then stretched out on the floor. "If only I had a blanket," he whispered.

He started to drift off to sleep when he heard a knock. At first he was not sure where the sound came from, then he heard it again. Someone was knocking at the door. He thought that it must be Karen, but he knew that it could not be since she was working until seven A.M. He wondered whether to answer the door. It could not be Sarz. Sarz did not know where Fitzsimmons lived.

But it was Sarz. "Fitzsimmons. Are you in there?" he called. He knocked again. "Fitzsimmons, are you all right?"

Sarz tried the handle but the door did not open.

A surge of adrenaline partially revived Fitzsimmons, but he was still in no condition to deal with Sarz. Slowly and quietly, he crawled to the kitchen. The knocking became more insistent. Without turning on a light, Fitzsimmons found the drawer which held the utensils, slid it open and took out a large carving knife.

"Come on, Fitzsimmons. You're sick. I want to help you. Open the door."

Fitzsimmons slipped the knife through his belt and crawled toward the front door. Now Sarz was shaking it by jerking the doorknob.

Without a sound, Fitzsimmons got to his feet and leaned his back against the wall next to the door. He slid the knife out of his belt and raised it above his head. Sarz turned the handle and put his shoulder into the door—once, twice, three times. It held.

"Answer me, Fitzsimmons. Are you in there?"

Fitzsimmons did not respond. He could hear himself breathing, and he felt his arm grow more and more heavy.

"Fitzsimmons?" There was a pause. "If you're not going to answer me, I'm going to assume you don't need help, and I'll leave. Fitzsimmons?" There was another pause. "Good night, then."

Fitzsimmons heard Sarz walk to the end of the hall and start down the stairs. He let his body slide down the wall until he was in a sitting position, and then he laid the knife on the floor next to him. After a moment, he picked up the knife and struggled to his feet. It had been too easy. He lifted the knife above his head and waited again. Suddenly, with no sound of warning, the door handle turned and the door vibrated as the full weight of a body was thrown against it. Fitzsimmons waited. Once more Sarz threw his body against the door, and once more it held. Then there was silence.

Fitzsimmons waited for a few minutes, and then he slid to the floor again. He sat with the knife in his lap.

"If he gets in through a window, I've had it," he whispered. But the windows were locked. He had taken that precaution after Karen's apartment had been entered.

After a few minutes, Fitzsimmons began to sweat again, and he felt chilled.

"If only I had a blanket," he whispered and then, still sitting, he fell asleep.

CHAPTER TEN

FITZSIMMONS WAS AWAKENED BY A KNOCK ON THE DOOR. THE room was bright with the morning sun and the carving knife was still in his lap. He tried to move, but he could not. There was another knock. He still felt drugged.

"Who's there?" he asked in a barely audible voice. He cleared his throat. "Who's there?" he asked again. This time his voice was loud enough, but it sounded thin. Fitzsimmons pictured Sarz on the other side of the door, and he wondered if he could summon the strength to fight him.

"Karen."

"Karen?" He shook himself awake and climbed slowly to his feet, putting his hand against the wall to steady himself.

"Are you alone?" he asked.

"Yes."

He fumbled with the lock until it snapped back, and then he turned the knob and opened the door.

A smile left Karen's face. She looked at once confused, hurt and angry.

"I thought you said you didn't drink," she said.

He looked at her stupidly. "I don't."

He realized that there was vomitus on his clothes. "I don't drink," he repeated.

Karen did not look as if she believed him.

"I shouldn't have opened the door," Fitzsimmons said.

"Are you sick?" It was more of an accusation than a question. Fitzsimmons shook his head. Karen looked devastated.

"You're going to have to give me ten minutes. Let me take a shower, then we'll go out for breakfast and I'll tell you why I look like this," Fitzsimmons said.

"Why can't you tell me now?" she asked.

"I want to get cleaned up. Do you want to come in and wait, or do you want me to come over to your apartment?"

Karen just stared at him. Her eyes were filled with disappointment.

"Come in, please," he said.

As she stepped through the doorway, her foot touched the carving knife.

"What's that?"

"It's a long story. I'll tell you as soon as I clean up."

Karen turned abruptly and walked out into the hall. "I'll wait in my apartment," she said over her shoulder.

By the time Fitzsimmons cleaned the bathroom, showered, shaved and dressed, almost a half-hour had elapsed, and he was feeling much better as he knocked on Karen's door.

Karen averted her head as she opened the door, and then she turned and walked to the window, so that Fitzsimmons could not see her face. He knew immediately that she was crying. He stood behind her and put his hands on her shoulders.

"Why are you crying?" he asked.

"Fate," she said.

"Fate?"

"Yes, my awful, awful fate."

"You're going to have to enlighten me," he said.

"Two drunks in a row," she answered. "A husband who would come home and pass out on the front lawn and now you. The only man I've trusted, the only man I've been with since I left my husband."

"I'm not a drunk," Fitzsimmons said.

She turned around to face him, and now the tears had been replaced by anger. "Don't tell me that," she said. "Don't lie to me.

Don't make excuses. I know a drunk when I see one. My father was a drunk, my husband was a drunk and you're a drunk. And you know what drunks are? They're grief. They're pain. They start off full of love and laughter and they end up sleeping in their own puke." She waved her hand as if to erase Fitzsimmons' image.

Without taking his eyes from hers, Fitzsimmons took a step back and folded his arms.

"The scars are deep," he said.

"You bet your life they're deep. They've cut right down to my soul." Karen's face softened and she began to sob.

Fitzsimmons smiled gently.

"What are you smiling at?" she shouted at him.

"I wasn't drunk last night," he said. "I didn't have anything to drink. I'm not a drunk. Never have been a drunk, and I wouldn't hurt you for the world."

Karen's face reflected her doubt.

"Do you think you can suspend your disbelief long enough to go out for breakfast and find out what really happened?" he asked.

"Are you lying to me?" Her voice was low, almost inaudible. "Don't lie to me," she pleaded.

"I'm not lying, Karen. I don't lie, and I never will lie to you."

Karen shook her head. "I just can't get back into that."

"Nobody's asking you to."

They found a place that served breakfast on Beacon Street. Fitzsimmons ordered scrambled eggs and bacon; Karen asked only for black coffee.

"I'd like to hear a little more about your marriage," Fitzsimmons said.

Karen looked up from her coffee. "I'd like to hear a little more about last night," she answered.

"I can tell you what happened, but I can't tell you why it happened," Fitzsimmons said. Karen looked down at her coffee. "There's a fellow I work with at TPI who has been bugging me for months to go out for a drink with him. He's an unpleasant guy, and I've always managed to put him off. But last night, my defenses were down, I wasn't paying attention. I was thinking about you, frankly, and I agreed to meet him at a bar after I got out of work."

Karen's eyes had become accusatory again, but Fitzsimmons ignored them.

"He's a very strange person. I think—and I don't know why—but I think he planned to harm me in some way. In fact, I had the feeling last night that he wanted to kill me, and that I barely escaped with my life. But I was drugged, and I just don't know how dangerous a situation I was in. And I don't know why in God's name he would want to hurt me. I have done nothing to him."

Fitzsimmons reached across the table and touched Karen's hand, and then pulled his own hand back before she could pull hers away.

"Try to listen to me," he said. "I can see in your eyes that you are comparing me with your father and your husband. Just try to listen to what I'm going to tell you." And, with that, Fitzsimmons recounted in every detail the prior evening, beginning with Sarz's invitation, including Sarz's description of the rape and murder of the young girl, and ending with his falling asleep clutching the carving knife. When he had finished, he could see that Karen's anger had left her.

"Is this true?" she asked.

"Karen, I would have to be a pathological liar to make it up."

"You're not a liar," she said. "But ... "

"But your father and your husband. I understand that. I understand how something can happen to us that taints our view of life and love and hope. I understand how difficult it can be to trust. But if we are ever going to get over whatever it is that has hurt us so deeply, we have to risk trusting."

"How ... " she started to ask and then stopped.

"How what?"

Karen shook her head. "I was going to ask how you know these things."

"I'm living them," Fitzsimmons said.

"So am I," Karen said. "You don't realize how deeply you've been hurt until it comes back at you as it did this morning. When you opened the door, it was like I was back in Detroit looking at Todd."

"Tell me about him," Fitzsimmons said.

"I met him while I was still in nursing school. He was studying for the bar exam. He was handsome and full of fun, and everybody believed that he would become a top trial lawyer. He was quick and he had the kind of mind that could always find a flaw in an argument, and he could always come up with a different explanation from what seemed to be the obvious one. He was made to be a lawyer. He drank, but it never seemed to bother him. He never got drunk and he never got argumentative or nasty the way my father did. He became a lawyer, I graduated, and we got married. And somehow during the first five years of our marriage he turned into a drunk. When we first met he could drink anybody under the table and still be pleasant and charming and get up and go to work the next day. By the time we were married five years he was coming home drunk every night. Sometimes he couldn't walk. Sometimes he couldn't talk. He never saw Amy, our daughter. He'd come in late and pass out and leave in the morning. And I couldn't talk to him about it. By the time Amy was five, he had been fired from a couple of law firms—he was out of control. He was like a storm, a hurricane. He was unpredictable and violent. He destroyed our marriage, and I was afraid he was going to destroy me and Amy—not physically, but mentally.

"I'd find him passed out on the front steps at six o'clock in the morning, and he would make up an incredible tale about what had happened to him. At first, I used to believe him, and then, gradually, I realized he lied. He lied about everything. I don't think he knew what the truth was. Sometimes, he did. Sometimes he'd get sober for a week or for a few days, and he would be so gentle and so apologetic and so full of promises and good intentions. And then he'd get drunk, and he would be worse than he was the time before.

"My life was dreadful. I was ashamed of him and ashamed of myself. I treated Amy like a poor relation. I don't know what happened to me. It was like Todd ruined everything that was loving in me. I had dried up inside. I had no love to give. I couldn't love Amy and I couldn't love myself. And when I realized that, I knew that I was losing myself and Amy, and that the only way we could survive was for me to leave Todd. More than that—to cut the ties between us—physical, emotional, legal, even geographical."

Karen nodded her head as if agreeing with what she said.

"It was a very bitter period in my life," she continued. "In some ways I think I was almost as sick as he was. I was always anxious, always worried. I tried everything to get him to stop drinking. Nothing worked. There was just nothing I could do for him. But once I left him, things started to get better, and as soon as I stopped worrying about him and about the neighbors and about whether we'd lose the house and all those other things, and I started to be concerned about my own well-being and Amy's, then I started to get better.

"I decided to start my life over, and I decided to do it in a new city. At first I didn't want another relationship. I just wanted to get enough money so I could buy a house, and Amy and I could live in the suburbs. But as I went along, I knew that I would want to get married again and that I would want to live a normal life. I do want a husband. I do want Amy to have a father, and all of a sudden I met you. You were good-looking, unattached, smart, gentle, but there was something else about you, too, and I knew it almost from the beginning. I couldn't put my finger on it, but I had the feeling that there was something there, something that could hurt the both of us." Karen stopped speaking. She looked intensely at Fitzsimmons and then she looked down at the table.

"And when you saw me this morning, you thought that what was wrong with me was the same as what was wrong with Todd," Fitzsimmons said.

Karen nodded.

"It's not," Fitzsimmons said. "That doesn't mean there's nothing wrong with me, but I don't have Todd's problem. After I lost my wife and Sarah, I left where I lived, too. I didn't think about starting a new life, I just wanted to get away from the old one. I traveled for a while and I wound up here in Boston. I had no intention of meeting a woman or getting married or doing anything. Those kinds of things never occurred to me. I just wanted peace and solitude. And then I met Peter, and for the first time in years, I had a friend, and I began to enjoy human company again. I never thought I would, but I did. We went to the theater and concerts and restaurants, and I began to become interested in life again. And then I met you—and you—well, you awakened something in me that I thought was dead."

Fitzsimmons hesitated, debating whether to go on, and then he continued. "I am not saying that I am not damaged. I am damaged. I'm not a whole human being. But you … "

He hesitated again. "It may be too early in our relationship to say this, but I'll say it anyway. You have awakened in me the desire to become whole."

They were silent while Karen pondered his words.

"You didn't drink," she said after a few minutes. It was not a question.

Fitzsimmons shook his head.

"We are two wounded people," she said.

Fitzsimmons nodded.

Karen smiled. "I didn't want to meet a wounded person. I wanted to meet someone who was strong and had absolutely nothing wrong with him."

"There may be somebody in Boston like that," he said.

"I think it may be too late," she answered.

"I hope so," he said.

It was not until they were on the way back to the apartment that they returned to the subject of the previous evening.

"Did you ever do anything to offend him?" Karen asked.

"Sarz? No, not that I know of. We're strangers. I don't think that before last night we had a total of ten minutes of conversation, but he hates me. I could just feel it oozing out of him. He loathes me. I don't think I've ever elicited that kind of feeling from another human being, and I don't even know him. It's really crazy."

"There's got to be something," Karen said. "He has to have some reason to hate you."

"Well if he does, I didn't give it to him."

"You hear about people having the need to confess. Do you think that could be it?"

"He wasn't confessing," Fitzsimmons answered quietly. He cleared his throat. "He wasn't confessing," he repeated in a more natural voice, "he was boasting."

"He seemed to single you out. Why would he boast to you?" Karen asked. She looked up at Fitzsimmons but he did not look back at her. He cleared his throat again and shook his head without speaking.

"Are you okay?" she asked.

"I'm all right," he said.

Karen took his hand and squeezed it. "What are you going to do about him?" she asked.

"I don't know," Fitzsimmons said.

"You could go to the police."

"I suppose, but it would be the same thing as when your apartment was broken into. The police wouldn't be able to do anything. There were just two of us at the table, and I was the one who staggered out of the place."

"What about the girl that he said he raped and killed?" Karen asked.

"I don't know. Given the lengths he went to, there probably isn't any way he could be tied to a killing. I suppose I could go to the police, but I don't know. Let me think about it."

They continued holding hands the rest of the way, and each was comforted by the touch of the other.

By noon, Karen was sound asleep. Fitzsimmons sat in a chair by the window studying her. She looked peaceful and untroubled, and her face seemed to have an underlying strength and determination that was not obvious when she was awake. He knew that whether Karen realized it or not he had committed himself to her. This was not merely a romantic exercise, nor was it love as he had previously experienced it. It was as though their relationship had skipped a stage.

It had been much different with Eileen. (He wondered if it was wrong to compare them or if it was just inevitable.) His relationship with Eileen had started with romance and anticipation. He had courted her and won her. It had been exciting and adventurous and magical. When he had asked Eileen to marry him, it seemed like the single biggest step he would ever take in his life. He was eager, but even in his eagerness he felt trepidation. They were almost strangers. They had only known each other for a few months. But it had worked. Perhaps they had intuitively known that it would, that they would complement each other. After they were married they had grown to know each other slowly and to accept their weaknesses and their failings even more slowly, but they had never shared adversity. They had never, hand in hand, faced the storm—a crisis which would have either broken their marriage or made it indestructible. Their common experience now seemed so superficial to Fitzsimmons. It seemed to him that they had been little more than children—naive, immature, somewhat silly.

"What were our ambitions? What did we think life was about?" he wondered half aloud.

Karen stirred but did not awaken. Fitzsimmons waited until he was certain that she was sleeping soundly and then he slipped from the room. At the doorway, he turned and looked back at Karen, and as he did he had a premonition of evil.

"Oh God," he whispered, "not again."

He shut the door to the bedroom gently, and started across the living room, but he stopped abruptly.

"The reality of it is that the son of a bitch wants to destroy me," he whispered. It was as if all the strength went out of him. His sagging body found the sofa. He sat staring at the rug with his shoulders hunched over his knees. He was being thrust back into the world of darkness, a world of uncertainty, a world without order and without rules, where lives could be snuffed out at the whim of a maniac and children faced indiscriminate terror.

Fitzsimmons did not move for almost an hour as he sought some defense against the fear and anxiety which paralyzed his mind. He had no defense; he had no answer to the world's insanity. For Peter Genaro, he knew, God's love was the answer. It was the cement which gave the chaos a mysterious unity and explained the unexplainable. For Fitzsimmons, there was no love and no cement, just disorder and pain.

Is there a God, he wondered, and does he involve himself in the affairs of men?

"Are you there, God?" he asked aloud. "And do you care?"

In the bright, sunlit room, there was only silence.

CHAPTER ELEVEN

FITZSIMMONS WENT TO WORK THAT AFTERNOON FEELING VERY uneasy. He had considered calling Barbara Wright and telling her that he was ill, but he rejected the idea. It would have been admitting that Sarz had power over him. Fitzsimmons did not know what to do about Sarz, but he would not run from him or avoid him. It would have been easier if Fitzsimmons had known with certainty that Sarz was a rapist and a killer. But Sarz was a master of ambiguity and his statements had a taunting, teasing quality, and Fitzsimmons was unsure whether it had been a bizarre barroom conversation with a practical joker or a confrontation with a monster. In either case, Fitzsimmons did not know what to do, and he felt intimidated by his own sense of powerlessness.

"Hey, how you feeling?" It was Sarz waiting for him by the time clock. His concern fell just short of being genuine.

Fitzsimmons looked him in the eye, and Sarz returned the look with a steady, even gaze.

"Are you what you say you are?" Fitzsimmons asked.

Sarz's smile mocked him. "Blessed are they, Fitzsimmons, who have not seen and yet believe," he answered.

Fitzsimmons put his card into the slot and waited while it was punched.

"How are you feeling?" Sarz asked again.

"What did you put in the drink?"

"Me?" Sarz asked. "I shouldn't be blamed because you can't handle your ginger ale."

Fitzsimmons started to walk away.

"Hey, you still haven't told me how you feel."

"I feel like I'm in the presence of someone who is very, very sick," Fitzsimmons said.

"You're an asshole," Sarz said. "You just don't understand."

"Understand what?"

"If you of all people have to be told, I certainly can't explain it to you." Little flecks of spittle flew from Sarz's mouth as he spoke. "Maybe one of these days it will dawn on you," Sarz said. He strode away before Fitzsimmons could say any more.

There was a depth to Sarz's ferocity which bewildered and alarmed Fitzsimmons.

"What the hell is this all about?" Fitzsimmons asked out loud. "Why should I, of all people, understand?"

"He's a bad man, Jay." It was Tommy. He had come up behind Fitzsimmons without Fitzsimmons noticing him. He looked up at Fitzsimmons with an intense but guileless expression. "He's the kind of guy that would poke the eyes out of puppies."

For the briefest of moments Tommy was very sober and very solemn. He scratched one of the tufts of beard on his otherwise silky smooth chin. "I hate him, Jay. He's bad." After a moment, Tommy's mood changed and a gleam came to his eye. "And he hates you. I hate him, and he hates you, but he doesn't hate me, and you don't hate him. That's funny, Jay. Ha, ha, Jay, you pervert. You don't even know enough to hate him. You're a nut cake, Jay."

Tommy, still laughing, started to walk back to the assembly room, but he stopped and turned back to face Fitzsimmons. "Hey, Jay, do you believe in hell?"

Fitzsimmons did not know what to make of the question or, indeed, any of Tommy's conversation. "I don't know," he answered.

"Well, you better," Tommy said. "Don't you know what Sarz's real job is?"

"What do you mean his real job?"

"Not his job. Not sweeping halls. I mean what he really does, his … his what-do-you-call-it, the things priests have."

"His vocation?"

"Yeah, Jay, his vacation, ha, ha, I mean his vocation."

Fitzsimmons shook his head. "No, I don't know. What is it?"

"He goes around proving the existence of hell," Tommy said with a withering stare. The gleam returned to his eye, and he turned his back to Fitzsimmons and walked away. After a few steps, he broke into three loud, high-pitched guffaws.

Fitzsimmons waited until he had disappeared into the assembly room, and then he followed him to look for Shanny.

As he entered the large work area, Fitzsimmons was struck again by the multitude of faces, and the varying degrees of intelligence and lack of intelligence which they displayed. Tommy sat ten yards away, apparently deeply engrossed in his work. Most of the others, too, seemed to care only for what their fingers were doing. What thoughts did they harbor behind those blank looks, Fitzsimmons wondered? Were they innocents, or were they like the rest of the world? And why had he, Fitzsimmons, chosen this underside of life? Most people hardly ever see someone who is retarded. Most people live in a world that is insulated from the sick and deformed, from the retarded and the deranged, from criminals and maniacs. Fitzsimmons, himself, had once inhabited that insulated world.

He walked into Shanny's office. Shanny was not there. Fitzsimmons picked up the telephone and dialed Peter's number. The priest answered. "I'd like to have another talk," Fitzsimmons said.

"Any time," the priest said.

"Tonight about eleven?"

"I'll be here," Peter said.

Shanny walked in and Fitzsimmons hung up. "Local call," Fitzsimmons said.

"That's all you can make on that phone," Shanny answered. "There isn't a whole hell of a lot to do tonight. There's only one stack to move into shipping."

"All right," Fitzsimmons said. "I'll be back in a few minutes. I want to run up and see Ms. Wright."

Barbara Wright was in a better mood than when he last saw her. When he knocked on her open door, she waved him into her office with a smile.

"Ah, John," she said, "How are you today?"

"I'm okay."

"What can I do for you?"

"Just a quick question," he said taking the chair she offered. "You said the other day that when I came to work here you checked my references?"

"Of course. We always do."

"Was it an extensive check? Did you dig into my background?"

"Extensive enough. We didn't want to pry, but we couldn't help learning something about your past. I know that you used to be a college professor, and I know about the terrible thing that happened to your family."

"Is that common knowledge here?"

"No. I kept it pretty much to myself. From talking to the people on Long Island, I got the feeling that you really didn't want people around here to know about your past. I respected that."

"Thank you," Fitzsimmons said. As he started to get up, his glance focused on the filing cabinets. He saw several drawers labeled 'Personnel Records' followed by alphabetical designations. His would be in the drawer labeled 'F-J'.

Ms. Wright also started to rise. "What makes you ask?"

"Oh, nothing, really. I just wondered."

"Something must have made you wonder. Did someone say something?"

"No. It was just a feeling I had. It wasn't important. You're right. I would just as soon nobody knew about my past. I just wanted to make sure that I was not the subject of idle curiosity," Fitzsimmons said.

"If you want something kept secret, don't tell anyone," his father used to say. His father had been a man of terse, sometimes cynical statements, a man who was not much enamored of life, but he had been right more often than he had been wrong.

As Fitzsimmons stepped out of the office he saw Sarz at the far end of the hall, stooped over a pail with his back to him. Just the presence of Sarz, even at that distance, made Fitzsimmons uneasy. He suspected that Sarz had found out—either he had heard it from one of the other employees or he had rummaged through the personnel records—but he had found out, and because of it, for some reason known only to Sarz, he hated Fitzsimmons. The suspicion gave Fitzsimmons a terrible foreboding. He had an enemy whom he had done nothing to, an enemy who hated him and who seemed to want to harm him. It was inconceivable, and yet his intuition told him that it was true. There was something unsettled between them, something that would have to be settled before he would be free of that foreboding.

Another disturbing thought came to Fitzsimmons. Sarz, wringing out a mop with his back to Fitzsimmons, was vulnerable. Fitzsimmons could walk quickly and quietly down the hall and with one strong blow disable him and have him at his mercy. The ferocity of the idea and the appeal of it startled Fitzsimmons. He wanted to rid his mind of it, but at the same time, the idea gave him a defense to his disquietude. It was a reassuring fantasy, one he could take comfort in.

Sarz, still bending over the pail, turned slightly and looked at Fitzsimmons as if he had known all along that Fitzsimmons was standing there. The two of them looked at each other for a moment or two—their faces were expressionless—before Fitzsimmons turned away and went downstairs to the assembly room.

By 4 P.M. the building was empty except for the two of them, and the air seemed heavy with their presence. Fitzsimmons avoided Sarz for the next three hours. He stayed mostly in areas that Sarz did not come into, and when Fitzsimmons did go through the office section, he strode through the hall quickly and lightly. He was not ready for a confrontation. As irrational as it seemed, Fitzsimmons feared that Sarz had a plan of action, a scheme aimed at hurting Fitzsimmons, but he had no clear idea why Sarz was plotting against him, and lacking that knowledge made him feel even more helpless. He did not know how to combat irrationality. Fitzsimmons was a man who had believed in order, and even though it had been clearly demonstrated to him that order was frequently an illusion and that chaos was often the reality, there was a part of him that could not recognize chaos and could not deal with it, and it was that part of him that paralyzed him.

Sarz was implacable. He had an agenda and a convoluted ethic which was beyond Fitzsimmons' comprehension. The fantasy returned. He could not merely throttle Sarz. That would only fuel the fire of his hatred. Fitzsimmons could strangle Sarz or break his neck. For an instant he let himself imagine having his hands around Sarz's throat, but only for an instant. He was constrained from even dwelling on the fantasy by his own ethic. He could not surrender to barbarism either in himself or in Sarz, and as he realized that, he began to feel better. He did not know what to do about Sarz, but he knew that he would not surrender to him. Whatever it was that Sarz had planned, Fitzsimmons would not be an accomplice, he would not willingly embrace chaos.

At seven o'clock, Fitzsimmons met Sarz at the time clock to let him out of the building.

Sarz was almost out the door when he stopped and turned. "How about coming by The Good Sports Cafe? We can finish our dialogue."

Fitzsimmons shook his head.

Sarz pursued him. "How about tomorrow night? You know we're not finished—the conversation is not finished."

"I know that," Fitzsimmons said, giving Sarz a steady look. "We'll finish the conversation. I'll let you know when."

"You do that. You let me know," Sarz said and went out into the street.

It was almost midnight when Fitzsimmons got to the rectory.

"I'm sorry to impose on you this way," he said when Peter opened the door.

"It's not an imposition," Peter said. "Come in and tell me what's going on."

The two men went into the study, and Fitzsimmons recounted the episode with Sarz and its aftermath with Karen.

"That's a strange story," the priest said when Fitzsimmons finished. "Of course, it's only part of the story, and that makes it hard for me to understand all its ramifications."

"I told you everything," Fitzsimmons said.

Peter shook his head gently, and Fitzsimmons averted his eyes. For a few minutes there was an uncomfortable silence.

"One of the things that bothers me," Fitzsimmons said at last, "is the ambiguity of the whole thing. I can't be certain that Sarz is what he says he is. I am not absolutely sure that he wants to harm me. He has given me no reason. He hasn't told me he hates me or even what it is—if there is anything—that he holds against me."

"He is taunting you, John, and taunters are masters of ambiguity. They bring you just short of the point where you will automatically respond with anger and aggression. They create uncertainty and ambivalence, and then they use your own negative emotions to disarm you. It's a trick common to the school yard and the prison yard."

"But why is he taunting me?"

"Don't you know?" the priest asked.

"No," Fitzsimmons said.

"Maybe he recognizes what he perceives to be a weakness in you, a weakness that he will go to any lengths to deny in himself. And one of the ways he denies that weakness is to exploit it in you."

Fitzsimmons pondered the priest's words. "How do you know that?" he asked after a moment.

"How does anyone know anything? Experience." Peter sat back in his chair. "You don't have to accept what I say. You won't hurt my feelings."

"I don't doubt you, Peter. You seem to have a knack for looking into people. I just wondered where you get this knowledge."

"It comes from paying attention," the priest said. "I've done a lot of that in the last twenty years or so."

Fitzsimmons knew that if he said nothing Peter would elaborate, so he waited in silence.

After a while the priest nodded as if assenting to Fitzsimmons' wish that he continue. "I have the opportunity to deal with a lot of wounded people—any priest does—but you have nothing to offer them unless you understand your own wounds. You've got to pay attention to pain and inadequacy, failures, sins. You've got to study them, and if you do that, you begin to understand sickness and evil and the inadequacies and failures and sinfulness of others—not as a judge, but as a fellow sufferer.

"A lot of people can't look at themselves. They're afraid that what they'll find will be too awful. We have these terrible standards. Even rapists and child molesters and killers have standards. They're different from ours, but they're standards anyway. This man that you're having the trouble with has standards, inner emotional and psychological standards that you somehow threaten. If you were not a threat to him, he would leave you alone. You see, the bully secretly identifies with the victim, but he is so terrified by that identification that he abuses the victim as a way of denying it."

"You're telling me that Sarz identifies with me, and he is doing whatever it is he is doing because I am somehow a threat to him?" Fitzsimmons said.

Peter nodded.

"I don't even know the son of a bitch," Fitzsimmons said, "and he doesn't know me."

The priest shrugged. "He doesn't have to know you, in the sense that you and I, for example, know each other. He just has to perceive something in you that he is afraid of in himself." The priest leaned forward again. He rested his elbows on the desk and his chin on the heels of his hand.

"That's just a general principle of human behavior as observed by Peter Genaro," Fitzsimmons said. "And you're probably right."

"The question is," Peter said, "what is it that he sees in you that makes him want to attack you?"

"I don't know," Fitzsimmons said.

The priest raised his eyebrows slightly.

"Do you know?" Fitzsimmons asked.

Peter shook his head. "How can I know?" the priest asked. "Part of the equation is missing."

Fitzsimmons looked at the rug. "This is not the first time in my life that I have been confronted by insanity," he said.

"Insanity? You think this Sarz fellow is insane?"

"Sane people don't go around doing the kind of things he says he does," Fitzsimmons said.

"How about evil people?" the priest asked.

"Evil?" Fitzsimmons said the word as if it was foreign to him.

"Yes, evil. There is evil in the world, John."

"You mean evil, like Satan?"

"I mean evil like murder and rape, genocide and exploitation, starvation and deprivation, committed by people to satisfy their own evil ends. And, yes, I mean a principle of evil—call it Satan, call it what you will—an evil that seduces and corrupts. I get the feeling that you look upon evil as a kind of accident, something that wasn't supposed to happen but did, an afterthought rather than an active principle. I think that you look upon evil as a flaw built into the universe, a mistake that God made—if you believe in God."

"Yes. You're right. That's what I think. I think God screwed up," Fitzsimmons said. "I believe in God, an uncaused cause, but this is not the best of all possible worlds. It was made badly, and I think it's naive to conjure up a picture of a being in a black cape with a Vandyke whispering in people's ears."

Peter smiled. "If you don't see that image as a metaphor—yes, it's naive. But it's more naive to believe that evil is not greater than men's power to commit it, not to perceive that behind inhumanity there is a cosmic, demonic force. Do you think that the barbarism of the Nazis was an aberration, a spontaneous and isolated incident—the work of some sick individuals? Certainly they were sick, but I think that your definition of sickness does not include freedom of choice; that, for you, sickness exonerates man from his action. The Nazis embraced evil. The men who showed mothers and children the way to the poison gas chambers embraced evil. The men who schemed to exterminate an entire race, not to mention all the others they killed, including an awful lot of Christians, were given over to evil. Yes, they were sick. Spiritually sick. That is what happens when someone embraces evil— he becomes spiritually sick.

"We're living in a mechanistic society. People ignore the spirit of man, they ignore the whole spiritual side of humanity. Sarz is spiritually sick, but he doesn't sound crazy. He is given over to evil, but he is not insane. He is bad. He is wicked. He is a child of darkness. It is the same darkness that spawned Hitler and Borman and Eichmann. It is the darkness of the Ku Klux Klan and drug dealers. And you and the whole world may deny it or laugh at it or see it as a man with a black cape and a Vandyke, but there is a principle of evil. There is a darkness that embraces men's souls, and it is real, and it has its own separate existence. It is an entity, a force, a thing to be reckoned with." The priest spoke softly, but with an authority and conviction that Fitzsimmons had not seen in him before.

"This fellow Sarz reminds me of a character in *The Divine Comedy*," the priest continued. "I don't know if you remember the part where Dante is walking though one of the circles in hell and he comes across a man who he knows is still living in Florence. Dante says something like, 'How can you be here? You're still alive.' And the man answers that sometimes men are so evil that God permits their souls to be taken to hell even before their bodies die, and allows evil spirits to inhabit those bodies until the time of death arrives," the priest said.

"Peter ... "

The priest waved him silent. "A metaphor. I'm not suggesting that Sarz is dead and an evil spirit inhabits his body. I am suggesting that he has given himself over to evil to the point that he has lost his humanity and cannot retrieve it. And so what is the difference whether he is possessed by an evil spirit or not? He might just as well be because it is the spirit of evil which moves him."

Fitzsimmons closed his eyes and massaged their corners with the thumb and forefinger of his right hand. "I don't know whether I grasp what you are saying."

"I am saying that there is insanity and there is wickedness and the two things are not the same. The insane man does what he does because he cannot do otherwise. He is not responsible. Sarz is altogether different. He is an evil man committing evil acts. He is not crazy; he is bad."

"Bad," Fitzsimmons echoed. It was neither a question nor an affirmation.

"Yes, bad. He is a child of darkness, and he is the servant of darkness," the priest said.

"It all sounds medieval to me," Fitzsimmons said.

"That's because men do not believe in what they cannot measure and what they cannot understand. They cannot believe in God because such a belief would make them subordinate. They cannot believe in evil because then they would have to believe in God and seek his help to overcome it."

"And you believe?"

"Of course, I believe. I'm a priest. I'm a servant of Jesus Christ." His tone was sharp as if Fitzsimmons had insulted him.

"Forgive me. I've known other priests who didn't, at least not in the way you're talking about."

"What do you mean?" the priest asked.

"I think that most people, priests included, don't think of Jesus as anything more than a remote and undemonstrable ideal. God for them, for me, is something set apart, a witness to the chaos, a scorekeeper, perhaps a being aloof from the pain of existence. For you, it's different. You're apocalyptic. For you there is a cosmic battle going on. The forces of light versus the forces of darkness."

"Of course, and we are all involved, even if we only stand on the sidelines and deny that there is a battle. The war has been going on since before history. It is going on at this moment. Sometimes it is obvious, sometimes it isn't, but it is always going on. This is an alien world, a world seduced by evil, and the irony is that we see evil and evil men like Hitler or Idi Amin or the countless men who thrive on manipulating and exploiting and debasing their fellow men, and yet we fail to see that there is a source of evil, a reservoir of evil which corrupts and sustains them. It is a cosmic battle. Evil has an immense power. Look at the disease, the hatred, the pain, the mean-spiritedness which abounds in this world. Look at the oppression and the exploitation. There is so much evil that most of it goes unrecognized. Most of it is accepted without a second thought."

"So what do you do about it?"

"What do I do about it?" the priest asked.

Fitzsimmons nodded.

"I embrace the good." Peter smiled. It was almost an apologetic smile, as if to say that he knew that Fitzsimmons could not comprehend what he was talking about. "I follow Christ."

Fitzsimmons shook his head. "You have something that I don't," he said. "You have a different frame of reference. You can, as you say, embrace the good. But what do I do?"

"I don't know," the priest answered. "I don't know how you can resist evil if you don't believe in it, and I don't know how you can embrace the good if you don't believe in it."

"Neither do I," Fitzsimmons said.

The two men were silent. The priest got up and went to the window, staring out at the blackness with his back to Fitzsimmons for several minutes, and then he left the room without speaking. Fitzsimmons considered leaving, but decided against it. He knew that Peter would return. In the meantime, Fitzsimmons found the study comforting. It was very still and had a peaceful air. He sat quietly, without thinking, his mind almost a blank. For the moment, Sarz was Peter's problem. Let him wrestle with it.

After about a quarter of an hour, Peter returned. He sat back down at the desk and measured Fitzsimmons with his eyes as if to see if what he had to say would fit.

"I believe that whatever comes our way in life—anything that happens to us—is an opportunity to grow as human beings, to become wiser and more human. But I see life from a perspective of eternity. I don't know what your perspective is."

Fitzsimmons slouched down in his chair and said nothing.

"No matter what you believe in, it is the duty of every human being to resist evil and not to cooperate with it. When you are confronted by evil, you must not submit to it. When we cooperate with evil, when we submit to it, we become part of it. I have already made the ultimate choices in my life. I believe that love is the most important act a human being can commit. Love is what defines us. If we love, we have the potential for wholeness. If we do not or cannot love, we are less than human. When we love, we embrace life. That is what is happening between you and Karen right now. You are embracing life, and when you embrace life, you are saying yes to life and to goodness and to truth.

"Some people seem to have more difficult roads than others. I suspect that you are one of them. I don't envy you, but I believe this: I believe that God has not forgotten you or turned from you. I believe that he is leading you to a life that has meaning, that he is bringing you out of a terrible darkness, and that in the end it will be all right."

"What are you telling me, Peter?"

"I'm telling you to hang on, to trust your instincts. They are good and God-given. Evil has within it the seeds of its own destruction. Sarz is no exception. He is a formidable enemy. I don't mean that you should underestimate him. But I know you, John. You are a good man. You believe in more than you think you believe in. You will get through this, and when you do, you will be better for it."

"I believe in more than I think I believe in," Fitzsimmons mused.

The priest leaned forward. "Tell me, what is it that you're hiding? What is that you want to talk about but can't?"

Fitzsimmons opened his mouth to speak but nothing came out.

"Whatever it is, it has not destroyed you. You have survived, and it is your belief which has sustained you. If you did not believe there was something better, you would have given up."

"My belief?"

"Your belief. And let me tell you something else. Belief and despair can exist side by side. There is a time that we hug our despair, that we cherish it. And there is a time to discard it, a time to look at it for what it is, a time to look at the past and to accept it and to be free of it. Don't let that time pass you by."

They were silent again for a long time. Finally, Fitzsimmons spoke. "But what about Sarz? What would you do if you were in my place?"

"I'd ask God for help."

"I mean, what would you do if you were me?" Fitzsimmons asked.

The priest pondered the distinction. "I don't know," he said.

CHAPTER TWELVE

THREE WEEKS PASSED. SPRING TURNED INTO SUMMER, AND THE PACE of the city slackened. Fitzsimmons hardly saw Sarz, and when they met, they nodded to each other and kept going. If they spoke at all, it was never more than a sentence or two. It was as though the incident at The Good Sports Cafe had not happened. Sarz never referred to it. He seemed to ignore Fitzsimmons, and the irony had left his eyes. Rather than being puzzled, Fitzsimmons was relieved.

"Maybe he was just drunk. Maybe it was some kind of elaborate practical joke after all, and maybe he decided to just drop it," Karen said.

It was Sunday, and they were sunning themselves on the Esplanade. She wore a red halter top and jean shorts. She sat on the blanket with her arms around her knees, and her hair fell loosely on her back.

"Maybe," Fitzsimmons said. But at a very deep level of his consciousness he knew it was no practical joke and that he was merely enjoying a respite from Sarz's bizarre behavior, but he did not want to think about it.

"I love sitting here with you," he said. "I must be the envy of Boston. I'm alive and I love it."

"I love it, too." She leaned over to him and touched him on the forearm. "You've given me something," she said.

He looked at her and nodded. "And I've gotten it back," he said.

Karen smiled. Her face was relaxed; her expression was tender, open. The anguish which had been hidden in her smile when they first met was gone. She was peaceful and radiant.

"Almost from the very first, I thought this would be permanent," Fitzsimmons said. "I was afraid to tell you that. I was afraid I'd scare you off."

"You might have. I was a little intimidated by you. I still am."

"Intimidated?"

"A little," she said. "We don't have an awful lot in common. I'm a nurse; you're a professor. You love music; I don't know Verdi from linguine."

"We have more in common than you realize," he answered.

Karen gazed at him thoughtfully, but she did not pursue the conversation.

"I don't know what to do about Amy," Karen said as they were walking back to the apartment house.

"In what way?"

"Well, school's almost out. I know she wants to come and live with me for the summer, and I want her, but ... "

"But what?"

"You're going to think I'm rather cold and calculating," she said.

"Risk it," he said with a smile.

"Okay. I've been putting off a decision to see what happened with us. I didn't want to jeopardize our relationship, and I didn't want to bring Amy into a situation she couldn't handle."

"And now?"

"Now I want her to come to Boston."

"Good. I've been looking forward to meeting her," Fitzsimmons said. As he spoke the words, even though they were true, he had a vague sense of misgiving.

"It may not be easy. She was affected by Todd—by me—by the whole ugly situation. She became very withdrawn. She was a child who never smiled."

"She'll be all right."

"I hope so, but I don't know," Karen said.

"Well, I do. Peter says the antidote for any evil is love. Nothing can withstand it. He's right."

As they crossed Arlington Street, a disheveled man approached them. He had not shaved in several days, and his clothes were rumpled and dirty.

"Pardon me, sir," the man said to Fitzsimmons, "can you spare a quarter?" He looked detached, as if a refusal would not bother him.

Fitzsimmons took the change in his pocket and handed it to the man.

"Thank you, sir. Sorry to trouble you," the man said.

"That's all right," Fitzsimmons said.

Karen waited until the man was out of earshot. "Some things can withstand love," she said.

"Maybe," Fitzsimmons said, "but not little girls."

Karen took his hand and squeezed it. "I'm going to call Amy when we get back to the apartment and tell her I want her here as soon as she can get here."

"Good," Fitzsimmons said.

They checked their mailboxes before going upstairs. Karen pulled several letters from hers. Fitzsimmons found a business size envelope with no return address. He folded it and put it in his pocket.

"Come on in while I call her," Karen said.

"Okay. But I don't want to be introduced to her over the telephone."

Fitzsimmons stretched out on the sofa as Karen dialed. He sensed her eagerness and her anxiety; in fact, he felt a little of it himself.

"Hi, mom ... I'm fine ... It's lovely here, too ... Yes ... Wonderful ... No, everything's wonderful ... Yes ... Yes, we spent the day together."

Karen turned to Fitzsimmons and winked. "Is Amy around? ... Oh, good. Let me talk to her ... Hi, honey ... I miss you, too ... I love you, too. How's school? ... How many days left?

"Wednesday? ... Do you want to come to Boston? ... I hope until you grow up and go to college."

Karen was smiling broadly, but her eyes were wet. She turned so that Fitzsimmons could not see her. "Grandma will take care of everything. Don't worry. I'll tell her to buy your ticket and put you on the plane, and we'll be at Logan Airport to meet you ... John and me ... He's my friend ... You'll like him. He's right here now. Do you want to say hello to him?" Karen smiled and turned back to Fitzsimmons. He took the telephone.

"Hi, Amy. I'm John Fitzsimmons. I'm looking forward to meeting you. Your mother has told me a lot about you ... Well, that she loves you very much and she misses you very much ... We'll talk about that when you get here, and don't worry, I'm not as bad in person as I sound on the telephone ... No, I'll bet you're not either," Fitzsimmons laughed. He handed the telephone back to Karen.

"I'm sorry," Karen said after she hung up the telephone. "I didn't know what to do."

"That's all right. I'm glad I talked to her. Now I won't be such a big surprise when she gets here."

"And what is it that you two are going to talk about when she arrives?"

"Oh that," Fitzsimmons said. "Amy wanted to know if we were just friends or if we are planning to get married."

Karen's smile reflected amusement, shock, and embarrassment. "She asked that?"

"Yes."

The embarrassment and the shock left her face and the smile faded until just a hint of it remained. "And what are you going to tell her?"

"I'm going to tell her that I love you." Fitzsimmons paused, weighing his words. Again, the words were true, but as he spoke them he became apprehensive.

Karen stood as if frozen, waiting for him to continue. The sunlight streamed behind her, making her skin seem very pale. As she looked at him, the uneasiness which he felt finally reached his face, and for the briefest moment he looked as if he was in agony.

"Is that all you'll tell her?" she asked.

He reached out and took her hand. "There are still some things in me which haven't been resolved. There are still some things I have to come to terms with."

There was a sadness in her, a sense of rejection which Fitzsimmons could feel, and his eyes reflected his own sadness.

"Damaged goods," Fitzsimmons said.

"What?" she asked sharply, anger rising in her voice.

"Me," Fitzsimmons said. "Not you. Me. I'm damaged goods."

He dropped her hand and started to leave, but then he turned back. "I can't apologize for myself, Karen. I'm doing the best I can. I wish that I were a completely whole human being, but there's still something broken."

He started for the door, but Karen stopped him. She put her body against his and looked up into his face.

"I love you," she said.

When he returned to his apartment, he found the envelope in his pocket. Inside it, there was a folded newspaper clipping but no note or letter.

"Body of Girl Found in Swamp," the headline read. Fitzsimmons felt his stomach churn. The respite with Sarz was over.

"The body of seven-year-old Helen Vitigliano was found in a swamp in Dorchester, a few feet from Morrissey Boulevard at 6:30 last night.

"Police said the child had apparently been sexually abused. However, they refused to elaborate pending the results of an autopsy which was scheduled to be performed late last night.

"The girl, a daughter of Mr. and Mrs. Mario Vitigliano, lived at 117 E St., Dorchester. She was a first grade student in Our Lady of Loretto School.

"The discovery of her nude body, shortly before sunset, ended a day long search by Boston, MDC, State Police, and National Guardsmen. Her parents had reported her missing Tuesday night.

"Police at the scene of the discovery said the victim's clothes were found crumpled into a ball about ten feet away from the body. They said no weapon was found.

"One source, who refused to be identified, said the girl appeared to have been strangled. The source said there were deep bruises around the girl's neck.

"Helen was reported missing at 8 P.M., Tuesday, after she failed to come home for supper.

"Her parents called police after telephone calls to the girl's friends proved fruitless. The Vitiglianos were in seclusion last night, and police said Ruth Vitigliano, Helen's mother, was under a doctor's care.

"The search for the missing girl began early yesterday morning. More than two hundred police and national guardsmen searched a radius of two miles from Our Lady of Loretto School. They worked their way methodically through vacant lots and empty buildings.

"The discovery of the girl's body was made by two National Guardsmen about two hours before the search was scheduled to be called off for the night.

"A crowd of about 150 onlookers, mostly friends and neighbors of the Vitiglianos, had gathered by the time the police ambulance arrived at the scene. The crowd was somber and quiet as the body of the young girl, covered with a gray blanket and strapped to a stretcher, was placed into the ambulance."

There was more to the story, some quotes from friends of the girl and the nun who was the principal of the school. The reporter who had written the story managed to convey the sense of hopelessness and despair the family suffered. At the end of the story there was a small headline—"Boy Still Missing"—and a two paragraph story about a Roxbury boy who had been missing for several months.

Fitzsimmons collapsed into the stuffed chair in his living room. The clipping was undated. The event could have taken place the week before or years before. He had no way of knowing, but he was touched nonetheless by the feelings and the pathos. Like the crowd, he was somber and quiet. He felt the void that Helen Vitigliano's parents felt, and he felt their frustration. There was an immense sadness within him, but he did not cry.

The interlude was over. Sarz had started again, and Fitzsimmons was at his mercy. Sarz could deal out the cards in any order and at any time he wished, and Fitzsimmons could do nothing except wait.

It was all so amorphous, so intangible. Sarz was invulnerable. There was nothing Fitzsimmons could connect him to. Fitzsimmons knew intuitively that the clipping came from Sarz, but Fitzsimmons could not prove it. Sarz had told Fitzsimmons that he had strangled a little girl, but Fitzsimmons could not prove that either. Doing anything seemed purposeless, and doing nothing would only underscore his helplessness.

Fitzsimmons got up and began to pace, walking back and forth across the room, occasionally glancing out the window. After a few minutes, he left the apartment. He paused in front of Karen's door, but then went quickly to the stairs and left the building. He went into a small variety store and used the pay telephone to call Peter.

"Do you have any friends in the police department?" Fitzsimmons asked.

"Several," Peter answered. "Frank Volpe was one of my best pals when I was a kid. He's a captain now."

"I'd like to talk to him, or maybe he could refer me to somebody else."

"What's going on?"

"I'm getting newspaper clippings again."

"I'll call Frank. I'll try to set something up for Monday. Is that too late?"

"No, Monday's fine," Fitzsimmons said.

As he walked back to the apartment, his mood changed. He felt lighter, as if a burden had been lifted. Perhaps, the police could do nothing about Sarz, but that didn't matter. At least Fitzsimmons was acquainting them with the problem. At least he was doing something.

As he walked down the hall to his apartment, Karen's door opened. He could tell by her face that her mood had brightened, too.

"Where have you been? I've been looking for you."

"I called Peter."

"You could have used my phone," she said.

"Next time. Why were you looking for me? Did you want to take me out to dinner?"

"I thought that would be a good idea," Karen said.

Fitzsimmons leaned over and kissed her.

"I'm so excited," she said. "I want to celebrate. My daughter is coming. I've got you. John, you can't imagine how good I feel."

"Want to bet?"

She squeezed his hand. "Come on. Go get ready. We've got reservations at Ma Maison."

"I'm going to get fat," he said.

"Enjoy it. When Amy arrives we're going to lose some of our freedom. Do you mind?"

"Not a bit. I'm looking forward to Amy. I guess I'm a little bit nervous about meeting her, but I'm looking forward to it."

"Don't be nervous, she'll love you. And you'll be good for her. You'll be good for each other," Karen said.

CHAPTER THIRTEEN

FITZSIMMONS WOULD NOT HAVE SUSPECTED THAT FRANK VOLPE AND Peter Genaro were old friends. They seemed to have nothing in common. Peter was lively and smiling. He had a spiritual aura and soft features that tended to blend together. His tendency toward being overweight showed a self-tolerance, an easy discipline, which was not evident in Volpe. The policeman was a perfunctory, matter-of-fact person. He was dark and lean, without being thin. His face was expressionless as if he had heard all the stories there were to hear and had stopped reacting to them years before. He was a neat man, but he was not conscious of style. He wore a brown plaid jacket with brown slacks and brown shoes with crepe soles. His shirt was a light green and his tie was mustard.

"I don't usually meet people privately," Volpe said after he and Fitzsimmons shook hands. "I only made an exception because of Father Pete."

"I'm sorry to bother you. I could have gone to the police department and seen someone there," Fitzsimmons said.

The policeman's stare was level and impenetrable. Fitzsimmons returned it. "Well I'm here now," Volpe said.

"Yes, and thank you so much for coming, Frankie," Peter said.

Volpe looked at Peter and then back at Fitzsimmons with a trace of amusement. "Nobody's called me Frankie in years," he said. "Father Pete and I grew up together. We were real pals when we were kids. We both planned to be major league ball players. And here we are. I track them down and he forgives them." He took a package of cigarettes out of his shirt pocket. "Now what's all this about?"

"I don't know what Peter has told you," Fitzsimmons said.

"Just that you had a problem I could help you with."

"Well, I do have a problem, and it's perplexing because I'm not absolutely sure it's a problem. There's a man who works with me who told me that he had raped and killed a child."

Volpe's attention seemed to be concentrated on the package of cigarettes which he held in his right palm. When Fitzsimmons did not continue, he looked up and asked, "Why aren't you sure it's a problem?"

"Because I don't know whether the man is telling the truth or whether it's some kind of sick joke."

"Is he the kind of person who makes jokes?"

"Not the usual kind. He's a strange person, very devious, very ambiguous."

Volpe listened impassively as Fitzsimmons recounted his experiences with Sarz. The policeman's face registered nothing except perhaps disinterest as Fitzsimmons spoke of the pornographic magazine, the conversation in the bar, the drugged ginger ale, and, finally, the newspaper clipping, which he handed to Volpe.

Volpe read the entire clipping before he spoke. "I remember this case," he said at last. "I was one of the investigating officers. The Italian community was outraged." He handed the clipping to Peter. "I'm sure Father Pete remembers it, too. He was an assistant at that parish ten or fifteen years ago."

Peter held the clipping without looking at it. He nodded as Volpe spoke.

"This is recent," Volpe said. "A year and a half or two years ago at the outside. I remember the reporter who wrote it. He's dead now. Had a heart attack about six months ago. Heavy drinker, heavy smoker. He never took care of himself. Hard worker, though. Pretty decent guy—for an Irishman."

Fitzsimmons could not tell if the remark was said seriously or was meant to be humorous.

Volpe put the package of cigarettes back in his shirt pocket without taking one. "We never solved this case, officially, at least. There was a twenty-year-old kid, a really strange kid, who we know did it. He was one of those loners, no friends, quiet. Lived at home. Strange parents, too. He had a record. Couple of indecent assaults on young girls, lewd behavior, that kind of stuff. But he cracked. Whether the girl screamed and he panicked or what happened, we'll never know. He hung himself. He left a note but his father destroyed it. Said it was none of our business. Then he turned around and sued the city. Said his son died as the result of police harassment. The case is still pending, and the son of a bitch may collect. But we knew the kid did it. And the old man knows the kid did it, too. That's why he destroyed the note.

"As far as that other one, I don't remember it. I don't know whether the kid was ever found or not," Volpe said.

"What other one is that?" Peter asked.

"The boy. That small story tacked onto the end of the one about the Vitigliano girl," the policeman answered, and turned to Fitzsimmons. "But in a city of this size, it's not all that unusual for kids to disappear. Some of them, probably most of them, want to disappear. They take off and go to live with a relative in some other city or they just take off. If they're reported missing and they show up a couple of months later, nobody bothers to report that they came back. Of course, sometimes it is foul play. Kidnappings happen. Usually it's a relative. A father steals his son or a mother grabs her daughter. And every once in a while some young kid will be kidnapped by a pedophile and he or she will never be heard from again. It happens."

Volpe had warmed to his subject and he seemed almost friendly. He took the cigarette package out of his pocket again. This time he slipped a cigarette out and put it in his mouth. He fumbled through his other pockets for a match. Then he stopped and looked at his watch. He took the cigarette out of his mouth and carefully put it back into the package.

"Now about this guy, Sarz. I can only tell you he didn't kill Helen Vitigliano. The kid who hung himself did that. We didn't have enough to charge him, but we would have if he had stuck around. We were building a very strong case against him, so strong that there really is no reason to entertain the possibility that someone else did it."

"No?" Fitzsimmons said. "Even though this guy tells me he killed a girl, and a newspaper clipping about a murdered girl turns up in my mailbox?"

"What he told you and how that clipping got in your mailbox may or may not be related. But whether he put that clipping there or not, he did not kill the Vitigliano kid," Volpe said.

Fitzsimmons nodded his head. "It would have been politically impossible," he said.

"Don't give me that shit," Volpe said. "Politics has nothing to do with it. I know who killed Helen Vitigliano. It was not this guy. But if he is a practical joker, it would make sense for him to pick this clipping. He must have known there's a lawsuit against the city, and he must have known what the reaction would be if you brought it to the police."

"He sure must have," Fitzsimmons said. "And do you suppose he saved this clipping for two years, just as a joke?"

"I don't know how he got the clipping, whether he saved it or whether he bought or found an old newspaper, but I know that he didn't kill the girl," Volpe said. He glared at Fitzsimmons but Fitzsimmons did not look away. Instead, he returned Volpe's hard look with a steady gaze. It was Volpe who finally looked away first.

The policeman turned to the priest. "I'll check this guy Sarz out, Peter, and I'll try to find out what his problem is. And I'll do that for you." Volpe stood up to leave, and Peter and Fitzsimmons both rose from their chairs.

"Thanks for coming by, Frank. Whatever you can do will be appreciated," the priest said.

Volpe glanced at Fitzsimmons. "I hope so," he said.

"Thank you," Fitzsimmons said. His words seemed to hang in the air.

Volpe nodded. "I'll get back to you, Peter," he said.

Peter shut the door behind Volpe and shrugged. "Frankie was always something of a hard-nose," he said.

Fitzsimmons smiled and let out a strangled laugh.

"It's funny how we keep people frozen in our mind," the priest said. "We forget how they change. When we were kids, Frank was open and friendly. In fact, he was quite garrulous, if you can imagine that."

"He's changed," Fitzsimmons said.

Peter smiled. "And the great thing about life is that he may change again."

"Well, if nothing else, at least I told somebody official about Sarz."

"You did your part," Peter said. "That's all you can do."

"It may not be enough," Fitzsimmons said.

"No, it may not. But you did what you are supposed to do, and you've given Frankie the opportunity to do what he's supposed to do."

"Well I hope he takes that opportunity. He would be the perfect match for Sarz. In a lot of ways he's just like him," Fitzsimmons said.

Tommy was the first person Fitzsimmons saw when he went to work that afternoon.

"Hey, Jay," the little man called. He hurried toward Fitzsimmons, his right toe pointing inward as he dragged his right foot. There was a conspiratorial look on his face. "I think Sarz is looking for you," he said in a low voice.

"Why?"

"I don't know," Tommy said grinning widely. "Don't you know, Jay?"

"I mean what makes you think he's looking for me? Did he ask you where I was?"

"No, Jay. He didn't ask me. But I can tell. I know about Sarz. I know what he's got on his mind. He wasn't looking to talk to you. He was just looking for you. He likes to know where you are."

"How do you know?" Fitzsimmons persisted.

The smile left Tommy's face. "I'm not a half-wit, Jay. I look like a half-wit. Don't I? That's all right. I look in the mirror and even I say, 'You look like a half-wit, Tommy,' but I'm not a half-wit. I only look like one and act like one. But I don't think like one. Inside this half-wit there's a whole-wit. Do you understand me, Jay?" Suddenly the mischievous smile was back on Tommy's face. "You half-wit. You're a half-wit, Jay. You look like a whole-wit but inside you there's a half-wit." Tommy began to giggle. "There's a half-wit struggling to get out." Tommy began to shriek with laughter. "But it's all right, you half-wit, you're part of the silent majority."

Tommy started to scurry away, but he stopped and turned back to Fitzsimmons. "I know what he's got on his mind. He's got you on his mind. He hates you, Jay, you half-wit."

"Why is that, Tommy?"

Tommy's face became very solemn. "He just hates you, Jay. That's all I know. Don't you know?"

"No," Fitzsimmons said.

"Well, you'll find out, Jay. One of these days."

Tommy's face became vacant as his thoughts turned to something else, and it was as though Fitzsimmons had suddenly disappeared. Tommy spun around and then, slowly, limped away.

Chapter Fourteen

Amy Easton had the quiet beauty that Renaissance painters liked to capture. There was a mystery beneath her serenity, a depth to the seven-year-old girl that Fitzsimmons could only wonder at. It was as if the tragedy of her father had aged her, and she knew that life had a potential for terrible pain and inexplicable sadness and that permanence is an illusion. Fitzsimmons had expected her to be hostile, but she was not. Instead, she was initially wary and distant. He did not mind. In fact, he preferred that to feigned affection. He knew that they would become friends because they had the common experience of tragedy. When they were together, which was quite often because of Karen's work schedule, Fitzsimmons respected Amy's distance. He refused to force conversation on her. If she wanted to talk, they talked, and if she did not, they were silent. Sometimes she would spend hours watching television while Fitzsimmons read, and sometimes Fitzsimmons would take her for a walk or to the movies or to a museum. She liked the Museum of Fine Arts. She was especially struck by the 16th century paintings of young girls.

"Do you drink?" she asked one day as they visited the New England Aquarium.

"No."

"Did you ever?"

"When I was young a couple of times. I didn't like it."

"Why not?"

"I felt like I was losing control. It was very unpleasant."

They continued to walk up the circular ramp that wound around the huge glass center tank.

"My father drank," she said.

Fitzsimmons nodded. They stopped to watch a large, gray fish move through the green water. Amy said nothing further, and Fitzsimmons did not pursue the subject.

Another time when Fitzsimmons took her out for a pizza, Amy said, "I hated Michigan. I loved my grandma, but I hated Michigan. It's so much nicer here."

"You must have missed your mom."

"Yeah," she said.

"I know your mom missed you."

"How do you know?" Amy asked.

"Because I saw her cry."

"I used to cry, too," Amy said. "I used to cry myself to sleep every night."

Fitzsimmons nodded.

On the way back to the apartment, Amy said, "Mom told me you were married once."

"That's right," Fitzsimmons said.

"And you had a daughter?"

"Yes."

"Where are they now?"

"They died."

"Did you ever cry yourself to sleep?" Amy asked.

"I've done my share of crying," Fitzsimmons said.

As they crossed Beacon Street, Amy took Fitzsimmons' hand. She dropped it when they got to the sidewalk.

"How old would your daughter be if she hadn't died?"

"Your age," he said.

A strand of blond hair had fallen over Amy's left eye. She brushed it away with her right hand.

"What was her name?"

"Sarah."

"That's a nice name."

"Sarah Anne Fitzsimmons."

"That's pretty," Amy said.

"She was a pretty girl."

"Do you miss her?"

"Not as much as I used to."

On Saturday morning, Karen slept late, and Fitzsimmons took Amy out to breakfast. It was fun for them both. They had identical orders—orange juice, pancakes, eggs over easy, and sausage. Fitzsimmons had coffee and Amy had hot chocolate with whipped cream on top. Fitzsimmons had started reading newspapers again, and Amy read the comics as he read through the first section. Amy wore a pink blouse and khaki shorts. Her hair was drawn back in a ponytail. As she pored over the comics she was unaware of the occasional admiring glance which was cast her way. One elderly woman, on her way back from the rest room, stopped at their table.

"I must tell you what a beautiful daughter you have," she said to Fitzsimmons, ignoring Amy as if the girl could not hear her. "She is so well-behaved and ladylike."

"Thank you," Fitzsimmons said.

"She thought I was your daughter," Amy said when the woman was gone.

"I hope you don't mind that I didn't bother to correct her."

Amy studied Fitzsimmons' face and then looked away. "That's all right. I don't mind."

After breakfast they went to the Esplanade and walked along the Charles River. The grass was dotted with people lying on blankets sunbathing, strollers filled the paths, and sailboats were bobbing along out in the river.

"I like this," Amy said.

"So do I," Fitzsimmons answered.

What Fitzsimmons said was true. He enjoyed the time he spent with Amy almost as much as the time he spent with Karen. It was a different kind of enjoyment. He felt his fatherly instincts, which had been aborted four years earlier, returning. Amy was easy to get along with. In ways she reacted more like an adult than a child. The scars left by the trauma of dealing with her father and being separated from her mother were not obvious at first. She was neither rebellious nor possessive. What at first seemed to be shyness turned out to be introspection and detachment. She seemed to expect nothing from him or, for that matter, from Karen. It became apparent to Fitzsimmons that she was like a guest who did not wish to offend her hosts. That did not surprise Fitzsimmons. Amy had been rejected by her father and left by her mother, and now her mother had a relationship with a man to whom she was not married. There was an ambiguity there which would make most children uncomfortable. What was more disturbing to Karen was the fact that Amy did not seem to care that there were no opportunities for her to meet girls her own age. This, too, seemed natural to Fitzsimmons. Amy was having a respite from an unpleasant past. She was in the process of healing. September and school would come soon enough, and Amy would re-enter the world of childhood. Perhaps by then she would begin to have enough confidence in their relationship to become self-assertive.

"You don't mind her being with us so much of the time?" Karen asked.

"Sometimes I wish we had more time to ourselves, but she's a good kid. I enjoy her. We're becoming friends."

"I know you are. She likes you. She tells me how nice you are."

"We complement each other," Fitzsimmons said.

It was midnight, and they were sitting in Karen's living room. Amy had long since gone to sleep.

"I went to see Peter," Karen said.

"Oh? Peter Genaro?" Fitzsimmons asked.

"Do you mind?"

"No. Of course not. I'm just surprised. Why should I mind?"

"Well, he's your friend, and I didn't tell you about it." Karen leaned forward in her chair.

"Sometimes I wonder whether what I'm doing is right. From everything you told me about Peter, he seemed so nice and understanding. You had a friend you could turn to and talk about things, and I need somebody like that. Do you know what I mean? There are some things two people can't get straight just by themselves. I don't have any real close friends in Boston. You're the only person I'm really close to here."

"It's good to have somebody to talk to, somebody with whom you don't have to worry about what they're thinking. Was he surprised?"

"A little, I think, or maybe not. I didn't even telephone. I just showed up at the rectory, and he treated me like I was a long lost friend. And I'm not even a Catholic—I'm not really much of anything. He really is a nice person. I can see why you're so fond of him."

"Can I ask what you talked about or would that be prying?"

"We talked about you. We talked about me. We talked about Amy. Actually, I did almost all of the talking; he just listened. I suppose that's what I needed—someone to listen while I sorted out my feelings."

Karen was silent for a moment, and Fitzsimmons waited for her to continue.

"I worry, John. I worry whether what I'm doing is right. Whether it was right to leave Amy with my mother. Whether it is right to have her here now. I wonder whether it is right to be a single mother having a relationship with a man across the hall."

"It's not that casual," Fitzsimmons said.

"No, I know it isn't. But I think about those things, and I wonder, 'Am I doing right? Am I doing wrong? Is this helping Amy or is it hurting her?' And there are other things, too. I wonder if I'm not using you, if I'm not just trying to put my life back together and if our meeting was more convenience than fate."

Fitzsimmons leaned his chin on the palm of his hand and looked at Karen.

"And I wonder if that's what you think," she said. "Do you know what I mean? Sometimes I think this is too good to be real. I think that maybe this is just an interlude, and I wonder what would happen if it ended. What would happen to me, and what would happen to you, and what would happen to Amy?"

Karen hesitated as if pondering whether to continue, and then she did.

"And maybe what I wonder about most is you. In some ways I know you very well, and in others you're a mystery. I have a feeling that there is a whole big part of you that I have never seen."

Fitzsimmons nodded as if in agreement. "What did Peter say?" he asked.

"He talked about trusting. He said I had to trust my feelings and that I had to trust you. And he talked about God and trusting God."

"He's a priest," Fitzsimmons said, shaking his head. "Sometimes I forget all about that."

"It came sort of as a surprise to me, too," Karen said. "He was wearing his Roman collar and everything, but I was really looking for human answers."

"Did you tell him that?"

"Yes."

"What did he say?"

"He just laughed. He said God was a human answer." Karen looked at Fitzsimmons as if expecting him to comment, but he said nothing.

"And I said to him, 'What about morality?' And he said, 'What about it?' And I said, 'Father, I'm divorced and I'm having a relationship with a man I'm not married to.' And he said, 'Morality is love. If you truly love, you cannot offend morality.'"

Karen crossed her legs and recrossed them.

"This isn't easy," she said. "It was easier talking to Peter about all this than to you, but he said I ought to talk it out with you so that's what I'm doing." Karen took a breath and exhaled. "You know, we just happened. All of a sudden we were. And I told him that, and he said, 'All right. Step back and examine your feelings.' And he asked me if I was running, and I said, 'No.' And he said, 'Are you using him to escape the past?' And I said, 'No' again. 'Is this just a sexual thing?' 'No.' 'Do you love him?'" Karen lowered her voice. "And I said, 'Yes.' And he said, 'I don't mean are you infatuated with him and captivated by him or that you take pleasure in him or that he is convenient.' And I said, 'What do you mean?' 'I mean, do you want to give to him?' 'Give what to him?' And he said, 'Self. Not just body but self. And are you ready to allow him to give up himself, to surrender to you and you surrender to him, to accept him as he is with his imperfections and defects?' "

Karen stood up and took a few steps across the room.

"I knew what he meant, and yet I didn't know what he meant. I have all these feelings inside of me. And I said to him, 'Not unconditionally. I'm ready to surrender, but I can't do it unconditionally. I would have to know that he is surrendering too, I just cannot give blindly. I just can't leap out into the dark if I don't know that I'm going to land safely.' And he said, 'None of us can. At least not at first. We must have trust to make that leap. We must trust ourselves and our feelings, and we must trust the other person. And then we have to make that leap of trust countless times in a relationship. When things don't go well, when the other person fails to meet our expectations, when the other person has an annoying habit or doesn't see things our way. Love tells us to leap and trust allows us to. We do it despite our anger and despite our fears. We act despite ourselves. That is love.' At least that's what he said."

"I believe that," Fitzsimmons said.

"He said that most people don't understand that love is an act of the will. It's a decision, not just an emotion," Karen said. "But he put the most emphasis on God. And he quoted the Bible. Something I didn't understand."

"What was it?" Fitzsimmons asked.

"He said, 'If God doesn't build the city, the builders labor in vain.' "

Fitzsimmons thought for a moment, and then shook his head. "I don't know what he meant either," he said.

"And he said one last thing," Karen said.

"What was that?"

"He said that there would come a time when you would forgive God, when you would understand that God is not the source of pain."

Fitzsimmons cleared his throat before he spoke. "You had quite a conversation," he said.

"He's not a person that stays on the surface. I see now why the two of you are friends. I feel like I could tell him anything and he would understand and that he would still like me."

Fitzsimmons nodded. "He would."

"And he thinks the world of you. He really does. He thinks you're special."

Fitzsimmons smiled, a half-embarrassed smile. "I can't for the life of me figure out why," he said.

Karen walked over to the sofa where Fitzsimmons was sitting and stood in front of him. "I can," she said. "There's something special about you, something different."

The next morning, Fitzsimmons rented a car to take them to Cape Cod. He parked in the street, went into the hall and pushed the button to ring the buzzer in Karen's apartment. As he waited for them to come downstairs, he spotted a piece of brown paper through the slot of his mailbox. He took out his key, opened the box and pulled out a folded piece of paper which had been torn from a brown paper bag.

When he unfolded it, he saw that one word had been scrawled on the paper in blue ballpoint: "Asshole." He crumpled it up and put it in his pocket.

"All set?" Karen asked from the top of the stairs.

"I'm as ready as I'll ever be," Fitzsimmons said.

CHAPTER FIFTEEN

VOLPE STUDIED THE CRUMPLED PIECE OF BROWN PAPER BAG. "When did you get this?" he asked without looking up, as if he wanted to ignore, as much as possible, Fitzsimmons' presence.

Fitzsimmons, in turn, studied the policeman without answering. Volpe wore a dark brown blazer with gold buttons and matching brown trousers. He had on a dark blue shirt with an even darker blue, almost black, knit tie. He finally looked up at Fitzsimmons.

"Saturday," Fitzsimmons said.

Peter had gone to get coffee and the two men were left alone in his office. It was Peter who had called Volpe, despite Fitzsimmons' argument that asking the policeman's help was futile.

"Let me keep it," Volpe said, pushing the piece of paper into the left side pocket of his blazer. "He must've guessed I was checking him out. People like him have a sixth sense about cops."

Volpe took a cigarette pack from his shirt pocket, and, in almost a single motion as if he wanted to avoid inner debate, slid out a cigarette, lit it, and inhaled deeply. "Or maybe it's not from him at all."

Fitzsimmons looked away from Volpe, as if he was no longer paying attention.

"He's not an easy person to gather information on. F. B. Sarz. He's got a driver's license. He's got a car. He's not a registered voter. There

are no current warrants out for him, and as far as I can determine, he
has no history of sex offenses. It's true that he frequents The Good
Sports Cafe, but there's no law against that."

Fitzsimmons glanced at Volpe and then looked away again.

"On the surface, there doesn't seem to be much to the man. He
works. His attendance record is good. He's discreet about his sexual
behavior. He may or may not be homosexual or bisexual or heterosexual. His neighbors hardly notice him. He is not a person who stands
out in a crowd."

Fitzsimmons' sigh was barely audible. "There is more to him than
there appears to be, Captain," he said.

"That may be, but if there is, he hides it well. Since he was eighteen, his life has apparently been uneventful."

"How about before he was eighteen?" Peter asked as he came into
the room. He was carrying a tray with a glass coffeepot and three
mugs.

"That's a different story. Usually I wouldn't check a guy back so far,
but there was so little information on this one that he became a challenge. I visited TPI, and I saw him working in the hall. As soon as I saw
him, I knew that at some point in his life, he did something. People
like him have a sixth sense about cops, and cops have a sixth sense
about people like him. So I decided to check with the Department of
Youth Services, and there was one old-timer who remembered him."

By now, Fitzsimmons was looking at Volpe. The policeman spoke
methodically, betraying no hint of self-congratulation.

"He had problems as a kid," Volpe said. "He was a little bastard the
day he was born, and he was a little bastard for most, if not all, of his
young life, with all apologies to you, Father Pete. He was one of those
kids who are strange. Even among juvenile delinquents, there are some
kids who are strange, and this kid was one of them. He even had a
strange name, Free Sarz. Free B. Sarz. I mean why the hell would anybody name a kid Free—especially one who spent a lot of his life
locked up. The other delinquents used to call him Freebee. Maybe the
joke was intentional. Maybe his mother was on welfare and he was all
paid for.

"Anyway, his mother was a prostitute, and she didn't do a hell of a
lot more for the kid than give him a name. She abandoned him when
he was eight. She just took off and never came back and never even

said good-bye to him. He lived on the streets for a while, not just a day or two, but a couple of months, until somehow or other they caught up with him. He was probably caught sleeping some place he shouldn't have been or stealing food.

"He was turned over to the Division of Child Guardianship and they placed him in a series of foster homes. He couldn't adjust. He was a truant and a stubborn child who kept getting into trouble. When he was ten he was arrested on a half-dozen charges of driving without authority and shoplifting. Driving without authority means he stole the car but he didn't plan to keep it or sell it. A juvenile judge committed him to the Department of Youth Services, and the DYS shipped him back out to foster homes, tougher foster homes, but he still couldn't adjust.

"When he was fourteen, he and another kid committed an armed robbery. They took a shotgun from the house they were living in, stole a car, and held up a drugstore. He spent some time locked up in juvenile detention centers and then he was sent back out to a foster home.

"Some kids like Sarz immediately graduate to state prison when they turn eighteen, and some of them quiet down. He was one of the ones who quieted down.

"Of course, if you asked the people at DYS they'd say Sarz calmed down because of a program they put him into. But that's a lot of crap," Volpe said.

The priest handed Volpe a mug of coffee. "What program, Frank?"

"While they had Sarz in a lockup, they tested him and found he had a high I.Q. I don't know how high, but I guess it was pretty high. Genius level, whatever that is. And they put him into a special program which was run by one of the local universities. After he entered that program he never got caught at anything again. But let me tell you, radicals, cop killers, and bank robbers have come out of some of those enlightened programs."

Volpe stopped talking for a moment and looked from the priest to Fitzsimmons.

"That's true. It's a matter of record. Pete, you remember that Irisher out of Walpole State Prison who got hooked up with those girl radicals and killed the cop?"

The priest nodded.

"So maybe while they were teaching him about philosophy, they also taught him how not to get caught," the policeman said.

"Did Sarz graduate from college?" Fitzsimmons asked.

"I don't know. The DYS lost track of him once he turned eighteen. They also stopped paying for the program at that time, too. So what happened to him? I don't know. But if he graduated from college I doubt very much if he'd be sweeping floors at TPI," Volpe said. He took a sip of the coffee and then a drag from his cigarette.

"But all of that aside, I don't think there is a program in the world that can untwist a twisted kid, and kids like Sarz are twisted. Most of them come from rotten environments, and something has been knocked out of them. I've never been able to put my finger on it, but they're missing something other kids have. I know this sounds bad, but it's true. They're animals, and they get treated like animals. They're locked up in cages, just like at a zoo. They're fed and exercised. Sometimes they watch television and sometimes they break things or they give themselves tattoos. I saw one kid who got sick of his tattoo and burned it out with cigarettes. They're tough, they're mean, but they can look and talk like choir boys."

Volpe paused again and looked from Fitzsimmons to the priest and back to Fitzsimmons. "So what can you do with these kids? Society won't let you keep them in jail. You can't shoot the little bastards. So you wait. You wait for them to grow up and rape somebody or kill somebody or rob somebody and then you throw them into prison with the big boys, where they learn a whole new code of behavior.

"Sounds pretty jaded, huh? If the liberals and the radicals could hear me now they'd be screaming 'fascist.' I'm just telling it the way it is, and I'm not blaming them. Maybe it's not their fault. But that's the way it is with them—not every kid that gets into trouble, but the hard ones, the ones that lost that spark, that sense of right and wrong. They are bad, bad news. And this guy Sarz sounds like he was pretty twisted.

"Not only was his mother a whore who gave him a strange name, but he had problems at some of the foster homes he lived at. One of them was run by a farm couple who were drunks. The husband was a real bruiser and he used to beat the shit out of the kids whether they stepped out of line or not. It was like Oliver Twist. Really. That's where Sarz and the other kid stole the shotgun. It's a wonder they didn't blow the guy's brains out. Oh, that happened. A couple of years later a kid blew the guy away while he was sleeping. But that was after Sarz left." Volpe put the stub of his cigarette out in an ashtray on Peter's desk.

"There's one other bit of information I got from the old-timer. When Sarz was eleven, he was a resident of a foster home run by a priest. It happened that this particular priest was queer. Sorry, Pete, but the guy was a fag, and he used to seduce the boys in the house."

"I remember," Peter said. "It all came out in the papers. He was a bad priest, a man who never should have been a priest. I think he got out of the country before he could be arrested."

"That's right. He went to Canada," Volpe said. "Now, nobody could say for sure that Sarz was one of the kids this guy slept with, because Sarz wouldn't talk about it. When they questioned him, he would not open his mouth. He wouldn't say yes and he wouldn't say no. His silence was absolute."

Volpe slapped his hands together with a sharp crack, which rang through the office. "Well, that's what I found out about this guy."

As Volpe was talking about Sarz's childhood, Fitzsimmons had listened intently. He had leaned forward in his chair with his elbows on his knees and his chin in his hands and stared unwaveringly at Volpe. Fitzsimmons did not change his position even after the policeman slapped his hands together.

"I knew he was sick," Fitzsimmons said. "I knew there was something churning inside of him."

"The priest may never have laid a glove on him," Volpe said.

"He may not have touched him physically, but he touched him," Peter said. "And if Sarz wasn't raped by the priest, he was certainly raped by something—maybe it was life itself—but whatever it was, he was violated."

The three men looked away from each other. Peter's eyes were on the painting of the Annunciation. Fitzsimmons looked out the window, and Volpe stared at the rug. It was Volpe who broke the silence.

"All that doesn't do you much good," he said to Fitzsimmons.

"It doesn't do me any harm either. At least I know something about the guy. It doesn't explain what he's doing … "

"If he's doing anything," Volpe interjected. The policeman's face was expressionless. Fitzsimmons studied it in vain looking for some clue as to what was in Volpe's mind.

"Yeah, if," Fitzsimmons replied. "It doesn't explain it, but it's a start. It begins to explain it. It fits. Do you know what I mean?"

A hint of disdain crept into Volpe's face. Fitzsimmons' eyes narrowed just slightly.

Peter looked quickly from Fitzsimmons to Volpe. "Did you draw any conclusions?" the priest asked.

"Conclusions?" Volpe asked, still looking at Fitzsimmons. "What kind of conclusions?" he asked, finally looking at Peter.

"About this fellow Sarz," the priest said.

"There really isn't anything I can conclude. If you mean do I think he stuck the piece of bag in Mr. Fitzsimmons' mailbox, the answer, not an official answer, is yes, he probably did. If you mean, do I think he raped the Vitigliano girl, the answer is, officially and unofficially, no."

"Anything else?" Peter asked.

"What else is there? The guy is making a pain in the ass of himself. The world is full of people who make pains in the ass of themselves."

"Why is he doing these things?" the priest asked.

"I just told you."

"But why these specific things?" the priest persisted.

"Because he thinks your friend is vulnerable to them. And I would guess he's right. Is he?" Volpe asked Fitzsimmons.

Fitzsimmons returned the stare. "Do you mean am I especially vulnerable to being drugged?"

"I mean to the newspaper clippings. You're not married, are you?"

Fitzsimmons shook his head.

"No children by a former wife?"

Fitzsimmons shook his head again.

"You don't have a record?" It was a question without the inflection.

Fitzsimmons shook his head again.

"Then why does this guy think you're vulnerable to this stuff?"

Fitzsimmons looked at Peter. He started to speak, hesitated, and then said, "That's a question he'd have to answer."

"You don't know?"

"Does it make a difference?" Fitzsimmons asked.

Volpe looked at his watch and then at Peter. "No pastries today, Pete? I feel short-changed."

"Excuse me, Frankie. Of course I've got pastries. I have some cannoli in the refrigerator. Let me go get them."

The priest got up quickly and left the room. Volpe waited only until the door was shut.

"You're something like this guy, Sarz," he said turning to Fitzsimmons. His face had taken on an intensity he had not displayed before. "I know that if I go back on you, I'll find something, just like I found something on Sarz."

Fitzsimmons did not avoid the policeman's stare. "In your own way, Captain, you're something like Sarz yourself."

Volpe glared at him. "What do you mean?" The policeman's voice was even, but his face had hardened.

"You have similar approaches. You use the same elements: disinterest, aggression, and intimidation."

"You didn't call me here to insult me, did you Mr. Fitzsimmons?"

"I didn't call you here at all, Captain. But I certainly don't want to insult you any more than you want to insult me."

"Pete, I don't think your friend likes cops," Volpe said as the priest swung the door open.

The priest looked at Fitzsimmons but said nothing.

"I was just making an observation," Fitzsimmons said. "It wasn't meant to be taken personally."

The priest offered a plate with cannoli to Volpe, who took one, and then to Fitzsimmons, who declined. "Oh, by the way, I have a message for you from an old friend of yours," Volpe said.

Fitzsimmons at first thought Volpe was talking to Peter. It was only after a moment that he realized that the policeman was speaking to him.

"A friend of mine?" Fitzsimmons asked. His tone was disbelieving.

"Yes, a Mr. Wallace. The academic dean at your university. He said to tell you they still want you back." Volpe turned to the priest. "Your friend is extremely well thought of back on Long Island."

Fitzsimmons stood up. His arms were at his sides, but his fists were clenched. "What?" His voice was sharp. His face was flushed with anger. "What … " he repeated the word, but was unable to say anything else.

"What?" Volpe echoed. For an instant he was surprised, but he maintained his composure. "What?" he repeated, this time with a trace of irony.

"How did you happen to talk to Mr. Wallace?" Peter asked Volpe.

"Just doing my job, Father Pete. I don't know your friend, and you haven't known him too long yourself. I just wanted to make sure that he is who he says he is. I didn't investigate him. I just checked his references, that's all."

Fitzsimmons started toward the door, but he stopped and turned to face Volpe.

"Wallace spoke very highly of Mr. Fitzsimmons," Volpe said. "He called him brilliant. Said he was one of the few people in his field who really had something to say. He said he would love to have him back."

Fitzsimmons waited until he was sure that Volpe had finished.

"Captain, I know that you went to a lot of trouble. Thank you."

"You don't have to thank me. I did it for Father Genaro," Volpe said, using the priest's last name as if to indicate that Fitzsimmons was not privy to the same intimacy with Peter as Volpe was.

"I know that," Fitzsimmons said. "I want to thank you anyway, even if it was an unintended service."

Fitzsimmons started for the door again, but again he stopped.

"Thank you, too, Peter," he said.

"Don't go yet, John. I want to talk to you for a minute or two," the priest said.

"And I've got to get back to work," Volpe said, standing up. "The cannoli were great and so was the coffee."

"You don't like him," the priest said after Volpe left.

"No," Fitzsimmons said.

"And the feeling appears mutual."

"Yes."

"Sometimes the help we get is not the help we expected," the priest said.

"What do you mean?"

"Well, I think we were both secretly hoping that Frankie could take some kind of action against Sarz. He can't or he won't, but still, doesn't the information he uncovered on Sarz help you?"

"As a matter of fact it does. It doesn't prove anything, but it certainly says something about the man. If nothing else it tells me I'm not wrong in blaming Sarz for the clippings or believing that he is capable of doing what he says he has done," Fitzsimmons said.

"In an ironic way it puts our minds at ease—at least partly at ease," the priest said.

Fitzsimmons nodded.

"But he also upset you."

Fitzsimmons nodded again.

"Why?" the priest asked.

"Because he knows, and because it's none of his business."

"Knows what?"

"About my wife and daughter."

"That they're dead?"

"That they were murdered."

"Murdered?" Peter's voice was so low that his question was almost inaudible.

"Butchered," Fitzsimmons said, without looking at the priest. "He knows that they were butchered. And he knows that Sarz knows, and he thinks that Sarz is just playing a cruel practical joke."

Peter was silent for a very long moment. "What makes you say that?" he asked, when he had finally collected his thoughts.

"Because it's true. He knows. He knows why I am vulnerable to those clippings. Believe me, he knows."

"John ... "

"When you get a chance, ask him," Fitzsimmons said. "Ask the son of a bitch. He was just like a cat playing with a dead mouse."

"John," the priest said. "John," he repeated.

"Do you think he spoke to Wallace and Wallace didn't tell him? Wallace is a gossip, and he is one of the most ingratiating people I have ever known. Your friend and Sarz have a lot in common—I told him that while you were in the kitchen. At the very core of their being, there is a cruel streak, something that takes delight in probing others' pain."

"John, he asked you about a wife and child. Why didn't you answer him?"

"The man knew. I am not going to share my pain with a sadist," Fitzsimmons said.

"Or anybody at all?"

"I've tried. I've tried to tell you. I've tried to tell Karen. As much as I have wanted to speak, I have been unable to. I don't know why. Maybe it isn't even the pain anymore. Maybe I just can't let go of it."

Peter stepped sideways so that he was in Fitzsimmons' line of vision, and Fitzsimmons was forced to look at him, an aging priest with gentle features who looked at him sternly.

"You will have to let go of it. Until you do, you will be crippled by it," Peter said.

"Crippled," Fitzsimmons repeated.

"It is your indictment of life and of God," the priest said. "It is your silent judgment against them both."

"Maybe," Fitzsimmons said. "Maybe." He shook his head. "Maybe they need to be judged."

"Isn't that what Sarz is doing? Isn't he calling God before the bench and finding him wanting? Isn't that what all sick people do?"

Fitzsimmons could not escape the priest's gaze, and so he returned it. He spoke quietly but sharply and as he spoke he pointed his finger at the priest.

"I am not the guilty party here. I am not the rapist; I am not the killer. Maybe I have been pointing a finger at God. Maybe somebody ought to point a finger at God."

"And if you could point your finger at God, what would you say to him?" the priest asked.

"I'd say, 'God, is it worth it?' I'd say, 'Look around you, God. Look at the blood and the madness and the pain, and tell me, is it worth it?' "

When Fitzsimmons finished speaking, the two men looked away from each other, and there was a long silence.

"You're the one who will have to answer that question," Peter said at last.

They fell silent again, glancing at each other occasionally.

"I've got to go," Fitzsimmons said after several minutes.

The priest nodded and followed him to the front door. As soon as Fitzsimmons stepped outside he turned and faced Peter.

He hesitated for a few seconds as if debating whether to speak. Finally, he did. "Perhaps you could join Karen and me for dinner tomorrow night?"

The priest, too, hesitated, as if he wanted to ask Fitzsimmons something. But all he asked was, "What time?"

"Well, let's see. Amy is going on that field trip with the Girl Scout Troop from this parish. I think they get back about six. How about meeting us at 7:30 at my apartment?"

"Sure," Peter said.

CHAPTER SIXTEEN

"FIRST THEY TOOK AWAY THEIR PEACE OF MIND. THEN THEY TOOK away their security, then their property, and then their freedom. Then they deprived them of their pride and self-respect, and finally they deprived them of their humanity. Then—only then—they took their lives."

Sarz smiled an enigmatic smile and toyed with the beer glass in front of him.

"They debased them—they even debased their bodies. It was the ultimate degradation. To the victims it was a nightmare. They were faced with an irrevocable progression, an unstoppable juggernaut. No matter how they scurried, no matter what they tried, they couldn't escape. They watched as their children's heads were bashed against walls and their wives were abused. They helped as gold was pulled from mouths and bodies were carted off to the incinerator. They helped their torturers and persecutors. And why? Because they could do nothing else. That's incredible, isn't it? And it was no accident. It was genius."

Sarz stared across the table as he took a long sip from his glass.

"People like you see beauty in paintings and sunsets. You look for perfection in architecture or poetry. You fail to see the genius and perfection in malice. You call people like the Nazis aberrations—freaks.

Evil is all around you, but you refuse to look at it. You noticed the Nazis because they almost took over the world. Yes. They almost did it. As impossible as that sounds to you, the Nazis almost took over the world. They were evil, but they weren't an aberration. Tamburlaine, Nero, Attila, Napoleon, Hitler. All cut from the same bolt of cloth. There is a war going on, and it has been going on since men have been men. It is as old as Cain and Abel, and it hasn't ended yet. Do you think it was an accident that Hitler's victims were Jews? God's chosen people?" His laugh was short—shrill and half-strangled.

"Do you understand what I'm saying? Life appears very stable. Law and order. Truth and beauty. Justice and honor. Love and mercy. But that is an illusion which conceals the underlying chaos. While we sit in this civilized atmosphere, there are monsters sprouting up all over the world. You never hear of most of them. Once in a while, one of them gains some notoriety. Idi Amin. What ever happened to Idi Amin? He was completely lacking in sophistication, but a monster all the same."

The noise from the bar came in waves, laughter, obscenities, shrieks. The smell of tobacco smoke was heavy and mingled with the smell of bodies. The Good Sports Cafe was packed.

"And how many killers do you think there are in this city alone? In this bar? How many people doing unspeakable things in the darkness and masquerading as upright citizens in the light? Oh, I love the darkness."

He waved his arm at the barroom full of people.

"There is an incredible amount of evil here—never mind the world. And do you know what? I am part of it. I am evil. I am part of the chaos waiting to swallow you up."

He laughed again, and again it sounded like a half-strangled shriek.

"One of the things I admired most about the way the Nazis handled the Jews was the sense of inevitability. There was no escaping and no appeal. The cruelty was methodical which made it even that much crueler. They weren't a bunch of deranged civil servants; they were clever and resourceful and evil. They divested themselves of weakness, of pity and empathy and morality. They were not bound by your absurd notions of kindness and self-abnegation. Domination and pain. Torture the bastards and glory in it. We are what we are. We are darkness. We are destruction. We are chaos."

He banged his empty glass on the table three times, and his eyes glared as he leaned forward in his seat.

"That's why I do what I do," he said, and lapsed into silence as he waited for the waitress to bring him another drink.

The two men studied each other, Sarz with a slight up turn at the corner of his mouth as though amused by the conversation and the noise and the smells, and Fitzsimmons, quietly and intensely, like an academic considering an abstraction.

Fitzsimmons had left work and came to the bar on impulse. He felt a need to clarify his position with Sarz. He wanted an end to the ambiguity and the feinting. Volpe had said that nothing could be done about Sarz, and he was probably right, but Fitzsimmons still felt drawn to confront Sarz and to try and define whatever it was that was going on and, if possible, to resolve it.

"You're not drinking—anything," Sarz said with a sarcastic edge to his voice.

Fitzsimmons shook his head.

"I'll have another," Sarz said to the waitress. "Nothing for him."

"You just said that's why you do what you do. What is it that you do?" Fitzsimmons asked after the waitress had gone.

"I've told you."

Fitzsimmons leaned across the table until his face was close to Sarz. "You didn't kill that girl," he said.

Sarz's face showed a trace of a smile. "How do you know that?"

"I know."

"Must have gone to the police," Sarz said, still with a trace of a smile.

"Must have."

The smile changed to a sneer. "Asshole," Sarz said.

"You're becoming repetitious," Fitzsimmons replied, slouching against the back of the booth.

"That was sort of an analogy," Sarz said. "Do you think I would tell you something that you could go to the police with and they could nail me on? The substance of what I told you was true. Do you understand?"

"No," Fitzsimmons said.

"The names and places were changed to protect the guilty. Now do you understand?"

Fitzsimmons nodded. "But where did you get that clipping?"

"I saved it."

"Why? That happened before we met."

"You still don't understand. You don't understand about the clipping, and you don't understand about me. Everything I tell you, I tell you for a reason. Everything I give you, I give you for a reason."

"That's what I don't understand. I don't understand your reasons and why or how they concern me."

Sarz smiled again, but now the sneer was clearly part of it.

"Why, Fitzsimmons," he said with an elaborate courtliness, "you are my Jew."

Fitzsimmons' expression did not change at Sarz's softly spoken words, but his calm expression hid feelings of panic and despair. Sarz's hatred of him did not make any sense. It seemed insane, and yet he understood, at a level deeper than intellect, its powerful reality.

"Why have you chosen me?" Fitzsimmons asked as softly as Sarz had spoken.

"When you understand that, you will understand it all," Sarz replied.

Fitzsimmons sighed. He looked around at the people crowded throughout the bar as if searching for an ally, and, seeing none, he turned back to Sarz.

"Is this just a game? Is this some kind of sadistic prank?" Fitzsimmons asked.

Sarz toyed with his glass for a moment and then looked across the table at Fitzsimmons.

"This is real," he said. "I am chaos. I am darkness. I am evil. Believe me. I am what I say I am." His speech had become slightly slurred, and his smile had the glint of intoxication.

"I'm not drunk," Sarz said as Fitzsimmons wondered whether he was. "You wish I were, but I'm not. But even if I were, what I say is true. You don't want to believe it's true because then you would have to look at the world and life in a different way. You want to believe that the world is basically good. All the evidence is to the contrary. In fact, the world is basically evil. And you don't know what to do about it. You can't embrace evil and you don't want to fight it, so you deny that it really is. You have that concentration camp mentality. You hang on and hang on, hoping that things will get better, and they get worse and worse. You are being crushed and you don't believe it. When will you believe it?"

Sarz half stood up in the booth and leaned his face across the table almost pushing it into Fitzsimmons' face. As he spoke little flecks of saliva flew from his mouth and hit Fitzsimmons' face.

"What are you going to do about me? You fucking asshole. What are you going to do?" The pitch of his voice had risen until it was almost a shriek, and his eyes glared with rage.

"I don't know," Fitzsimmons answered quietly.

"Don't you understand that I hate you? I despise you. I want to see you crushed. I am a real and present danger. But you, you asshole, you do not understand hatred. You do not understand evil. And because you don't understand it, you don't believe it exists."

The anger suddenly left Sarz's face, and he sat down.

"That's why you are my Jew," he said calmly. "Because even as you are being destroyed, you will be whistling in the dark. You'll be saying, 'He won't harm me. It won't happen to me. I've done nothing.' That's what they said as they walked into the gas chambers.

"And they hadn't done anything. They were innocent. They didn't deserve what was happening to them. It was evil. They didn't deserve it, and you don't deserve it. But it happened to them, and it will happen to you. That is what evil is all about. It strikes those who don't deserve it."

"And you didn't deserve it either," Fitzsimmons said.

"What?"

"You didn't deserve it either," Fitzsimmons repeated.

"What didn't I deserve?"

"Your life. A mother who was a prostitute and who abandoned you. A foster home run by a queer priest."

Sarz was stung. His eyes narrowed as if he had been slapped.

"Well, well, well," he said, nodding his head. "Well, well, well."

"Free B. Sarz. What the hell kind of name is that?" Fitzsimmons asked. His tone was gentle, not taunting.

Sarz continued to nod, as if recognizing something.

"No child deserves what you got," Fitzsimmons said.

"Well, well, well. The victim is not completely passive. The victim can strike back."

"I'm not striking back," Fitzsimmons said. "You're striking back. I just don't understand why I'm the target."

"How did you find out about me?" Sarz asked quietly.

"A cop checked you out. He talked to somebody at the Department of Youth Services who remembered you."

"They still remember me?" Sarz asked.

"One of them did," Fitzsimmons said.

"Who?"

"I don't know."

The two men lapsed into silence. They sat without looking at each other, absorbed in their own thoughts and insulated by the noise of the bar.

"So you think that explains me," Sarz said. His speech was clear. He now showed no sign that he had been drinking.

"It puts you in perspective," Fitzsimmons replied.

"Perspective. You see where I'm coming from, and you think you know where I've been."

"Yes, I do," Fitzsimmons said.

"An amateur psychologist."

"I don't have to be a psychologist to understand you."

"Understand me?" Sarz asked with a tone of incredulity. "Understand me?" The incredulity became tinged with anger.

"A bright young boy whose mother was a whore who hated him and showed that hatred by giving him a strange name and then abandoning him—taking his revenge on a sick world—running from reality into books—trapped by a self-image that was so bad, so despicable that the only way he could bear it was to construct a philosophical system based on evil rather than good. Yes, I think I have some understanding of you." Fitzsimmons spoke quietly and deliberately, staring unwaveringly into Sarz's eyes.

Sarz started to nod again. "Free B. Sarz. The kids thought she called me that because we were on welfare, but that wasn't the reason. 'The only time all year that I fucked for nothing and I got you,' she used to say. And I used to feel guilty because she fucked for nothing and I was conceived."

He stopped nodding.

"You're right. You are right. It took me a long time to deal with that. I tried to deny it. I tried to make believe I was somebody else, until finally I met this guy. He was a mean son of a bitch. A faggot. And he said, 'You are what you are. Accept it. Stop paying for it. Make others pay. Fuck them. Don't worry about them. Let them worry about you.' So I'm Free B. Sarz. And I don't worry about you or anybody else, but you damn well better worry about me."

"I do worry about you," Fitzsimmons said. "I don't know where fantasy ends and reality begins in you. If I knew that, I would know what to do about you. And when I find out, I will do something about you."

He paused and scrutinized Sarz's face as if seeking a clue to what was hidden inside of him.

"I want you to understand something, Sarz. I am passive because of the circumstances and not because of fear or because of any predilection toward passivity. If you are what you say you are, you are like a truck that's out of control. You destroy indiscriminately. I'm not like that. Now to you the difference between us may appear to be the difference between power and weakness, but it's really the difference between being a maniac and being a human being. I don't apologize for the way I am. I am not, as you want to believe, a fucking asshole. I am a decent human being. You are something else. You are a distortion. You have been consumed by sickness. Whatever you are, you are not decent, and you are not properly human."

They were engulfed with sound from the screaming jukebox and the crossfire of shouted conversations. They stared at each other. Sarz did not respond.

Fitzsimmons slipped out of the booth and stood next to the table and pointed his finger in Sarz's face.

"You are not going to win this thing," he said and turned to leave.

"Fitzsimmons," Sarz shouted after him and waited for him to turn around. "Your hands are tied."

"By what?"

"By morality," Sarz said. "I can't lose."

Fitzsimmons turned again and headed for the door.

"You should be on my side," Sarz shouted. "You asshole, you should be on my side."

CHAPTER SEVENTEEN

THE NEXT MORNING FITZSIMMONS GOT UP EARLY SO THAT KAREN could sleep late. He had promised to take Amy out to breakfast and then bring her to St. Camillus where the bus was leaving for the parish Girl Scouts' day-trip to Old Sturbridge Village.

Fitzsimmons was tired. He had lain awake long into the night thinking about Sarah and Eileen and Sarz, and when he did fall asleep, he dreamed that Sarz was standing in his old bedroom sneering at him, and he saw the blood again and he awoke, sweating.

During the course of the night, in between snatches of sleep, Fitzsimmons reached a decision, and he got out of bed dreading the day to come. That evening, he would be together with Karen and Peter and he knew that it was time to share the past with them. He was terribly reluctant and terribly anxious to do it. The past was like a volcano within him that had been sealed, and he was afraid of the eruption that would take place when it was unsealed. And yet he knew that the discussion was inevitable. He knew when he first met Peter that someday he would have to tell him about the past, and he knew, too, when he first met Karen that a time would come when he would have to tell her. And he recognized that along with his dread and his resistance, there was also a sense of anticipation and a sense of release that, at last, the time had come.

But there was something else, too. During the night, he realized that Karen did not understand just how deeply Sarz hated him and wanted to harm him. Fitzsimmons had not intended to keep it from Karen. He had become so used to keeping painful things to himself that he had not acquainted her with all the details of Sarz's hatred for him. They had discussed Sarz after Fitzsimmons had been drugged, but Fitzsimmons had not told her that he was a continuing threat, and now he worried about Karen's reaction. Would she feel that he had deliberately avoided telling her? Would she be overwhelmed not only by Sarz's hatred but by the terrible nature of his own personal revelation? Perhaps she would. Perhaps he should have told her about Sarah and Eileen the night they went dancing. Perhaps he should never have let their relationship begin without telling her. She could have walked away fairly painlessly then. Now, they would both suffer. Amy, too. The three of them would suffer. Even so, he hoped he would be able to stick with his decision and get it out once and for all.

Amy was already dressed and waiting when Fitzsimmons knocked on the door to the apartment. As they walked toward Beacon Street, Fitzsimmons realized that Amy had softened him. In one sense she had blunted the past's power to wound, and she had made it possible for him to have occasional memories of his wife and daughter—tender memories of holding hands and hugging, of laughter and love. Amy had evoked those gentle images. His association with her had enabled his mind to leap over the nightmare image of the final day and safely recall the good times.

As they were finishing their breakfast, Amy leaned across the table and asked, "What time is it now?"

"Ten of eight."

"Shouldn't we get going soon?"

"We've got time," he answered. The bus wasn't leaving from St. Camillus until 9:30. "Let me have another cup of coffee and a glance at this newspaper and we'll head up to Brighton."

Amy looked worried.

"You're not going to miss the bus," Fitzsimmons said. "If worse comes to worst, we'll take a cab—in fact, why don't we just take a cab anyway?"

Amy smiled. "Can I have another hot chocolate?"

"Sure."

In the paper there was talk of nuclear warheads, a possible teachers strike in September, and a shark sighted off Nauset Beach in Orleans on Cape Cod. Fitzsimmons shuffled through the paper quickly, reading the headlines and the first paragraph or two of each story until he got to page 10. There, a short story under a two-column headline caught his eyes. "Boy's Body Found Buried in Vacant Tract." Some kids playing in Dorchester had come across the body of a child in a sandy lot near the water. They had been playing pirates and were looking for buried treasure. Quite by accident, they found the body of the boy which had been buried under about two feet of sand. The body was badly decomposed but police estimated the boy was between ten and thirteen years old and had died within the past six months. The cause of death could not be immediately determined. Police were checking to see if any boys had been reported missing from the area during the past year. They hoped that an identification of the body could be made from clothing and dental records.

"Are you ready now?" Amy asked.

There was hardly any traffic and the cab made good time. Neither Fitzsimmons nor Amy spoke. Fitzsimmons' mind kept returning to the story about the body. He found himself imagining how the boy died. He guessed he was strangled. The police probably would have been able to tell if he had been stabbed or shot or bludgeoned to death. The clothes would have been bloody or the skull would have been crushed. Fitzsimmons remembered the conversation he had with Sarz the night Sarz had drugged him. Sarz had talked of raping and killing a young girl, how the girl, all alone without any friends or family, had come to understand the enormity and the mercilessness of evil.

"Are we almost there?" Amy asked.

"A couple more minutes," the cab driver said.

Fitzsimmons closed his eyes and without wanting to, he visualized the boy being strangled—the terror in his eyes, his struggling body.

"Oh God," he whispered involuntarily.

"What?" Amy said.

"Nothing," Fitzsimmons answered.

As Amy was about to get on the bus she pulled at Fitzsimmons and when he bent down she hugged him. He returned the hug and she clung to him for just a moment.

"Are you sure you want to go?"

"Yes," she said. "It will be fun."

"Do you have enough money?"

"Yes."

"Here," he said and handed her ten dollars, "bring your mother a souvenir."

Karen was still asleep when Fitzsimmons got back to their building. He let himself into her apartment quietly and peered through the doorway into her bedroom. She lay on her side facing the door with the sheet pulled up to her shoulders. Her face was calm, without expression, and her skin seemed pale against the white pillowcase and her dark hair. Her breathing was light, almost imperceptible, and there was a faint scent of perfume in the air.

She opened one eye and looked at Fitzsimmons. "Anything wrong?"

His face was ashen and he leaned against the door post.

"No. Nothing," he said. "I didn't mean to wake you."

"Did Amy get the bus okay?"

"Yes."

"Well are you going to come over here and give me a wake-up kiss?"

As he walked toward the bed, the other images faded from his mind.

Later, she said, "I think you should have a blood sugar test. I bet you're hypoglycemic."

"Why?" Fitzsimmons asked.

"The way you looked when you came into the room. I thought for a moment you were going to faint. And it's not the first time."

"Blood sugar is not the problem," he said.

"How do you know?"

"I just know."

"Then what is it?"

Fitzsimmons shrugged. "I've invited Peter over this evening. I thought the three of us could have dinner."

Karen sat up and looked at him as if she wanted to say something, but instead of speaking she got out of bed and went into the bathroom. Fitzsimmons, too, got out of bed and got dressed. After a few minutes, Karen reappeared.

"What time does Amy get back?" she asked.

"About six."

"I have to go out," Karen said. "I have some shopping to do. I'll meet her."

"Do you want me to come along?"

"No," she said. "That's all right. It's not the kind of shopping that would interest you."

Fitzsimmons nodded.

After she left, Fitzsimmons went for a walk, fighting off a feeling of sadness tinged with a mild depression. Karen's mood had changed. One moment she had been bright and gregarious and the next she had been terse and aloof. It was as though she had a foreboding, as though she knew it would not be a pleasant evening. This was, Fitzsimmons supposed, the jumping off point, and he wondered if she was ready, if she had the strength, or even if she cared at any deep level.

"We are the shallow society and this is the disposable age," he said aloud, reverting to his old habit of talking to himself.

His thoughts hung about him like the heavy, gray sky, and in the center of them was Karen's mournful face. It began to rain lightly. He didn't have an umbrella, but it didn't matter. He walked on and after a while he found himself at the Esplanade walking along the Charles. The river was calm, almost smooth, and as the raindrops hit the gray water, they sent out perfect little circles which seemed to bounce into each other without absorbing or being absorbed. Is that what was happening here, he wondered? Were he and Karen just bumping into each other without being transformed, without becoming a new entity? Or was that look on her face just his imagination? Was he just projecting his own fear or desire that their relationship could not survive his revelations?

He sat down on a wet bench and stared across the river. There was safety in shallowness. There was less potential for feeling either pain or pain's opposite. There was less potential for life. It would be ironic if after four years of clenching his teeth and forcing himself to go on, he just surrendered and swam out into the middle of the river and did not swim back. "Avanti Dia, Scarpla," he thought. "Before God, Fitzsimmons," he whispered. It would be easier. Call it quits. What would God say? Would he say anything? Would he even care? Or would he say, "What took you so long?"

The alternative was saying "yes"—to life, to Karen, to Amy, even if Karen decided to look elsewhere for a relationship, "yes" to whatever insanity Sarz would perpetrate, and "yes" even to the past. Fitzsimmons did not know if he had it in him.

He spent most of the afternoon staring at the river, reflecting as snatches of his life passed through his memory—not the vivid memories which had stayed with him for the past four years, but more ancient ones, memories of childhood—wearing a white shirt and a red tie as he attended the first grade parochial school; standing on the altar in a black cassock and a white surplice and trying desperately not to laugh as he and two other altar boys watched a priest officiate at a requiem Mass; driving for the first time by himself. Countless images ran through his mind, and he let them run without analyzing them. He saw moments of joy and moments of pain, little triumphs, little failures, a series of episodes in which he was the connecting link. Was there meaning? Was there significance to life? He could not tell; he could only wonder. There did not seem to be any significance to his. He was not important. If he had never been born the course of history would not have been altered.

"What am I doing here? What are any of us doing here?" His gaze left the river and drifted up to the clouds. "It doesn't make any sense, God," he said.

As soon as he spoke a verse from Isaiah ran through his mind, "As the heavens are above the earth, so my thoughts are above your thoughts." Fitzsimmons got up from the bench. His clothes were soaked through and he was tired. He went back to his apartment and slept.

He slept so soundly that it was a long time before he became aware of the ringing. After a while he sat up on the sofa and listened. It was coming from across the hall. Finally it dawned on him that it must be Karen. He let himself into her apartment and picked up the telephone.

"Oh thank God," Karen said.

"I was asleep. What's the matter?"

"Amy didn't come back with the Girl Scouts."

"They left without her?" Fitzsimmons asked. "Didn't the chaperones count heads?"

"There was a mix-up. One woman thought she was with another woman—I don't know—they were confused."

"Did you call Old Sturbridge Village?"

"She's not there."

"How about the police?"

"They're checking. John, something bad has happened," Karen said. She was sobbing.

"She'll be all right," Fitzsimmons said. "Nothing will happen to her. It's okay."

"How do you know?"

"I just know. I feel it. Where are you?"

"At Peter's."

"Is he there."

"Yes."

"Let me talk to him."

After a moment Peter came on the line.

"Can you drive Karen over here and stay at the apartment in case Amy calls while we drive your car to Sturbridge?"

"Of course I can," the priest said.

After he hung up the telephone, Fitzsimmons began to pace. He walked into the kitchen and back into the living room. Then he walked back into the kitchen. His head was bent and as he walked he slapped his half-closed right fist into the palm of his left hand.

His mind was blank. He paced as if in deep concentration, but he thought of nothing. He was conscious only of the anger growing within him. Finally he stopped at the doorway to the kitchen.

"Do I have to kill him?" he asked aloud.

He began to pace again, and again he slipped his half-closed fist in the palm of his left hand.

"Must I kill the son of a bitch?" he asked. He turned and walked back into the living room. The apartment door was open and Amy was standing in the doorway, clutching a long white envelope and a plastic bag. There was a young couple standing behind her.

"Amy!"

"Hi."

"Amy!" Fitzsimmons exclaimed again.

"I missed the bus," she said.

"I know."

"We thought we'd get her home before anybody missed her," the young man said.

Fitzsimmons rushed over to Amy and put his arm around her.

"We were coming to Boston anyway," the man said.

"That was very nice of you. Why don't you come on in? Amy's mother should be here soon. I know she'll want to thank you. She was very worried."

"We tried to call here before we left, but there was no answer, and Amy forgot the name of the church that she left from," the young woman said. She smiled and Fitzsimmons liked her immediately.

"St. Camillus," Fitzsimmons said.

"That's it," Amy said.

When Karen and Peter arrived fifteen minutes later, Karen clutched Amy and sobbed.

"Oh, thank God," she said. "Thank God. I prayed and prayed. Peter prayed with me. Oh, thank God. I was so worried."

"We tried to call here, but there was no answer," the young man said.

"I went to Brighton early," Karen said to Fitzsimmons. "I wanted to talk to Peter."

Fitzsimmons looked over to the priest who had a half-smile on his face.

"We have to leave," the young man said.

"We can't thank you enough," Karen said. "And you, too, Father Pete. You're a rock."

"That was another Peter," the priest said.

"But you, too. You're a rock," Karen said.

"She's right," Fitzsimmons said.

After the young couple left, Karen asked Amy if she was hungry.

"We stopped at Howard Johnsons on the turnpike. They tried to call you from there. I had fried clams."

"Did you have enough money?"

"Yeah. John gave me some extra. Oh, I forgot. I got something for you." She opened the plastic bag and took out a plate with a wooden bridge painted on it.

"It's a souvenir," she said. "It's for you."

Karen hugged her.

"It was John's idea," Amy said.

"Well it's beautiful. Thank you both."

"Oh, I have something for John, too," Amy said. "It's not a souvenir. Somebody at Old Sturbridge Village gave it to me and told me to give it to you. Do you know anybody there?"

"No."

Any handed him the sealed, white business envelope.

Fitzsimmons took it but did not open it.

"Amy, why don't you go and take your bath. I'm going to make dinner."

"Don't make me any, Mom."

When Amy had gone, Fitzsimmons opened the envelope. Inside there were several newspaper clippings. With just a glance he knew what the headlines said without reading them. "Pentagram Killer Axes Mom, Tot," said a huge headline that had appeared on the front page of a New York tabloid. "English Prof Discovers Bloody Scene," a smaller headline said. There was a picture of Fitzsimmons with his face in his hands. He tried to stuff the clippings back in the envelope, but Karen put her hand on his.

"May I see them?" she asked.

She took them and sat on the sofa next to Peter. The two of them examined the clippings in silence while Fitzsimmons stood looking out the window with his back to them.

CHAPTER EIGHTEEN

As Fitzsimmons stood looking at the soft twilight outside the window, the scene of that Thursday afternoon four years earlier came back to him as vividly as when it happened.

He had come home in midafternoon after teaching a class on Chaucer. When he found the front door ajar, he was stung by fear and the premonition that something painful awaited him. He swung the door open and called out the names of his wife and daughter.

"Eileen. Sarah," he called. The magazine rack in the living room had been knocked over and old copies of *Time* and *The Saturday Review* had spilled across the rug.

"Sarah," he called. "Eileen." His premonition became stronger as he walked quickly through the dining room to the kitchen. The drawer which held the large utensils had been pulled out and overturned on the white linoleum. The knife rack had been ripped from the wall. That, too, lay on the floor. The largest knife was missing.

"Eileen," he screamed. His voice was on the edge of hysteria. "Sarah. Sarah." He raced from the kitchen and ran up the stairs to the second floor. The telephone table in the hall had been overturned and there was blood on the rug. Without thinking he righted the table, hung up the telephone, and placed it on the table.

"Sarah," he said. It was almost a whisper. "Eileen? Eileen?" He walked slowly into the master bedroom. The carpet was spongy beneath him, thick with dark pools of red. "Oh, God," he heard himself say. His voice seemed remote and insulated from him. "Oh God," he said. The words hung in the silent room.

Eileen lay face up on the bed. Her throat had been slashed, and her right breast had been cut off. Her clothes had been torn from her body, and she was naked except for a sleeve to her blouse which was still on her right arm and her panties which hung from her left ankle. Sarah lay on the floor next to the huge knife. She was fully clothed. Her eyes and tongue bulged from her face. A pair of panty hose cut into her neck. On the wall, drawn in blood, was a pentagram.

Fitzsimmons stood motionless in the bedroom for what seemed a long time. It could have been only seconds or it might have been minutes. As he stood there, parts of him were sealed up, parts of him were frozen and parts of him died. It was not until he felt a great wave of madness coming over him that he turned and left the room. He clung to the banister as he staggered down the stairs, as if by clinging to it he could hold on to his sanity. He went to the kitchen and tried to dial the operator on the telephone, but he could not do it. He could not concentrate long enough to insert his finger in the zero hole and bring it around to the stop and release it. He tried five or six times and each time he either released the dial too soon or let his finger drag so that the dial did not return smoothly. He dropped the receiver to the floor and went out to the sidewalk in front of the house. Two high school boys, on their way home with their books, saw him and stopped. They looked at him with apprehension, as if they could see the madness in him.

"Help me. Help me," he cried. "Call for help. Telephone. Help me."

"Are you all right?" the taller youth asked.

"No," Fitzsimmons said. "Oh God, no. They're butchered. Help me. Call the police."

"Let's get out of here," the other boy said. "This guy is whacko."

"Oh, God," Fitzsimmons called out as if to heaven, "Make them help me."

"All right, mister. All right. Take it easy," the taller boy said. "We'll help you. Is that your house?" he pointed toward the open front door.

Fitzsimmons nodded.

"Do you want to go inside?"

Fitzsimmons shook his head. "Use the telephone in the kitchen. Call the police. Don't go upstairs."

"What's upstairs?" the shorter one asked.

"They're dead."

"Who's dead?"

"The joy of my youth," Fitzsimmons said. He could feel himself succumbing to madness. He was hysterical. He didn't care. "Ad Deum qui Iaetificat Juventutem meam." He had learned the response as an altar boy when he was eight years old.

The two boys looked puzzled.

"You stay here," the taller one said to his companion. "I'm going next door to call."

"Hurry up," the other boy answered.

Then Fitzsimmons had sat down on the front steps and waited for the police to arrive.

He turned from the darkness outside the window to face Karen and Peter. They had stopped looking at the newspaper clippings some minutes earlier. They were both silent, both waiting for him to speak.

"There you have it," Fitzsimmons said.

"Let's talk about it," Peter said.

"What's there to say?" Fitzsimmons asked.

"Everything," the priest answered. "Talk about it. Karen and I want you to talk about it. Tell us from the beginning to the end. Everything." He was not asking; he was commanding.

Fitzsimmons sat down in the easy chair facing them. He looked at Karen, and then Peter, and then Karen again.

"All right," he said. "From the beginning." He leaned forward and put his forearms on either knee and stared down at the rug, glancing up only occasionally.

"I had what I considered to be a noble and uncomplicated life. I was doing what I wanted to be doing with people I wanted to be doing it with. I was successful and I was well liked. I was already an associate professor and my prospects were good. I was married to a beautiful woman who loved me and whom I loved, and I had a wonderful little four-year-old girl, Sarah. She was pretty, friendly, intelligent, and unspoiled—everything I wanted in a daughter. Amy reminds me of her. Amy has brought back so many memories, so many good memories. "I used to say, 'Sarah, you're going to break a lot of hearts when you grow up.' 'No, I won't, Daddy,' she'd say. 'No, I won't.' "Fitzsimmons' head sank and he looked straight down at the rug. He cleared his throat. "I had a little sailboat that I used to sail in the Long Island Sound and I had an MG—plenty of free time to pursue music, to go to the Met, and money to travel. Both Eileen's parents and mine were pretty well off. Sometimes I think they tried to outdo each other in their generosity.

"Looking back at it now, my life was shallow, almost hedonistic. Eileen and I were liberal and earnest and we were committed to each other but not to much else, not to anything outside ourselves. I don't think we were superficial. I think we were just immature. We hadn't experienced much of life. We meant well, but our goals were just extensions of our egos. I can see that now. I couldn't then. I'm not condemning myself. I thought that the important things in life were success and enjoyment, and I thought that really was all there was to it. I thought I knew as much as I needed to know, that I had cleared all the hurdles and that the rest of life was all downhill.

"And then my world ended. Just like that, he said and snapped his fingers. "At one moment everything was pretty much the way I want-ed it, and at the next moment I had nothing. I came home one after-noon just minutes after a madman had left my house. He had raped my wife and butchered her in front of my daughter, and then he strangled Sarah. After four years, I still see Sarah's purple face and bulging eyes. I see my naked wife spread-eagled with only one breast and the black and blue marks on her stomach and thighs. I see the red pentagram on the bedroom wall, and I feel that desolate numbness in my stomach as though someone had clubbed me.

"Inside of me there was a terrible panic. It was a feeling of being trapped and wanting to escape. I didn't know how to deal with it—the police, my family, her parents, my friends, the school. I couldn't deal with any of them. They were all kind and understanding. At least they seemed to be. I didn't know what any of them were really feeling. I didn't care. I was drowning inside. My brain was being submerged by waves of despair and rage and fear and isolation. I was on the brink.

There was a huge blackness which hovered around me. I knew I could sink into it. I knew I was on the verge of being overwhelmed by insanity. I had never understood madness before. I had always thought Ophelia was theatrical and nothing more. But I could feel myself drawn to madness. I was attracted by it and repelled by it and terrified that I had no alternative but to succumb to it.

"Even now I don't remember all that went on. Some things stand out. The funeral. The large, bronze casket and the small, white one. Television cameras, reporters. A police lieutenant who smoked cigars. But I don't have a coherent memory of it. I cannot put the events in sequence. The moment I saw the blood something happened to my mental processes. Perhaps I went a little mad, or maybe it was shock, but a lot of the next few weeks was like hallucinating. Some images are very clear, larger than life. Others are blurred and distorted.

"I remember standing on the shore of the Long Island Sound in the middle of the night. The moon was bright so that you could see the boats and the outline of the land. Everything looked blue. For a moment I felt very close to my wife and daughter, as if they were there with me, one holding each hand, and I was calm. Gradually the feeling of their presence left. I was alone. There was no one with me or for me. There was no one who could share or understand my anguish or my desolation. There was a great emptiness within me. The center of my life had been destroyed. Meaning and hope were gone. There was nothing. I had nothing to hold onto, neither inside of me nor outside of me.

"I looked up at the night sky. It was filled with stars, and I thought how distant and cold they looked. They were like God. Aloof and impassive. Uncaring, really. Splendid but uncaring. I knew that I had come to the shore to end my life. I had heard that drowning was a peaceful, even a beautiful way to die. I don't know whether that's true. But I loved the water, its vastness and its sounds, and I thought that, perhaps, I would sail my boat out toward Connecticut, and sometime during the night, I would secure the tiller and slide over the side and let the boat sail on."

Fitzsimmons paused. He had been speaking slowly, listening to his own words, as if what he was saying was a revelation to him, too. He stretched back in his chair and looked up at the ceiling as if it were the sky and the stars. He gazed at it for a very long moment. Peter and

Karen waited without speaking or moving.

"But then I thought that suicide would, in a way be condoning what had happened. It would be like saying to God, or whatever is responsible for life, that I agreed with the principle of violence that had destroyed my wife and daughter, that I embraced a universe of madness and death. And I did not and I do not. So right there, on the shore of the Long Island Sound, with the water lapping up over my shoes, I made a vow. I vowed I would not kill myself and that I would not go mad. I would not be a part of the insanity and the depravity of the universe. I condemned it, I condemned whoever or whatever was responsible for it, and I decided to withdraw from life—not to kill myself but to be aloof from it. I guess part of that was out of philosophical conviction, but part of it was out of necessity. I was filled with rage and despair and I could not deal with either one of those feelings. I had tried. This must have been several months after the killings, because I had had a number of sessions with a psychiatrist.

"He told me that I would have to release the rage—that I would have to let go of it and let it out or it would destroy me, but I knew it would drive me over the edge if I released it. He also encouraged me to have sex, but I couldn't. I wasn't interested. The sexual drive had left me. It had been contingent upon Eileen. We had been one flesh. Indiscriminate sex was beyond me. It seemed to me selfish and mechanical. I could not have sex with a woman with whom I was not emotionally bound, and there was no woman with whom I could become emotionally involved. It was out of the question. Something inside of me had shriveled up. There was no beauty in life, no warmth, no reason. Parts of me were dead. I could not laugh, I could not even smile. I could not be interested in another human being, or anything, really. English literature became barren. I had lost the sense of shared experience which is necessary between a teacher and student. I was living in another dimension. It was arid and gray, and the only noise came from insane ideas.

"I had a terrible fear of going berserk. When I was a child, I had a friend whose father did that. He was a policeman in New York City, and one night when he was on his beat, he went crazy. He took out his service revolver and began shooting people in the street. When he ran out of bullets, he pulled a fire alarm, and when the trucks came he grabbed an axe and started swinging at people, raving and screaming, until finally they disarmed him. I was afraid of doing something like that. I didn't think I could, but that cop probably didn't think he could either, and he did."

Fitzsimmons looked up at Karen as if hoping she would tell him to stop. Her face was very sad, and she stared at him, mesmerized by his words.

"I had no place to turn. Psychiatry could not help me, and religion seemed like it was just a lot of anemic formalities. I had only myself and very little of that. I felt utterly without strength. I could only clench my jaw and fight off the monsters within me. I had never been so utterly isolated. I was terrified and helpless, but I was determined not to succumb. I couldn't teach. I just couldn't pick up my life and continue. There was a buzzing in my head. I couldn't concentrate. It felt like a steel band was wrapped around my skull and that it was digging into my temples. I couldn't sleep. I tried drinking but I became more depressed. After a while I decided to leave. I sold everything: the house, the car, the boat, and I left Long Island. But traveling didn't help. I wasn't interested in sightseeing; I just wasn't interested in anything. One night I was on a Greyhound bus heading through Texas; I decided that if I was going to survive, I would have to do something to occupy myself, something that would be physically exhausting. I got off the bus in Houston, and the next day I got myself a job in construction. It was a huge housing development in a suburb. I did bullwork. I carried lumber and pipes, and I cleaned up—all unskilled work, and after work, I took up running. Day after day, I would work hard and then I would run. I would go to bed exhausted, and I would lie there and push thoughts out of my mind, hoping to fall asleep. At first I could sleep for only two or three hours at a time, and some nights I wouldn't sleep at all. But I would get up and go to work, and in the evening I would run, and after months and months, my sleep pattern improved. By that time I had lost thirty pounds. I weighed one hundred and fifty-five. I looked like someone who had spent a year in a concentration camp. But I didn't go insane and I didn't commit suicide. I don't know when the buzzing in my head stopped. A year perhaps. It took even longer for that feeling of tightness around my temples to go away. In all that time, I did not make one friend. I did not have a single conversation of any substance with another human being. I had become one of those people who seem to be on the periphery of humanity, the eccentrics, like the bag ladies and winos, people who hang around bus terminals, with their staring eyes and gaping mouths, or the men who live alone in rooming houses and never go out. Misfits, the flotsam and jetsam of society. That was me. I had become an outcast.

"I understood that one hot, summer day. I was walking around the construction site, feeling the sun on me, and I looked over at a group of men who were lined up at a canteen truck. They were laughing and joking and having a hell of a time for themselves. I knew at that moment that I was different. Something inside of me had dried up. They had a dimension that I had lost. I had become an outsider. When I was younger, before the murders, I used to look at the outsiders and I used to pity them and wonder how people could be like that. There was an old man that I used to see on Third Avenue in New York City. He used to wear all his possessions—a half-dozen wrist watches, ten rings, two overcoats. It was obvious that he wasn't poor. He was different—isolated and strange—like the others who were into themselves. And there I was in Houston. I had crossed over the line. I had gone from being one of us to being one of them. My grandfather used to call them the lame, the halt, and the blind—the crippled members of society. I knew what it was like to be a convict or an inmate in an insane asylum or a retarded person. 'Fitzsimmons,' I said to myself, 'you are a changed man. Maybe you have gone mad after all.'

"The construction job had done all it could for me. I was sleeping, and I wasn't torn by rage. That afternoon, I found the clerk of the works and I quit and I left Houston."

Fitzsimmons started to stand up, but he thought better of it and remained in the easy chair.

"I left Houston about a year and a half after I lost them. I had changed. My brain had stopped buzzing, and I was pretty sure that I wouldn't go berserk. But they were still with me and the pain was still intense because I had not given them up. I had not surrendered them to death and to eternity. That sounds strange, but it's true. I didn't think about them very much, I trained myself not to. But there was a hunger in me, and anticipation, as if I expected to meet them someplace, bump into them on the street. I would walk past a store and see the back of a woman, and if her hair was the right color and she happened to have a child with her, I would think for a moment that it was Eileen with

Sarah. Just for a fraction of a second. It happened, not frequently, but it happened often enough so I knew that I had not accepted the ultimate reality of their deaths. I had accepted that they were gone, but part of me had not accepted that they were gone forever. I carried a photograph of them in my wallet. I never looked at it, but I was conscious of it being there, and somehow through that picture they were still alive to me. I wandered around for another year and a half, working here and working there. I did all sorts of things—construction, kitchen work, deck hand, maintenance man—and all that time, I kept the picture in my wallet. But I never looked at it. I ached. After more than three years, I still ached. I was like a monk. I had no real human contacts. I was empty inside except for that ache. Usually I could ignore it. I would refuse to admit that I felt it. I would busy myself. I would run—move to another city. It never really went away, and I knew it would never go away as long as I kept that picture in my wallet. One night in Quebec, on that boardwalk that overlooks the St. Lawrence River, I took the picture out, and I looked at it, for just a few seconds—my wife smiling, my daughter looking up at her—and I cried. I leaned against the railing and I cried and I cried and I cried. And then I ripped the picture up into the smallest possible pieces, and I threw the pieces out into the wind and watched them swirl away and down.

"Out in the river there was a freighter heading toward the Atlantic. I watched it until it was out of sight. The next morning I took a bus to Boston. I've been here ever since."

Fitzsimmons took a deep breath and then exhaled.

"There you have it—the tragic history of John Fitzsimmons," he said.

"Are we the first people you have told all this to?" Peter asked.

"Yes."

They sat in silence for several minutes until, finally, the priest spoke.

"You didn't say anything about the killer. Did they find him?"

"Yeah. They caught a man about a month later. He was in the act of raping a woman in front of her two small children when her husband came home. The husband subdued him, almost killed him."

"How did they know he was responsible for the deaths of Eileen and Sarah?" Karen asked.

"They found my daughter's locket in his room, and there were some other things. He was a devil worshiper and he had drawn a pentagram in blood on the wall next to his bed. And he saved newspaper clippings of the murders—not just Eileen and Sarah, there were four others."

Fitzsimmons stopped speaking and stared down at his feet. Then he looked up at Peter.

"I saw him once, in court, the day the judge ruled he was insane. We looked into each other's eyes, and I could tell he was overjoyed to see me. The expression on his face didn't change, but I could see the delight in his eyes. There was a cruelty there ... it's inexpressible. There was something implacable, something ... "

"Demonic," the priest said.

"Yeah, demonic," he replied.

Fitzsimmons looked across the room and saw Amy standing in the shadows of the bedroom doorway. When she saw that he had noticed her, she walked over to him and hugged him.

"I forgot you were taking a bath. How long have you been there?" Karen asked.

"Pretty long," Amy said. She stood next to the sitting Fitzsimmons with her arm around his shoulders.

"Well, now you all know," Fitzsimmons said. He looked from Amy to Karen. "It's just as well," he added.

Karen stared at him without nodding.

CHAPTER NINETEEN

AFTER THEY HAD EATEN AND AMY HAD GONE TO BED, THE THREE OF them lingered quietly at the kitchen table, sipping coffee but leaving untouched the pound cake Karen had bought at a supermarket. They had been quiet, too, during the meal, each thinking over Fitzsimmons' story, each digesting it bit by bit—even Fitzsimmons, for it was also the first time he had heard the entire story, and it added to his perspective and put more distance between himself and the day of the murders.

"There's more to talk about," Peter said, breaking the long silence.

"I know," Fitzsimmons responded.

"We don't have to do it right now."

"It may as well be now," Fitzsimmons answered.

"Is Amy still up?" the priest asked.

"She's sleeping, and her door is closed. She had a long day," Karen said.

Peter picked up a spoon and gave his coffee a single stir. "What do you make of those newspaper clippings?" he asked.

"Sarz," Fitzsimmons answered. "It had to be him. There's no other explanation."

Peter nodded. "And what about Sarz? How dangerous is he?"

"If he is what he says he is, then he is very dangerous," Fitzsimmons said.

"What does he say he is?" Karen asked.

"He says that he rapes and murders children and that he wants to destroy me."

"He rapes children?" Her voice was strained and high-pitched. "My God. Is that what he says?"

"Yes."

"And he murders them? And he wants to destroy you?"

"That's what he says."

Karen had become quite pale. "You never told me that," she said.

"I've never been absolutely certain. It's all been so nebulous," Fitzsimmons said. "I don't know whether he separates fantasy and reality. I'm never sure about him. I can't even say with absolute certainty that the newspaper clippings came from him," Fitzsimmons said.

"Why does he want to destroy you?" Her voice was calm now, but her face was white and filled with anxiety.

"I don't know why," Fitzsimmons said. "I have done nothing to the man."

"Nothing at all?" Karen asked.

"Nothing."

"John," she said leaning across the table, "there has to be a reason."

"I suppose so, but I don't know what it is. I don't know whether this guy is crazy or sick or what he is. He has a fantasy about evil. He identifies with people like Eichmann, and he sees me as a victim. He says he plans to take away everything I value, and then he plans to destroy me."

"Everything you value?"

Fitzsimmons looked into Karen's eyes and nodded.

"Amy?"

He nodded.

"Me?"

He nodded again.

"Oh, my God, John," she said. She looked at Peter and then back at Fitzsimmons as if for an explanation or a denial.

"But how did he pick you?" Karen asked.

"I don't know. Maybe he picked me at random. Maybe I was just handy."

"No," Peter said. "There is nothing random about him. He went to a lot of trouble to get those clippings, and even more trouble to manage to get them to Amy in Sturbridge. Had you told him about Amy?"

"I have never discussed anything of my personal life with him."

"But he knows about it. And he must have followed you and Amy today. He may have been following you for some time. This is not a random project," the priest said.

"No," Karen said. "No, it isn't. But that doesn't matter now. I just want to know what you're going to do."

"We've been to the police. That hasn't accomplished much," Fitzsimmons said. "I don't know if it would do any good to go back to them. I mean we can't prove anything. Amy didn't even get the envelope from him. She said a little boy gave it to her. So as far as I can see, there's no way Sarz can be tied to this, and even if we could tie him to it, I don't know that he's committed a crime. What could they charge him with? Sending me newspaper clippings?"

"Even if there's nothing the police can do right now, there are steps we can take," the priest said.

"Like what? I can't kill the son of a bitch," Fitzsimmons said.

"No, you can't," Peter said. "But we can make sure that Amy and Karen are protected."

"The two of you could confront him. You could talk to him," Karen said. "You could force him to stop doing these things."

Fitzsimmons shook his head. "It wouldn't do any good," he said.

"Why not?"

"He's not like us. He doesn't feel the same way we do. To him this is a chess game. He spends a great deal of time plotting every move he will make and figuring out every move I will make. What you are suggesting is something he has already anticipated. He expects it. He is waiting for me to come and threaten him or plead with him or beg him. And whatever I do or we do along those lines I'm sure will have no effect on him."

"You don't know that," she said. "It's worth a try. It can't hurt."

"Oh, yes, it can. I've already seen him. I've already confronted him. It just fed into his sadism. I'm not going to do that anymore. I'm not going to play it his way. I'm not going to threaten him. I'm not going to plead with him. I'm not going to beg him."

"What are you going to do?"

"I don't know."

Karen looked at Peter as if to an ally.

"John is right," the priest said. "There is no compassion in this man or what you and I would consider reason. Sarz is obviously taking pleasure in stringing this out. Going to him would increase his gratification. It would be playing to his strength."

"What can we do then, nothing?" Karen snapped.

"No. There are things we can do, but I think that first, the most important thing we can do is understand just what we're up against," Peter said.

Neither Karen nor Fitzsimmons spoke.

"The first thing that we've got to get straight is that he's an evil man. He's not like some people we've met who are basically decent people who sometimes act badly. You can reason with those people. You can appeal to their better nature. He doesn't have a better nature. He has no interest in the welfare of others. He is only concerned with gaining his own ends. That's all that matters to him. He sees other human beings as objects to have power over. He wants to dominate, and for him ultimate domination is destruction of another human being. Emotional destruction, spiritual destruction, and, finally, physical destruction. Evil people are all the same. They all want to dominate. And the more evil they are, the more they want to dominate. And they're ruthless. They use any means to accomplish whatever it is they want—seduction, manipulation, intimidation—and all the time they project an image of invincibility and inevitability."

Fitzsimmons nodded, and the priest put his hand up to indicate he had not finished.

"So much for Sarz. What about us? We're just the opposite. We have compassion. We're not ruthless. We don't want to hurt others or to have power over them. And when we come across somebody like Sarz, we are overwhelmed. We don't know how to react. We can't believe that there are people like him. So what most of us do, if we can, is to get out of his way. Evil is just too frightening, too intimidating. But sometimes we can't get out of the way. Sometimes we are the target, and there is nothing more difficult in life than to be the target of evil. Nothing.

"But even though it's a terrible position to be in, it's not an impossible position. Evil is not omnipotent and evil is not inevitable. It would have us think that, but evil is a liar. Its most basic premise is a lie. Its very foundation is a lie. No matter how powerful it is or appears to be, it is never all-powerful. In fact, it carries within it the seeds of its own destruction."

Peter looked at Karen and then continued. "When we are intimidated by evil, we strengthen it. We tend to let it dominate our thinking and our reactions. So it's important that we put evil in perspective and keep it there."

"And one more thing," the priest said, turning to Fitzsimmons. "There may be an analogy between Sarz and you and the Nazis and the Jews, but you are in an entirely different situation. The Jews were captives in an alien society. They were, in fact, powerless. You are not. There is a difference between not being able to do anything and not knowing what action to take."

Fitzsimmons seemed to reflect on the priest's words before answering. "It's not a question of not knowing what action to take, Peter, it's a question of not knowing if there is any action I can take—short of killing him," Fitzsimmons said. "I mean what else can I do?"

"You can refuse to be seduced or manipulated or intimidated."

"I suppose so," Fitzsimmons said. "But I don't see that that will make much difference."

"Well, for one thing, it will prevent him from accomplishing the thing he wants most."

"To destroy me?"

"To rob you of your dignity," the priest said. "I don't know why he hates you, but I know that he is more concerned with destroying your spirit than he is with destroying you physically. If he destroys you spiritually, any other destruction is anticlimactic; it's like sweeping up the garbage."

"Spiritually?" Fitzsimmons said in amazement. "Spiritually? Doesn't he know that I've been spiritually dead for four years?"

"You're not dead spiritually," the priest said, shaking his head. "Wounded, perhaps. Alienated. But not dead. Spiritual death is when you give up. It's when you let evil win. It's when you embrace the darkness."

Karen had stopped listening some moments before.

"Father Pete, I can try to put evil in perspective. I can try not to be intimidated or manipulated, but what's that going to do? That's not going to stop him," she said.

"No, it won't stop him. But it won't help him either, whereas if you are intimidated, then you strengthen him. You become his ally and your own enemy."

Karen stood up, but she did not move away from the table.

"There has to be something else we can do," she said.

"There is," Peter answered. "You can turn to the source of good—the real power. You can ask God for help."

"You mean pray?" she asked.

"I mean ask him to step in and take over. Ask him to handle it," the priest said.

Karen looked at Fitzsimmons. His face was gaunt, and he turned his face away from her.

"Like he handled it the last time?" he asked coldly.

"It's only a suggestion," the priest said. He, too, stood up. "You've had a trying day."

The three of them moved through the living room to the door to the hall. Peter opened the door and hesitated.

"I'll remember you in my Masses," he said.

"Thank you," Karen said.

Fitzsimmons did not reply, but his mouth wore an ironic half-smile.

"You don't think much of that, do you, John?" Peter asked.

"Believe what you want to believe, Peter," Fitzsimmons said. "But I know that whatever is done about Sarz will have to be done by me. I'm not going to get any help. That's the way he's arranged it. I think I've known that from the beginning."

"Do you remember what you said happened after you found your wife and daughter and went out into the street?" the priest asked.

"About the high school kids?"

"Yes. Do you remember? You said they were scared and that they wanted to run away."

Fitzsimmons nodded.

"And you called out, 'God, make them help me.' And they helped you."

Fitzsimmons said nothing.

"I'll remember you in each of my Masses," the priest said. He went out and closed the door behind him.

CHAPTER TWENTY

"I FEEL BETRAYED," KAREN SAID. AS SHE STOOD LOOKING AT Fitzsimmons, she seemed both sad and angry. Fitzsimmons turned his eyes away from her and said nothing.

"Do you understand that?" she asked. He remained silent.

"When I married Todd, he was a time bomb. I didn't know it then, but I found out later. I had no idea how in love he was with alcohol. He concealed that from me, but had I known, and if I had had any sense, I would have walked away."

"And me?" Fitzsimmons asked.

"I had no idea about Eileen and Sarah. You told me they were dead. You might have even told me they were killed. But I thought they died in an automobile accident or a fire. I didn't know that they were murdered."

Fitzsimmons put his hands in his pockets and stared at the rug.

"I didn't conceal it from you. I tried to tell you about it a couple of times, but I just couldn't speak about it. I just could not get the words out. There was something here—" He put his right hand on his throat. "—that would not let them out."

"And Sarz? What about him? Apparently he was sending you anonymous clippings before we even met."

"But I didn't know it was him," Fitzsimmons said.

"He threatened to destroy you."

"That was later, and I didn't believe that he could do it."

"And Amy and me?"

"Until tonight, I did not realize that his hatred for me could endanger anyone but myself."

They stood six or seven feet apart, facing each other in the brightly lit living room.

"How couldn't you realize that?" she asked. "How could you of all people not realize that?"

"I don't know. Maybe I just couldn't believe that anyone who is rational can be what Sarz says he is. Maybe I was just insulating myself from him. Maybe I didn't want to believe him. I don't know. But I know that I have been honest with you. I haven't consciously concealed anything from you. Even now, in retrospect, I don't know what I could have told you. Does it make any difference that my wife and daughter were murdered by a maniac? Or that newspaper clippings were stuck in my mailbox? Or that someone I work with hates me? Or even that he says he kills children?"

"Yes, it does," Karen said. "Yes, it does," she repeated. "Don't you see it? Don't you see that you're a man who invites tragedy?"

Fitzsimmons' body gave a sudden involuntary start, and he turned his face slightly as if he had been slapped.

"A man who invites tragedy," he repeated. His face was drained of color, and his body seemed almost limp. He looked as if he were about to become physically ill. He started toward the door without speaking.

Karen reached out and grabbed his arm, but he pulled it away.

"I need air," he said.

"Wait, John," Karen said.

He turned to face her, and, for the briefest instant, she saw that his eyes were filled with terror and panic and anguish, and she knew that that was how he must have looked when he found his dead wife and daughter in his bedroom.

"John," she said and put her hand out to touch him, but he took a half step backward.

"Let me not conceal it from you," he said. "There are still times when I feel like I'm skating on the thin edge of sanity."

He was able to smile slightly, and the color began to return to his face.

"Damaged goods," he said.

"I'm sorry I said that," she said. "But I had to. Do you understand?"

"More than you know," he answered.

"What do you mean?" she asked.

"I mean we've come to a critical point," he said. "Perhaps it's time to make some choices."

Fitzsimmons looked very tired and still somewhat pale. He spoke softly, but he spoke with conviction, and he looked unwaveringly at Karen. She, returned his steady gaze. Her face, which initially expressed concern, now began to reflect anger and defiance.

"What kind of choices?"

"I think we have to decide what kind of relationship this is. Is it just a casual relationship or is it something more than that?"

"Casual?" Karen asked, with obvious anger. "Is that what you think this is?"

"I don't," he answered. "I'm not a casual person."

"And you think it's a casual relationship for me?" She folded her arms and glared at him.

"That's what I'm trying to find out," he said and now there was a sharp edge to his voice. "Is this an instance where, if you have any sense, you'll walk away?"

"I've had a lot of pain in my life, John. And so has Amy. I know you have, too, and you've borne it somehow. Maybe you have a greater capacity for it than I have. Or maybe I have to be concerned for more than just me."

She looked away from him. He thought she was about to smile and then he realized she was on the verge of tears.

"Oh, God, God, God. Don't you see where I'm coming from? Don't you know the hell I've been through and the hell Amy has been through? And I get out of one hell and suddenly I'm facing another hell, maybe worse than the first one." She did not give way to tears, and her tone became more assertive.

"I have been beaten and screamed at and embarrassed and humiliated. I have lived on fear and anxiety and the constant uncertainty of never knowing if a sick puppy or a drunken brute would come through the door, never knowing when I would be embarrassed or hurt. I lost my self-esteem. I lost my tenderness. I lost myself and my daughter. Maybe my pain wasn't the same as yours, but it was real and it was destructive. My life was pain and darkness, and so was Amy's. Until today, I thought that was part of the past. Until today, I thought my life was back on track, that it would be orderly and sane and well balanced. I'm not a casual person either, and I certainly didn't look upon this as a casual relationship. But I have a daughter and I have myself and I don't know. Do you understand all that?"

"I understand," he said. His tone was gentle and consoling.

"We're both upset. We're both tired. Maybe this isn't the moment to make choices," Karen said.

"And maybe it is the right moment, precisely because we are tired and we are upset," he said. "I can understand how you feel, and I don't blame you for feeling that way. Believe me. But let me tell you how I feel. I don't invite tragedy. I don't ask for it. I don't want it. I've been dogged by it. God knows that. But it has not been my doing. Oh, there's a part of me that says that somehow I was responsible for what happened to Eileen and Sarah, that things like that only happen to people who deserve it. But that's not true. It's a lie. It's a lie when I think it, and it's a lie when you think it, or when anybody thinks it. But it's such a powerful lie that it can almost overpower me as it did a minute ago.

"Now what am I supposed to do about this tragedy, this evil? Should I give up? Should I have gone off in the sailboat in the middle of the sound? Should I never love a woman again? Should I become a kind of eunuch?

"I turned away from life—not on purpose. It was all that I could do at the time. And now I've turned back to life, and you and Amy have had an awful lot to do with that. I love you both. You have awakened passion in me. You have taught me how wonderful it is to want to possess another human being and be possessed by her, and Amy has awakened a father's love in me, a tenderness, a gentleness. She has freed me to love the memory of my daughter, to forget that final image and remember her with her arms around my neck and her cheek against mine. I would not willingly hurt either one of you. You don't want a life of pain. I understand that. You want to be free of fear and anxiety. I understand that. And if you decide that I'm too much of a liability, I will understand that. It will hurt, but, as you say, I have a certain capacity for pain, and the pain will pass."

Karen sank into a stuffed chair.

"And if you decide to end it, then that would be my decision too. You don't want to go back to the life you had with your husband, and I don't want a relationship that is tentative. I want someone who will be there on sunny days and when the storm hits, whether it's my storm or her storm."

When he finished speaking, Fitzsimmons walked over to the chair and bent down and kissed Karen on the cheek. It was wet with tears, and he realized that his eyes, too, had tears in them.

Karen's head was bowed and she did not look up. He waited for a moment and then turned and left the apartment, closing the door quietly behind him.

As he walked across the hall he heard the telephone ring in Karen's apartment. He inserted the key in the lock to his door, but he did not turn it.

After a moment the door to Karen's apartment opened and she stepped into the hall. Her troubled face told Fitzsimmons who was on the line.

"There's a man on the phone who says he wants to talk to you," she said.

Fitzsimmons went back into her apartment and picked up the receiver. "Hello?" he said.

The voice on the other end said one word. "Asshole." There was a click, a short silence and then a dial tone.

Karen stood in the doorway. "That was him, wasn't it?" she said.

He nodded.

Karen's body sagged against the doorway. "I'm not as strong as I look," she said.

"Neither is he," Fitzsimmons replied.

He walked over and put his arms around her and held her as she cried silently. A terrible rage began to well up in him, but he said nothing to Karen about it.

PART TWO

PART TWO

CHAPTER TWENTY ONE

THE OLD WHITE HOUSE HAD THE AIR OF A FALLEN VICTORIAN woman: regal, despite being out of favor. It had been fashionable for at least half a century, and then, after World War II, the neighborhood lost its affluence as the residents moved to the South Shore. Sometime after that, the house had been carved up into seven apartments—three on the first floor, three on the second, and one on the third. Sarz's apartment was at the rear of the first floor, the north side of the house. The rooms got little light during the day, and during the night Sarz kept the lights dim, giving the place a funereal atmosphere. One whole wall of the living room was lined with books. On another wall, two large prints of nude boys hung on either side of the door to the bedroom. The boys had soft, almost effeminate bodies, and their stares were seductive, almost wanton. On the opposite wall was a smaller print—Goya's *Saturn Devouring His Son*—a grotesque work, almost a caricature of the naked wide-eyed god greedily eating a man's body, doll-sized in comparison to his own. The god's eyes stared out blankly toward the two soft boys. Next to the Goya print was a black and white photograph of a man's face. He, too, stared, but his look was neither wanton nor greedy. It was cold and unnerving. It was the look of a man who routinely judged others to be of no significance. Beneath the picture, a three by five card with a type-written inscription had been tacked to the wall.

At ten o'clock Saturday morning Sarz heard the knock on the door. He was still in bed, but he was already awake. He reached over and pulled a filtered cigarette from the cigarette package that lay on the bed table. He lit the cigarette, inhaled deeply, and let the smoke escape from his nose. There was another knock. Sarz inhaled again, and again he let the smoke escape slowly. He threw the sheet back and stretched his naked body, reaching with his toes toward the bottom of the bed. On the third knock, he slid his feet leisurely to the floor and stood up. He walked to the door of the bedroom, snatched his bathrobe from a hook, and walked barefoot and naked through the living room, dragging the robe behind him.

"Who's there?" he asked in a sharp, argumentative voice.

"Peter Genaro."

"Who?"

"Peter Genaro."

"What do you want?"

"I want to talk with you."

Sarz put the bathrobe on and tied it. He opened the door as far as it could go with the safety chain attached and peered out. The short, moderately overweight priest was dressed in a black suit with a Roman collar. His dark brown eyes stared back unyieldingly at Sarz.

"What the fuck do you want?" Sarz asked.

The priest's face remained impassive. "I told you. I want to talk with you."

"About what?"

"Are you afraid of me?" the priest asked.

"Afraid of a fucking priest?" Sarz asked incredulously.

"Then why don't you let me in?"

Sarz shut the door. After a moment, he opened it wide. "If you want to come in, come in," he said.

Sarz was silent as Peter looked around the room, first at the prints of the nude boys, then the Goya print and finally the face of the man with the cruel eyes. He walked over to the last picture and read the inscription on the file card aloud:

"Our battle is not against human forces but against the principalities and powers, the rulers of this world of darkness."

The priest turned to face Sarz. "That's from St. Paul," he said.

"Yes," Sarz replied with a slow, sardonic smile. "Letter to the Ephesians, I think. Sort of puts it in perspective."

"Yes, it does," the priest agreed.

Sarz went over to a recliner chair by the window and sprawled in it, putting his naked left leg over the left arm of the chair and wiggling his toes.

"Well, what do you want?" he asked.

"You've seen me before," the priest said, studying Sarz's face.

"Oh?"

"I'm a friend of John Fitzsimmons. I was outside the church yesterday when the Girl Scouts were leaving for Old Sturbridge Village."

Sarz looked bored. "This sounds like ragtime to me."

The priest continued to look at Sarz but said nothing.

"Is that all you wanted?" Sarz asked.

"No. There are two things I came for. First, I hoped you would explain to me what you have against Fitzsimmons."

Sarz shook his head.

"It puzzles me," the priest said. "It doesn't make any sense."

"What's the second thing?"

"I came for you."

"You came for me? Well, here I am, and it's just as I suspected, every one of you fucking priests is a faggot."

"I came to see what I could do to help you."

"Help me?" He pulled his leg off the arm of the chair and put both feet on the floor.

"Yes."

"Help me?" Sarz asked again. "Why would you want to?"

"It's my job to help people, and in your case it's owed to you."

"What do you mean, owed?"

"As I understand it, you had a nasty experience with a priest when you were a child."

"You know about that, too?" Sarz said. "That's a really well-publicized piece of debauchery, but it's no big deal, getting buggered by a priest when you're twelve. I wasn't a Catholic anyway."

"Neither was he, not in any real sense," the priest said. "And it was

a big deal. Children look to adults for guidance, for help, for suste-
nance. What he did to you was evil. It harmed you, it harmed him, it
harmed the priesthood, and it harmed the Church."

A look of irony left Sarz's face. He seemed to weigh the priest's
words carefully.

"I was an outcast, a state ward. People could do whatever they
wanted to me. I was just a piece of meat. Nobody gave a shit."

"That's why I'm here—to tell you that someone should have cared.
You were owed that. You should not have been treated like a piece of
meat. I have come to atone for that."

"I'm beyond that," Sarz said.

"Beyond what?"

"Beyond atonement. Beyond whatever it is you are offering me."

"Beyond forgiveness?"

"Yes. Beyond forgiveness. I am like the fallen angels. I can't go back,
and I don't want to. You cross a line. Little by little you leave certain
things behind, certain feelings, certain desires. You renounce them."

"Like remorse and guilt?"

"Yes, and the desire to please, the desire to give. I lost them a long
time ago. For me that was freedom. I was free to be what I am without suffering for it."

"And what are you?"

"I'm one of the bad guys," Sarz said gently. "That's the way I am. It's
the way your God wanted it. You and I are at opposite ends of the
scale. We are at war. That's why we can talk like this. We understand
one another. Fitzsimmons would not understand. He doesn't believe in
evil—or goodness for that matter. He is neutral."

"Is that what this is all about?" the priest asked.

Sarz shrugged. "Most people are neutral."

"Then why is Fitzsimmons so special to you?" the priest asked.

Sarz stared evenly at the priest for what seemed a long time.

"He's only a pawn," Sarz said, and the ironic smile returned to his
face. "Some people are destined to be crushed, and some are destined
to be crushers. He is destined to be crushed."

Peter pondered the words without replying.

After a couple of minutes Sarz stood up. "You can stay if you feel
like having sex," he said, fingering the gold chain around his naked
neck.

Peter, too, stood up. He looked once again at the photograph of the man with the cold, staring eyes, and then he turned toward the door.

"Nothing more to say?" Sarz asked.

Peter looked back at Sarz and then at the photograph. "Who is that?" he asked.

"I can't remember his name. I had it but I lost it. He was an SS man. I clipped that out of a magazine. There was something about the eyes that I liked."

"You truly are a child of darkness," the priest said.

He reached for the door handle, but Sarz's hand was there ahead of his.

"Don't come back here," Sarz said. His tone was gentle. "I don't like priests. I really don't. Someday I may crush a priest."

Peter looked him directly in the eye. "I have no fear of you," he said. "I belong to Jesus Christ. I am beyond any power that you may have."

"Is that a challenge?" Sarz asked. His smile was almost friendly.

As he stood waiting patiently for Sarz to open the door, Peter continued to stare Sarz in the eyes.

"It's not a challenge; it's a fact," Peter said. "You are the one who should fear."

Sarz turned the handle and pulled the door open.

"Me?" he asked.

"Even the demons know that God is One, and tremble," Peter said. He stepped into the hall, and Sarz watched as he walked through the gloomy passageway to the front door and then disappeared into the bright daylight.

CHAPTER TWENTY TWO

IT TURNED HOT DURING THE EARLY AFTERNOON, AND IT STAYED hot into the night. When Sarz left his apartment, he could hear the voice of the announcer telecasting the Red Sox game coming through open windows from the other apartments. He went behind the house to an aging green sedan and opened the trunk. He pushed a spade aside and reached under a large piece of canvas until he found a flashlight. He shut the trunk, checked it to make sure it was closed securely, and then he got into the car and backed it out of the driveway. He cruised for about two hours. At first he drove on the periphery of black neighborhoods, and then through poor white neighborhoods, slowing whenever he passed groups of young people clustered on street corners. Later he drove to Revere and went past the beaches, scanning the sidewalks, looking, looking.

After about two hours, he drove back to Boston. He parked his car three blocks from The Good Sports Cafe, locked it and began walking toward the bar. The street was empty, with only an occasional car going by. He had gone about a block when he felt someone tap him on the shoulder. He clenched his fists, ducked and turned to face Fitzsimmons who stood with his arms folded. Sarz relaxed and let his hands drop.

"What do you want?" Sarz snapped. His voice was edged with contempt.

Fitzsimmons glared at him but said nothing.

"What do you want?" Sarz asked again, and again his voice was sharp and contemptuous.

Fitzsimmons' only response was a continued glare.

"First the priest and now you. A pair of assholes."

Sarz turned to walk away, but as he did Fitzsimmons' left hand shot out and grabbed him by the throat. His right hand smashed into Sarz's rib cage, and then it, too, grabbed Sarz's throat. He pulled Sarz's face toward his and stared down into his eyes. Sarz's knee came up sharply, but Fitzsimmons' hips were turned and the blow struck harmlessly on his thigh. Sarz tried to clutch Fitzsimmons' head, but Fitzsimmons kept twisting it, breaking Sarz's grip, and all the while, he squeezed Sarz's throat tighter and tighter, his thumbs digging deeper and deeper into his neck, and all the time he stared into Sarz's eyes. They became wider and wider, and then they lost their focus and rolled back into his head. A gurgling sound came from Sarz's throat, and his body went limp, and he stopped struggling. Fitzsimmons continued to squeeze.

"You phony bastard," he said. "You sneaky son of a bitch." He glared into Sarz's face looking for a response, but there was none. Finally, he let go of Sarz's throat and his body fell to the sidewalk.

"You son of a bitch," Fitzsimmons hissed through clenched teeth and kicked Sarz in the side. "You son of a bitch," he repeated and kicked him again. He reached down and grabbed his shirt and pulled Sarz's face up towards his own. Sarz appeared to be dead or unconscious.

"Wake up, you bastard," he screamed and delivered a strong backhand across Sarz's face. "Wake up," he screamed and slapped him across the other side of his face. Sarz did not respond.

"Then die," Fitzsimmons said. He released the shirt. Sarz fell back to the sidewalk, and Fitzsimmons pulled his foot back to kick the motionless body once more.

"Kill him," a woman's voice urged.

Fitzsimmons hesitated and then put his foot back on the sidewalk without kicking Sarz. He turned to look at the woman. It was the waitress from The Good Sports Cafe, the one, he presumed, who had drugged his ginger ale. Her face no longer reflected a vague ennui. Her body was taut and there was a fanaticism in her eyes as she looked down at the immobile Sarz.

"Kill the bastard," she urged. "Kill him." She reached out and clasped Fitzsimmons' upper arm. "Do it. Do it," she whispered with an almost sexual intensity.

Her urgings had the opposite effect on Fitzsimmons. The rage drained out of him, and he felt contaminated by her words and by her presence. Now he, too, was immobile as he stood looking down at Sarz.

"Aren't you going to kill him?" she asked plaintively, as if her passion would not be fulfilled.

Fitzsimmons bent over Sarz and looked at his face. Blood was coming from both sides of his mouth, and both his eyes were beginning to swell. He reached down and felt Sarz's neck for a pulse and found it.

"Is he alive?" she asked.

"Yes," he answered. He remained bent over Sarz, studying the unconscious man's face.

"If you want to do it, I won't tell anyone," she said. "Hey, I'll walk away if you want me to."

"No," he said. He stood up straight, but he continued to stare down at Sarz.

"You might not get another chance," she said.

Fitzsimmons continued to stare at Sarz without answering.

A man had come out of the bar and started to walk toward them. When he saw there was trouble, he crossed the street. Several cars passed but the drivers paid no attention to them.

"If you're not going to do it, you'd better get out of here," the woman said.

Sarz began to stir.

Fitzsimmons looked at the woman. The fast life had taken its toll on her. She was in her mid-thirties, but she was only a step away from middle age. In the streetlights, her heavy eye shadow made her look pale and tired, almost ill. The first three buttons of her blouse were unbuttoned, and Fitzsimmons noticed the hint of her naked left breast.

"Are you going to work now?" Fitzsimmons asked her.

"No. I'm finished. I was heading home. You can come with me, if you want."

"Thanks," he said, "but I can't."

Sarz groaned.

"Aren't you going to leave?" the woman asked.

Fitzsimmons nodded, took a last look at Sarz and started to walk away.

"Hey," the waitress called after him.

Fitzsimmons stopped and turned around.

"Watch out for him," she said, pointing to Sarz.

When Fitzsimmons was out of sight, Sarz struggled to his hands and knees, and then rose unsteadily to his feet. He wiped the blood from his mouth with his hand and examined his streaked red fingers. He spit red onto the sidewalk, and looked at the waitress. She moved a few steps back and watched him in silence.

"Hysteria," Sarz said, nodding his head in the direction that Fitzsimmons had taken. "How do I look?"

"Like somebody just beat the shit out of you," the waitress said.

"Yeah. Somebody beat the shit out of me. Not the first time, either." He glared at the waitress as if he wanted to strike her, but she was beyond his reach. Without saying anything further, he left her and walked to his car.

The waitress stayed where she was, watching Sarz drive away until he turned a corner, and then she walked back to The Good Sports Cafe.

Chapter Twenty Three

By the time Fitzsimmons walked three blocks, his pulse rate dropped and his adrenal glands quieted. After another block, he began to tremble despite the heat, and by the time he walked five blocks, he was oppressed by feelings of guilt and self-loathing. He had very nearly killed Sarz. If the waitress had not come along, he might have killed him. He had not intended to. He had only wanted to intimidate him, to make him give up the maniacal game he was playing, but something happened to Fitzsimmons once his fingers were around Sarz's throat. Fitzsimmons had become drunk with rage. As he stared into Sarz's bulging eyes, he felt a towering sense of power—the power to end life by a simple act of the will. His rage seemed heroic, an unreckoned force which was suddenly released and turned his impotence into omnipotence. His thumbs had dug deeply into the muscles of Sarz's throat, and he had heard the gurgle, like a death rattle, as Sarz lost consciousness, and he had been without pity. Indeed, he had been transported by a savage joy. He had allowed himself to lose control.

The knowledge that he was capable of killing and that he could be overwhelmed by emotion to the point of taking a life unnerved him. He had found a dimension of himself that he had not known existed—it was dark and it was violent and it was frightening.

"You didn't think you had it in you," Peter said. "Why not? God knows that a reservoir of latent anger must have been building in you from the moment you discovered Eileen and Sarah. Certainly you had every reason to be angry."

"But I was insane," Fitzsimmons said. "I didn't have any say in the matter. When I grabbed his throat, it was like someone else took over—another side of me, a vicious, inhuman side. And I know now what Sarz meant when he talked about the feeling of power that you have when you take a person's life. I had that feeling of power. I had his life in my hands, literally."

"But you stopped strangling him. You let go," Peter said.

"Yes, but if that woman hadn't come along, I might have kicked him to death."

"Maybe," Peter said. "Maybe."

"And now I feel like him," Fitzsimmons said. He hung his head.

"Bullshit," the priest exploded.

Fitzsimmons' head snapped up. He had never before heard Peter use a vulgarity.

"I said, 'bullshit,' " the priest repeated vehemently. "You are a man who has been attacked, again and again and again. Your wife and your daughter were killed. You have been hounded by a sinister man, who drugged you, stuffed newspaper clippings in your mailbox to torture you, and, finally, followed Amy to Sturbridge. You have been the subject of an evil campaign, a studied malevolence, and you reacted fiercely, angrily—humanly."

"But I'm not even sure that he really is the person behind all this," Fitzsimmons said.

"Yes, you are. You may not have prima fade evidence, you may not have a court case, but you know—intuitively—and you're intuition is correct."

"How can you be so sure?"

"I went to see him at his apartment today. There is almost a visible aura of evil about him. I've only met one other person like that in my life," the priest said.

"I thought we agreed that talking to him wouldn't do any good," Fitzsimmons said.

"Yes, I agreed that confronting him wouldn't do any good," the priest said with a look of amusement. "I didn't go there to confront

him. I felt a responsibility for him. I'm a priest. A bad priest con-
tributed to whatever he is today. I went on a pastoral mission."

"Pastoral?"

Peter nodded somberly. "I'm a priest, John. Part of my job is to go
after lost sheep. Even he understood that."

"A lost sheep," Fitzsimmons said, almost to himself.

"He is more than a lost sheep. He has been swallowed up by his own
malignancy," the priest said. His eyes measured Fitzsimmons for a
moment and then he continued. "You are not at all like him, at least
not in the way you think. You are not a vicious man, and that is why
you are trembling because you are afraid of what you could have
become. What you have in common with Sarz is self-sufficiency and
self-righteousness. That's what you've been swallowed up by."

They were seated in Peter's office, Fitzsimmons in the high-backed,
covered chair and Peter behind the desk. The priest had been to a wake
and still wore his black suit with the Roman collar.

"Neither one of you wants to hear about God—but that's as far as
the similarity goes. Sarz has embraced evil."

"You talk about evil as if it had an objective existence," Fitzsimmons
said.

"Doesn't it?" the priest asked. "Think about it for a moment. Think
of the Holocaust. Think of the dictatorships of the right and the left.
Think of the things that Sarz says he has done to children. Evil transcends Sarz. It transcends all evil men. It's not that people cannot recognize that, it's that they don't want to."

"Sarz said the same thing to me, almost in the same words,"
Fitzsimmons said.

"As Sarz said, he and I understand each other. Sarz may even understand that next to evil, the thing people fear most is good. Good
requires a commitment, a surrendering of self. That's against our
nature. The very last thing we want to do is surrender self."

"Surrender self to what?" Fitzsimmons asked.

"To the good."

"You mean God," Fitzsimmons said, and there was an edge to his
voice.

"The good, by whatever name you want to call it."

"God," Fitzsimmons said.

"If that's the name you want to give it."

"And you're suggesting I surrender to him?"

"I'm not suggesting anything. What I'm saying is that when faced with the reality of evil, the only real choice we have is to turn to the good. And to do that we sometimes have to readjust our attitude toward God. For some of us that means—as strange as it may sound—forgiving him."

Peter paused again and contemplated Fitzsimmons from across the desk.

"I'm not suggesting that you do that, I'm just trying to explain things as I see them," Peter said.

"Good," Fitzsimmons said, and there was a finality to his tone.

Peter was not deterred. "John, there is a world of people who never face up to evil or good. They think that life is an end in itself. They spend their lives looking the other way, never facing the grim under-pinnings of reality. They grab at everything but commit themselves to nothing and end up believing that they've been cheated. They think life mocked them when it was really the other way around—they mocked life."

Peter shook his head.

"You are not like that, John. You're not disillusioned; you're angry. You've been traumatized. You have fallen into the trap of believing that evil is the fault of the good. God is to blame for everything bad that happens. I don't like murder or rape, nuclear weapons, radicals, reac-tionaries, communists, fascists, terrorists, bombs, oppression, starvation, disease, and death. Did it ever occur to you that maybe God doesn't like these things either?

"We become so pompous and judgmental—so self-righteous. We look down our noses at God. We say, 'God, when you made the uni-verse, you did a pretty lousy job. You really screwed it up.' But it's not God who screwed it up. God isn't raping and murdering. He's not oppressing people and starving them. He's not torturing them and denying them basic human rights. It is not God who embraces evil. It is men. Men do that. We do that, and we do it without any help from God. We blame God for war, but we credit ourselves for peace. We blame him for hatred and congratulate ourselves for love. We are so shortsighted. Why don't we understand that unless he wanted to make men automatons, he had to give them the option of looking down their noses at him—yes, even the option of committing rape and murder."

"Option, my ass, Fitzsimmons said. "That guy who killed my wife and daughter didn't have an option. He wasn't part of a transcendent evil—he was just plain crazy. He spent his whole childhood being abused. His father used to lock him up in a closet for days without food and without water. For days, he would sit in darkness with only his stinking feces to play with. Whatever was human in him was twisted and distorted until there was a madman in a seven-year-old body. The body grew up but the madman remained and had no choice."

Peter leaned forward in his chair. Fitzsimmons had never seen him so intense. "He was the product of evil and not the product of good. Maybe he didn't have a choice, and maybe Sarz never had a choice, and maybe they did," the priest said. "But you have a choice, and most people have a choice, and somewhere, sometime, somebody had a choice which resulted in the seven-year-old boy becoming a madman and Sarz being twisted into a monster. At the very least someone had the choice—maybe a lot of people had the choice—to help them, and they let it go by. That's what we do. We do nothing. We see evil and we are shocked. We decry it, and then we look away from it—we ignore it. We put ourselves above it and above a God who permits it to exist. And that makes us the highest good. Let me tell you, John, if I am the highest good, or you are the highest good, the existentialists are right—all of this is absurd, because alone, in the face of evil—real evil—by myself I am powerless, and by yourself, you are powerless.

"Even if you had killed Sarz tonight, you would not have destroyed evil, you would merely have eliminated one of its manifestations—a drop in the bucket—and you would not have erased the previous evil that Sarz committed, whatever that is. You would have been like a man who blows out a match while an inferno rages."

Fitzsimmons nodded. It was true.

"And what is worse," Peter continued, "in a very real way you would have become like him."

"I already have. I feel tainted by what I did. I feel like I've lost something," Fitzsimmons said.

"You haven't lost anything," the priest said. "You have just gained an awareness. It is only when we are awakened to our potential for committing evil that we can stop being self-righteous."

"We?" Fitzsimmons asked.

"Yes, we. You, me, the rest of us," Peter answered. "Do you think priests are immune from human nature?"

The priest smiled, almost sadly. He seemed to be debating whether to say more. Fitzsimmons waited without saying anything.

"People think that when you take the vow of celibacy, the sex drive vanishes," he paused again, and again he continued. "What I am going to tell you, I have only told one person outside of the confessional, and he was a priest. I'm not ashamed of it, but I don't wish to scandalize the Church."

Fitzsimmons nodded, as if agreeing to keep the priest's secret.

"I've had my temptations," Peter said. "When I was in my mid-thirties, there was a woman. I'm not sure how it happened. We worked together at the parish I was assigned to. She was an organist. Vivacious. Beautiful. Full of life. At first we didn't care for each other much. I think we each felt threatened. She wanted to do things her way; I wanted them done my way. It was ego. But gradually we got over that. We came to respect each other. It was innocent. We kidded each other. She was married. I was a priest. There was something wrong with her marriage. He husband was neurotic. He had a couple of nervous breakdowns; he was in and out of the hospital. He was a nice man, but he was full of fear. He couldn't hold a job, and I guess after a while she lost respect for him. I don't think she meant to. I think it happened without her even realizing it. They had two children, two beautiful little girls."

Peter stared out the window as if he could visualize them. He looked back at Fitzsimmons, and Fitzsimmons could see that, even after all these years, the memory was not without pain.

"I was still a young priest, but I was nearing the point of no return—that second line that celibates cross when they accept at the deepest level of their being that they will never be like other men, that they will never know the pleasures of loving a woman and of having children. When you haven't turned forty, and you see the elderly priests, some of whom seem so barren, life can look pretty gray. But I wasn't thinking about it—not consciously. I wouldn't have entertained those thoughts. I wanted to be a priest.

"But there is a part of me, John, that wanted something else. There is a part of me that wanted to be warmed by a vibrant woman, that wanted to hold her and caress her and love her. It had nothing to do with my will. One day by accident—we were in the rectory, in my office—I reached for a book on a shelf as she turned and our bodies met—joined is a better word. She was against me, and I was against her, and I did not step back, and she did not step back, and my arms went around her, and her arms went around me. Our bodies melded. I could feel all the things I had never felt—her breasts pressing into me, her inner thigh against my leg. I felt this great roaring wave within me. It swept up my intellect, my will, my emotions, my twelve years as a priest, and it carried me away. It was so powerful; I was helpless. And she was as carried away as I was. I think we were both prepared to have intercourse right there in my office. Right there on the rug.''

Peter smiled again, this time gently, tolerantly. "But before we could get to it, before we could rip each other's clothes off and indulge ourselves in front of all those statues and holy pictures, the housekeeper, old Miss Riley, came bursting in. And I almost didn't care. It hardly made any difference that I had an audience, at least for the first few seconds. The old lady was dumbfounded. She loved me like a son. I don't think she believed what she saw, so she acted as though it wasn't happening.

" 'We're having pork chops tonight, Father,' " Peter said, trying to match her brogue, and then he laughed. "I don't mean to laugh. At the time it was terrible. I wouldn't have laughed then, but now I see the comic elements—the two of us clinging to each other and yet trying to pull ourselves apart, and this old lady standing there chattering as if what was happening was an accepted everyday occurrence. We did finally separate, and I told Miss Riley, thank you and that I was looking forward to her pork chops. I went and sat at my desk, and Carol stayed at the bookcase blushing and smoothing her hair.

"Miss Riley only stayed for another moment, but it was enough. Sanity returned. 'That was the grace of God that just walked in and out of the room, Carol,' I said when Miss Riley left. 'It has given us a moment to reflect, a moment to see if we really want to do this thing.' 'I know,' she said. 'I can only see pain and heartbreak,' I said. 'I know,' she said, and she left my office without another word."

Peter stood up and walked to the window as if trying to walk away from the emotion that had risen within him.

"She was a beautiful woman, a lovely person," the priest said. He turned around and faced Fitzsimmons. "But that's not the point. The point is the experience devastated me. I knew that if Miss Riley had not come in, I would have broken my vow of celibacy, and, indeed, I had already broken it in spirit. I became very depressed. I felt like a hypocrite, especially when I heard confessions. I believed that I had violated everything I held sacred, that I had sullied the most important thing in my life, and that I had let God down."

Peter paused, reliving those feelings, and then he continued.

"I suffered for months. I felt like an apostate. I went to confession, but it didn't seem to help. To the world I looked like a saint, and to myself, I looked like a demon. When I could stand it no longer, I searched out an old priest friend of mine, and I bared my soul to him. He told me what I am telling you—no one is immune from error or from the dark turbulence of human nature. No one. He told me that I was self-righteous, and he was right. For years I had sat in the confessional shaking my head and saying to myself, 'Thank God I'm not like that. Thank God I'm not a thief. Thank God I'm not a drunk. Thank God I'm not an adulterer. Thank God I'm not like other men'—just like the Pharisee, and I never realized it. That was the main reason for my depression—my self-righteousness had turned on me, and I was scourging myself with it.

"After the old priest told me I was self-righteous, he told me that I hadn't let God down. 'God doesn't depend on you; you depend on God. When he created you, he knew your frailty, and he created you anyway. Pick up your bed and walk. Your sins are forgiven.'

"That was a turning point in my priesthood. It taught me an awful lot about humility and charity, and it also taught me a lot about myself. I stopped judging others. I stopped preaching to them. I began to listen to them and realize that their sins are my sins and my sins are their sins. I saw that we all need forgiveness, we all need consolation, we all need help. Every one of us is wounded, and every one of us is culpable. It was then that I became a disciple. I realized that I'm no great shakes. If it weren't for the grace of God, I'd be out there sleeping with the women of my parish and probably stealing from the parish funds to pay for my assignations."

"Come on, Peter. You know better than that."

"No, I don't," the priest said. "I know that if Miss Riley hadn't walked in on us that day, Carol and I would have become lovers, and I suspect that if that waitress had not turned up when she did, you might have killed Sarz. I don't believe in coincidences. You can believe what you like, but I believe those two people were the instruments of God's grace."

"I don't know about that, but you're probably right about one thing," Fitzsimmons said. "I think I have been self-righteous. I have set myself apart from and above other men. I don't think I did it purposely. It's just an attitude that I've always had. I don't even know where it came from."

"It's part of being human, and we never really grow until we understand that," the priest said.

"Tough lesson," Fitzsimmons replied.

"But a valuable one."

"And you're right about God," Fitzsimmons said. "I do blame him."

"I know," Peter said with a smile. "Bum rap."

Fitzsimmons rose to leave.

"Take my car," Peter said. "You can return it tomorrow."

"That's all right," Fitzsimmons said.

Peter tossed him the keys. "It's after eleven. Karen must be anxious about you."

"You're right again," Fitzsimmons said.

Peter's car was parked in the driveway at the rear of the rectory, and they walked through the kitchen to the back door.

"Good-bye, John," Peter said as Fitzsimmons went out.

"One last thing," the priest called out as Fitzsimmons reached the driveway.

Fitzsimmons stopped and looked back at the priest.

"Yes?"

"You've got endurance, John. That's a wonderful virtue. Hang on to it."

The priest stood in the doorway outlined by the kitchen light, and his face was in shadows.

"I will," he said.

"Hang on," Peter said again.

"I will," Fitzsimmons repeated.

CHAPTER TWENTY FOUR

SARZ WATCHED AS THE BLACK CHEVROLET TURNED INTO THE STREET and drove off. He took a last deep drag on his cigarette and flipped it into the gutter. When the tail lights had disappeared, he exhaled a heavy stream of smoke and picked up a duffel bag, which had been lying on the ground next to him. He walked out of the shadows, crossed the street, and went up the walkway to the front door of the rectory.

"What can I do for you?" the priest asked. He did not seem surprised to see Sarz standing there, and his tone was neither hostile nor welcoming as he stood behind the partly opened door. "I want to talk," Sarz said.

The priest glanced at the bruises on Sarz's face. "All right. Come in," he said and swung the door open to admit him.

"Would you like some coffee?" the priest asked as they entered the study.

"No thanks," Sarz said.

A lamp on the priest's desk was the only source of light in the room, and Peter walked over to the wall switch.

"Well, let's have some more light then," the priest said.

"My eye hurts," Sarz said. "Do you mind just leaving it?"

"Not at all," Peter answered. He sat down behind the desk and Sarz put his duffel bag on the rug next to a chair that was in front of the desk and sat down.

"What can I do for you?" Peter asked.

"I'll take an ashtray."

Peter opened the top, right-hand drawer to his desk and took out a small, glass ashtray. He leaned over the desk and handed it to Sarz.

"Were you outside long?"

"About a half hour."

"You could have come in while John was here."

"We've already talked," Sarz said. He gazed at the priest steadily, dispassionately.

"I know about that," Peter said.

"We'll talk again."

The two men fell silent in the dimly lighted room. Sarz continued to stare at the priest, but Peter was not disconcerted. He stretched back in his swivel chair and focused his eyes on the ceiling plate that covered an old electrical box from which a chandelier had once hung.

After a little while, the priest broke the silence. "Why are you here?"

"I have come to kill you," Sarz said. His tone was even, matter-of-fact, and he leaned forward in his chair as if to better see the priest's reaction.

Peter sat upright. He looked back into Sarz's eyes. They were sharp, predatory eyes, which betrayed just a hint of delight. He knew that Sarz was waiting for him to show fear.

"I've thought about killing a priest for a while now," Sarz said. "But I didn't want it to be an indiscriminate thing. I wanted it to be relevant."

"Relevant?"

"Yeah," Sarz said. "I didn't want it to be just any priest. I didn't want it to be a faggot priest or a priest who shouldn't be a priest. I wanted a priest who is committed. A real priest."

"Most priests are like that. The other kind are few and far between—the exceptions that prove the rule."

"That may be. Anyway, I know that you're a real priest, and now that he has raised the level of violence, I have to respond, and by killing you I achieve two things. I destroy a priest, and I remove his friend, the person he turns to in a crisis."

Peter looked away. His eyes focused on the reproduction of the Renaissance painting of the Annunciation that hung over the filing cabinets. The young, virile angel knelt before an even younger virgin whose head was bowed humbly to the will of God. He was announcing the great mystery. If it were not for that mystery, an event that happened two thousand years earlier, Sarz would not have come to kill him.

"I knew a man who kept track of every woman he had sex with," Sarz continued. "When I knew him, his conquests totaled one hundred and seven. I've kept track of the number of people I've killed. It pales by comparison. You'll only be number seven."

There was a terrible stillness in the room as the two men looked at each other. The dim light and its green tone gave them a surreal aspect as if their conversation was taking place on another plane.

"My soul magnifies the Lord," the priest said, quoting the young virgin who had received the message.

"What does that mean?"

"It means that if it is God's will for me to die at your hand, then I embrace his will."

Sarz took a package of cigarettes from his shirt pocket, removed a cigarette and lit it. "Perhaps you don't understand what is happening here," he said, blowing the smoke out toward the priest. "You're not going to leave this room alive. You're going to meet your fucking God tonight."

"I've anticipated the meeting for many years. I look forward to it."

"I am going to destroy you. When I leave here you're going to be a thing. Do you understand that?"

"You're not going to destroy me. You don't have that power."

Sarz took a switchblade knife from his pocket and pushed a button on the side of it. The blade sprang open. It was seven inches long. He pressed the point against his left forefinger as if to test its sharpness and then he placed the knife in his lap.

"We'll see," he said.

"I knew when I saw you this morning that I was looking upon the face of evil. I even suspected that you would be the instrument of my death," the priest said. Peter was restrained and businesslike, even understanding. He leaned forward and put his forearms on the desk.

"Seven people?" he asked.

"Six," Sarz said. "You'll be number seven."

"And the others, were they all little girls?"

"Little girls?"

"The ones in the newspaper clippings that you sent to John Fitzsimmons."

"Oh, those little girls," Sarz said. He seemed embarrassed. "No. I didn't kill them. I don't care about little girls."

"Then why did you send those clippings to Fitzsimmons?"

"Just to torture him. To play with him. He had a little girl that was killed. I wanted him to keep feeling that."

The priest glanced down at his hands and then looked back at Sarz. A look of disgust mingled with anger spread across his face.

"Don't look at me like that you son of a bitch."

"Like what?"

"Like you're better than me."

The priest shook his head. "I have never met anyone worse than you," he said.

They both looked at the knife lying in Sarz's lap.

"Your experience has been limited," Sarz answered.

"No. I've met some pretty horrible people. Sick, crazy people. Bad people. I don't think I have ever met anyone who was as intentionally evil as you."

"Sure you have," Sarz said. He crossed his legs carefully to keep the knife from sliding from his lap. "You've met them. You've been friendly with some of them. You just don't recognize them. They don't reveal themselves. They do what they do in darkness, out of the public eye. They seem well intentioned, but they mask their arrogance and their hatred. They exploit, and they take joy in it, but they hide their hands. If I did not choose to reveal myself, you would have no idea of my evil. I would just be another pretty face."

Sarz waited for a response but there was none. "Oh, I've met them. In the combat zone, at strange parties in strange houses. After a while, you instinctively know the really bad ones. They are so jaded. They take pleasure in others' pain. They love to debase others. That's how they get their rocks off. And the really bad ones love to violate the innocent. To violate a ten-year-old girl with a bunch of people standing around watching. To crush that innocence, to watch the despair and sickness come into those young eyes. And you know what is worse? It's for a man to rape a young boy. A big, hairy man to thrust … "

Peter raised his hand to silence Sarz.

"You may as well hear me out. You may as well let me tell you what that does to a young boy," Sarz said. When the priest did not answer, Sarz continued. "It acquaints him with the true nature of the universe. It is the ultimate proof that God is a bastard. I know. It was one of yours that taught me. And I have taught others. And I have gone one better. When they were sick with revulsion, when they thought the worst had already happened, I showed them they were wrong. I put my hands around their necks and watched their eyes pop. I watched their disbelief turn to panic and their panic turn to horror. And there was no one to help them. Not God, not their parents, not the police. No one. They died with horrified eyes."

Peter looked up. His eyes and Sarz's eyes met. "Little boys—eight-year-olds, nine-year-olds. Sometimes even ten or eleven, if they still have that innocence about them." Sarz smiled thinly.

"But what does this have to do with John Fitzsimmons?" the priest asked.

"I figured you would understand," Sarz said. "He is an affront to me. Evil is not to be ignored. You can't just walk away from it like it does-n't exist. There is a magnificence to evil. There is an absoluteness about it, an irrevocability. Do you know there have been boys that I didn't kill, boys that I didn't rape? They were the ones who did not submit, the ones who said, 'Fuck off, you faggot. Get lost you creep.' They lived. It was the ones who were too scared to do anything but let me zipper down their flies, the ones who cried when I violated them. They were the ones who died. All six of them. Every one of those pussies died."

As Sarz spoke he became more and more intense. He pointed his index finger at Peter to give emphasis to his words, and he raised his voice to a slightly squeaky pitch.

"His wife was raped and murdered. His daughter was murdered. And he acted like one of those pussies. He sobbed and he walked away. He just wanted to forget about it. He did nothing. I mean, he did nothing. I hate victims. I hate them when they do nothing. When they cry and do nothing," Sarz said, jabbing his finger again and again at Peter.

"You mean you never cried and did nothing?" Peter asked.

Sarz's hand dropped, and the intensity left his face.

"When that priest seduced you in that home for delinquents, for example," Peter said.

"I cried," Sarz answered, becoming reflective. "I think it was one of the last times I cried. It was certainly the last time I believed in any-thing good. After that I understood that goodness was a screen people used to manipulate other people. But I didn't forget it. And I didn't walk away and do nothing. It was one of the things that changed me for good. Freebee Sarz. That's my name. Freebee. My mother was a whore. She gave it away and she got me. So she named me Freebee. I had a whore for a mother and a faggot for a priest. And when that son of a bitch was finished playing with me, and when I was finished crying, something happened inside of me. I started to grow up. And somewhere along the line, I decided that I was sick of being a victim, of, shall we say, getting it up the ass. I said to myself, 'That's it. I've taken it and taken it, and now I'm gonna give it. I'm sick of paying. It's time other people paid.' "

As he spoke the intensity returned, and again he emphasized his words with short jabs of his finger. "And they have paid. And you'll pay. And Fitzsimmons will pay—sometimes I want the whole fucking world to pay."

Moment by moment and word by word Sarz was allowing his rage to build. His voice was raised to a squeaky pitch again, and his face was animated and angry. "I want the whole fucking world to pay, but I don't have that power. So I have to pick and choose. And I choose to make the victims pay. The snotnosed victims. The ones who get crushed with tears in their eyes, who don't fight back. The pussies." He sat back in the chair and his body relaxed, but the fierceness remained in his eyes.

"Fitzsimmons just walked into TPI. I thought I recognized him but I didn't know from where. When you're like I am, you take an interest in big murders, especially when they make the national news. So I checked his personnel file, and then I remembered. The college professor who walked away. Just walked away like it never happened. Never even complained. Never said, 'Shoot that son of a bitch. Kill the bastard.' He just had that vacant look in his eyes."

"What could he have done?" Peter asked.

"He could have done something. He could have screamed. He could have stood up and said they should cut the guy's balls off. They asked him should they reinstate the death penalty. And he said, 'No.' He said the guy was crazy. It wasn't his fault. That's all. It wasn't his fault. Well, who the hell's fault was it? It's somebody's fault. Somebody's to blame. Somebody. God. Somebody should pay."

Sarz paused as if waiting for Peter to say something, but Peter only stared at him in silence.

"He was crushed and he did nothing. He was crushed and he just walked away. He gave up everything. A college professor who wound up sweeping floors. I despise him. I have contempt for all victims."

"And this whole campaign—the clippings, drugging him, following Amy—all because you despise victims."

Sarz nodded his head. "Victims in general. Him in particular." He recrossed his legs carefully so that the knife remained balanced on his lap. "If he had just reacted, I probably would have left him alone. But he didn't. I kept pouring salt on his wounds and it was like he was dead. It began as a diversion but the more he failed to react, the more consuming it became until it grew into an obsession."

"But he did react," Peter said.

"Too late. Too late," Sarz waved his hand as if to erase the priest's words. "Tonight is too late. All that did was seal his fate."

"He reacted before tonight," the priest said. "He came to me. He went to the police."

"What could you do? What could the police do? Nothing. And he knew they couldn't do anything. So he put up with it. I even told him what would happen. I told him he was my Jew. I would take everything from him, even his self-respect."

"You're mixed up," the priest said. "He didn't do anything because he was afraid he was wrong about you."

"Bullshit. He's a victim."

"He's a very courageous man. Now that you've come out of the shadows, I don't think you'll be able to play your game with him any more."

"Bullshit. He's going to become the ultimate victim. He'll kill himself." Sarz picked the knife up by the handle. "When I am finished with him, he'll kill himself." Sarz started to get up from the chair.

"I want you to know that for whatever you are about to do, I forgive you," the priest said.

"You forgive me."

"Yes."

"But just for what I'm going to do to you. Not for what I've done to the other six or what I will do to Fitzsimmons."

"I can't forgive you for the others. I can only forgive you for myself," the priest said.

"I thought you had the power to forgive all sins," Sarz said, in a half-mocking voice.

"I do," the priest said. "But I can only forgive those who want to be forgiven. To have the burden lifted, you must want the burden lifted."

"The burden?" Sarz asked with a half-smile.

"Don't you find it a terrible burden to be what you are? You're a prisoner to your own rage. You're a prisoner to the darkness in your soul."

The smile was gone from Sarz's face. It had been replaced by a wounded look.

"It is a burden," Sarz said in a whisper. "It's amazing that you recognize that. I carry it with me all the time. Other people have burdens but they can get rid of them. I have to carry mine. Day after day."

"Do you want to be set free?"

"Free?" He pondered the words, and for the briefest instant, his eyes softened, and his features lost their hard edge. But it was for an instant only. In a moment, he had become the predator again. "No. I don't want to be set free. Nothing can set me free. I am what I am."

The moment had come, and Peter knew it.

"Even in this darkness, Lord, I know that you are with me," he said in a voice that was firm and full of conviction.

Sarz shrieked, and before Peter could move, he dove across the desk knocking the priest backward in his chair and falling on top of him. As they crashed to the floor, Sarz stabbed the priest in the face again and again. The knife point struck the cheekbone, the nose and then penetrated the right eye, which began to hemorrhage. Sarz stumbled to his feet. The priest was still breathing. He plunged the knife into Peter's neck and ripped his throat open. The blood spurted out as if he had opened a tap.

It poured over Sarz's shoes and saturated the rug. Sarz leaned back against the desk. He was breathing heavily, and the sound of his gasps filled the room. He looked down at the priest. His face was a mass of blood. The man who had sat at the desk a minute or two earlier was hardly recognizable. He was lifeless now. Just as Sarz had predicted, the priest had become a thing.

"Peter," a voice called from beyond the closed study door, "are you in there?"

Sarz raced around the desk, jumped to the door and pulled it open. An elderly man in pajamas stood in the doorway staring at the blood-covered Sarz with his mouth open.

With his left hand, Sarz reached out and grabbed the man's pajama shirt and pulled him toward him. With his right hand he plunged the knife into the man's stomach.

"Why?" the man said in astonishment.

Sarz stabbed him again.

The man staggered forward. "Why?" he said again.

"Die, you son of a bitch," Sarz said. He plunged the knife into the top of the stomach and up under the rib cage to the heart.

The man collapsed to his knees. His eyes were still wide open and there was still a question on his lips. He fell face forward to the floor.

Sarz pushed the point of the knife into the old man's back and between his ribs several more times to make certain the man was dead, and then he stepped away.

The back of the old man's pajama shirt was saturated with dark, red blood, but it did not pour from him as it had from Peter. Sarz stepped into the hall. The light at the top of the stairs was on. He walked quickly to the front door to make sure that it was locked and then he went back to the study, picked up his duffel bag and began to explore the house. He went from room to room with the duffel bag in one hand and the knife in the other. He checked the basement and every room and every closet on the first floor and then he went up the stairs to the second floor. Again he checked every room and every closet. Finally, he went up into the attic to make sure there was no one there.

When he was certain that no one else was in the house, he found a bathroom on the second floor. In the mirror he could see that his clothes were soaked with blood. He left the bathroom door open and stripped his clothes off, throwing each piece in the bathtub. When he was naked, he sat down on the covered toilet and took off his pair of sneakers and his socks. They were also covered with blood and he threw them on top of the heap of clothes in the tub. Again, he examined himself in the mirror. There was blood on his hands and on his face, even in his hair. He turned the shower on, stepped in and pulled the curtain. Quickly but thoroughly, he washed every inch on his body and his hair. He stepped out of the tub, and wrung out his clothes and dropped them back into the tub. Then he took a large towel and dried himself and his hair.

When he had finished, he opened his duffel bag, took out clean clothes, socks and sneakers and got dressed. He looked in the mirror again. His hair was still wet. He found a hair dryer in the cabinet beneath the sink and dried his hair and combed it. He took the wet clothes from the tub and put them in the duffel bag. He rinsed the tub and wiped it with the towel and carefully wiped the shower faucets. He put the towel and the hair dryer in the duffel bag and zipped it closed. When he was certain he had left nothing in the bathroom, he turned out the light and went downstairs.

He stood in the hall and looked into the study. The old man's body lay where he had left it near the door, and he could see the priest's legs protruding from behind the desk. Sarz entered the study, carefully stepping around the puddles of blood. He unzipped the duffel bag, put the ashtray in it, and zipped it up again. On the way out of the study he flipped the light switch off with his elbow. He went to the front door and wiped off the lock and handle with his handkerchief. Then he walked though the kitchen and left the rectory through the back door. He stayed in shadows until he got to his car. He opened the driver's door, but the interior light did not light up. He got in and drove away. He went for a block before he turned the headlights on.

He went directly to the city's 'Combat Zone.' Despite the late hour, there were still many people on the streets: women with long, dyed blond hair, and short skirts who were heavily made up and stared boldly at men who drove the streets, men in business suits— studying the picture boards outside pornographic movie houses and reading the advertisements for "live peep shows"—sailors in twos and threes, laughing and swaggering, men with shiny black shoes with pointed toes, and tight-fitting pants.

Sarz pulled down a side street and parked the car. He opened the glove compartment and took out a folded green plastic bag, the kind used to line garbage cans. He unfolded it and after a moment's difficulty succeeded in separating the two sides so that the bag opened at the top. He pushed the duffel bag into the bag, and tightened a plastic-coated twist to seal it. He got out of his car and took the bag by its neck and walked casually down the dark, narrow street looking into each alley as he did. After less than a hundred yards, he spotted a dumpster near the rear door of a bar. When he was certain that no one was watching him, he walked to the dumpster and flipped the plastic bag up and over its side. It fell on top of a lot of other neatly tied plastic bags.

He walked off briskly and spent the rest of the night drinking in bars frequented by pimps, prostitutes and drunks.

CHAPTER TWENTY FIVE

FITZSIMMONS CLIMBED UP THE FIRE ESCAPE TO THE ROOF TO GET out of the apartment and away from his thoughts. He had been up all night, and he felt it. His neck and shoulders ached as if he had been carrying a yoke. His eyes were heavy, but he knew he was not ready to sleep. As the rising sun turned the sky from dark to blue, the city was still quiet, no sounds of traffic, no voices in the hallways or on the streets, only silence as the dawn's radiance broke over the sprawling mass of buildings. He felt as if he were the only human being in the city who was out of bed and awake. He felt alone, all alone, as he had after his wife and daughter had been buried and the police had gone, and the reporters had gone, and his friends had gone. He was alone with that terrible inarticulate voice inside him, the voice which stormed and raged and cried but was too distressed to express itself in words.

He leaned against a brick chimney and watched as the sunlight slowly defined the city. Peter was dead, and Fitzsimmons was powerless.

He had known that Peter was dead as soon as he drove around the corner. Police cars lined the curb in front of the rectory, and across the street there were three vans from television stations parked one behind the other. Clustered along the sidewalk in front of the church, there were groups of people who talked to each other but kept their eyes on the rectory. It was all very familiar. Part of Fitzsimmons wanted to drive on, away from Boston, away from Massachusetts, away from everything—to escape before he could be certain that anything had happened, but he knew there was no escaping it. He pulled Peter's car into the driveway behind an unmarked police car which gave itself away because, although it was a new Ford, it had black sidewalks.

"Hey," a voice shouted at him as he parked the car.

He knew it was a policeman without looking. He shut off the engine and got out of the car, and as he did, he felt an emotional numbness descend upon him—a detachment which allowed him to view what was happening almost as if he weren't taking part in it.

"Hey, you can't park there," the policeman shouted again. He came running down the sidewalk to the driveway.

"It's the pastor's car," Fitzsimmons said.

The cop stopped and took a long look at Fitzsimmons. "Who are you?"

"A friend of his."

"And that's Father Genaro's car?"

"Yes."

"What are you doing with it?"

Fitzsimmons didn't answer. He looked around and saw a priest staring at them from the front door and another uniformed policeman who had started toward them.

"Come with me, please," the officer said.

As the two began to walk up the sidewalk to the house, the priest hurried down the front steps and approached them. He looked to be a year or two older than Fitzsimmons. His face was very somber, but his eyes were gentle and comforting.

"I'm Kevin O'Donnell," the priest said putting his hand out.

"John Fitzsimmons."

"I thought so. I saw you drive up in Peter's car. I thought it could only be Mr. Fitzsimmons, Peter's friend."

"What's this," a man shouted from the doorway. A long filtered cigarette hung from his mouth. He was wearing a suit and tie.

"He says he's a friend of the priest. He just drove up in the priest's car," the officer said.

"Bring him in here," the man said, taking a drag on his cigarette.

As he entered the hall, Fitzsimmons' eye caught Volpe's. The detective was standing in the office near the door. At his feet there was a huge bloodstain on the carpet. Volpe glared at Fitzsimmons for a moment and then looked away.

Fitzsimmons floated through the morning, feeling almost nothing, looking upon the scene from a great emotional distance. It was some time before he realized that he was in a state of shock, and he only came to the realization because Kevin O'Donnell was so solicitous. The priest seemed to know all about Fitzsimmons and to be very concerned about the effect that Peter's murder would have on him. He seemed to hover about Fitzsimmons anxious to do something for him, offering him coffee, trying to engage him in conversation, and generally making him aware of a friendly presence.

Fitzsimmons was at the rectory for more than three hours. He was questioned four different times by three different questioners, and all the while Kevin O'Donnell stayed nearby.

Volpe had treated Fitzsimmons in a tender, almost brotherly way, but despite his tenderness, Fitzsimmons recognized that Volpe had escaped being touched by the death, as if the police officer had seen so much death and so much violence that it never surprised him or hurt him no matter where he found it. There was a gentleness about Volpe but it was a practiced gentleness that masked a cold toughness.

"I would rather hurt," Fitzsimmons thought, even though his emotions were still shielded by his shock.

"I promise you, we will get the son of a bitch," Volpe said.

Fitzsimmons had nodded, as he had four years earlier. Death was implacable and unanswering. Getting the priest's murderer would not change that.

"What about the other man?" Fitzsimmons had asked.

"A retired priest who lived with Pete. The housekeeper was lucky she didn't live in the rectory. Do you have any ideas about this? Did Pete ever mention anybody who troubled him?"

Their eyes met, and Fitzsimmons' gaze was steady under Volpe's probing stare. He shook his head. "No."

"What about this guy that was giving you the hard time?"

"Sarz?"

"Yeah. Pete called me about him. He wanted me to speak with him about those clippings you got the other day. It didn't seem that there was anything substantial to talk to him about, though."

Fitzsimmons nodded. "Peter told me that he went to see Sarz yesterday."

Volpe jotted something down in a small notebook and then went back into Peter's office.

After Fitzsimmons waited in the hall for another hour, Volpe came back and told him he could leave. Kevin O'Donnell insisted on driving him home. He made Fitzsimmons take his telephone number and promise that he would call so that they could have lunch together.

It was not until Fitzsimmons was back in his apartment that the immensity of death confronted him again. As always, it was absolute and unfathomable.

The sky had turned a bright blue. Fitzsimmons' view of the horizon was blocked by the buildings, but in his mind's eye he could visualize the great fireball rising up from the Atlantic, and as he did, he realized that he had not been able to escape his thoughts by coming to the roof. He turned to go back down, and he saw that Karen had followed him and had been watching him.

"Hi," she said. "I guessed that you would be up here."

"I thought you were sleeping."

"I haven't slept all night. I've been thinking." There was a finality to her tone, and Fitzsimmons knew that she had come to a decision.

"And?" he asked.

"I thought about Peter and you and me and Amy. I feel like I've lost a friend or a close relative and I only knew Peter for a little while. I can imagine how you feel."

Fitzsimmons closed his eyes. The pain was written on his face.

"And I think that Sarz killed Peter."

Fitzsimmons nodded again without opening his eyes.

"Because he knows it would hurt you. And I'm afraid for you and for me and for Amy. It's insane. It's so insane."

"I think it's time for you to leave."

"And go where?"

"Back to Detroit or anywhere away from Boston."

"I'm afraid to go," Karen said. "I'm afraid to stay, but I'm afraid to go. Especially alone."

It was light enough now so that Fitzsimmons could see all the care and weariness in her face. He wanted to go to her and comfort her, but he felt an emotional barrier between them.

"Would you come with us?" she asked.

"I have to stay here."

A look of anger flitted across Karen's face. "Why?" she asked.

"I'm tied to this thing. I can't escape it. I'm tied to Sarz and to what he is doing. I don't know why he hates me, and I don't know with certainty who he has killed or what exactly he has done, but I know that he is evil and that his evil is pervasive. I feel like I'm caught in a storm at sea. I can't run from it. All I can do is ride it out."

Karen bent her head and raised her clenched fists to her forehead. "Is that all? Is that all you can do? Ride it out?"

"And wait," Fitzsimmons said.

"Wait?" Her voice was disbelieving.

"Yes. Wait," Fitzsimmons said. "I thought of killing him, but I can't do that, and I don't know what else I can do."

Karen started down the fire escape but stopped. She looked up at Fitzsimmons. The anger had drained from her.

"I know you can't leave. I don't understand it, but I know you can't leave." She started down the fire escape again but stopped again. "And I can't leave either. And neither can Amy. All I thought about last night was running. Running, running, running. And Peter. Running and Peter. I can't run. I have been trapped in this thing, too. We're trapped."

"I love you," Fitzsimmons said.

Karen's face was somber, and Fitzsimmons could see an unspoken accusation in her eyes. "You'd better," she answered, and for a brief moment an anemic smile softened the lines of worry in her tired face.

Fitzsimmons stayed on the roof after Karen climbed back down. He was very weary now. His state of shock had worn off some time during the afternoon, and he had been attacked by grief and anger and frustration. He felt as if he had engaged in an epic battle and now was spent, and yet he knew the battle had hardly begun. He knew that he had to summon energy from somewhere in order to continue.

He remembered how Sarz had boasted of the way in which the Nazis had stripped the Jews of their peace of mind, and then their property and their families, and finally of their very selves. If Sarz had killed Peter, he was in the process of doing to Fitzsimmons what the

Nazis had done to the Jews. If Fitzsimmons could be certain that Sarz was a killer, if he had absolute proof that the man was planning to destroy him, then, Fitzsimmons thought, he might be able to kill Sarz, or at the very least, Fitzsimmons could be certain of where he stood. He realized that uncertainty was also a weapon for Sarz, because Fitzsimmons knew that as long as there was any lack of certainty, he could not unilaterally eliminate Sarz.

"I am beginning to understand," Fitzsimmons thought. The city, which he loved, had become an alien place, a dangerous place. There was no authority to which he could appeal because the authorities had to act within the constraints of the law, and it could not be shown that Sarz had violated the law.

"I'm beginning to understand how they felt," he thought.

He knew that the analogy was not complete. The Jews had faced an immeasurably greater evil, a demonic manifestation that was unparalleled, and they had been powerless because of politics and geography and a world which looked the other way, and they had been trapped by their own goodness, by their belief in justice and their inability to comprehend the depths of evil which consumed their adversaries.

Fitzsimmons was trapped by uncertainty and by moral restraints which were deeper than intellect and will. They were a part of his nature. The very things which distinguished him from Sarz, the things which made Fitzsimmons human, were the very things that worked to Sarz's advantage and worked against Fitzsimmons. And yet, Fitzsimmons knew that he could not abandon morality. In the face of an irrational evil, an evil which Fitzsimmons had done nothing to merit, Fitzsimmons simply did not know what to do.

He looked up at the wide, blue sky. Its brilliance seemed infinite, its depth unfathomable.

"Is goodness helpless?" Fitzsimmons asked aloud. "Is decency powerless?"

CHAPTER TWENTY SIX

THE MAHOGANY CASKET WAS CLOSED. IT LAY ON A CATAFALQUE IN front of the altar, and a gold-framed, eight by ten photograph of Peter rested on top of it. The picture was a formal portrait, the kind taken for diocesan newspapers. Peter wore a black suit and Roman collar and his demeanor was serious, although the kindness in his eyes was obvious. A small crucifix stood next to the picture.

Two lines of people extended down the main aisle of the church from the coffin to the vestibule doors. At the foot of the altar, several priests and members of Peter's family waited to receive those who had come to pay their respects. One of the priests was Kevin O'Donnell. He patted hands and nodded somberly, and occasionally he smiled; sometimes, he laughed.

Fitzsimmons had never been to a priest's wake before, nor could he remember having seen so many priests and nuns collected in one place. Some of them knelt in prayer in pews or at the side altars, but most of them clustered in little groups chatting intently. There seemed to be two distinct moods in the church. The people who were waiting to pass the coffin were somber and quiet while those who had already passed it seemed to be relaxed and sociable. Fitzsimmons,

Karen and Amy hardly spoke or even looked at each other as they
waited for the line to move.

Light from the setting sun strained through the stained glass windows, casting rose, blue and green rays across the rows of pews and giving exotic tints to the faces of those who passed through them. Soft,
almost muted organ music gently carried throughout the church. It
was distinct without being obtrusive, and it did not compete with the
constant hum of conversation. The large, iron crucifix was suspended
by wires above the altar. The dead, metallic Christ hung in silence. His
head, crowned with thorns, had fallen across his right shoulder. Off on
a side aisle, Angelina, the woman who owned the restaurant in the
North End, was talking to a nun. For just a moment her eyes met
Fitzsimmons'. She smiled consolingly and then looked away, but that
was enough to penetrate the rush of feelings and fragmented impressions that Fitzsimmons was experiencing, and he was grateful for that
little sign of friendship.

By the time they reached the coffin, tears had begun to fall down
Karen's cheeks, and her right hand clutched Fitzsimmons' left hand
tightly. The three of them stopped before the picture of Peter, and
Karen laid her left hand on the top of the coffin. Amy took
Fitzsimmons' other hand in hers and stared hard at Peter's picture.
Fitzsimmons closed his eyes and waited for them to move. As soon as
they were past the coffin, Kevin O'Donnell stepped forward to greet
them. He reached out and took Karen's free hand in both of his.

You must be Karen," he said, smiling warmly. Karen's sad smile
could not conceal her surprise at his knowing who she was.

"And this must be Amy," the priest said.

"How do you know me?" Amy asked.

"From Peter. Father Genaro. He told me about you all. He thought
the world of your mother," the priest answered.

He guided them down the receiving line, and introduced them to
Peter's sisters and his nephews and nieces, and then he brought them
up on the side of the altar and introduced them to a very well tailored
priest who, it turned out, was a bishop named Cavanaugh. He was a
man about sixty years old with wavy, white hair and a strong, handsome face. He appeared to be in excellent physical condition.

"We were going to hold this at the cathedral," Bishop Cavanaugh
said, "but Father O'Donnell convinced us that Father Genaro would

have wanted it here. And, of course, Father Domenico's body was returned to the Worcester Diocese. Poor guy. He worked in that diocese ever since they split off from Springfield. When he retired, he got Father Genaro to let him live at St. Camillus so he could be close to the libraries here. He wanted to write a book on the history of the Church in New England. Did you know Father Domenico?"

"Just to say hello to," Fitzsimmons said. "He kept a pretty low profile."

"Sometimes elderly priests are like that. They feel out of place. Although Father Domenico used to help out with the Masses," the bishop said.

There was a long silence.

"The cardinal should be here soon," the bishop said. "This has troubled him deeply. I hope you can stay. There'll be some prayers. It won't take too long. The Mass is tomorrow. That, of course, will be our most important time of prayer."

"We'll stay," Fitzsimmons said.

"Meanwhile, Bishop, let me pull these folks away from you for a few minutes," Kevin O'Donnell said.

"Please do. Nice to meet you all, and thank you for coming," the bishop said.

Father O'Donnell took them through the sacristy and out in back of the church. Dusk was falling and there was a stillness in the air.

"We can go to the rectory for coffee, if you like," the priest said.

"This is nice right here," Karen said, and Fitzsimmons nodded in agreement.

"I'm afraid I surprised you," the priest said.

"You did," Karen answered, "I couldn't imagine how you knew who I was."

"Peter and I were very close. He was my spiritual director. He was very fond of you, John. I think he thought of you almost as a son, and he loved you, Karen. He thought you were very brave."

"How do you know all this?" Karen asked.

"That's an interesting question. In fact that's what I wanted to talk to you about," the priest said. "I've known about you, John, for quite some time. Peter used to talk about you often. Usually in general terms. I knew that you had the same interests, and he enjoyed your company, but he never told me much about you. Then on Saturday— the afternoon of the day he died—he called me up and talked to me for a long time about the three of you. I was a bit puzzled by the conversation. I knew that he had called me specifically to tell me about you, but I had no idea why, and when I asked him why, he said, 'I just want you to know these things. They're my friends and you're my friend. Perhaps you can be their friend.' I think Peter had an awareness that death was near."

Fitzsimmons nodded. "When we said good night on Saturday night, there was a finality about it."

"So here we are," the priest said. "I was a friend of Peter's and you were friends of Peter's. And I have a feeling that it would please Peter if we could go out to dinner, say in a week or so."

"Sure," Fitzsimmons said.

"I'll give Karen a call. Peter even gave me her number," the priest said, with a smile. "But I want you to have my number, too," and he handed a card to Fitzsimmons.

The next morning, as Fitzsimmons approached the steps leading up to the church it was as if he were back on Long Island. There seemed to be television cameras and police everywhere. Men in suits and women in expensive clothes and carefully molded hairdos stood on the steps talking into microphones, while men with jeans, sneakers and beards aimed cameras at them. Other people, younger men and women, also wearing jeans and sneakers, scurried around with clipboards in their hands, pointing, whispering, running. There was something detached and inhuman about them. They were there to record and observe and not to mourn, and they were a scene unto themselves, a scene within a scene. Fitzsimmons held Amy's hand in his left hand and Karen's hand in his right, and he walked quickly up the steps looking neither to his left nor his right.

His mind was flooded with images from the past and the present as if, as he walked through the large, open doorway, he was simultaneously experiencing two separate events. The location was different and the faces were different, but the emotions were identical and there was an eerie sameness to the crowd and the ceremony. His impressions of the past were so strong that Fitzsimmons could barely notice what was going on. He had never consciously remembered the funeral of his wife and daughter—he had closed that memory off as soon as it happened. Now it came back, so powerfully that he could almost see the two coffins, one large, oak casket and a small, white one, in the center aisle. He was dizzy and his palms were sweating. He clutched the missalette and twisted it into a cone.

Karen leaned over to him. "Are you all right?" she whispered in his ear.

Fitzsimmons nodded.

"Are you sure? You're awfully pale." Her right hand circled his left wrist and her index finger pressed on his pulse.

"I'll be okay," Fitzsimmons whispered. His throat was dry and his voice cracked. He coughed. "I'm all right," he whispered and his voice was stronger, and at once color began to return to his face.

Karen patted the back of his hand, and Fitzsimmons took a deep breath and exhaled. He would be all right. The shock was passing, and by the time the Mass started Fitzsimmons was able to look around and concentrate on what he saw. The church was mobbed, but Fitzsimmons was only able to pick out a few faces that he recognized from the wake. The casket was at the head of the center aisle. It was closed as it had been at the wake, and for one brief moment Fitzsimmons imagined Peter's vested body with his badly damaged face lying inside the coffin, and then his mind drifted away, back to Long Island and the two caskets, back to images of Eileen and Sarah, happy images and painful ones, and as the Mass began, Fitzsimmons was oblivious to the procession of fifty priests, the cardinal and several bishops, which moved up the center aisle past the casket and then filled the altar.

It was not until Kevin O'Donnell had mounted the pulpit that Fitzsimmons' attention focused on the present.

"I want to set the record straight this morning," Kevin O'Donnell said as he began his eulogy. His tone was conversational and personal as if he was speaking only to one person instead of the hundreds who had become utterly quiet.

"In that coffin lies the body of Peter Genaro. Father Peter Genaro. He was my friend. He was my counselor. He was, perhaps, the best man I have ever known. He was everything you could ask for in a priest. He was wise and loving, gentle and compassionate, strong, courageous and full of life. He was a true disciple of Jesus.

"But on Saturday night, he was brutally stabbed to death, and now his mangled body lies in that casket, and we are grieved. And it may seem to you that evil has triumphed. It may seem to you that evil always triumphs, that the exploiters and the terrorists, the people with bombs and guns, the ones without pity and without mercy always win, and that good men and women—the people who love and serve each other, the people who want to feed the hungry and clothe the naked—always lose. You may think, without even realizing it, that Peter Genaro lost just because of the way he spent the last few moments of his life.

"Well, let me set the record straight. Let me tell you a little bit about Peter. He was a man whose cup was filled until it ran over and filled other cups. He was a man who changed lives—for the better. He changed my life. At a very critical point in my life, he taught me what was real and what was important, and he introduced me to the transforming power of God's love. He changed a lot of people's lives." The priest paused for a moment as if caught up in a memory, and then he continued.

"There is a story that Peter told me once that I want to pass along to you. Peter and his father were very close. They were great pals. But in the late fall of Peter's senior year in high school, about a month before Christmas, Peter's father had a heart attack and he died. There was no warning. In the morning Peter had a father, and that night he didn't. Well, Peter was devastated. He was deeply hurt, and he was very angry. He was angry with his father for dying, and he was angry with God for letting him die. He became disinterested in life. He didn't care about school or sports. He didn't care about anything. His mother was worried, his teachers and friends were worried, but he didn't care.

"Until one spring morning as he was leaving for school and he saw some tulips sprouting up in front of his house. About a week before he died, his father had planted those bulbs with a good deal of delight— relishing his hopes for spring. When Peter saw the tulips, it was as if he saw his father because those tulips were a sign that somehow his father was still present in his life and that his father's love transcended the grave. His father had planted tulip bulbs in the ground, but he had also planted seeds in Peter, seeds of love and wisdom, compassion and dedication, seeds which, like those tulips, sprang up and produced wonderful fruit—a hundred-fold.

"So on that spring morning, Peter realized that even though good people die, their goodness doesn't. It continues on after them. That was true of Peter's father, it is true of Peter," Father O'Donnell said. His eyes roamed over the congregation almost as if he were trying to make eye contact with each person there.

"And so the good lives after him," the priest continued, "but what about Peter? Well, if all there is to Peter is that poor body lying in the casket—if this is all there is—a world where success is measured by power and self-gratification—then Peter was a foolish man because he thought of others rather than himself. But I tell you this, and I tell it to you with certainty; Peter has come into his inheritance, he has found reality at last. Even as we struggle with our sorrow, he has found freedom and joy. I tell you this from the deep knowledge of my heart: Jesus Christ is the savior of men. And God knows we need a savior. Jesus Christ is the savior of Peter Genaro. And he has saved him, and that, for Peter, is all that matters."

Father O'Donnell paused to allow the congregation to digest his words, and then he continued.

"Peter Genaro was a good man. I know because he was my friend. When I needed someone to turn to, I turned to Peter. He was understanding and compassionate. He was wise, forgiving and good. He was a man whose energy was fueled by love.

"When you leave this church today, mourn a world in which goodness is murdered by evil, where arrogance and pride are virtues and compassion and humility are signs of weakness. Mourn a society which cannot hear the message of Jesus Christ, a lost world which does not wish to be saved. But do not mourn Peter. In a world of darkness, he clung to the light, and the light has seen him through. He has finished the race. He has won the crown. And the very evil which sought to destroy him, has instead caused him to step through the doorway of eternal life. So now, we can say with Paul, 'O death, where is your victory? Death, where is your sting?' "

The church was still as the priest left the pulpit and took his seat among an altar full of priests. The cardinal sat in a throne-like oak chair behind the altar. He was a personable looking man in his fifties whose gentle manner was offset by hard, probing eyes. His gaze had measured Father O'Donnell throughout the eulogy, and now as the congregation meditated on the priest's words, Fitzsimmons thought he could read approval on the cardinal's face.

After several minutes of silence, three priests rose and began preparing the altar for the cardinal, who was the principal celebrant, to continue the Mass. As they did so the organ began to play. It was joined by a children's choir singing the Panis Angelicus.

The music brought Fitzsimmons back to the Long Island funeral, and he was lost somewhere between the present and the past for the rest of the Mass. When the casket was rolled down the aisle past him, he came out of his reverie, and he realized that he had experienced three funerals that morning, Peter's and Sarah's and Eileen's. He had been too numbed four years earlier to experience his wife's and daughter's funeral, but the experience had been stored away in an unconscious part of his memory, and it had surfaced during Peter's funeral, and as it surfaced it healed.

During the Mass, he underwent a final catharsis. He remembered and he loved, without pain and without anger and without despair. He saw Sarah very clearly, not as a dead and brutalized victim, but as a beautiful, young girl with thin, blond hair and wide, green eyes, smiling and reaching for him. And he saw Eileen as a warm and loving woman, with a tenderness in her eyes and a touch of sorrow, but also smiling. He had a feeling that both Sarah and Eileen were present, that they had an objective reality and that they had acquired a wisdom which was superior to his and that they understood and accepted joyfully what he did not. As he stepped into the aisle to leave the church, Fitzsimmons felt at peace. It was as though Peter was with him, assuring him that everything was all right.

It wasn't until he was almost to the door that he noticed Sarz, who was shuffling down the aisle, deep in thought. Fitzsimmons had never before seen Sarz's face in an unguarded moment. He looked shaken and troubled. Their eyes met, but Sarz was so deep in his own reflections that at first he did not recognize Fitzsimmons. When he did, his face stiffened and he turned his head away without acknowledging him.

It was the only time Fitzsimmons had ever felt that he and Sarz shared a common humanity. For the next week, the memory of the look on Sarz's face consoled Fitzsimmons. For the first time he had seen the crack in Sarz's armor. The man was vulnerable—to what, Fitzsimmons did not know—but Sarz was vulnerable. Fitzsimmons had seen the doubt and misgiving in his face.

CHAPTER TWENTY SEVEN

AFTER THE FUNERAL, THEY DECIDED TO GO AWAY FOR A FEW DAYS. Fitzsimmons called Barbara Wright at TPI and told her that he, Karen and Amy were going to Long Island for a visit. He rented a car, but they did not go to Long Island. Instead, after Fitzsimmons made certain that they were not being followed, he drove onto the Southeast Expressway and headed for Cape Cod. They had stayed in Falmouth on their first visit, and this time they wanted to go farther out to a less populated area. They did not make motel reservations, deciding to leave it to chance where they would stay.

After they crossed Cape Cod Canal on the Sagamore Bridge, they took Route 6 to the Hyannis exit. They were surprised by what they found. Hyannis might as well have been a city. Its streets were crowded with cars, its sidewalks with people, and bars and motels were everywhere. They didn't even stop. They followed Route 28 along the coast through Dennis Port, Chatham and Orleans until it ended, and they found themselves back on Route 6 driving next to a bay where dozens of sailboats raced under the light blue sky.

"This is really where the National Seashore begins," a woman at the Eastham tourist information center told them. "In fact, the Visitor Center for the Cape Cod National Seashore is just down Route 6 about a mile and a half. You'll like it. They have bike trails and hiking trails, they even have a walk for blind people. And if you like the ocean, you'll really love this whole area. We have the real ocean. Up cape, at Hyannis and Falmouth they call it ocean but it's really the Nantucket Sound. From here to Provincetown you have one long ocean beach on the east side of the cape and one long bay beach on the west side of the cape."

They found a motel on Route 6 not far from the Visitor Center. They put their bags in the room and began to explore immediately. The woman was right. It was lovely. As they drove to the ocean they passed along miles of open fields dotted with scrub pine and oak and cedar. The beach stretched as far as they could see. The pounding white surf roared and broke over the smooth yellow sand. People crowded into the foaming surf and some swam out past the breakers. But thirty yards out the ocean was empty to the horizon except for a few fishing boats.

The sun seemed much brighter and its rays much warmer than it had in Boston, and, as they threaded their way through the blankets, beach towels, and umbrellas, the three were conscious of being very pale while everyone else on the beach seemed either tanned or sunburned. Although the beach was crowded near the parking lot, they found that by walking a few hundred yards they escaped the throng and had an area largely to themselves.

Karen and Amy walked down to test the temperature of the water, and Fitzsimmons spread a blanket and stretched out. The sun was strong and warm on his bare back as he felt its therapeutic rays soak into the muscles in his shoulders and neck.

"You coming in?" Amy asked.

"Later," he answered without opening his eyes. "First I have to let my skin get hot."

"Okay. We'll be waiting for you."

After a few minutes, Fitzsimmons' mind was cleared of any thoughts. His only consciousness was of the sun and the luxurious feeling it gave his body. Then, slowly a cloud came into his mind. At first he ignored it, but as it took shape he found that he had to focus on it. What he saw was Sarz's face as he was leaving the church, that face in an unguarded moment. What was in it, Fitzsimmons wondered, as he strove to read Sarz's expression. Was it fear? Was it sorrow?

Fitzsimmons concentrated with all his power on that face. Still he could not fathom its expression. Something was going on inside of Sarz, but Fitzsimmons could not tell what. He jumped up and joined Amy and Karen at the edge of the surf. He did not want to think about Sarz if he could avoid it.

They came back to the beach that night after they had dined at a steak house in Orleans. The ocean was calm, almost still, and the moon hung low over the water, cutting a golden swath through the sea. Amy had taken off her sneakers and was walking ahead of them. Down the beach about a hundred yards a group of people was gathered around a fire.

"This is really marvelous," Karen said. She held his hand and smiled.

"Mmm," Fitzsimmons said. "There's something mysterious about the ocean. It's so vast and it has its own rules. It does what it wants. When we were here this afternoon, I was thinking how puny we are. Here's this huge ocean thousands of miles wide and thousands of miles long, and here's a thousand people dipping their toes in its edge. And if there were a storm they wouldn't even do that. And if there were a very bad storm it would be dangerous just to be on this beach."

"It's like you never know about things," Karen said. "Something so beautiful and nice can turn into something fierce and dangerous. Sometimes I think the whole world and everything in it is like that."

"Everything?"

"Just about," she said and let go of his hand.

"You? Me?" Fitzsimmons asked.

"I don't know. I think we can change. We start off to be one thing and we end up being something else. Look at Todd. He started out wanting to be a lawyer and a husband and a father and he ended up being a bum. You started out to be a college professor and you end up working in a factory for the handicapped. And I wanted to be a nurse and a mother, someone who was strong and effective, and I turned out to be a frightened runner."

"The last chapter hasn't been written yet," Fitzsimmons said.

"I know, and I'm afraid of what it will say."

Fitzsimmons turned from the ocean and faced her. He took her hands in his. "It will say that in a very difficult time we had the good sense to love each other. That we faced the storm together."

"And we got dragged under by the waves?"

"Maybe," Fitzsimmons said. "But there are worse things."

"Like what?"

"Like letting fear destroy our love. Like turning away from each other." They looked back at the ocean. "I've been thinking a lot about Peter."

"So have I," Karen said.

"Whatever happened in his study, I know that Peter died being Peter. He wasn't intimidated. Whatever fear he had he overcame, and he wasn't compromised by evil. He didn't bow to it or beg from it, and he didn't become infected by it. That's what upset me after I attacked Sarz. His evil was infecting me. I was becoming like him. I was using violence and hatred. Peter didn't do that. I'm sure of it. And I'm not going to do that any more. I am not going to become like Sarz. I would rather die than be like Sarz."

Karen listened, but she did not answer.

"I am not going to change," Fitzsimmons said. "I am not going to be calm and loving one moment and turbulent and dangerous the next. Whatever happens, Karen, I'm going to be a decent human being."

"I know that," she said.

"Good, because I love you, and I want to marry you."

Karen looked up at him with eyes which held both tenderness and anguish.

They stood in silence. Amy ran back and forth along the water's edge. After a while she stopped and looked at them, and then she ran over to them.

"What's up?" she asked.

"What makes you think something's up?" Karen answered.

"I can tell by the look on your faces."

"We're just trying to decide some things," Karen said, and she turned away from them and began to walk up the beach.

Amy took Fitzsimmons' hand as they began to follow about ten yards behind her. For a while they walked in silence, feeling the sea air on their faces and listening to their feet crunch the sand.

"Were you talking about getting married?" Amy asked.

Fitzsimmons smiled.

Amy squeezed his hand. "Were you?"

Fitzsimmons laughed. "You don't miss a thing, do you?"

Karen heard Fitzsimmons laugh and stopped to allow them to catch up. As she waited she looked out at the ocean. There was a sad, gentle smile on her face, a pale echo of Fitzsimmons' laugh, and she seemed to Fitzsimmons to be far away. Behind her, the lighthouse sent its signal out to sea: two white beams and one red, two white beams and one red. The signal was unvarying and true. Sailors could see it and know exactly where they were, where the danger lay, and how to avoid it.

"That must be a comfort to them," Fitzsimmons thought.

The next day they went to Nauset Beach in Orleans. The sun was bright and hot. The sky was a faint blue, and the surf was rough and surging white. There was no haze or clouds. Everything was clear and sharp. Out near the horizon a schooner with bright, clean sails moved slowly across the sea. The beach was crowded and, it seemed to Fitzsimmons, mostly with attractive women. He had forgotten what beaches were like, all the bronzed bellies and the long legs, and Fitzsimmons enjoyed the freedom which allowed him to be a casual voyeur. There was something delightful about being surrounded by so many attractive bodies.

They walked for almost two hundred yards before the crowd began to thin out and they found a comfortable spot for the blanket. The three were still pink while most of the other people on the beach were tanned. Karen's mood had changed. During the morning, the aura of sadness had left her, and she no longer seemed distant. She wore a yellow bikini and paid no attention to the glances she received as they walked down the beach.

"You'd better be careful. You could get a bad burn today," she said to Fitzsimmons as he lay down on the blanket.

"If I fall asleep, turn me over every fifteen minutes," he said.

It was luxurious, feeling the sun's rays massage his body. He closed his eyes and he felt a wonderful sense of security and peace. Karen poured suntan lotion on his back and began to work it into his skin, and he was filled with a warm sensuousness. He let out a soft grunt.

"You like that?"

"I'll like it better tonight."

"Oh yeah? How are we going to manage that?" They had rented one room with twin beds and a cot which Amy slept on.

"Love will find a way," Fitzsimmons said.

Karen smiled. "I hope so," she said.

That night Amy found a new friend, and she went with the girl and the girl's parents to play miniature golf. Karen and Fitzsimmons were invited but they begged off. The other couple, who seemed friendly and knowing, made it clear in their strong New Jersey accents, that they would not press the issue. Karen and Fitzsimmons experienced an exhilaration that comes only with freedom. They were alone, Amy was safe, and no one knew where they were. Being in the motel room was like being on a deserted island. They were free to love without fear, without anxiety and without interruption. It was splendid.

Later when they were dressed and waiting for Amy to return, Karen asked, "Do you mind having a nine-year-old around all the time?"

"Not at all," Fitzsimmons said.

"You want to marry a woman with baggage?"

"Amy's not baggage. The parallel must have occurred to you, too. I wouldn't tell her this because I think it would put her off, but finding Amy is a bit like finding Sarah. She's a lovely young girl. She's bright, she's friendly, she's unspoiled. In her own way, and without knowing it, she has done as much to restore me to the human race as Peter or you have."

"She thinks the world of you, John."

"It's mutual," he said.

Fitzsimmons awoke before sunrise. Amy was asleep on the cot, and Karen was sleeping in the other bed. He lay still, wondering what had awakened him. He tried to remember what he had been dreaming about, and then it came to him. He had been dreaming about Sarz, and at once he saw Sarz's face with the expression it wore as they were leaving St. Camillus. What did it mean? What had been going on inside of Sarz? Fitzsimmons pondered that face with its troubled expression for what seemed like a long time.

"Maybe something happened. Maybe it's over," Fitzsimmons thought, and he rolled over and went back to sleep.

It was a recurring thought during the next few days. He didn't mention it to Karen, but from time to time as they were enjoying the late summer sun, Fitzsimmons would gaze up at the clear sky or stare out to sea and he would think, "Maybe it's over. Maybe it's all over."

It was just a few days short of September when they came back to Boston. Here and there a leaf had already turned color, the Red Sox were preparing for a home series with the Yankees which would make or break their pennant hopes, and the city and Beacon Hill were once more filling up with students. Commonwealth Avenue, especially, showed that the fall semester was beginning. Fraternity flags rustled in the late August breeze, and students seemed to be everywhere carrying books and boxes and furniture. They awakened an excitement in Fitzsimmons. He found that he could remember campus life without the sting of tragedy blocking all its joy, and he decided he might like to try his hand again at teaching. Before going back to work, he visited Boston University, Northeastern and Boston College. He was not looking to join a faculty full time. He just wanted to teach a course or two, perhaps a seminar course. His credentials were excellent, and even with a layoff of four years, the deans he spoke with at the schools were interested—not, of course, for the fall semester, it was too late for that, but they were interested. Fitzsimmons told them he would even be willing to teach a night school course, and they all seemed anxious to accommodate him.

The joy that Fitzsimmons had seen in Karen's face while they were on the Cape disappeared when they returned to Boston. She became quiet again and seemed to detach from him.

He was filled with enthusiasm when he told her about his job prospects, but her own enthusiasm was muted.

"I'm glad," she said, after studying his face for a moment, but he could see that returning to his profession was no longer the issue it once was.

"You know, I may teach a course and find out that I really don't want to go back to it," he told her.

"That's all right. I know you're not going to sweep floors much longer."

"How do you know that?"

"I just know," she said. "Aren't I right?"

"Yes," he said, "you're right."

She was right, and Fitzsimmons did not really understand it. Something had changed inside of him, and he traced it back to Peter's funeral. There was an irony in it. He loved Peter, and he missed him, and he knew that as time passed he would probably miss him more.

But he had not been devastated by his death as he had by the deaths of his wife and daughter. Instead, something within Fitzsimmons had been healed. He had turned a corner, and he had a longing to participate again, to do something, to be of service.

Perhaps it had something to do with the parable of the tulips, Fitzsimmons thought. He suspected that Peter had planted in him things of which he was still unaware. Indeed, he was just beginning to understand that Peter's importance in his life had gone beyond mere friendship. The priest had restored in Fitzsimmons an awareness of goodness. He could no longer believe that there was only evil and disinterest in the world. Peter was proof that there was goodness. The priest had helped bring Fitzsimmons out of his inner blackness, not so much by anything he had said but by his attitude and his approach to life. Peter embraced life. He believed that it had intrinsic significance, and he believed that a true human being was defined by love and by nothing else. For Peter life itself was a gift, something to be savored and cherished, something to be embraced and not something to flee from. Peter had accepted life without qualification and without condition. He thought it was as wonderful to live on the bad days as it was to live on the good. Fitzsimmons was sure that the priest had maintained that conviction even when he was being attacked and killed.

"Can I accept it all?" Fitzsimmons asked himself. "Can I accept murder and insanity as part of the price of living?" He did not answer the question because he did not know the answer to the question. He knew now that to truly accept life one must accept evil as well as goodness. It was mysterious, perhaps beyond comprehension, but it was so. Peter, by his own example if not by words, had taught him that he could never be really happy unless he said 'yes' to everything—to death, disease, anxiety, fear, pain, defeat, love, health, hope, happiness and triumph.

That night as Fitzsimmons lay in bed he remembered a scene from his childhood.

"The trouble with getting a dog is it's going to die," his father had told him when he was a young boy. "Do you still want a dog even though you know it may get run over? And even if it doesn't, sooner or later it will die."

"I still want one," Fitzsimmons had said.

After three years, the dog was run over by a truck. Fitzsimmons was heartbroken.

"Do you want to have a wife even though she may get butchered? And even if she doesn't, your relationship will end either in death or divorce? Do you still want to marry her?" In his imagination, it was his father's voice asking a variant of the question he had asked so many years ago.

"Do you want to live?" This time it was Peter's voice. "Are you ready to try life again?"

He pictured Karen sleeping in her apartment, her black hair against the pillow, her light, steady breathing. She had been silent on the subject of marriage since he mentioned it on the beach, and he had not raised the question again.

He was ready. He was not sure if she was.

The week passed quietly. His mailbox had been empty when they returned from the Cape, and it was empty when he checked it each day. The newspaper clippings had stopped. Fitzsimmons saw very little of Sarz. When they did meet, in the hall or on the staircase, they barely nodded to each other and never spoke. Even so, Fitzsimmons was convinced that something had happened to Sarz to change him. The malice was gone from his eyes; the taunting look had disappeared from his face. Now he looked introspective and troubled. Despite himself, Fitzsimmons felt a bit of compassion for Sarz, and the feeling puzzled him. How could he feel compassion for the man he believed killed Peter?

On Friday, Fitzsimmons learned that Sarz had quit. Sarz had called Barbara Wright at the office that morning and told her that he was finished. He gave no notice and offered no explanation. Fitzsimmons was delighted with the news, and as he made his rounds that night, he found himself singing aloud.

It was a quiet week at home, too. They were marking time on Beacon Hill. Waiting. They never talked about what they were waiting for, but they were waiting. In his heart Fitzsimmons knew he was waiting for enough time to pass so that he cold be sure it was really over. He knew that Karen did not share his optimism. She, too, was waiting, but she was waiting for her fear to be vindicated.

CHAPTER TWENTY EIGHT

IT WAS NOT OVER. FITZSIMMONS KNEW THAT AS SOON AS HE HEARD the knock on the door early Saturday morning.

Karen stood in the hall, half-asleep, wrapping herself in her bathrobe. He looked at his watch. It was 6:30.

"There's somebody on the telephone who says it's important that he talk to you."

Fitzsimmons did not bother to go back to the bedroom for his slippers. He walked barefoot across the hall and into Karen's apartment.

"This is it," the voice said.

"This is what?" Fitzsimmons responded.

Karen was leaning against her bedroom door just waiting for the conversation to end so that she could go back to sleep.

"This is the end of our confrontation." Fitzsimmons recognized the voice as Sarz's.

"You mean it's over?" Fitzsimmons asked. It was an asinine question. He knew it was not over. But the words came out anyway.

"Almost. Not quite. There's just one more thing."

"What's that?"

"It's fairly drastic," Sarz said. "I don't think you're ready to hear it."

"Are you drunk?" Fitzsimmons asked.

"No. I'm not drunk. I've had a few. Just enough to keep me warm. Fire escapes can be chilly on late August nights."

"Why don't you go to bed and let me go back to sleep?" Fitzsimmons said.

"You're not paying attention, you asshole. Don't you listen?"

Fitzsimmons' mind went back to Sarz's last sentence. "Fire escape," he thought.

"Listen? I'm listening," he said.

"I was on her fire escape last night, for a long time. I had a couple of pops while I was waiting."

"Waiting for what?"

"Waiting to grab the little girl."

Fitzsimmons could feel the panic being unleashed inside of him.

"Grab what girl?"

"You asshole," Sarz said. "What girl do you think? The one you take out to breakfast on Saturday mornings."

Fitzsimmons dropped the telephone and bolted across the room and opened the door to Amy's bedroom. Her bed was empty and her window was wide open.

"What's wrong, John? What's going on?" Karen called after him.

"Oh, God," Fitzsimmons said. "Oh, God."

"John. What's the matter?"

"Sarz has Amy."

Karen's face filled with terror. "What?" she screamed, running to the bedroom.

Fitzsimmons had become very pale. His body swayed as if he were about to faint.

"Sarz took Amy. He snuck up the fire escape last night and kidnapped her," he said.

Karen's eyes were wild. She ran past Fitzsimmons to the window and looked out onto the fire escape.

"Oh, my God," she echoed. "Oh my God."

Fitzsimmons went back to the living room and picked the telephone off the floor.

"Why have you done this?" he asked.

"That's not the question," Sarz said.

Fitzsimmons let the hand which held the receiver drop to his side.

He felt utterly helpless, frustrated, defeated. He put the phone back to his ear.

"What is the question?" he asked.

"The question is, what do you have to do to get her back?"

"All right. What do I have to do?"

"You have to make a sacrifice," Sarz said.

"What sacrifice?"

"The ultimate sacrifice," Sarz said.

Fitzsimmons was silent.

"Did you hear me?" Sarz asked.

Fitzsimmons shook his head.

"Are you there, you asshole?" Sarz shouted.

Fitzsimmons felt the old madness beginning to stir within him, but he fought it back. "I'm here," he answered.

"Well, then, let's understand each other. This is the situation. I have the little girl, and I can do whatever I like with her. You understand that, don't you? And you understand the kind of things I like to do, don't you?"

Fitzsimmons was silent.

"I've told you what I do to little girls. I'm not sure you believed me. But I bet you believe me now, don't you?" Sarz's voice was sharp, his tone taunting.

"I believe you," Fitzsimmons said.

"That's good. Now as I see it, you have two alternatives. You can walk away and do nothing and let me amuse myself with her, or you can do what I want you to do and save her."

"What do you want me to do?"

"I thought I already mentioned that," Sarz said. "I want you to give your life for hers. Isn't that what ultimate sacrifice means, English professor?"

"How can I do that?" he asked quietly. He looked up. Karen was leaning with her back against the wall staring at him with horror-filled eyes.

"I already told you. Kill yourself."

Fitzsimmons was silent.

"You don't have to do it this moment. I'll give you some time to think it over. Let's see. This is Saturday, and it's a few minutes after six. You can have until nine o'clock Sunday night. But if you're not dead by then I will amuse myself with the girl. Incidentally, you might not want to wait all that time. She's pretty frightened. Shitting her little pink panties."

Sarz paused and when Fitzsimmons did not respond, he said, "Well?"

Fitzsimmons felt a flood of rage and despair, and he felt that he was about to be swept away by the turbulence inside of him, but he maintained his exterior calm. "What is this going to accomplish?"

"It will balance things out," Sarz said. "Either way it will balance things out."

"How?"

"One way or the other you will be destroyed. Either you will destroy yourself to save the girl, as you should have destroyed yourself four years ago, or you will do nothing, and the knowledge that you permitted me to debase her and kill her will destroy you."

"Why are you doing this? What are you going to get out of it?" Fitzsimmons asked.

"Justice. Vindication. Satisfaction."

"Justice?" Fitzsimmons throat was tight and the word squeaked through. "Justice?" he could barely speak the word.

"That's right. Justice. You can't understand it, but that's what I want. Justice. My justice. It will be a judgment."

"Against whom?"

"Against God," Sarz said. "I will break you. I will destroy you, and I will say to God, 'Look at all you've given him. Money, education, family. And look at the shit you have given me. A whore for a mother and a sailor for a father. A queer for a priest and a jail cell for a home. And he broke and I didn't. I never broke.' "

"You broke," Fitzsimmons said.

"Never," Sarz said.

"You were broken beyond repair a long time ago."

"Fuck you. You sound like that priest."

"My friend? Peter?"

"Yeah."

"You didn't break him," Fitzsimmons said.

"I slashed the son of a bitch right into eternity."

"But you didn't break him. You may have killed him, but you didn't break him. You didn't crush him."

"No," Sarz agreed. "But I'll break you."

Fitzsimmons said nothing.

"Now listen to me. I told you I killed the priest because I wanted you to know that. I killed him right in front of those holy pictures. Right in front of the Pope and the Cardinal and the Blessed Virgin. And I killed the old one, too. And then I used his shower and changed my clothes and threw my bloody clothes and the knife away.

"If you want any other details, I'll be happy to give them to you, because I want you to understand that I did indeed kill those priests. And I want you to understand that I have indeed killed children. Not girls. Boys. Lots of them that nobody ever missed. Not their parents or their friends. Not anybody. And I want you to know these things because I want you to believe that I will do exactly what I say I will do to this girl, and that the only way you can protect her is to sacrifice your life for her.

" 'Greater love hath no man than that he give up his life for his friends.' That's what you're going to do. And you are going to do it by nine o'clock Sunday so that I'll be able to see it on the eleven o'clock news. That means you are going to have to do it in a fairly spectacular fashion. You can immolate yourself on the Common. You can blow your brains out in front of the Shubert Theatre. I really don't care how you do it. Just do it.

"Are you still there?"

"I'm still here," Fitzsimmons said.

"Then let's be clear on one other thing. I am never going to be arrested. I am never going to spend another minute in a jail cell. That means if the police come looking for me the girl dies. If I just think they're coming for me, she's dead. Do you understand that?"

"I understand."

"Good. I'll look forward to the news."

"How can I be sure that you'll let Amy go?"

"You can't. You'll just have to trust me."

"How can I be sure you haven't killed her already?"

Sarz thought for a moment. "I'll call you tonight and let you talk to her."

Sarz hung up, and Fitzsimmons stood holding the telephone. He turned to Karen and he looked into her eyes expecting to see blame there, but he did not.

"He'll call tonight and let us speak to Amy," Fitzsimmons said.

"What does he want?"

"He wants me to kill myself."

"What are you saying?"

"He says the price to get Amy back is me. He wants me to kill myself by nine P.M. Sunday or he'll kill Amy."

"John, that's insane. It's … it's … "

"Diabolical," Fitzsimmons said.

"What are we going to do?"

"I don't know."

The telephone receiver had begun to emit annoying beeps. Karen reached for it.

"Don't call the police. He said he'll kill her if the police come after him, and I believe him."

She dropped the receiver back on the bed. It continued to beep.

"Then who can we call?"

"Nobody," Fitzsimmons said. He picked the receiver up and placed it gently back on its cradle.

"We've got to get help," Karen said. "There must be somebody we can call. There must be somebody we can turn to."

Fitzsimmons shook his head.

"If only Peter were still alive," Karen said.

"Sarz said he was the one who killed him."

"I knew it," Karen said. "I knew it. And I knew it was directed at you."

Fitzsimmons nodded.

"Is Amy going to die, John?"

Fitzsimmons took her hand in his. She looked terrified and vulnerable, her eyes were submissive and pained. She looked as if she expected to be struck

"No," he said. "Amy won't die."

Relief flooded her face, but only for an instant. "And you, John?"

"I don't know," Fitzsimmons said. "A year ago if I had been told I could help somebody by committing suicide I would have jumped off the nearest bridge. We'll do something."

"Something?"

Fitzsimmons saw the anger and the despair change Karen's expression. He wanted to comfort her and he wanted to give her assurance, and he knew the best way that he could do that was by remaining calm. So he maintained a calm exterior. But inside he was not calm. Inside, he felt himself drawn to the edge of madness. His brain was screaming, but it was so loud and so screeching that he could not understand what it was saying. He walked over to the window. "Hold on," he said to himself. "Hold on."

"John. She's with that man right now. What's he going to do to her?"

"Nothing," Fitzsimmons said without turning from the window.

"How do you know?"

"He has a thing for little boys, not girls. He told me." Fitzsimmons heard the words come out, calmly and logically. They seemed disassociated from him. "Is that me speaking?" he asked himself. He felt waves of terror pounding inside his brain.

He turned from the window and almost stumbled.

"John," Karen said with alarm.

He put his hand to his forehead. "I'm okay."

She went to him and led him to a chair.

"John," she said again.

He looked up but he did not answer. The screaming inside of him had grown louder. He had never experienced such inner chaos, even when he found his wife and daughter. He was now sure he was going mad, and that within moments he would be lost inside of himself.

"Oh, God," he said.

Karen took his hand in hers. "It will be all right," she said.

"Oh, God," he said again, his voice rising and becoming shrill. "God, help me."

He leaned back in the chair and closed his eyes. His lips were clenched and his face was twisted in agony. Karen's troubled eyes rested on his face for an instant and then darted around the room as if looking for an escape. There was none. She looked back at Fitzsimmons and her face mirrored the agony in his. She dropped his hand.

"I'm going to put on some coffee," she said. She turned to leave the room.

"Jesus," Fitzsimmons whispered. "Jesus. Jesus. Jesus."

Karen hesitated, not knowing if Fitzsimmons was even aware of her presence, and then she went into the kitchen.

Fitzsimmons stopped trying to fight the rush of madness within him. Instead he let his body and his mind go limp. At first his body jerked, but then it relaxed and as it did, the screaming in his mind softened and very slowly he felt the chaos drain out of him, until all he heard was the echo of his prayer, "Jesus. Jesus. Jesus."

CHAPTER TWENTY NINE

FOR SEVERAL MINUTES AFTER SHE ENTERED THE KITCHEN, KAREN stood by the sink without moving. She was paralyzed by her own fear and by an implacable sense of helplessness. She was filled with panic and uncertainty and her mind was besieged by wave after wave of emotion—anger followed by fear followed by anxiety. She wanted to take immediate action, to do something to get Amy back, but there seemed to be nothing she could do. Tears streamed down her cheeks, but she made no sound.

After a while, still crying, she loaded coffee and water into the coffee maker, turned it on, and started toward the living room, but she stopped and walked back to the sink without looking through the doorway. She could not bring herself to look. She could not bear to see that distracted expression on Fitzsimmons' face—the same expression he had worn the night she first met him, when he stepped into her apartment and discovered that a robbery had been in progress. Then she had not been bothered by that look, but now she knew what it meant. It meant that Fitzsimmons was shaken to the very core of his being, that he was emotionally overwhelmed, that he was incapable of dealing with what was going on. Her husband had looked like that before he was fired from his law firm. The look indicated more than weakness; it indicated a broken spirit.

It was always this way. At decisive moments, the men she had known were crippled. Her husband and her father by alcoholism, and now Fitzsimmons by the violent shadows of his past. They had never been there. Never. When she needed help, when she needed strength they collapsed, and if she tried to rally them, they turned their wrath on her. It was always hopeless, always futile. Nothing could be done. She had no weapons. She could only be silent and avert her eyes. She wanted to scream, to run into the other room and club Fitzsimmons, to beat him into action. But Karen, too, was crippled, by a lifetime of showing no reaction, by a lifetime of keeping silent and averting her eyes.

She began to sob. Amy had been kidnapped, and Fitzsimmons was helpless. Something had to be done, if Fitzsimmons could not do anything, then she would have to act. She grabbed a dish towel, wiped her face, and turned to go into the living room.

Fitzsimmons had already stepped into the kitchen. He appeared to have recovered himself. The distracted expression was gone. Instead, he seemed calm.

"Don't call the police," he said, anticipating her intention. "They can't help us."

There was color in his face. He seemed to have returned to normal.

"We can't do anything alone," she said.

"Yes we can. We're not helpless," Fitzsimmons said. "We'll find Sarz."

Karen's face betrayed her disbelief. "How?" she asked.

"We'll start by going to his apartment. And if he isn't there, and I don't think he is, we'll track him down from there."

"And if we find him? What then?"

"We'll get Amy back," Fitzsimmons said.

"How?"

"Any way we have to."

Karen was not affected by Fitzsimmons' sudden confidence. "John, let's call the police," she said.

"If you want to do it, then do it. In the short run it will make things easier. We can escape responsibility. We can give this burden to the police and let them do what they have to do. But if we call the police, I know that Sarz will kill Amy. It's that simple. Something has happened to him. I don't know what, but he's changed. I think he sees this as an ending. I think he's ready to die. I think he may even want to die."

"But first he wants you to die, too," she said.

"Yes, he does. He wants to annihilate me, and then he wants to mock me."

Karen stared at Fitzsimmons as if she had been hypnotized.

"I would sacrifice myself for Amy. I would die so that she could live. But I can't kill myself. Even if I could and I took my own life it would mean complete victory for him and utter defeat for me. I know that he would kill Amy just to make sure that my death was meaningless."

Karen sat down at the table and rested her head in her hands.

"I don't know what to do," she said.

Fitzsimmons reached out and touched her shoulder, and Karen began to sob.

"First, the two of us are going to accept the responsibility for getting Amy back. We are not going to call the police. Second, we are going to locate Sarz. And third, we're going to bring Amy home."

Karen looked up. She had stopped crying. "Do you really think we can do that?"

"Yes. Sarz is not invincible. We'll find him."

"But suppose we can't?"

"If we have no hope of finding Sarz, we'll go to the police," Fitzsimmons said.

"Suppose we just call the police now and tell them what's going on and ask them to wait until tonight or tomorrow morning before they do anything?"

"Do you think they'd wait?" Fitzsimmons asked.

"No," Karen answered. "And you're right. He will kill her. Do you really think we can save Amy?"

"I know we can. I know we're going to."

Fitzsimmons took a cup of coffee back to his apartment to drink while he shaved and dressed. When he returned to Karen's apartment, the thought of food crossed his mind, but Fitzsimmons had no appetite.

"I want to rent a car and go to his apartment," Fitzsimmons said.

"Wait for me. I'll go with you."

As Karen was getting dressed Fitzsimmons drank another cup of coffee, and by the time she came into the kitchen the knot was gone from his stomach. It was replaced by hunger. He found a couple of bagels in the refrigerator and wolfed them down.

It was almost nine by the time they drove out of the car rental agency on Stewart Street. Fitzsimmons drove through the light rain directly to Hyde Park, and without much trouble found Sarz's street. He drove past the house and parked about fifty yards away. They sat watching the house and listening to the rain strike the roof of the car. There was no activity on the street except for an occasional passing car. After about fifteen minutes, a car stopped and a stout woman in her late fifties got out and went into the house. No one came out.

"We can't sit here all day," Fitzsimmons said. "I'm going to go check his apartment."

"I'm coming," Karen said.

The mailbox with Sarz's name on it said apartment 1C. Without knowing why, Fitzsimmons was surprised that Sarz's apartment was on the first floor. He had unconsciously expected it to be on an upper floor. Fitzsimmons tried the front door and found it was unlocked. The long, dark hallway was lined with soiled wallpaper. It had a faintly foul odor as if the walls had absorbed the smells of hundreds of sweating, unwashed bodies as they went in and out of the apartments. Fitzsimmons and Karen followed the hall toward the rear of the building until they came to the door to Sarz's apartment. It was wide open. Fitzsimmons knocked, and the woman whom they had seen enter the house earlier came out of the bedroom and walked over to the door.

"You want something?" she asked.

"We're looking for the guy who lives here," Fitzsimmons said.

"Are you friends of his?"

"No," Fitzsimmons said.

"Well, thank God for that," the woman replied. "He is a strange one," she said, pointing to the picture of the SS officer.

"He sure is," Fitzsimmons said. "He's got something that belongs to us, and we're trying to find him and get it back."

"Well, he's not here now, and I don't know when he's coming back. I'm just the cleaning lady. I don't have anything to do with him except to clean the place once a week."

"Do you know where he went?" Karen asked.

"No. I was just glad that he wasn't here when I came this morning. What's he got of yours?"

"A book. A first edition. One of a kind. It sure would put my mind at ease if I knew it was here."

The woman did not respond.

"Would you mind if we just took a quick look for it?" Karen asked. "We won't take it. We just want to see if it's here."

"What's the book?"

"*The Tragic History of Doctor Faustus* by Christopher Marlowe," Fitzsimmons said.

"What's it look like?"

"It's black and so big," Fitzsimmons said, indicating a width of eight or nine inches with his hands.

"I haven't seen anything like that," the woman said.

"It's probably in his bedroom," Karen said.

"I can take a look, if you want," the woman said.

"Thanks a lot," Fitzsimmons said.

The woman went back into the bedroom. They followed her and stood at the doorway and looked in.

"There's only these on the bed table," she said holding up two paperbacks.

"No," Fitzsimmons said.

"How about under the bed?" Karen asked.

"The only thing he has under the bed is a little, black box that he keeps locked up," the woman answered.

"Well, thanks anyway," Fitzsimmons said.

On the way out, Fitzsimmons took a quick look at the door lock. It was a snap type and not a deadbolt. It would not be difficult to get back inside.

"If I'm still here when he gets back, what do you want me to tell him?" the woman asked.

"Well, if you should see him, tell him that we came for our property and we'll be back later."

"I'll do that," the woman said.

"Thanks."

Karen and Fitzsimmons returned at noon. This time they did not pause at the front door. They went straight in and straight to the door of Sarz's apartment. Fitzsimmons took out a tire iron which he had slid inside of his pants and bent back the molding at the lock. He inserted one of Karen's credit cards and turned the doorknob. The door opened, and they went into the apartment and shut the door behind them. Fitzsimmons found the box underneath the bed and, using the tire iron, he was able to pry it apart. There was not too much in it. There was an old snapshot of a woman smoking a cigarette, a copy of a birth certificate which gave his name as Free B. Sarz, and several newspaper clippings. One announced the resignation of the assistant director of the State Department of Youth Services. Another was a story of the closing of a foster home run by a priest. The priest, who was being sought by police on moral charges involving boys under his care, was believed to have fled the country. The third and last clipping told the story of a man who was killed by police after he shot a guard in a bank holdup.

"I'll bet this is his mother," Fitzsimmons said pointing to the picture. "This foster home is the one where he was seduced by the priest. This guy who was killed must have been a friend of his, and the man who resigned must have been someone he hated or someone whom he liked. If that's possible."

He turned the box upside down and three bullets fell out on the floor.

"That's all. Bullets and no gun. Which probably means he has the gun."

"And nothing else?"

"No," Fitzsimmons said.

"Then we're nowhere," Karen said.

"Perhaps." He went to the closet and looked inside of it. There was nothing in it but clothes.

"He's got to have something else here. Somewhere. He saved all those newspaper clippings he sent me. He's got to have a hiding place."

They went through every inch of the apartment. They took apart the bed, they opened up chair cushions, they emptied the cabinets in the kitchen. They looked in the toilet tank and under the sink. They could find nothing.

"Let's get out of here," Karen said when they had returned to the living room.

"He's a collector. Somewhere in this apartment he's got trophies. I know it."

On an impulse, Fitzsimmons lifted the picture of the SS officer from the cheap paneling which lined the wall to see if there was a compartment behind it. There was not. Only a cloth picture hanger was glued to the paneling, the kind that is used when using a nail is to be avoided.

Fitzsimmons rehung the picture and walked across the room to the picture on the opposite wall. It was a print of Goya's *Saturn Devouring his Son*. A wild-eyed, naked giant held a body in his hands. The head and right arm had already been eaten and the giant was about to bite into the left arm. It was a stark work against a black background. Clearly Goya's later vision was one of horror and the grotesque. Fitzsimmons lifted the painting from the wall. There was nothing behind it except the nail which had been driven into the paneling to hang the picture.

"Why would he use a nail here and go to the trouble of gluing a picture hanger over there?" Fitzsimmons asked aloud.

He went back to the picture of the SS man and took it down again. He pushed the paneling and found it was not snug against the wall. Either it had not been nailed well or it had not been nailed at all. Fitzsimmons took the tire iron and forced the edge of it between the paneling and the piece next to it and tried to pry it away from the wall. It came away surprisingly easily. In a moment the piece, about a foot wide, fell to the floor. It had been held up by double-sided tape. Behind where the picture of the SS officer had hung, there was a hole in the wall and in the hole was another small, metal box. This one was also locked. Fitzsimmons took it out and pried it open. He found a wad of ten dollar bills held together by a rubber band, some newspaper clippings, a half-dozen photographs and a folded piece of paper. Fitzsimmons took out the piece of paper and dumped the rest of the contents on the floor. He unfolded the paper and read aloud from it.

"You found it. You figure it out." It was signed, 'F. B. Sarz.'

The most recent clippings were stories of the murders of the two priests. There were also clippings of stories of missing boys and one, which Fitzsimmons remembered reading, about a boy's body which was found in Dorchester.

"He killed all those people," Karen said.

"Yes."

Fitzsimmons brushed the newspaper clippings to one side and began to examine the photographs. They were mostly pictures of nude boys, sometimes standing or lying alone and sometimes playing with each other. Two of the boys appeared to be sleeping. One stared up from a shallow grave. The last picture was of Tommy Quercio. He was standing against a brick wall and masturbating. He had an impish grin on his face.

"Good grief," Karen said as she looked over Fitzsimmons' shoulder.
"Yeah. Good grief. This one I know. He works at TPI." Fitzsimmons
stood up.

"Is he retarded?" Karen asked.

"Yeah. Sort of."

"That's awful," Karen said, turning away from the picture.

"It's symptomatic. It doesn't surprise me. Sarz feeds on the abnormal. He worships the grotesque."

"I hate this room," Karen said. "I can almost feel his presence here.
It's almost tangible."

Fitzsimmons stuffed the pictures and the clippings back into the
box and closed it.

"I want to get away from here," Karen said.

They left the picture of the anonymous SS man staring up at the
room from where it lay on the floor.

CHAPTER THIRTY

IT WAS STILL RAINING, AND THE CITY SEEMED GRAY, FLAT AND uninviting. The mood inside the car was grim as Fitzsimmons and Karen drove back to Beacon Hill with the metal box lying on the seat between them. Its presence had the same effect upon them as if a third person, an ominous stranger, was sitting in the car, and they were silent for most of the drive. It was only when they were a few blocks from the apartment that Karen broke the silence, at first only to sob.

"I feel like I'm going to break apart, like my mind is going to unravel," she sobbed. "Oh, my God, if I feel this way, how does Amy feel?"

"It will be all right," Fitzsimmons said.

"If only we had someone to help us, someone to appeal to." Karen searched for alternatives. "If only Peter were alive."

Fitzsimmons nodded.

"How can someone be so bad?"

"I don't know," Fitzsimmons said.

"These kinds of things shouldn't happen," she said angrily. "Who allows these kinds of things to happen?"

Fitzsimmons saw the anguish on Karen's face and said nothing, and except for an occasional sob, Karen was silent again until they got to the apartment. Once inside, Karen's despair filled the living room. It was so strong, it was almost palpable, and Fitzsimmons could feel its seductive power, luring him to succumb to it, to embrace it, and to give up.

Instead, he turned the metal box upside down and let its contents fall on the rug. The picture of Tommy Quercio grinned up at him, and Fitzsimmons sat down on the sofa and stared back at it.

"Why don't we have some coffee," Fitzsimmons said, ignoring the aura of Karen's torment. She left the living room without speaking, and Fitzsimmons wondered if, in her distraction, she heard him. He started to get up to follow her but changed his mind and sat back down and continued to stare at Tommy's picture.

After a few minutes Karen came back into the room and sat next to him on the sofa. Fitzsimmons did not look at her.

"His name is Tommy Quercio," Fitzsimmons said, as he continued to stare at the picture. "He's half retarded and half existentialist. He's in his forties, and sometimes he sounds like a child and at other times he sounds old and disillusioned."

"You can see that in his face. It's like there are two personalities in that face," Karen said. "What happened to him? Was he born like that?"

"No. He was born normal. I think he was probably a pretty bright kid, but he was in an accident when he was in the sixth or seventh grade. He was walking to school with a friend of his—a girl in his class. She started across the street without looking—walked right into the path of an oncoming truck. Tommy sacrificed himself for her. He rushed in front of the truck and pushed her out of the way. She wasn't touched, but he received permanent brain damage. She grew up and he didn't, and he's very conscious of that—that the girlfriend he saved abandoned him because of his injury—and very conscious of his handicap. I had a naive view of people like Tommy. I thought that they weren't aware of their handicaps—that they didn't know what they were missing. Tommy knows, and it upsets him. And he lets people know it.

"His favorite targets are priests and ministers. If a clergyman comes to TPI, the staff is supposed to make sure that Tommy doesn't get close to him. If Tommy spots one, he goes right after him. He has a theological side, and he attacks clergymen on their own ground. He tells them that they're phonies, that they don't talk about God as he really is. He says that if God were good there wouldn't be all this evil in the world—that a good God wouldn't allow children to become half-wits."

Karen pondered Fitzsimmons' words, and then seemed to dismiss them. "That's an awful picture," she said.

Fitzsimmons reached down and picked it up.

"I wonder where it was taken?"

"Maybe at Sarz's apartment," Karen said.

"No. Look at the wall behind Tommy. It's bare. There's no wall like that in his apartment."

Fitzsimmons started to rise from the sofa, but stopped halfway up, paused, and then sat back down. "Karen, this picture is the key. Wherever it was taken is where Amy is."

Now he did stand up, and he began to pace back and forth in front of the sofa. "A few months ago I was talking to Tommy—I don't even remember about what—but he asked me if I had ever been up to Sarz's room. And I said 'no' that I didn't even know where Sarz lived. And Tommy laughed this crazy laugh, and told me I was a funny guy. I didn't know what he was talking about. But it was as though Tommy knew something that I didn't. Tommy wasn't talking about Sarz's apartment. Sarz must have a room someplace else that he uses for assignations, and I'll bet it's not on the first floor. He asked me if I had been up to Sarz's room—that's why I was surprised that Sarz's apartment was on the first floor, but this room isn't. Tommy has been there, and he can tell us where it is."

The telephone rang and Fitzsimmons walked across the room and picked up the receiver.

"Hello," he said. There was no response.

"Hello," Fitzsimmons said again. And again there was silence on the other end. Fitzsimmons hung up. "He must be keeping tabs on us," Fitzsimmons said.

Karen put her face in her hands. "Oh, God. Oh, God, why don't we just go to the police?" she said.

Fitzsimmons felt the pall of despair fill the room again.

Fitzsimmons pulled Karen's hands away from her face and held them. She refused to look up at him. Instead, she stared down at her knees.

"We are not going to give in to fear," Fitzsimmons said. "I am not and you are not. Fear is useless. What we need is trust."

"Trust?"

"Yes, trust. I know in my heart that if we have the courage to do it, we'll get Amy back. But I know that if we don't have the courage, then we won't. If we go to the police and Amy is killed you will be haunted by that for the rest of your life."

"And if we don't go to the police and Amy is killed, I will never forgive you. Even if I wanted to forgive you, I couldn't. I'm not even sure I can forgive you if we get Amy back," Karen said. She glared at Fitzsimmons, and the tears were gone from her eyes. They had been replaced by a mixture of sadness and anger.

Fitzsimmons was stung. He dropped Karen's hands. "That will be up to you," he said. "You can decide that later."

Karen studied Fitzsimmons. Whatever it was that had immobilized him a few hours earlier no longer bothered him.

"But we're not even sure we can find them. You only think you can," she said.

"I know that they are in the room where this picture was taken. In fact, I promise you that if they're not there we'll go to the police."

"You promise?"

"I promise."

She thought it over for a few seconds. "All right," she said. "Can you find Tommy?"

"He lives in a halfway house for the mentally handicapped in Dorchester. Barbara Wright had me drive him home in her car one afternoon when he missed his bus."

"Do you want to take a cup of coffee with us?" Karen asked. "It's made."

"Let's," Fitzsimmons said and there was relief in his voice. Karen had heard him and had made the coffee. She was functioning.

Tommy wasn't there and neither were most of the other residents of the halfway house. They had gone on a day trip to Hampton Beach.

"Even in this rain?" Fitzsimmons asked the woman who ran the house.

She was a fidgety, scrawny woman, who sucked deeply on a king-sized cigarette and acted as if something untoward might happen at any minute.

"Why not? They weren't going to go swimming anyway. They enjoy the bus ride and some of them like to go to the arcades," she said.

"What time will they be back?"

"By five if it keeps raining, but if it clears they probably won't be back until seven—I hope," the woman said.

Fitzsimmons looked at his watch. It was only ten minutes before two.

"What do we do now?" Karen asked as they walked back to the car.

"Wait," Fitzsimmons said.

"I can't wait, John. I'll have a breakdown," Karen said.

"No you won't. You're doing fine."

"I'm not doing fine. I feel like I'm coming apart."

"You're supposed to feel that way. You're a mother. You'll be all right."

Karen grabbed his arm and stopped him. "How do you know?" she demanded.

"I felt that way for three years," he answered. "Come on. I think I know somebody who can help."

Karen got in the car without asking to whom Fitzsimmons was referring.

Fitzsimmons drove to St. Camillus in Brighton. When she saw the church, Karen looked at him in bewilderment bordering on fear, as if she suspected that Fitzsimmons' mind had snapped and he had come to see Peter.

"Kevin O'Donnell is here. Don't you remember? He said that he was going to be the interim pastor, just to get the parish over the hump."

"Oh," Karen said. "No, I don't remember."

The priest greeted them with warm enthusiasm as if he had been anticipating their visit. His manner changed when he realized that Karen, at least, was emotionally tattered.

He reached out and took her hand. "What's the matter?" he asked softly.

She began to cry uncontrollably, and he gently embraced her as her face dug into his chest. The priest stroked her hair as if she were a child, and he looked to Fitzsimmons for an explanation, but Fitzsimmons was affected by the sight of Karen. Tears also welled up in him, and at first he could not speak. He shook his head, and cleared his throat.

"Amy has been taken," he said.

"Taken?"

"Yes."

"By whom?" the priest asked.

"By the man who I think killed Peter."

"The one who's been persecuting you?"

"Yes."

They were all still standing in the doorway.

"Let's go inside," the priest said. He led Karen down the hallway, away from the study, to the living room, and Fitzsimmons followed.

The priest brought Karen to the sofa and sat down next to her. He looked up at Fitzsimmons. "What happened?" he asked.

"I think it would be best if Karen told you," Fitzsimmons said. "If you'll excuse me for a few moments."

Fitzsimmons ignored the puzzled look on the priest's face as he waited for a reply.

"Sure," Father O'Donnell said. "Go ahead."

Fitzsimmons went to the kitchen and stayed there. After about twenty minutes the priest came and found him looking out the kitchen window at the rain.

"You wanted an independent judgment," Father O'Donnell said.

"I wanted her to tell you about it without my being there. I thought that it would help her."

They walked back into the living room. "Let me see if I have this straight," the priest said. "This man Sarz kidnapped Amy. He wants your life, John, in exchange for hers. He says that if you go to the police he will kill her."

Fitzsimmons nodded. His face was impassive.

"You believe you can find out where he is, and if you can, you propose to take action by yourself."

"That's right," Fitzsimmons said evenly.

"And Karen, you're not sure what to do."

"No, I'm not," she said. The tears had helped her. She looked drained, but the fear and distraction had passed.

"I'll help you in any way I can. If you decide to go after Sarz, I'll go with you. If you decide to go to the police, I'll stay with you," the priest said.

"But what should we do, Father," Karen asked. "Should we go to the police or not?"

"That's a decision you have to make."

"What would you do if you were in my place?" Karen persisted.

"I don't know. I don't think anyone who is not a mother can know how a mother feels in your situation."

Karen began to show her frustration.

"Karen, I can't make this decision," Father O'Donnell said.

"No, but you can help me make it," she said, with an angry edge to her voice. "What if you were in John's place?"

The priest was troubled. He shook his head as if trying not to speak, but he spoke anyway.

"If I were in John's shoes, I would do exactly what he wants to do," the priest said.

There was a long silence.

"And you'll help us?" Karen asked.

"Of course," the priest said. "I'll go with you right now. Just let me call someone to say the five o'clock Mass for me."

"You don't have to do that, Father," Fitzsimmons said. "We'll go see Tommy and you can meet us after the Mass at Karen's apartment."

The priest looked at Karen. "Is that all right?"

She took a key from her pocketbook and handed it to him. "Will you stay even if we're not back by the time you get there?"

"Of course. I want to do whatever I can. I'm at your disposal."

Fitzsimmons and Karen started to leave.

"Wait a minute," the priest said. "I want to say a prayer before you go," he said. The three of them stood in a circle and held hands.

"Father," the priest said aloud, his eyes raised to the ceiling, "we turn to you in our pain and anxiety. We hold your children—Amy and Karen and John—up to you and we put them in your loving care and protection. We know you will not lose them because we do this in the name of your Son."

Even though the rain did not let up, the residents of the halfway house did not get back early. Fitzsimmons and Karen waited in the car for an hour and a half, and then, at Fitzsimmons suggestion, they drove to a McDonald's. Karen only nibbled on her hamburger, but Fitzsimmons wolfed down his food and drank three large cups of black coffee. It was almost six thirty by the time they left. Karen stopped at an outdoor pay telephone and called her apartment. Father O'Donnell answered, and she told him where they were and asked him to wait there.

When they got back to the halfway house, Tommy was watching a Red Sox road game on television with a group of other people who lived at the house, and he came out of the large, common room reluctantly. He was surprised to see Fitzsimmons and he seemed distant, perhaps suspicious, and not very comfortable in the presence of Karen.

"Hello, Jay," he said. "Are you looking for me?"

"Yes, Tommy. This is my friend, Karen."

"Karen," Tommy said, smirking, as his mood changed. "You like Ks, huh, Jay?"

Fitzsimmons was mystified. "K for strike out?" Fitzsimmons asked, but Tommy ignored the question.

"I didn't think you had any friends, Jay," Tommy said with a leering grin.

"Well I've got you, Tommy."

The smile left his face. "You're a funny guy, Jay. What do you want me for?"

"I want you to tell me where Sarz's room is."

Tommy's face became taut. "What room?"

Fitzsimmons took the picture out of his pocket and palmed it, and then showed Tommy his palm so that only Tommy could see the picture.

"This room," Fitzsimmons said.

Tommy grinned fiercely. "A good likeness, huh Jay?"

"He really captured you," Fitzsimmons said.

"Did you show it to her?" Tommy asked, nodding his head toward Karen.

"She's seen it."

"You're a dirty guy, Jay," Tommy said. He was blushing.

"Tommy, where's the room?"

"You've never been up there, Jay?"

"No."

"Sarz said you had."

"When did he say that?" Fitzsimmons asked.

"When he took me up there. He said you went up there all the time and jerked off." Tommy was grinning again, and he sneaked a glance at Karen. "He said you were a dirty guy, Jay. Just like him."

"Well he lied. Whereabouts is this room?"

"It's all the way down at the end of the hall. It's the last room on the right. Wait till you see it. It's like a regular whorehouse. It's even got pictures on one of the walls. Hey, Jay, do they have girls in whorehouses?"

"Yeah."

"That's what I thought. But Sarz just has pictures of boys."

"What hall are you talking about?" Fitzsimmons asked.

"The hall on the third floor."

"At TPI?"

Tommy nodded. "Half-wit," he whispered to no one in particular.

"The third floor is closed," Fitzsimmons said.

"Sarz says that's because he owns it."

"Is the hall empty?" Fitzsimmons asked.

"No, they got all sorts of crap stacked up in it. Boxes and chairs and a couple of machines. It's all pushed up against one wall. And it's all dirty."

"How big is Sarz's room?"

"It's like Ms. Wright's office. How come you want to know, Jay?"

"I'm just curious."

"Yeah, you're curious, Jay. You're a curious guy," Tommy said. "Is that all, Jay?"

"Is there a lock on the door to the room?"

"Yeah." Tommy was looking back into the room where the television set was. "Is that all, Jay?"

"Yeah, that's all. Thanks, Tommy."

"Hey, Jay," Tommy said, "How about giving me that picture?"

Fitzsimmons started to hand it to him but changed his mind and put it back in his pocket. "I'll give it to you later," he said.

Tommy looked at Karen and blushed again. Then he turned and limped back into the room with the television set.

"Are they all like that?" Karen asked when they were back in the car.

"Who knows? I don't know what goes on in their minds. Maybe they all are like him but they can't articulate it. Tommy calls them half-wits, but he thinks we're all half-wits."

When Fitzsimmons came off the Southeast Expressway he did not head toward Beacon Hill. Instead he drove into the North End and parked the car.

"Why don't you drive for a while," he said.

"Where are we?" she asked.

"A couple of blocks from TPI. I want to get a good look at it as you drive by. Even if Sarz is looking out the window, he won't be able to see into the car from the third floor."

Karen drove slowly past TPI but there was nothing to see. The building looked empty and silent. Fitzsimmons noticed for the first time that some of the windows on the third floor had been painted black, and among them were the windows to the room at the end of the hall. She took a left turn and Fitzsimmons scanned the rear of the building. There was no sign of anyone being inside it.

"Well?" Karen asked.

"It looks pretty quiet," Fitzsimmons answered.

After a few hundred yards she started to speed up.

"Hold it," Fitzsimmons said. "Let me out."

"What's the matter?"

"I thought I saw a car in that alley."

Karen backed the car up, and they looked down the alley. At the end of it, a taillight and a few inches of green fender protruded from behind tall stacks of pallets. Fitzsimmons looked back toward TPI. It would be impossible for Sarz to see them. He got out and walked down the alley to the parked car. It was Sarz's.

He walked through the rain back to the car, and Karen rolled down the window. "Now we're sure," he said. "He's up there, and Amy's with him."

"Yes," Karen said, "She's up there. I know it. I can feel it. Oh, thank God. Thank God. At least we know where she is."

Fitzsimmons opened the door and she moved across the seat as he slid behind the wheel.

"I want to wait until it gets dark before I go in there," Fitzsimmons said. "I want to get as close to him as possible before he knows I'm there. If you want we can go back to the apartment for a while."

"I don't want to leave here without Amy," Karen said. "I want to make sure he doesn't take her someplace else."

"You're right," Fitzsimmons said. He pulled the car over to the curb and shut off the engine. Instead of heartening her, the proximity to Amy had filled Karen with even more anguish and uncertainty.

Fitzsimmons reached over and touched her hand. "We're halfway there," he said. "In a few hours, this will be finished."

"And Amy will be all right?" she asked, in a voice filled with doubt.

"Amy will be all right," he said.

"How are we going to do that?" Karen asked.

"We'll find a way," Fitzsimmons said. "Let me just sit here for a while and think about it."

CHAPTER THIRTY ONE

SOMETIMES THE RAIN PICKED UP AND SPATTERED THE CAR WITH A driving staccato and sometimes it was no more than a heavy drizzle. They sat quietly, feeling the cool dampness without looking at each other. The rain comforted Fitzsimmons. He could not say why, but as he watched the rivulets wash down the windshield he felt a security that was reminiscent of childhood. There was a safety in rainy days, he remembered, a somber safety. You knew that after the chill and the wet, there would be warmth—a hot tub, a dry bed, and peaceful dreams. He was ready for peaceful dreams, an eternity of peaceful dreams. He used to think that people died when they had nothing left to do or when they decided that they would do no more. At least he had felt that way about himself. In the past, when he was teaching at the university, he believed that when he no longer had a goal, he would die, and so he was always careful to have a goal. "I'm not ready yet," he would say when the thought of his own impending death came to him. "There are things that I still have to do, God. I'm not ready yet. Let me raise my daughter. Let me write a book. Let me do something important. Then I'll be ready—when I've done something." And always the thought of death would leave him, and he would be safe from it—safe because he believed that if he thought about death and assented to it, it would happen, but if he did not think about it and did not assent to it, it wouldn't. Time had seemed to prove him wrong. For four years he had had no goals, and when the thought of death came to him he had assented to it, embraced it so long as it was not at his own hand. But death had ignored him.

Fitzsimmons suspected that death would ignore him no longer. It was not a premonition, it was not even a feeling. It was, perhaps, an awareness that his life span had reached its thinnest point and that it might very well snap before it bridged tomorrow. He sighed deeply and felt Karen's eyes upon him, but he did not turn to her. It would be over tonight. Before midnight. This long, torturous episode which began when he walked into his home to find his wife and daughter slain and continued through his half-mad odyssey in the world of darkness, continued even into his awakening, his resurrection and his friendship with Peter and his love for Karen and Amy. This episode was about to close. He would be free of it, free of the pain of the past and free of the burden of evil. He had not succumbed. He had held on. He felt a sudden burst of joy. He had done something noble, without meaning to, without understanding it. He had looked evil and insanity in the face, and he had refused to yield. He had done the most a man could do, he had stood his ground, and it didn't make any difference whether he was crushed or would be crushed or not. He had refused to surrender, and that was all that mattered. It did not even matter if anyone else knew. He knew. God knew. His life had a certain completeness now. Perhaps he had had a goal all along. Perhaps he had only wanted not to succumb.

He fought back a strange sense of exhilaration. He needed to think. He had to come up with a workable plan of attack. In his mind he outlined the three things that he knew he must do. First he had to get into the plant without setting off the alarm system and alerting Sarz. Second, he would have to get to the third floor in the darkness, again without alerting Sarz. And third, he would have to somehow subdue Sarz and free Amy. It seemed at once very simple and impossibly difficult. He fought the feeling of despair which quickly replaced his euphoria. He had learned as a young man not to try to do difficult things all at once but rather to break them down into steps. His father had taught him not to worry about accomplishing the final goal and instead to worry only about achieving the first step.

TPI had an alarm system which was activated and deactivated with a key that fit a special switch at the front door. He had the key. There was a problem, however. When the key was used to turn the alarm system on, it also turned on several red lights, one at the front door, one at the side door, and one at the loading dock. If he deactivated the alarm, the lights would be turned off. That could tip off Sarz to Fitzsimmons' presence. Fitzsimmons would not be able to turn off the alarm system. He would have to get into the building without triggering it. The only way to do that would be to enter through a second floor window, or one of the small windows near the loading platform that were about twelve feet off the ground. He remembered the pallets in the alley. If he stood one on end and then stood another on top of it, he could easily reach a window near the loading platform and he could pry the window open with the tire iron.

"All right. That's the first step," he said aloud.

Karen folded her arms across her chest and hunched her shoulders. She looked at him quizzically but said nothing. He explained his plan for getting into the building, and then he opened the glove compartment and took out a copy of the car rental contract he had signed. On the back of it he sketched the floor plan for the building and showed Karen how he could move through the plant in the darkness without making any noise. He had walked the floors hundreds of times; it would only require recall and caution to get to the third floor without making noise.

"And then what?" Karen asked.

"Then I'll just have to see what happens and do the best I can."

"This seems so futile," Karen said.

The despair was there again. Fitzsimmons could feel it build in her and overflow. "Why don't we just go to the police? We know where she is. Let them do their job."

Anger replaced the other feelings in him.

"Do you really want to go to the police?" he asked sharply.

She didn't answer.

"You've seen the pictures. You've seen the newspaper clippings. You know he killed Peter. He doesn't expect to escape from this thing. He has no intention of letting Amy go free. This is all coming to an end. Sarz is coming to end. It's only a matter of who he takes with him. If we go to the police, Amy is dead and Sarz is dead. And if we don't,

Amy may still be killed, and I may be killed, too, but at least there's a chance that I can save her. I'm willing to accept the responsibility for that. I'm not willing to surrender my responsibility to the police or anyone else when I know it will cost Amy her life. Do you understand what I'm saying? Right now you and I are under heavy stress, heavy tension. Part of us wants to escape from that. What I am asking you to do is to accept the stress and accept the tension. Accept even the possibility that we will fail because the only chance we have of succeeding is to risk failure. I can't stop you from doing whatever you want to do. If you decide that you have to go to the police, then I'll go with you, even though I believe it will mean Amy's death."

Karen stared at her knees without answering.

"But we've been through this before and this is the last time we can go through it." Fitzsimmons' tone was hard and cold. "Choose to try and save Amy with me or choose to go to the police. But don't sit here and go back and forth. We both need all the help and all the support we can give each other. We don't need to waver and second-guess ourselves."

"She's my daughter."

"I know."

"I have no more strength."

"Yes, you do," Fitzsimmons said. "You have a whole reservoir of strength. Use it."

The wind picked up and whipped the rain against the car. Karen stared straight ahead, unmindful of it.

"We're both stronger than we think," Fitzsimmons said. "Sarz is not going to prevail. We will prevail."

"You believe that," she said.

"Yes, and if you will allow yourself to, you'll believe it, too."

Fitzsimmons put his head back against the seat and gazed straight ahead. He remembered a conversation that he had had with Peter. Fitzsimmons said that the role of society was to deal with evil. Peter had argued that in the end, the battle against evil was always a matter of individual action, that each human being was defined by how he or she chose to act when confronted by evil. Fitzsimmons knew how Peter had acted. He would never have surrendered or pleaded for his life. Life meant too much for him to have his continued existence depend on submitting to evil.

Again Fitzsimmons felt drawn to death. There was a delicious peace to it, a luxurious freedom. The rain cascaded down the windshield and gusts of wind battered the car. The day had become even more dark and gray. Boston was somber, chilly and wet.

"The world is such an inhospitable place," Fitzsimmons thought. "Why do we want to stay here?"

He glanced at Karen. She seemed so remote, as if the two of them existed on different planes. He had a knowledge that she did not have. This was an alien world. There had to be something better somewhere else. And if there was nothing? If this was all there is? Fitzsimmons shrugged mentally. The end was in sight. He could not afford the luxury of metaphysics.

CHAPTER THIRTY TWO

As twilight approached, Fitzsimmons switched the key on and started the car. The wipers swept silently back and forth across the windshield. Karen sat huddled in her raincoat, staring straight ahead, oblivious of them.

"You have to leave now," he said.

Karen started as if coming out of a trance. "What?" There was a trace of alarm in her voice.

"You have to be at the apartment when he calls."

She nodded.

"Father O'Donnell is there. That will help," Fitzsimmons said.

"Sarz will want to talk to you," Karen said.

"Tell him I went out."

"He'll want to know where."

"Tell him you don't know. Tell him I was distracted, upset," he said.

They exchanged glances. The memory of Fitzsimmons sitting help-less on the sofa was still fresh for both of them.

"Tell him I said I'd be back by nine o'clock."

"All right."

"And insist on talking to Amy."

"Don't worry about that," Karen said.

He opened the car door, but she put her hand on his arm so that he would not get out.

"I want you to agree to something," she said.

"Okay."

"You have to wait until I get back here before you go into the building."

Fitzsimmons took out his wallet and gave Volpe's card to Karen, with Volpe's home telephone number written on the back.

"There's a deli four blocks from here. Call Volpe and tell him it's imperative that you be able to reach him later on tonight. Tell him that I am asking him to be available in the name of Peter's friendship. But don't tell him why. No matter what he says. No matter how he threatens or cajoles. Tell him you will call him around 8:30 and explain everything. After you call him come back here and let me know what happened."

Karen looked intently at Fitzsimmons as he finished speaking. "All right," she said. "But I want you to promise me that you'll wait until I get back here before you go into the building."

"We'll talk about that when you get back," Fitzsimmons said.

"Why?"

"Because of the logistics of the thing. Go call Volpe and then I'll explain it to you," Fitzsimmons said.

"Suppose Volpe agreed to come here by himself to help us?" Karen asked.

"He can't do that. He has to follow the rules. And it's not important that he be here until after I get to Sarz, anyway. I just want him here as a fail-safe."

"A fail-safe?"

Fitzsimmons returned her look with a calm, steady gaze.

"Don't even think about it," he said. "Just keep your mind on what you have to do."

She looked away, and Fitzsimmons got out of the car.

"You might call your apartment again and let Father O'Donnell know you're coming."

After Karen drove away, Fitzsimmons walked down the alley to Sarz's car. He smashed the driver's side window with the tire iron and reached in and unlocked the door and opened it. He pulled the hood latch release and walked around to the front of the car and raised the hood. He stared at the engine for a moment, and then, using the tire iron again, he popped off the clips which held the distributor cap in place and removed the rotor, dropped it on the pavement and struck it with the tire iron. The rotor was made of plastic and it splintered under the force of his blow. If Sarz was going anywhere, it would have to be on foot.

Karen returned in ten minutes.

"I reached Volpe," she said.

"What did he say?"

"He said he wouldn't be available unless I told him what it was for."

"What did you tell him."

"I told him that he'd better be. I told him it involved Peter's killer and my daughter, and if he wasn't available, that when this is over I'd go to the managing editor of *The Boston Globe* and tell him the whole story."

"And?"

"Then he said we shouldn't try to handle this by ourselves. He said we should let him help."

"What did you tell him?"

"I told him I'd call him back at 8:30. I didn't argue with him. I told him our minds were made up. I thought about what you said, about Peter and about those pictures. You're right. Volpe would bring a whole brigade of policemen over here—I knew it just by the way he was talking—and Sarz would kill Amy.

"I want my daughter. I was hesitant before because I was unsure of you. The way you looked this morning I thought you were going to go catatonic on me. But when I was talking to Volpe, I realized I had to trust you. You love Amy. Volpe is a stranger."

The decision had changed Karen. Her doubt and indecisiveness were gone.

"I'm trusting you with my daughter's life," she said. "If I could do it myself, I would. But I can't do it myself. So I'm trusting you."

As Fitzsimmons stood in the rain looking at Karen through the open car window, he felt a wave of sadness. They had become estranged.

He ignored his feelings.

"By the time you get to your apartment, a cop will be waiting there for you. Don't give in. I'm going to break into TPI at 8:45, and at exactly nine o'clock, I'm going to confront Sarz. You have to have

Volpe here by then. Ask him to wait a few minutes before he comes in after me."

"Will he do that?"

"I don't know," Fitzsimmons said.

"And what exactly are you going to do?"

"I don't know that either," Fitzsimmons said.

"This would be easier if everything weren't so ... " She could not find the right word. "Vague," she said finally.

"I know it would. Things are always so much easier if all the alternatives are well defined and all the possibilities known in advance. This just isn't like that," Fitzsimmons said.

A new awareness came into her eyes, an awareness that this might be their last meeting. Fitzsimmons recognized it at once.

"You'd better get back to the apartment," he said. Their eyes met again.

"Good-bye," he said.

They neither kissed nor touched.

"Good-bye," she answered. She rolled up the window, put the car in gear and, looking straight ahead, drove away.

After Karen left, Fitzsimmons stood in the rain waiting. He thought about sitting in Sarz's car, but he could not bring himself to do that. He would rather get wet. Karen was right. Everything was vague and insubstantial. He had no clear course of action except to get to Sarz. He did not even know what would happen once he got there. He did not know what he would say or what he would do. But he knew that he would not kill Sarz. He would not do him violence.

Something had happened inside of Fitzsimmons the night he had strangled Sarz. He had had a painful awakening, a recognition that evil did not exist only outside of himself, it was within him, too.

At first the knowledge had been sickening. He had felt tainted by it. But gradually he let go of the guilt and came to a new understanding of himself.

Being evil, he now knew, was part of being human. What distinguished good men from bad men was that good men refused to submit to the evil within them. Although they were infected, they refused to surrender to the disease. In fact, some people were so successful at resisting evil that they did not seem to be infected at all. Peter, for example. But Peter had been subject to the same negative forces that live in other men. Peter had very nearly committed adultery in his own rectory. He had at one time been judgmental and self-righteous. But he had learned from his own weakness. It had given him a new perspective, and Fitzsimmons, too, had gained a new perspective.

As much as he was sickened by Sarz, as much as he wanted to stop him and save Amy, Fitzsimmons did not judge him, nor did he want to take revenge on him. Revenge. The concept had just now surfaced in his mind. Revenge for Sarz being Sarz. Revenge against the maniac who had changed his life. The maniacs were the ones who were seeking revenge, in their sick, twisted fashion. Revenge must be part of the human sickness—the sickness which made men kill or fear, made them hate and envy, made them judge and feel superior.

"I'm infected," Fitzsimmons said aloud. "We are all infected."

The rain came down harder and the wind picked up. Fitzsimmons was cold and wet and alone in the empty street.

"I am infected," he said again. "This whole world is infected."

CHAPTER THIRTY THREE

THE MAN WAS WAITING IN THE HALL AS KAREN ENTERED THE apartment building.

"Mrs. Easton?"

"Yes."

"I'm Detective Reardon from the Boston Police Department."

He was in his late twenties, slender, a man who appeared to be in excellent physical condition. He was well dressed with a blue blazer, slacks, button-down blue shirt, and striped tie. He seemed friendly and concerned.

"Are you all right?" he asked her.

Karen knew that she was vulnerable. She was afraid that she would trust him.

"May I see some identification?" she asked.

Reardon pulled out a wallet and flipped it open to show her a Boston Police Department badge.

"Okay?" he asked.

"What do you want?" she asked.

"You talked to Captain Volpe?"

"Yes."

"Well, that's why I'm here. There's a man waiting up in your apartment. Shall we go up?"

"Hello, Father," Karen said as the priest opened the door. He was not dressed in clerical garb. Instead, he wore chinos, a knit navy blue sport shirt and loafers.

"How are you doing?" he asked.

"I'm all right," Karen said.

"Father?" Reardon asked. "Are you a priest?"

"Yes, I am," Father O'Donnell responded and introduced himself.

Karen crossed the room to the window. There was still light outside.

"Has anyone called?" she asked.

"No," the priest said.

"Do you want to tell me what's going on?" Reardon asked.

"I already told Captain Volpe."

"Well, it won't hurt to go over it with me."

In as few words as possible Karen explained the situation. Reardon listened without interrupting, but he shook his head almost continually.

"You're making a mistake," Reardon said. "It's understandable, but it's a serious mistake."

Karen did not reply.

"Do you have that note and those pictures you were talking about?"

Karen went and got the material they had taken from Sarz's apartment.

Reardon quickly leafed through the pictures.

"All right," he said. He suddenly seemed angry. "This has gone far enough. Where is this guy?"

Karen looked at the clock. It was a quarter past eight. She looked back at Reardon. He was now a formidable opponent.

"Lady, I'm in no mood for bullshit. I want to know where this guy is and I want to know right now."

The priest looked at Karen as if waiting for a cue, but Karen did not return his look.

"Get out of here," she said to Reardon.

"What?"

"I said get out of my apartment. You are not welcome here."

Reardon's aggressiveness evaporated. He raised his hands slightly as if half ready to surrender.

"No need to get angry, ma'am. I'm just trying to do my job. You may not think so, but I'm actually trying to help you. That guy who has your daughter—he's your enemy, not me."

"Then stop acting like my enemy. If you want to help, you can. But right now the only way you can help is to sit down and be quiet. If you can't do that, then leave." Karen's tone was civil but determined. For just a moment, Reardon's eyes revealed that her words stung him, it was only for a moment.

"Madam, I'm a professional police officer. There are lots of ways I can help you. Sitting down and shutting up isn't one of them. If it was up to me, I'd say the hell with you and leave. But it's not up to me. I've been ordered to stay with you, and that's what I'm going to do."

The telephone rang and Reardon started towards it.

"Don't touch that. I'll answer it. You stay away from it," she said. Reardon stopped, and she passed in front of him and picked up the telephone receiver. "Hello?"

"Let me talk to the victim," Sarz said.

"Who?"

"The victim. Fitzsimmons."

"He's not here."

"Where is he?"

"I don't know."

Reardon looked up and moved closer to the telephone.

"I've told the son of a bitch what will happen," Sarz said. "Does he think I'm just fucking around?"

"He's under a lot of pressure. I think he's on the verge of a breakdown. I know he wants to talk to you. He said he'd be back by nine."

There was silence on the other end of the line.

"He said that if you called, I should insist that you let me talk to Amy. He said he wouldn't do anything if you didn't."

"Lady, if you're bullshitting me, this kid is going to pay for it. Do you understand that?"

"I understand. But I want to talk to her."

There was another silence, and then Amy's voice said, "Mommy?"

"Oh, Amy. It's so good to hear you."

"It's good to hear you, too, Mom," Amy choked as she spoke, fighting back sobs.

Karen, too, had to fight off tears. "I love you, Amy. John loves you. Everything will be all right."

"That's it," Sarz said. "End of conversation. Tell the victim to do it, or I'll do it."

"Hold it. Don't hang up. John said he wants a guarantee."

"What kind of guarantee?"

"He wants to be sure that I'll get Amy back."

"He knows my terms. He knows what I will do if he doesn't do what I want. That's all there is to it. If he kills himself you get her back. If he doesn't, you don't. That's it. This is not negotiable," Sarz said and hung up.

"You know, lady, had you been cooperating we could have traced that call and found out where he is," Reardon said.

"That's not the problem."

"You're certain that you know where he is?"

Karen looked at her watch. It was twenty past eight.

"You are being completely irresponsible. You're jeopardizing your daughter's life."

The temptation was still there, the desire to surrender to authority, to put Amy's fate in someone else's hands, just as Fitzsimmons had said, to give up the responsibility. Karen faced the inner tension and stared it down. She did not trust Reardon. She did not trust Volpe. Their interests were not her interests. They wanted to do their jobs. Karen wanted to get Amy back. She knew that Reardon would not leave her alone now, so she would not be able to go back to TPI before Fitzsimmons entered the building. He would climb through the window in twenty-five minutes and in forty minutes he would face Sarz. She could hold off Reardon and herself for that long. She hadn't smoked in two years, but now she had a strong desire for a cigarette.

"Do you have a cigarette?"

Reardon pulled a pack from his shirt pocket and offered it to her. She took one but did not put it in her mouth.

"You're taking an awful lot on your shoulders. You've seen these pictures. This guy is an animal. He's demented. And you're not going to let the police help you?"

Karen looked at her watch. Thirty-nine more minutes. The second hand would have to sweep the face only thirty-nine more times. She could handle that and Reardon.

At this time of night they could drive to TPI in twenty or twenty-five minutes. That meant they could leave in fourteen minutes. She looked at her watch—in thirteen minutes.

"Excuse me," she said. "I want to use the bathroom." Reardon shook his head again.

Karen flushed the unlighted cigarette down the toilet and then she turned the sink faucets on and sat on the side of the tub. After a few minutes she shut the faucets off and looked at her face in the bathroom mirror. She spent time in front of the mirror every day, putting on her makeup, brushing her hair. But now she was doing more than looking at herself, she was examining her face, trying to see what was behind it, and it was as if she was looking at another person, someone whom she didn't know.

"Mrs. Easton. Are you all right in there?" Reardon called.

"I'll be out in a minute." She looked at her watch. They could leave in seven minutes. She looked in the mirror again. The face that stared back at her was the face of a woman. It was sharper, more certain, more determined. It was not the face of someone who would be intimidated, or someone who would surrender. Maybe she was stronger than she suspected.

"We'll leave here in five minutes," she told Reardon when she came out of the bathroom.

"Oh? Where are we going?"

"To pick up John. And then we'll go to where Sarz has my daughter."

"And where's that."

"You'll see when we get there. Do you want to call Captain Volpe, or do you want me to?"

Reardon called Volpe. After talking to him, he gave the telephone to Karen.

"Look, Mrs. Easton. I think it's time you listened to reason," Volpe said.

"Captain, we're on a tight schedule. We'll call you in twenty-two minutes and tell you exactly where to meet us."

"Mrs. Easton, you're assuming a terrible responsibility."

"I know," she said and put the phone down.

"Are you ready?" she asked Reardon.

"Where are we going?" Reardon asked after he had started the car. Karen was about to say, "The North End" when she noticed the police radio. If John could figure out where Sarz was keeping Amy, Volpe might be able to also if he knew the general area.

"Go up here and turn left," Karen said. "We'll do this block by block."

Reardon picked up the microphone. "This is car seven-two-seven."

"Yes, seven-two-seven," a woman's voice replied.

"Would you inform Captain Volpe that I have Mrs. Easton with me, plus a Father O'Donnell from St. Camillus Church in Brighton, and I'm turning west onto Pinckney Street?" Reardon said. He was clearly exasperated.

After a few more minutes, Karen realized that she had to give Volpe time to get to TPI. Angelina's restaurant was only a few blocks from TPI. She would have to take a chance.

"You can tell Captain Volpe that we are going to meet John at Angelina's Restaurant. Do you know where that is?"

"Yes, lady," Reardon said barely suppressing a host of negative emotions. "I know where Angelina's is."

There was a pause. Reardon no longer felt the need to be civil. "Any asshole in the city can tell you where it is," he said.

CHAPTER THIRTY FOUR

IT HAD BEEN DARK FOR THE BETTER PART OF AN HOUR, AND Fitzsimmons was glad for the darkness and for the solitude. It gave him time to piece things out, to re-examine himself, to look at his fears and at his motives, and to try to make some kind of value judgment about himself. He did not think he would survive the night, but the reality of his own death did not frighten him. He was ready, perhaps too ready.

His clothes were soaked through. The rain beat on his hair and face. Water streamed down his forehead into his eyes and mouth. Despite the cold and the discomfort, the rain felt good, and he felt good. He felt cleansed. The thought that the terrible chapter which began with the murders of his wife and child would end tonight was never far from him. He could see no logical connection between the deaths of Eileen and Sarah and what was happening now, but he felt an emotional, unconscious connection. There was a sense to it which his mind could not grasp but which his soul understood.

It was almost time, and Karen had not returned. Fitzsimmons guessed what had happened, that Volpe or some other policeman was with her, and that she would have to stay away until nine o'clock. It was just as well. Amy was Karen's daughter, but it was accidental that they were involved. This struggle was not Karen's. It was something between Sarz and Fitzsimmons and between Fitzsimmons and life. Karen was no more than an innocent bystander. Or was she?

"Are we all innocent bystanders?" Fitzsimmons wondered. "Or are we all in it up to our necks?"

He stared out into the blackness.

"Into what up to our necks?" he asked.

"Into life," the inner voice answered.

He looked at the luminous dial of his watch. It was time.

He dragged a skid from the alley to the rear of the TPI building and then went back and got another one. He leaned the first skid against the wall and set the second one on top of it at just enough of an angle that it would not topple back when he climbed it. He dropped his raincoat to the ground, stuck the tire iron in his belt, and very slowly and gingerly climbed the skids until his hands could reach the window which was about fifteen feet off the ground. As he had expected, it was locked. He punched a hole in one of the small panes of glass with the socket end of the tire iron and then he slid the blade of the iron through the hole and forced open the lock. He raised the window, brushed the glass off the sill and climbed inside. The darkness seemed absolute, but he knew that it wasn't, and he waited until his eyes registered even the most nebulous forms before he lowered himself to the floor.

Once there he imagined the room as if it were daylight. His left hand felt the old maple wooden desk where the bills of lading were signed. In his mind's eye, he saw the aisle which ran from the desk past rows of boxes to the main aisle which led to the fabrication rooms. He guessed it was about 40 feet to the main aisle. He inched away from the desk until he could feel the boxes with his right hand and then he began to walk very slowly toward the main aisle.

At about twenty feet his shins hit a box which was lying out of place. He had been walking so slowly that it hardly made a sound. He felt his way around it. Ten feet more and he found the corner and turned into the main aisle. He looked at his watch. It had taken him five minutes to go thirty feet. His time would have to improve. He dropped to his hands and knees and began to crawl toward the fabrication rooms. There were no obstacles in the aisle and he was next to Tommy's chair in less than a minute. It was about fifty feet to the next turn, and another fifty feet from there to the door to the stairway which led to the offices.

Fitzsimmons stood up and moved more quickly now, very certain of his surroundings even though he could see almost nothing. He was almost to the next corner when he walked into a table which had been pulled out in the aisle. The edge of the table struck him below the waist and below his outstretched hands. There was a loud clatter as several objects, glass and metal, fell to the oil-soaked floor.

Fitzsimmons listened without moving. The echo raged in his imagination. He waited for some sign that Sarz was aware of his presence, but he heard nothing and saw only blackness. He looked at his watch. It was eight fifty-three. He worked his way back to the doorway from the loading room and found the light switch and flipped it on. The room was empty. The table he had bumped into had been pulled out to block the entire aisle. A metal bowl and several glasses had fallen to the floor when he struck it.

Fitzsimmons moved quickly across the room to the door which led to the stairway. He turned the lights off, and opened the door. The stairwell was in complete darkness. He waited a minute for his pupils to widen, but when they did he could still see nothing. He felt along the wall for the light switch and flipped it. Half way up the first flight of stairs, Sarz had formed a barricade with three office chairs and balanced a metal lamp on top of them. Fitzsimmons carefully dismantled the barricade and climbed to the landing. There were no obstacles between the landing and the second floor.

It was eight fifty-six. Fitzsimmons ran up to the second floor and turned on the lights for the stairs that led to the third floor. The way to the landing was clear, but Sarz had blocked the final stairway with stacks of precariously balanced desk drawers. Fitzsimmons set them aside, trying not to make noise, but at this point he was not sure if it made any difference. Sarz probably knew where he was, and if he didn't he would in another minute or two.

He climbed the last few stairs, opened the metal fire door and stepped into the dark third floor hallway. He had never been on the floor before. Because it was unused, and because it was impossible to enter from outside the building, the floor was not on the rounds he made as a watchman. Fitzsimmons groped along the wall trying to find a light switch, but when he found it and switched it to the on position nothing happened. He switched it on and off several times. It made a loud clicking noise, but the lights still did not go on. Fitzsimmons opened the fire door and let light into the hall. All the doors off the hall were shut, and the hall itself was empty. Fitzsimmons let the door swing shut again.

"Sarz," he called out into the darkness, "I've come for Amy."

There was no answer.

"Sarz," he called again. And again there was only silence.

Doubt began to cross Fitzsimmons mind. He wondered if perhaps he was not wrong, that Sarz had taken the girl somewhere else. But it was only a momentary doubt.

Fitzsimmons began to inch toward the first door on the left. "Come on, Sarz," he called. "I want to see Amy." He slid his hand against the wall until he felt the pane of glass in the door. He tried the knob, and it turned. He pushed the door open and stepped into the room, found the light switch and turned it on but the lights did not work in that room either. He stood very still and listened. There was no movement, and he could hear no one breathing in the room. He stepped back out into the hall, and began to move toward the next door.

"John," Amy shrieked. Her voice came from a room at the far end of the hall.

"I hear you, Amy," Fitzsimmons shouted back.

A moment later, a door at the end of the hall opened, and a dull light illuminated the hallway. Fitzsimmons strained his eyes but he could see nothing in the room except the far wall. He walked slowly toward the doorway, and stopped about ten feet from it.

"Amy?" he called.

He heard a high-pitched whine, the kind that children make when their mouths are covered.

"As long as you're here, why don't you come in?" Sarz asked. He was still out of sight.

Fitzsimmons walked slowly to the doorway and peered into the room. Sarz was sitting with his feet up on a desk to the right side. Amy was directly opposite him. She was standing with her arms taped behind her back. Her mouth was taped shut with white adhesive tape. She looked very vulnerable, but he could see the relief in her eyes. Fitzsimmons went over to her and removed the tape from her mouth. Her face was gaunt but determined. It seemed to say that she had already lived through her worst fears. As she looked at Fitzsimmons her eyes filled with tears.

"I knew you'd come," she said. "I knew it." She looked triumphantly at Sarz, but he paid no attention to her.

Fitzsimmons began to untape her wrists.

"That's enough," Sarz said.

Fitzsimmons did not stop.

"I said that's enough," Sarz repeated. The chair squeaked as Sarz got up, but Fitzsimmons did not turn around until Amy's hands were free.

Sarz shut the door and stood in front of it as Amy's wrists dropped to her side. There was a slight smile on his face as though he were genuinely pleased to see Fitzsimmons.

"Nothing's happened to her, yet," Sarz said as Fitzsimmons looked at Amy.

"Is that true?"

Amy nodded.

"Good," Fitzsimmons said, turning to Sarz. The gun, he noticed, was in Sarz's belt.

"I wondered if you'd come, if you'd be smart enough to figure out where I was. Not that you would have to be very smart to do that. Although, I have to admit, when your girlfriend told me you were about to have a nervous breakdown, I almost believed her. It seemed the natural thing for you to do. Did you bring a gun?"

Fitzsimmons shook his head.

"So you came up here unarmed except for that tire iron in your belt?"

"That's not a weapon," Fitzsimmons said. "It's a tool."

"Yeah, of course. A burglarious tool used to break and enter in the nighttime," Sarz said. He snapped the lock on the door behind him. "Sit down."

Fitzsimmons remained standing.

"You have delivered yourself up to me. Only a complete asshole would do that." He looked over at Amy. "So this is your savior, huh? Well, your savior is an asshole, kid."

"No, he's not," Amy said.

"She's a girl of few words," Sarz said.

Fitzsimmons studied Sarz without replying.

"Did you just come here to look?" Sarz asked.

Fitzsimmons did not answer.

"Well, are you going to say something?"

Fitzsimmons wondered how much time had elapsed since he last looked at his watch. Two or three minutes? He listened, but he could hear nothing outside the building.

"This is where it ends," Fitzsimmons said.

"What ends?"

"You. What you've been doing. The people that you have killed. You. You end here."

"If I do, then you do, too. And so does the girl."

"Why is that?"

"Why?" Sarz asked, his voice slightly raised.

"Yes. Why?"

"Because you're an asshole," Sarz said. He seemed consumed by hatred.

"There's a world full of people you think are assholes," Fitzsimmons said. "Why am I special?"

Sarz waited before answering, as if he were thinking over what he was about to say, but his eyes never left Fitzsimmons. "We're so different. I'm not sure I can explain it to you. I don't think you can understand me or what I'm going to tell you. You'd have to have been where I've been. I'm not like you. When people hurt me, I hurt them back. When God hurts me, I hurt him back. I don't put up with anybody's shit, people's or God's. Do you understand that? This world and everything in it is rotten. But most people don't see that. They see me. And they say I'm rotten. They saw me as a three-year-old and they said, 'Freebee, you little bastard, you're rotten.' They have been saying that to me my entire life, 'Freebee, you're a rotten little bastard.' And I have answered them. And I keep answering them."

"How can you answer them? They're right. You are rotten, you're malignant. You are consumed by evil."

"Evil?" Sarz asked. "Evil? Evil is just another way of saying fuck you. That's what evil is. You never met anybody like me before did you? There's a world full of people out there blowing little boys, and some of them are priests, and some of them are ministers, and some of them are scoutmasters. And you've met some of them. But you haven't met anybody like me. I'm a rare one. I'm a jewel compared to the rest of them. Have you ever looked at the tear-stained face of a child after he has done something sordid, after the passion is gone, if there was any passion, and there is only the certain knowledge that he has done something that has contaminated him, something filthy? You look at that face trying to wash itself clean, trying to free itself from the last ten minutes, saying, 'No, no, no. I don't want that to have happened.' But it already did. It already happened. The semen has already dribbled away. The morning face of innocence has been tainted by depravity. And the child is drowning in the terror and disgust of its own guilt."

Sarz glanced at Amy. "Then I look into those eyes, and I judge them. Should this one live? Is there anything there besides fear and disgust? Oh, sometimes you run into a little faggot. No fear, no disgust. You're bad, little boy. I judge them differently. But the other ones, the ones with fear and disgust, the crying ones, I look at them and I despise them. They should not live; they have no right to live. Life is not for whiners; it's not for those who want to run away. Life is for those who will seize it. And the others? I dispatch them. With this hand," Sarz raised his right hand until it was even with his chest. "I squeeze them until their eyes bulge, until there is no longer disgust in them, just that terrible panic that comes when they understand I am not going to release them, that there is no mercy, that they will, in the next few seconds, die."

Sarz dropped his hand and there was silence in the room. Fitzsimmons had forgotten about Karen and Volpe.

"That is my moment," Sarz said. "It is addictive. When I was about seven years old, I poked out a kitten's eyes. The kid with me was disgusted. He was sick. I wasn't. I watched the kitten struggle until it no longer amused me, and then I strangled it. It was the first living thing that I strangled. It started me on my life of crime." Sarz smiled, not broadly, but fondly, as if he were reminiscing with a friend.

Amy looked at Fitzsimmons and he reached out and took her hand.

"It is addictive," Sarz said with his eyes on Amy. "I like to see things die, especially young things. To have the power of death is something I take great pleasure in. You probably can't understand that."

"It ends here," Fitzsimmons said.

"Believe me, Fitzsimmons, you won't end it."

"One way or another, it ends here," Fitzsimmons said.

"It will never end," Sarz said. "It will go on and on, just as it always has."

"Your participation in it ends tonight," Fitzsimmons said.

"Maybe," Sarz said. "I'm getting tired anyway. The joy is gone. But I'm glad you came. I have hated you for so long—ever since I realized who you are. You were hiding. You ran away from life and hid. Ever since then I have thought about you and toyed with you and tortured you and waited."

"I don't understand that. I don't understand your obsession with me," Fitzsimmons said.

"You are an affront to me. I don't like people who let things happen to them and do nothing about it. I hate people who go silently to their destruction. It's like assenting to all this. It's like saying, 'All right world, all right God, you can abuse me. It's all right. I'm not going to say anything.' You're a classic example of that—uncomplaining passivity. You're like a dumb animal that gets beaten and offers no resistance. Oh, you growl for a moment. For just an instant. You attacked me on the street. You could have killed me, and that waitress wouldn't have said a word. She would have helped you. She hates me. And we wouldn't be here now. This girl wouldn't have spent a long day of terror, and you wouldn't have to die. But you don't know how to strike back, or you don't want to strike back. I have been slaughtering people like you since the world began."

Fitzsimmons could feel impending death. He looked at Amy. Her face seemed frozen. Her mouth was open and she was staring at Sarz. He wondered if she knew how close it was to the end.

"Your answer was to rape and kill little boys. Mine was to choose not to participate in life. Your answer was evil, mine was all I could do at the time."

"Where are they?" he asked.

"Who?"

Sarz shook his head. "The police."

"They've got to be out there someplace," Fitzsimmons said.

"Did you call them?"

"Of course. You don't think I would let you continue, do you?"

"I wondered about that," Sarz said. "I mean what difference does it make to you? You don't give a shit about life, I mean a real shit. You don't care. So what difference does it make to you what I do to other people? You chose not to participate. Those are your own words. Don't you understand that I got pleasure out of what I did? So what difference does it make to you? Why ruin it for me? Why meddle?"

Fitzsimmons did not answer.

"It doesn't matter. You're right. It ends here. But it's not you who is ending it. It's God."

Sarz looked at the disbelieving Fitzsimmons and nodded.

"That's right. God. It happened at that priest's funeral. Your friend that I killed. It was like I had a vision. Maybe it was only my imagination, but it was like a vision. During the eulogy, I had an image of all those dirty little bastards that I killed. Everyone of them with their tear-stained faces and their guilty eyes. And God was washing them clean. Every one of them. He was gentle and kind and tender and loving. And everyone of those little bastards was smiling."

"So you lost," Fitzsimmons said.

"Yes, I lost. Of course I lost. Look what I was up against," Sarz said, "but it is some consolation to me that you came here."

They stood in silence. Fitzsimmons knew that Sarz was right. He was a murderer and a rapist, but what he said was true. Fitzsimmons had never said 'yes' to life. He had always held back. He had only gone into the water ankle-deep. The silence was interrupted by a noise, dull and far off. Sarz slid across the door until his back was in front of the wall, and the door handle was next to his left hand. His right hand touched the gun in his belt, but his hand dropped back to his side.

"They must have gotten the key to shut off the alarm. They should have guessed that I would have rigged something up, just in case."

All three of them, Sarz, Fitzsimmons and Amy listened for another sound, but they could hear nothing.

"Your coming here is a consolation to me," Sarz said.

Fitzsimmons nodded.

"I'm still not sure why you came. You knew I would kill you. You knew that I would kill her, too."

"Yes," Fitzsimmons said. "But I didn't want her to step into eternity alone."

There was another sound of falling metal, this time louder and closer, and Fitzsimmons stepped in front of Amy.

The two men stared into each other's eyes. Fitzsimmons felt very detached from himself and from what was happening. By the noise, he figured that Volpe and his men must be close.

"After he shoots me, he won't have time to shoot her," Fitzsimmons thought.

It was all very abstract to him. Was it because he was in a state of shock, he wondered, or was it because he still didn't care? Was Sarz, finally, only an instrument of death, and had Fitzsimmons, in the end, sought it out?

Amy squeezed his hand with all her strength until her fingers dug into his skin.

"It's all right," Fitzsimmons thought, "It's almost over."

There was a loud noise in the hall. It sounded very close to the door, and then Volpe's voice called, "Fitzsimmons, are you in there?"

Sarz pulled the gun from his belt and pointed it at Fitzsimmons.

Fitzsimmons stared in Sarz's eyes. "Yes," he called back, "we're in the room at the end."

Sarz raised the gun to shoulder level and fired. The bullet caught Fitzsimmons in the chest and sent him staggering back against Amy. He felt his knees start to buckle, but he managed to stay on his feet. His eyes never left Sarz's.

Sarz raised the gun again, and again he aimed at Fitzsimmons, this time at his face. The door burst open next to Sarz, and Volpe and a uniformed policeman were poised on the other side of the doorway, ready to jump into the room. For an instant, the scene was frozen. Sarz was leaning against the wall next to the door aiming the gun at Fitzsimmons, and Volpe and the policeman were staring at the blood soaking into Fitzsimmons' shirt.

Fitzsimmons' and Sarz's gaze never wavered. As they looked at each other, they weighed the possibilities, and in that split second, they both knew what the choices were. Sarz could kill Fitzsimmons and be captured or he could kill himself. There was only time for one shot, and one shot might not even kill Fitzsimmons. The first hadn't.

Sarz tore his raging eyes away from Fitzsimmons, and in one motion, as he turned to look at the doorway, he put the barrel of the gun into his mouth and pulled the trigger. The force of the shot stretched him onto his toes before he crumpled to the floor.

CHAPTER THIRTY FIVE

HE REALIZED LATER THAT HE HAD BEEN IN A STATE OF SHOCK. Moments seemed unconnected. Images were frozen and out of proportion to each other—Volpe glaring at him with a cigarette in his mouth; Kevin O'Donnell praying over the dead Sarz; Amy weeping silently and staring at Fitzsimmons as Karen clung to her.

His chest had been covered with blood, and his breathing was difficult and painful. He wondered if he was dying, but he did not ask the men who gave him an injection and pressed large, gauze pads on his wound and prepared to put him on the stretcher. He wanted someone to talk to him, but no one did. They were all busy. He hoped that Karen would touch him or speak to him, but she did not even look in his direction. He put his head back and closed his eyes.

"It's over," he thought. "The hell with them."

He felt a hand touch his hand, and he tried to open his eyes, but he was so tired and so relieved that he could not open them and it did not bother him that he could not.

John," a voice said. "John."

Was it Karen's voice or Amy's or both their voices? There was a soft, small hand inside of his. He squeezed it, but his eyes remained closed.

He came around as they secured the stretcher in the ambulance.

"Am I dying?" he asked a young man in a dark blue shirt.

"I don't know," the man said. "I'm not a doctor."

After the back doors of the ambulance closed, he sensed someone beside him, and he heard Kevin O'Donnell praying out loud, and then he felt the priest anoint his forehead with oil.

"I guess maybe I am dying," he thought. The thought did not disturb him; he was resigned to it, almost completely resigned to it. After all, he had won. Amy was alive. Sarz was dead. And Karen was distant, perhaps gone. If he was dying, that didn't matter. If he was dying emotional pain was an anachronism. Everything was an anachronism. He no longer had to struggle. He no longer had to care. Slide into the abyss. Darkness, silence, peace. But if he slid, if he surrendered, then Sarz was right about him. He was a man who held life at arm's length, a man who never said 'yes.'

"I am a man who has received the greatest gift that can be bestowed—life itself—and I have never unwrapped the package," he whispered.

"John?" the priest asked.

"Yes," Fitzsimmons said, but this time he spoke only to himself. "I accept it. Whatever it is, wherever it goes. Pain, death, rejection, love, life, being."

He opened his eyes.

"What?" the priest asked.

"Love. Life. Being." Fitzsimmons answered. He breathed deeply and closed his eyes again.

When he awoke, there was a tube coming out his nose. He saw an intravenous bottle hanging from a stand at the side of the bed, and nurses moving back and forth across what he dimly realized was the intensive care unit of a hospital. Reason told him that if he had made it this far, he would survive. He had an impulsive desire to share that knowledge with a nurse. He tried to call one, but no sound escaped his lips. It was only then that he realized that he was still under the effects of anesthesia, that his mind was drugged and that whatever he was feeling was not quite real. He tried again to call a nurse, and this time a hoarse, low sound was emitted from his parched throat, but it was not loud enough to attract attention. He decided that it was just as well, that he would rather be alone for a while. He closed his eyes and went back to sleep.

His recovery was rapid. Within twenty-four hours, he was out of intensive care and installed in a private room on the fourth floor of the hospital, where he slept or dozed most of the time. Karen appeared with Amy and then reappeared, never staying for more than a few minutes, and never saying much—solicitous but distant—her gratitude tinged with resentment. Even though Fitzsimmons had difficulty focusing his attention because of the painkillers he was still receiving, he was aware of the awkwardness in her presence, and he suspected that she had reached a decision.

The police came, too. First a young detective and later Volpe, who brought a tape recorder along. They were courteous without being friendly, as was Fitzsimmons. They were not allowed to stay for more than a few minutes, and so their visits seemed incessant, although, in reality, they were three or four hours apart.

Despite Karen's reticence and the persistence of Volpe and the younger policeman, Fitzsimmons began to be aware of a tremendous sense of release. It was as if a great catharsis had taken place and all the weight of his past life had been lifted from him. He was, he knew, free of the burden of the deaths of Eileen and Sarah, and he was free of the foreboding that Sarz had caused him. He was also free, to some extent, he realized, of self. He had become detached from himself—at least it seemed that way—and he did not think that it was due solely to the drugs he was receiving.

When the drugs did wear off, Fitzsimmons found that his new sense of detachment was real, but he also found that it did not make him immune to pain, either physical or emotional. By his third day in the hospital, he was able to sit up, and although he was conscious of pain on the left side of his chest as he breathed, he was still able to enjoy being able to view his new freedom despite its limitations. He could look out the window, and even though he could see almost nothing at all outside, just part of a building and a great deal of sky, he reveled in knowing that the sun was shining, that the city was filled with brightness, and that the air was warm and clear.

He was in a very buoyant mood when Amy came through the door, and even her sad, serious eyes did not dampen his euphoria.

"Hi, Ame," he said, using a diminutive of her name for the first time.

"Hi," she answered, still not returning his smile.

"Where's your mom?"

"Outside."

She walked over to the bed and put her arms around his neck. He felt her tears on his cheek.

"I love you," she said.

"And I love you," he answered.

"I know you do," she said.

"And I'm all right. I'm fine. I'll bet I won't be here for more than a few days. They've had me out of bed, and they say that everything is great."

"That's good," Amy said.

She began to sob, and Fitzsimmons put his hand on her back and patted her.

"It's all right, Amy," he said.

"But you don't know," she said.

The smile had left his face, and he could feel the tears coming to his eyes.

"Yes I do."

"That I have to say good-bye?"

"Yes."

They hugged each other for a long time, and their tears mingled. Finally, Fitzsimmons kissed the top of her head, and Amy left the room.

Fitzsimmons cleared his throat and pulled the sheet up and dried his face. He had just dropped the sheet when Karen entered the room. Instead of coming to the bed, she walked to the window and looked out. When she turned to face him, her eyes, too, were sad, but they were distant.

"Did you talk to Amy?" she asked.

"Yes."

"What did she say?"

"Good-bye," he answered.

"She's very upset," Karen said.

"So am I."

"I'm leaving Boston. I'm going back to Detroit," Karen said. She had not been looking at Fitzsimmons, but now she did.

"I just can't endure it anymore. My father was an alcoholic. My husband was an alcoholic. And you are someone who attracts tragedy. I love you—I don't even know if I love you. Something has happened to me. When he took Amy, he might just as well have put a stake through my heart. And when I saw you in the living room, you were crippled. You were just helpless. I've seen too many helpless men. Something happened to my feelings."

"I know," he said. "I felt it."

She started toward the bed but stopped and looked toward the door.

"Before you go," Fitzsimmons said, "I want to say something."

Her face was impassive. He had the impression that she thought that whatever he would say was only a hurdle between her and the door.

"I am not your father, and I am not your husband. I will not apologize for being who I am or what I am," his voice sounded angry and sharp, but he could not moderate it. "I have weaknesses and strengths, but I know that whatever else I am, I'm a decent human being who is capable of loving and accepting love.

"I thought—I still think—that you and I had something lasting, something which could withstand the onslaught. And no human being escapes the onslaught. But those who withstand it are the ones who, when they find love, when they find goodness, cling to them in the face of everything else because love and goodness are the only things that matter."

"There are other things that matter," Karen said quietly. "Amy matters. Our security matters."

"Security is an illusion. No one is really secure," he said.

"Some people are more secure than others," she said.

"An illusion. But if you want to trade your life for it, that's up to you."

"Yes, it is up to me," she said. Now there was an angry edge to her voice, too. She started toward the door.

"Karen," he said, and his tone softened. "Let's not end this in anger."

She turned toward him, and he saw that the anger had gone from her face and her eyes had filled.

"I love you," he said. "If this is the end, let it end with a kiss."

She came to the bed and bent down. Her perfume and her presence flooded his senses, and he felt the rush of desire. Their lips touched, tentatively, as if they were relatives carrying out a perfunctory rite, and she pulled her head away, turned and silently left the room.

CHAPTER THIRTY SIX

EITHER KEVIN O'DONNELL HAD AN UNCANNY SIXTH SENSE OR Karen had spoken to him before she left, because during the next week he visited Fitzsimmons at least once a day and some days two and three times. His excuse was that he had come to the hospital to visit sick parishioners, and that was partly true, but Fitzsimmons also knew that the priest wanted to help him through a difficult time.

It didn't take them long to get to know each other fairly well. Both of them spoke freely about themselves. The priest talked about how he had decided on his vocation, his friendship with Peter, and his hopes for himself. And Fitzsimmons talked about his youth, about Eileen and Sarah, and about Karen and Amy. Frequently, especially after the first few days, the conversation would turn to Sarz and the day of the kidnapping and Sarz's death. Very gradually, perhaps without even knowing what they were doing, the two men studied those events detail by detail, as if trying to uncover some element that they suspected, but were not certain, existed.

"Did Karen talk to you before she went back to Detroit?" Fitzsimmons asked, the day before he was scheduled to be released from the hospital.

"Yes. As a matter of fact she asked me to look in on you. I was planning to anyway, but she was concerned that you have a friend."

"Did she talk about the morning that Sarz kidnapped Amy?"

"No. Should she have?" the priest asked.

"Well, a big part of her reason for leaving Boston was the way I reacted after I got the telephone call from Sarz."

"She didn't mention it," the priest said.

"After I spoke to Sarz and realized he had Amy, I was crushed. I was emotionally paralyzed. I could feel darkness closing in on me. I could feel my mind disintegrating. I sat on her sofa and I was filled with panic and depression and hopelessness. It was as though everything negative in my personality turned on me and assaulted me. I was almost catatonic. And she saw me like that, and it was too much for her. There were just too many painful associations for her."

"But you didn't stay on the sofa," the priest said. "You certainly didn't look catatonic when I saw you that afternoon. And you did rescue Amy."

Fitzsimmons smiled, and then he laughed. "Yes," he said. "But the impression that I made on Karen when I was on the sofa must have been so strong that everything else became secondary to it."

The priest was thoughtful for a moment. "What happened?"

"What do you mean?"

"Well, you obviously didn't become catatonic, and you didn't stay on the sofa."

It was Fitzsimmons' turn to be thoughtful. "You're right. I didn't stay on the sofa. I don't know what happened. One minute I was almost catatonic, and the next minute I was in the kitchen telling Karen that we would get Amy back."

Fitzsimmons' eyes wandered away from the priest and he stared out the window at the sky.

"Just like that?" the priest asked.

"Yes, almost," Fitzsimmons said. "But there was something else. I prayed—sort of." He looked surprised. "I had forgotten all about that."

The two men were silent for more than five minutes. Finally, the priest turned from the window and looked at Fitzsimmons.

"Well, you've come through it," the priest said.

Fitzsimmons laughed. "By the skin of my teeth," he answered.

"And the grace of God," the priest said. "And is it all resolved?"

"As much as it has to be," Fitzsimmons said.

"We never really do get a completely clear understanding of it all, do we?"

"I guess not," Fitzsimmons said. "I have a sort of friend who may be right about us. He thinks we're all half-wits."

Father O'Donnell laughed. "Is he a theologian?"

"Just about. He works at TPI. He's got a mental disability. He was injured as a kid, and parts of him grew and parts of him didn't. He has to shave some parts of his face and other parts are as clean as a baby's as if they never aged. And his mind is like that. Some parts of it are retarded and some parts are profound."

"And he thinks we're all half-wits?"

"Well, not all. He didn't think Sarz was a half-wit."

"I wonder what he would have thought of Peter?"

"Yeah. I wonder," Fitzsimmons said.

"Maybe the very good and the very bad know something about life that the rest of us don't," the priest said. "Maybe your friend is right about most of us."

"Yes—through a glass darkly," Fitzsimmons said.

At that moment Tommy Quercio pushed the door open and limped into the room. He ignored the priest and looked fiercely at Fitzsimmons.

"My God, Tommy!" Fitzsimmons said.

"Hey, Jay, you half-wit. You beat him. I didn't think anybody could beat him. He was a bad guy, Jay."

Fitzsimmons nodded.

"How did you get here, Tommy?"

"I just came. I took the bus. Don't you think I can take the bus?"

"Is this the friend you were telling me about?" Father O'Donnell asked.

"Yes, it is. Tommy, this is Father O'Donnell."

Tommy gave the priest a sideways glance without acknowledging him.

"You're a half-wit, Jay," he said, shaking his head. "Are you hanging around with these guys now? The men in black?" His face gleamed as he looked out of the corner of his eye at the priest.

Fitzsimmons ignored the question. He realized that, in a way, tragedy had made them like members of the same family. They had a freedom to say things to each other that other people did not.

"There may be more to this than we thought," Fitzsimmons said. "Maybe God does more than watch."

Tommy's face hardened.

"I don't want to hear it, Jay. You've been talking to the men in black. They make that stuff up."

The gleam had left Tommy's eyes and there was no irony in his face. He looked much older and quite weary.

"See ya, Jay." He turned his back on them, pulled the door open and then he limped out into the hall letting the door close slowly behind him.

The silence left by Tommy's departure was profound. After a while, the two men realized there was nothing left to say.

"Well, okay then, John," the priest said, extending his hand.

But before they could shake hands, the door burst open and Tommy limped back into the room. He looked shyly at the priest and then at Fitzsimmons, his eyes glowing with mischievousness.

"Hey, Jay," he said excitedly, "blessed are the half-wits, for theirs is the kingdom of heaven."

And then the enigmatic Tommy Quercio spun around and in a limping half-gallop disappeared shrieking down the hall.

EPILOGUE

AT TEN THE NEXT MORNING, WHEN FITZSIMMONS LEFT THE HOSPItal, he experienced a curious mixture of euphoria and sorrow. The day was sunny, warm and dry, and after almost two weeks in an air-conditioned room, he found freedom and excitement in the fresh air. The streets of Boston were jammed with automobiles and trucks. Life was everywhere, and Fitzsimmons felt a part of it. As he stepped into the taxicab, he remembered that when he got back to his apartment, Karen and Amy would be gone, neither would he have the consolation of a friendship with Peter. He would have to start from scratch.

"Not so bad," he said to himself. "At least I can start."

He had already decided to put his old life behind him. He had called TPI and told them he would not be back. At first he thought he would move to another apartment in Boston, but now he thought he might pack his bags and get on a plane—fly to a new city, perhaps in New Mexico or Arizona, a place where there would be light and space.

The sadness rushed at him as he entered his apartment building and climbed the stairs. Acting on impulse, he stopped and knocked at Karen's door, but there was no answer. He knocked again, but he could sense that the apartment was empty, and it made him more deeply aware of the irrevocability of Karen's decision. He went into his apartment and shut the door behind him, and the emptiness of the apartment reinforced his sadness. He who had lived in isolation was no longer used to being alone. He who had coveted solitude now had a powerful longing to be with people, to talk to them, or at least to see them.

After only a few moments he decided to take a last walk around Beacon Hill and perhaps go past the State House and walk through the Common.

He left his apartment and retraced his steps, down the dim staircase and through the even dimmer musty hall, past the mailboxes, and, at last, out into the street. As he stepped into the light, he noticed a child with her back to him and a woman in the backseat of a cab leaning forward to pay the driver. He started up the street, but after a few steps, he stopped.

Amy was standing next to the cab. She seemed transfixed, staring at Fitzsimmons as if he were a stranger. Karen's head was down as she got out of the cab, and she was unaware of Fitzsimmons' presence until she looked up. She, too, looked at him almost as if he were a stranger.

Fitzsimmons looked from Karen to Amy and back to Karen, and as he did his face was filled with joy. That was all the signal Amy needed. She flew to him and hugged him. Karen stood a few feet away. She was somber and pale.

For a moment, Fitzsimmons suspected that she had returned only to retrieve something she had forgotten in the apartment and that she had not wanted to see him. He continued to hug Amy, but the joy left his face.

"I had second thoughts," she said. "I was wrong."

Fitzsimmons extended his arm; she came to him and clung to him.

"Thank God for second thoughts," he said.

And for a long time the three of them stood on the sidewalk and hugged each other.